FLEEING PEACE

Liere and Senrid: The First Adventure

SHERWOOD SMITH

Other *Sartorias Deles Stories in this arc* by Sherwood Smith

The Spy Princess

Sartor

Senrid

A Stranger to Command

Crown Duel

ISBN 978-1-61138-730-8

❀ Created with Vellum

FLEEING PEACE

You, my child, shall blossom,
Like the buds below.
I will be your thorn stem,
You will be my rose.

Chapter One

Everyone's heard the legends about how a heroic little girl named Sartora saved the world, but few know what really happened, or about the equally heroic friends who helped her. The only thing those youngsters had in common besides their age was that none of them —including Sartora—regarded themselves as heroes.

Good or bad, change takes getting used to, Leander Tlennen-Hess thought when he woke up and remembered that he was still a king.

Sometimes good or bad were tough to define, he thought as he rubbed the line in his cheek that the book he'd fallen asleep against had pressed. It was good that he was now king of Vasande Leror because it meant that his stepmother Mara Jinea was gone. It was going to take time to recover from the damage she'd done to the kingdom, and that kind of edged over into the bad things, because no matter how long Leander worked every day, the list of things people insisted were of the first importance just kept getting longer.

The room he'd claimed as his study was like ice. He braced himself, threw off his blanket, and hopped through the cleaning frame, which restored his clothing and his body to freshness, even if it didn't do anything about the cold.

It was a good thing that Vasande Leror was so small. He pulled on a sturdy linsey-woolsey tunic over his other clothes s he reflected on how a kingdom as large as Marloven Hess to the west, for instance, would have a list that much longer.

Leander paused before the west window, rubbing his arms, and thought of Marloven Hess's new king, Senrid, also fifteen years old. If he was still alive. Whenever Leander felt the least sorry for himself, he thought of Senrid over there in that enormous kingdom full of warriors, and the tasks that *he* must be facing.

Leander grimaced. It was a bad thing to have to share a border with Marloven Hess. But it was a good thing that the Marlovens had had so much internal trouble they probably wouldn't have time to go conquering again anytime soon. Only, was it a good thing or a bad thing to think that what was bad for someone else was good for their neighbors?

In an effort to warm up, he ran down to the kitchen, where he found his step-sister, Kyale, just sitting down to a meal at the secondary prep table. From the snap in her silvery-blond brows, and the downward turn to her small mouth, she was not in a good mood.

He pretended not to notice. Maybe he could coax her out of the sulks. "Good morning, Kitty. Going out to take advantage of the good weather while we still have it?"

Kyale Marlonen looked up at Leander in exasperation.

She couldn't *believe* it! How could somebody so *smart*, and so *hard-working* (he worked a lot harder than the grownups, in her opinion, and why didn't he give more commands since he was now the king?), and so kind, be so *ignorant*?

"Leander," she said, lowering her voice so the kitchen staff couldn't hear her. "That was the most boring New Year's Week *ever*. Horrible as my mother was, at least she gave parties. *I* could give parties. I would *love* to give parties, if only you would hire some servants. A *princess* should *not* have to eat in a *kitchen*. Nor should a king!"

As soon as the words—the very sensible, practical words—were out, his green eyes got that glassy look again. She had learned to distrust that look. Instead of saying, "You're right, Kitty!" he was going to talk in that horrid explaining voice.

"Because we don't have anything in the treasury, any more than we did last month."

"Why not? Don't the guilds pay taxes? I know they do—you were boring on for *ever* about which of my mother's taxes to get rid of and which ones to keep, all last summer, before those disgusting Marlovens attacked. And I *know* you kept *some* taxes."

"But we won't see any revenue from those until next year, or maybe after. Our debts are too large."

"Debts?" Kyale set her fork down. "How could we have debts? Kings don't *have* debts. Everybody owes *them* money. They're not supposed to owe anything. That's why they're kings. They protect the land, and make rules. Like taxes." She glared over her breakfast at Leander, whose head had bent forward, so all she could see was his black hair. And that was another thing, his hair was shaggy, hanging over the collar of that terrible old tunic—she was sure she'd seen him wearing it when he was an outlaw. When was he going to *look* like a king?

Her voice sharpened. "Leander, you *know* it's true."

Leander looked up from buttering his corn bread. "This is what I know today. There is no money in the treasury for decorating this castle, or hiring more people, beyond what we'll need to finish repairing some of the worst damage the Marlovens did, and to get through the rest of winter. We're going to have to make do."

"Then why don't you tell that disgusting Senrid that *he* should help those repairs that *his* disgusting warriors did? Because I know you write to him."

Her voice climbed toward shrill. Leander recognized the fear of being left alone underneath the jealousy. Kyale's mother had been a horrible person, using her daughter as a convenience for hostage and magical purposes. He had to give Kyale time.

"I've only written to Senrid twice, about border matters. Marlovens don't make reparations. Their view of the world is just too different."

"Then it's time for Senrid to learn," Kyale stated.

Leander shut his eyes, his appetite gone. He knew better—but either he answered, or she'd keep at it endlessly. "Kyale."

She scowled. She hated it when he used her name instead of "Kitty," which was her favorite nickname in the world. One she'd picked herself.

"Kyale," he said again. "If you want to help me govern, and that would be great, you've got to learn something about governing. I can give you a book on how we in Vasande are related to the Marlovens not all that long ago, but if you don't want to fix your ignorance, then have a great day. I've got to get to work."

He picked up his cornbread and his fast cooling eggs, and retreated up to his study, her shrill, angry voice chasing after, "Who are you calling ignorant? You're ignorant of proper manners! You don't live in that nasty, muddy outlaw forest camp anymore, so why can't you at least . . ."

As Leander walked through the kitchen, the cook and helpers went on with chopping and mixing and checking the big brick bake-oven, as if they hadn't heard the argument. The latest argument.

When he reached the back stairs, which was the shorter way up to his study, Kyale's small figure appeared in the doorway behind him, her silken skirts swaying, her silvery blond hair swinging.

"And you could at least take a day away from work," she yelled. "You were more fun as an outlaw!"

"That's enough, now, your highness." That gruff voice was Llhei, her governess, who had managed to give Kyale what little upbringing she had when Queen Mara Jinea wasn't around. Leander caught a glimpse of Llhei's comfortable form in her long Sartoran robe, and the back of her neat gray head, as she shepherded Kyale along the hall in the other direction.

"But it's the truth! And I'm so *bored*, Lhei, and Leander *never* does *anything* fun anymore, and what's the use of being a princess if I have to eat in the kitchen, and nobody *ever* comes to see us?"

"Like I told you, you have to be a friend to make a friend."

"I thought those Mearsiean girls were my friends, but . . ."

Their voices faded as they turned the corner next to what used to be one of the grand reception chambers, only most of the decorations had been stripped and carried off after Mara Jinea's defeat, by her former hirelings.

When he reached his study, Leander grimaced at the barren gray stone above his book shelves. The truth was, if he could go back to living in the forest, he'd grab the opportunity in a heartbeat. Even in winter. So far, the castle was scarcely warmer than outside, especially as they could only afford a few Fire Sticks. Feeling guilty about the sizable sum he'd spent on magic books, Leander had divided the Fire Sticks between Kyale, the kitchens, and the rooms where Arel and his stonemasons and wood carvers were doing the repairs. He kept none for himself.

He piled the eggs onto his corn bread and carried the sandwich to the window, where he could munch and look out at where big, burly Alaxandar drilled the castle guard—all twenty-odd of them. They couldn't defend the castle against a determined assault, as they'd learned a few months back. The Marlovens hadn't even broken a sweat. But, as Alaxandar said, "We'll go on as we mean to, because not to try is worse."

"Leander?" That was tall, shambling Arel, five years older than Leander at twenty, and newly made a master carpenter. He'd taken over as castellan. He balanced some kind of wood-smoothing tool on one thin shoulder as he wiped his pointed nose on his sleeve. "Sorry. Caught a cold. There's someone here to see you."

"Thanks."

Arel's quick footsteps retreated down the hall toward the back stairs. Leander wolfed down the last couple of bites and followed more slowly, wondering why Arel had come all the way upstairs to tell him, instead of snagging him at the kitchen—oh, of course. To avoid Kyale, who fretted when Leander's old gang forgot to say 'your majesty' or bow, or perform any kind of protocol.

Leander's mood was somber as he descended to the parlor, which was the only other room with a Fire Stick. Leander knew the off-duty servants used it, as it was the most comfortable room in the palace, where they'd gathered all the nicer furnishings, rugs, and cushions not carried off or destroyed during the trouble.

He was expecting another angry guild messenger, or a town representative; what he found waiting was a girl his age, quite as tall as he was, with black eyes and long, stringy black hair.

"Hibern?" Leander stopped where he was, surprised and alarmed. "Did Senrid send you? Is there . . ."

"A war party on its way?" Hibern said, her sardonic smile reminding Leander briefly of Senrid, though the two did not resemble one another in the least. Maybe it was a Marloven characteristic. "No." She waved her hand at her clothes, which belatedly Leander noticed. She did not wear the dull colors Leander was used to seeing on the few Marlovens he'd encountered. She wore a blue robe as an outer layer.

"You've joined the Sartoran Magic Council?"

Hibern laughed. "I'm a long way from that. But I am a magic student just the same. I have a tutor." Her smile vanished. "And things are so desperate right now that they're putting us students to work as they train us." She waved a skinny hand at the walls. "I'm on my way to see Senrid. But I stopped to warn you to strengthen all your protective wards. There is troubling news from Sartor—"

"Fern!" Kyale danced in, smiling happily. "I didn't know you were here!"

"I just arrived," Hibern said. "Was talking magic with Leander first, then I wanted to find you."

Kyale flushed with pleasure. "Came to see me?" Her happiness faded. "Magic with Leander? That horrible Senrid is not attacking, is he?"

"No, he's not attacking anybody."

"How about executions? Every day before breakfast?" Kyale asked snidely, and Leander shut his eyes.

Hibern turned her palm down, and made a little pushing motion that Kyale and Leander both recognized as a typical Marloven gesture. "Not a one."

Kyale smiled broadly. "Well, then! If there's no danger, may we offer you some breakfast? We have cinnamon rolls, and I can order you some eggs, or they could make you oatcakes. I remember you people like to eat oats."

Hibern's thin face was usually serious, emphasized by her straight brows. She looked younger when she flashed a grin. "I don't need any food. It's much later in the day where I was before my transfer. But I wouldn't mind something hot to drink."

"I will give the order," Kyale said importantly, and then ran out, because she didn't want Hibern to know that there was no servant on duty to give any orders to.

"I apologize for the insults," Leander said awkwardly.

"Oh, I don't mind. My country was not very good to yours, nothing can change that. Or change how you and Senrid first met. What I choose to remember is what a big help Kitty was to us, in spite of that bad beginning."

"She was glad to have helped," Leander said, adding at Hibern's smile, "though maybe not at the time."

"I know. I remember." Hibern's quick grin flashed again. "I think her insults were actually good for Senrid, in a weird way I'm not even sure I can explain."

"Maybe because they were funny, but not a threat? He's lived under threat so long," Leander said. "At least, that's what I figured out after those few days he was here."

Hibern pursed her lips. "I cannot say I know him, either. A very few meetings, for short periods, and often we end up arguing about dark magic and light. But you might be right." She glanced at the door. "Anyway, whatever she says, I know that Kitty means well. And whatever *he* says, Senrid actually wants to mean well. I think."

Leander wondered if she meant *I hope*. "He kept telling me that light magic is weak. Ineffectual."

"I think he knows that that's not true, it's just that light magic has so many safeguards. And he hates mages—and rulers—who claim that light magic is preferred by those who are morally superior."

"'Lighters.' That's what he called us."

"Me as well." She touched her robe.

"Are there any mages or kings who use dark magic who don't make war?"

"He says he can remain neutral."

Leander grimaced at the Fire Stick burning away. Beneficial light magic. Though dark magic could make Fire Sticks as well, he'd heard. How close were the two spells?

"The reason why I'm not a student at the mage school is that Mage Council believes that those who use dark magic can't remain neutral," Hibern said. "And I was born in a kingdom where not only dark magic is used, but the Council has no influence."

Leander had learned very early that the word 'dark' was a symbol, suggesting the absence of light, the void that comes when one has used up magic potential. The form of magic called 'dark' was powerful, dangerous, and its spells mostly meant to destroy. The term 'light' signified the careful, layered use of magic that is meant to stay in balance with the magic potential of the world. Like the steadily burning sun. 'Light' had also come to symbolize harmony toward others, something most dark magic users scorned as euphemisms for expedience and self-righteousness.

While Leander stared sightlessly out the window, remembering Senrid's scorn for light magic, the pale, wintry light highlighted the emerging bones of his face. *He's going to be handsome if he releases the Child Spell,* Hibern thought. *I wonder if he ever noticed.*

She had to laugh at herself; a year ago, *she* wouldn't have noticed. Now that was beginning to notice such things, she'd put the non-aging spell on herself, considering it to be just in time.

Maybe someday she would lift the spell and let her body finish making itself adult. But she was in no hurry. Great magic was her goal—world magic—and she did not want the clouding of sense that came with that mysterious, dangerous thing called attraction, which had caused her mother to blast her plans and marry a selfish dark mage, just because she'd, ugh, *fallen in love.*

Hibern hated thinking about the mess her family had become. She said, "Here's what I just learned. There's something really bad out there, far worse than mages and rulers arguing about who lives in harmony and who doesn't. Norsunder is trying to make a rift near Sartor. It's big—the biggest ever. All the mages in the two schools and independent are going there to fight it."

"A rift," he whispered.

The magic to make a rift was rare, and almost impossibly powerful. It meant nothing less than a tear in the fabric of the real world, opening into Norsunder, which lay beyond space and time. The cost in magic potential was truly terrible. Light magic did not make rifts.

"A big rift?" Leander's throat went dry. "That can only mean they want to bring across big armies. *Centuries* of warriors."

Hibern said, "That's if they make the rift. Here's what's important right now. There are Norsundrians in the world now. Searching. No one knows what for, but it's happening *right now*."

The quick patter of Kyale's step sounded outside the door. "I ordered some hot chocolate," Kyale said importantly.

Llhei appeared, obligingly carrying an old kitchen tray covered with a folded table cloth, and set with the fine porcelain that Mara Jinea had left behind; Leander had wanted to smash all those dishes, but Kyale had grown up with them, so here they were, in use.

He waited until Kyale had meticulously poured out hot chocolate for two, using her very best manners, and while Kyale asked after Hibern's family connections in Marloven Hess, Leander slipped out and ran upstairs to scout out whatever he could find in his new library about rifts.

Chapter Two

New Year's Week was over, and Senrid Montredaun-An, fifteen years old and newly king of Marloven Hess, had managed to survive the week without being assassinated.

It was a good beginning—but it was only the beginning.

He stood at the window of his new study and looked out over the jumble of snow-quilted rooftops, blue-white in the pale early-morning glow. The extensive royal castle and its training academy annex, two citadels within the citadel of his capital city, appeared from this height to be peaceful enough. The sentries roaming the walls moved with the steadiness of habit. No furtive glances or fingered weapons hinted at plots.

Senrid knew without getting out a spyglass that the city walls would look the same. Probably somewhere, someone was plotting against him. Marloven history was full of plots, successful or not. But so far, nobody seemed to have enough support to get rid of him and set themselves up as king, in spite of his age and lack of experience.

Yet.

But he couldn't let himself worry about hypothetical threats, not when there was a real threat just south of his border, where a number of Norsundrian warriors had camped.

His clock chimed six times, as elsewhere bells tolled the dawn watch. All normal sights, sounds, and yet he sensed trouble. So far, his instincts for trouble had been too accurate to ignore.

The internal alarm of transfer magic prodded him mentally—someone he'd given access had just arrived. He relaxed enough to draw a deep breath. A cold draft of displaced air blew across his face, carrying with it the scents of cinnamon and burning wood.

Hibern appeared by transfer. She was late, for the first time since they'd begun meeting in secret to discuss magic.

While she blinked away the transfer-vertigo, Senrid said, "Something's wrong. Is it your father?"

Hibern rubbed her eyes, partly to get rid of the transfer blur, and partly because she was tired. "My father is busy ordering magic books to try to find a cure for my brother." She didn't say *for what he did to my brother*, but they both knew it was true.

Senrid decided against saying anything. Hibern's father had been the cause of Stefan's insanity through the experiments that Senrid's regent, Uncle Tdanerend, had ordered him to perform. Tdanerend had wanted a way to control minds.

Specifically Senrid's.

Hibern said, "As for why I'm late, I stopped to warn Leander what I'm about to tell you. But listen, Senrid. You're going to be on your own."

"I've been on my own."

Hibern glanced across the wide desk at Senrid as she considered her words. Short, blond, and round-faced, he looked much younger than fifteen—until you noticed his eyes. They had the focus of someone older, someone who had had to watch for threat and danger from too early an age.

She was glad he wasn't an enemy. "Senrid, there's one thing I've learned from my studies so far. You can't remain neutral, not in the greater battle—"

"It's not my battle. I have enough to do to get control here, and keep it," he interrupted.

Hibern opened her hand in agreement. They were both Marlovens. They knew how much trouble a youth would face, especially one who'd been denied formal military training, in establishing control of a warrior kingdom like Marloven Hess.

She gave him the same report she'd given Leander.

Though the two boys were the same age, and both had learned magic while trying to survive machinations by adults, Senrid was far advanced in magic over Leander, though it was dark magic. His life had depended on it.

Senrid got up and walked to the window and back. "Norsunder's coming through the rift for what?" he asked at last, then took an impatient turn around his study. "Never mind. Has nothing to do with me, unless they're coming to my kingdom. There'd have to be more of them than that camp on my south border. So you're here to tell me you won't be able to meet with me anymore? For now, or is it 'ever'?"

Hibern sensed the real question: trust. She opened her hand as she said, "My tutor is taking me to Sartor to help close that rift."

In other words, not a matter of trust.

"Thanks for the warning," Senrid said.

Hibern braced herself for the jolt of transfer magic and whispered the spell. She vanished with a ruffle of displaced air.

The next morning, Leander was poked out of his dreams by two of his magic alarms: the sound of clacking sticks, and the sharp scent of pine.

The clacking sticks meant one person: the cruel, ambitious Mara Jinea.

The pine smell meant that someone had broken the protective ward he'd put over the castle against dark magic.

As he fought his way into last night's clothes, he thought miserably that the horrible thing about expecting trouble is that you always hope it will be later. You can try to be ready, but unless the enemy actually send you a note saying *Just to let you know we'll be attacking next Thirdday at noon,* it's always too soon.

"She's back," Leander whispered, his breath clouding.

He clawed his hair out of his eyes as he ran to the window overlooking the courtyard.

Sick at heart, he saw Norsundrian warriors forcing the two gate guards inside, their weapons taken, their hands on their heads. At least they hadn't been killed outright: that had to mean that Mara Jinea intended to stay, to resume being queen. She'd keep them on as menials.

He hopped impatiently as he pulled his socks on, then he shoved his feet into his forest mocs, and ran down the hall to Kyale's room. In the pale light of impending dawn, her bed was a mound of lumps— somewhere in there she was asleep with at least half her cats.

"Kyale," he whispered fiercely.

Kyale groaned as the middle mound jerked upright. Kyale flung the covers off, rumpled in her embroidered night dress. She sat in the middle of a moat of at least six cats, some still in pie-rounds. Others leaped down and vanished through the door, tails twitching.

"She's back," Leander said.

Kyale's mouth rounded, then she leaped out of bed.

"Change into something sturdy and warm. I need to test the magic she's ruined before I can figure out what to do," he said.

He raced out to warn the servants, but skidded to a stop when he heard Mara Jinea's distinctive drawl, "No, don't touch them, unless you intend to do the cooking and cleaning."

Captured—all of them. Leander's insides gnawed with regret. He couldn't save them, and he knew he was the main target. He'd talked about this endlessly with Llhei and Alaxandar, and both had insisted: *If She comes back, you run. You are our only chance of getting aid.*

He pounded to his room, grabbed his coat and the pack of overnight supplies he'd always kept ready, wishing he could get the fresh bread he smelled, but at least he had a traveler's loaf.

He whispered a test spell as he ran to Kyale's room, where he found her dressed and ready, her eyes enormous. Sure enough, his border had a magical overlay of some kind. Norsunder was good at that kind of binding. He could probably break it, but then they'd be able to track him.

He eyed Kyale. Nothing could convince her to wear sturdy trousers and tunic in winter, but at least that gown looked warm. He took her hand and transferred to the border destination he'd made ready during autumn. When the transfer reaction wore off, he said, "You are safe here. I have to go back to release the magical traps I made."

Kyale said fiercely, "I hope you made some good ones."

"Oh yes," he assured her. "I'll return shortly."

Transfers feel a lot like being shoved off a roof. You know how to land, but it still hurts every bone and muscle.

Leander braced himself and transferred to the second destination he'd prepared, back in the castle, inside the closet off the room Mara Jinea had once used as her magic chamber.

And sure enough—he heard her voice, but the second voice shocked him cold.

"... find the brat?"

That harsh, angry voice belonged to Senrid's horrible uncle, who had been the Marloven Regent, some said after knifing his own brother in the back. Leander believed it. Tdanerend Montredaun-An *enjoyed* cruelty, that much Leander had experienced personally.

"He's gone, of course," Mara Jinea said. "Coward transferred out moments ago, probably squealing in fear as soon as he heard us down below."

"You should have broken the wards first."

"I couldn't," she retorted impatiently. "He had a tangle of them. One on every door. But I'll find *him* as soon as he does magic. He will be my prime exhibit when I warn the populace just what the reward for disobedience is. It should last all day."

Tdanerend uttered a humorless laugh, more like a bark. Leander grimaced, hating the memory of that voice, the violence in every sentence the man uttered. "I don't see why they won't let me make an example of Senrid . . ."

More mumbles. Cursing? Leander wondered if he'd heard enough.

" . . . until the northern rift is made." Tdanerend's voice rose.

Leander started. What was that about a northern rift? Hibern had said that Norsunder was making one in the south, hadn't she?

A third voice joined the two villains. This voice was completely different, a mellow tenor with a musical accent. "You really ought not to be discussing these plans with your intended target listening eagerly ten paces away."

The shock of that made Leander jump, knocking against an old footstool. He transferred out so fast that Mara Jinea only found the footstool, and traces of recent magic.

Kyale whirled around when he appeared, then bent over, hands on his knees, as he fought the clawing nausea and joint pain of two transfers in a row.

Her hands rose to her mouth, then she whooshed out a sigh. "Where were you? Why did it take so long?"

"Come on." He straightened up, his limbs shaky. "They'll be here soon, and we can't transfer by magic anymore. We'll have to travel overland to the nearest city, and find a mage."

And so began a cold, dreary, frightening trek.

They reached the border road a short time later. For a while they walked peacefully, but the wind kicked up, making the ice creak in the stream alongside the road, and the evergreens roar. Those sounds and the snow muffled the hooves of a Norsundrian rider, who happened on them so fast all Leander had time to do was push Kyale behind a bush and fling himself into a snow drift as he fumbled for the knife he'd stuck in his pack.

Their trip would have ended there, along with their lives, if the Norsundrian hadn't been one of those strange ones whose mind was completely subsumed by some horrific magic: he looked like someone's dad, except for the blank lack of focus of his eyes, his silence as he pulled a sword and tried to kill them, and the chalkiness of his expression that suggested he had been bespelled at the point of death, surrendering his will to avoid dying.

Leander evaded the man's steady, lethal swings: his orders clearly were to kill anyone he found. Leander backed up, ducking and bobbing, jabbing high so the blank face lifted, until he found what he'd been looking for: a stream. He leaped, the Norsundrian swung—and slipped on ice, falling with a crash into the frigid waters.

Leander let out a whoop of triumph—and his feet slid out underneath him. He landed on one knee, the pain making the world go white. But he flung himself forward, his arms reaching the snow. Kyale ran to the edge of the stream. With red-faced effort, she hauled him off the cracking ice.

They staggered away, leaving the Norsundrian floundering in the icy water as he fought for breath. His horse had run off.

They cut across country, heading for a stand of pine, under whose thick canopy little snow had dropped, so they made no footprints in the thick duff.

In forest, Leander knew how to move fast and well. Ignoring the pain in his knee, he kept them moving until nightfall.

They camped in a shelter of fallen rock, shared the dry journeybread, and Kyale curled up in her cloak and tried unsuccessfully to make herself comfortable. Cold, achy, still hungry, she burst out, "Where are we going, anyway? And don't tell me I wouldn't know it because I never study the map. I want to *know*," she snapped. "Even if I've never heard of it."

Leander sighed. *Here it comes.* "You've heard of it. Choreid Dhelerei. Senrid's capital."

Senrid woke from deep sleep by the invisible skull-rap of an internal magic-alarm.

He thrashed into his clothes, then raced barefoot down the dark halls to his study, ignoring the wintry cold. Glowglobes flickered into life on his entrance. He crossed the room in two flying steps, slammed open a book that always lay waiting, and performed the assessment spells he'd set up. The lack of response forced him to the grim certainty that someone very powerful indeed had not only nullified his newly made castle-wards, but those protecting the kingdom as well.

In a single spell.

He sank down into his chair, contemplating the power that had been behind the spell.

A footstep at the door brought his gaze up. Uncle Tdanerend no longer wore a Marloven uniform, glittering with his ancestors' medals, in an effort to enhance his prestige. He was dressed in the gray and black of Norsunder.

Tdanerend could not enter past the powerful door ward, but he could look in. He could talk. His dark eyes narrowed with malicious triumph. "A nice piece of magery, eh?"

Senrid's heart thumped loudly in his ears, but he would have died rather than show any fear. "*You* didn't break that ward. If you'd ever had that much mastery over magic you'd be on the throne right now." *And I'd either be dead, or your mind-blank servant.*

"Detlev's power is my power," Tdanerend said, his tone even—unlike the old days, when his vile temper flashed at the slightest cause. "And that's why I'm here. I am retaking my throne, and Norsunder is backing me. You have a choice, boy. Detlev wants you. Either you conform willingly, and become useful, or your worthless life ends."

Senrid crossed his arms. "Horseshit."

Tdanerend shrugged. The lack of his characteristic ready anger illustrated most effectively how Detlev of Norsunder's magic had subsumed his will. The skin roughened on the outsides of Senrid's arms as his uncle said in that same even tone, "The two brats from Vasande Leror are probably on their way here. It will be considered a gesture of compliance if you detain them for us. Compliance will earn you a certain amount of freedom."

He touched the transfer token lying on his palm, and vanished.

Senrid stared at the place where he'd been, then he summoned the night-duty runner to carry a three-word message to his commanders: *It has begun.*

An hour later, glowglobes lit the top floor of the royal castle and a new fire crackled in Senrid's study, giving off warmth. Senrid was the only one in civilian dress, and under age, but he was the focus of attention as he walked back and forth before the fireplace, his words—and thoughts —headlong.

" . . . I don't know what happened in Vasande Leror, but from what Tdanerend said, Kyale and Leander escaped. Tdanerend seems to think they will come here. If Detlev wants me to knuckle under by betraying them, then that means we've got until the two show up. After that, you can expect my uncle, probably at the head of that force in the south."

Commander Keriam, head of the Cavalry Academy, said, "I didn't think we'd be at war so soon."

Senrid shook his head impatiently. "It's not war. Yet. Those Norsundrian warriors on our southern border are for scare, and probably for occupation. Look, if they wanted the land, they would have crossed the border already and they'd be busy killing us right and left. Instead, there's all this maneuvering and magical stuff with my uncle. That means something else is going on. Some goal bigger than Norsunder and us whacking each other with swords."

Keriam's grizzled head bowed a little as he made the gesture of assent. He did not understand magic at all. What he did understand was the whacking with swords. Whatever Norsunder planned, Marloven Hess and its army would eventually be a part, or why show up at all?

"So do we muster?" Gherdred, the old cavalry commander, asked. He, too, knew about war with other nations—none better, as he'd ridden with Senrid's grandfather when he'd tried to push the borders back to where they had been when the Marlovens were strongest. But war with Norsunder, the fearful and myth-enshrouded enemy beyond time, beyond death, left him feeling like an academy scrub.

They all did. Senrid could see it—he felt it as well. He'd been worrying at it since autumn, when he first decided to take his kingdom back from Tdanerend. For the past month he'd bombarded Hibern with questions about the greater battles between Norsunder and the world's guardians, so about this subject he knew more than his war leaders.

But it wasn't enough.

"I don't think so," Senrid said. "Not for a magic-backed ploy. We still might have to fight." He thought to himself, *Though we'd never win.*

Keriam frowned. "Then we let them walk in and take us, without even lifting a sword?"

Senrid turned to face him. "You fight, you die. Detlev's magic alone will see to that. I don't want a kingdom of dead, and I am gambling on the fact that Detlev doesn't want a ghost land, either . . ." Once again he was pacing, back and forth, wheeling quickly, talking fast. "Of what use is that? If they kill you with enchanted weapons, you don't quite die—that's what the records all say. You to the part of Norsunder beyond time and space, to await their pleasure in using you, but they have to have a rift to bring you back into the temporal world. I'm sure of that much. And you lose will, which means you lose initiative—all the things you've been trained to use."

Keriam said slowly, "If it's true they want us whole, then we might have time on our side."

"That's what I think," Senrid said. *That's what I hope.* "They're going to need armies in our world if their rifts don't work. If they try to recruit us, then we turn on them and fight. But their main effort, according to Hibern, is to create and maintain a big rift in Sartor."

They stirred, one shaking his head, another rubbing his chin.

"Back to us. Tdanerend is ensorcelled. It's not *him* anymore, it's Detlev controlling him. He wants to sit on the throne—that's about all of his will that's left. If you act like nothing is changed, I really think there won't be any battles, any fighting. Yet. It's a gamble, because you know I can't promise anything."

"And?" one of the foot commanders asked, folding his arms.

"Sit tight," Senrid said. "But be ready to act."

"What if Tdanerend commands us to attack Perideth or Telyerhas or one of the other kingdoms?" Gherdred asked. "In the name of Norsunder?"

Senrid sighed. "That's what I mean by acting." He saw that only Keriam followed his mental side-step, so he said, forcing himself to slow down, "If they let my uncle play at being a conqueror-king, then yes, you're going to face that choice. If what I think is true, and Detlev is in control—Detlev or some other big blade who has some kind of big plan— then he's just going to want you in place for the gathering of forces on a world scale. But you have to be careful. Detlev is not stupid enough to believe for a heartbeat that your lack of resistance to Tdanerend means you can be trusted."

Senrid watched his war leaders, who had trained all their lives to defend the kingdom. He had just asked them to effectively surrender without lifting a sword. Heartsick with anxiety, he waited for their reaction.

Gherdred flicked his hand open, and Keriam said, "And the benefit of non-resistance is . . .?"

"I think . . . I think the first struggle is going to be magic. Even if we had three times our numbers, we can't fight that. Detlev may be a war leader—the history books hint at that, though he might have used other names—but we *know* he's a deadly powerful mage."

He paused.

Keriam looked up. "And you?"

"I'm going to run." Senrid's tone was bitter. "What they've done to Tdanerend they have to be planning for me. Would you follow my commands if Detlev took over my mind and caused me to order you against every kingdom around us, fighting until you are dead?"

They exchanged uneasy glances.

"It would not be you," Gherdred said slowly.

"How would you know? *I'm* terrified of *that*." Senrid flung his hands wide. "I'd rather be put against a wall and shot." He mimed cranking a crossbow.

In spite of his age, they took him seriously. They all knew that Senrid had never had much of a boyhood, living under the constant threat from his uncle. Senrid's courage was already legendary, though he didn't know it.

"I was Detlev's prisoner, that last day before we defeated my uncle. The only reason I'm here is because one of Detlev's mage enemies came to my aid, but I don't expect that twice. And I can't stand against him alone."

When his leaders began to utter reassurances about how smart he was, how hard he'd worked, Senrid curbed his temper. They were loyal, they meant well, but they didn't *understand*. "Don't you see? Norsunder exists outside of time. Detlev's had the equivalent of *four thousand years* to concoct some lethal magery. So here's my job. I've got to get out into the world and find magic allies strong enough to help me take him on by magic. "

He paused again; the commanders' reactions were subtle. No more than a stirred boot, a hand still rubbing a jaw, but Senrid knew that the mention of Norsunder dismayed them. None of them knew magic, for Marloven law was strict about the military and magic-wielders being separate—except for the ruler.

Keriam finally said, "So if we do get orders to march under Norsunder's banner, then we are free to organize, mark out Tdanerend's Norsunder guard, and act at once." He snapped his fingers.

Gherdred's old face tightened. "We will raise our banner one last time —and strike it."

To the Marlovens, that meant a fight to the last warrior, who takes his knife to the banner and then to himself. "But we don't want that, because glorious as it sounds, it just means we lose," Senrid said. "So we're going to try a ruse. Let Detlev see from a distance that you've fallen into line under my uncle again. Maybe he's so busy he'll think that Marlovens have fallen obediently back to the old ways. And I mean the old *bad* days of factions, duels, sloppy drills. Slow moving because regs about how the horses are shod are more important than anything else. Use up as much time as you can if you get orders. I'm hoping that the mages training Hibern are going to be keeping Detlev on the hop magic-wise."

They saluted, fist to heart.

"So you will keep yourself from Detlev's hands in your search for allies, will you?" Keriam asked, not hiding his worry.

Senrid straightened up and grinned.

It was a toothy grin, arrogant and challenging, and his uncle had detested it since Senrid was small. He appeared to be little threat, standing there, short and slight, in his plain white linen shirt and dark trousers and riding boots, for he refused to wear a uniform he hadn't earned.

What the old commanders saw in that face and form was a glimpse of his coldly determined grandfather, but in his light voice, and in his manner, there was an echo of his brilliant father, who had been the first Marloven king to talk of justice in many, many years. That taste of a new concept of government, so brief before Tdanerend's knife in the back had ended Indevan's life, had lingered during the long, grim years of regency, to surface when Senrid had at last faced his uncle and proclaimed a return to Indevan's Law.

But now, in the face of far greater threat?

"I intend to make Detlev sorry he ever crossed our border."

Chapter Three

Kyale's throat hurt from yelling, pleading, and yelling. Leander wouldn't budge.

She stomped along, angry not just with Leander, but with the entire universe. Her brother had just managed to get their little kingdom back to peace again, and they *deserved* to live happily ever after. They did *not* deserve the sudden shock of her horrible mother returning, with Norsundrians at her back, to retake her throne.

"I still think we should go directly to Hibern," she stated, as she had at least a dozen-dozen times.

"We can't, Kitty," Leander said yet again. "She is not there."

He felt oppressed as well as cold. The gray sky seemed to hang just above his reach, the clouds about to drop an avalanche. His leg ached.

Kyale trudged unhappily at his side, her shoulders hunched and her arms held against her body. Why were boys so *dense*? "All right, so we go there to wait. Or somewhere else! *Why* are we going into Marloven Hess's horrible capital? We should go *anywhere* else! Who nearly got me killed just a few months ago?" she retorted.

Leander suppressed a sigh. How many times had they had this conversation?

"Senrid," he said. "But obviously he changed his mind. You spent a month with him afterward, and he didn't kill you!"

"That's because he needed something from me."

Leander sighed. "Who saved both our lives when his uncle stampeded into Vasande Leror with the east end of his army?"

"Senrid could have changed his mind again, now that he's got his own kingdom and his skunk of an uncle is gone," Kyale announced.

He's not gone, Leander thought, but he hadn't told Kyale what he'd overheard right after Mara Jinea appeared.

"And Marloven Hess is twenty times bigger than Vasande. Fifty! And it has that huge nasty army, and they're all evil Marlovens, so *no one* is going to help us if you're wrong. If we go straight to Hibern's, even if we have to wait for her to come back from wherever she is, at least we know she's on the right side."

Leander gritted his teeth against reminding her that Hibern was a Marloven, too. Kyale was exaggerating, and she knew it.

The real problem was jealousy. She worried that Leander and Senrid would become friends, and leave her out. Most of the people in her life had left her out, except for Llhei, who wasn't family.

Kyale quieted only when they spotted someone their age driving a weaver's cart, who cheerfully offered them a ride. She didn't complain about the boy, even though he was a Marloven, or about being squeezed in with a load of wet-smelling carded wool, not after he invited them to spend the night at his family's farmhouse. "We're always taking in travelers on their way to the royal city," he said.

"Probably to be used as target practice," Kyale whispered, but in Crestellian, and she didn't *really* mean it. She was thankful not to have to walk, and looked forward to the prospect of hot food.

Though a princess shouldn't have to do any of those things.

❧

It was noon when they first spotted the pale, honey-colored stone towers of Choreid Dhelerei, Senrid's capital. By mid-afternoon they trudged through the city gates among people with wagons and carts.

Leander scanned the alert sentries walking back and forth along the walls. As they passed through the gate, walking behind a string of slow carts carrying wicker-baskets of vegetables, no one gave them a second glance.

He knew it would be different when they attempted to enter Senrid's castle.

"Which way is the royal castle?" he asked as they walked into the great crossroads just inside the gate. Several streets gave off the wide, cobbled expanse.

Kyale hunched her shoulders and peered around. "There," she muttered, pointing at the towers to their left, visible above the rooftops. Choreid Dhelerei covered three round hills, the royal castle being on the highest, and the city spread southward over the others.

They reached the castle gates. Sentries walked alertly along it, but again, they totally ignored the two—though the man right after them got halted, as someone called, "Your business?"

Kyale was relieved. For her, notice meant threat, but Leander sensed something very wrong, and his neck tightened.

They approached the grand assembly areas where Marloven kings of old had held court, but not one of the black-and-tan uniformed warriors, or the runners in their longer tunics, paid them any heed.

Leander stepped in the way of a boy his own age carrying papers. The boy's gaze flitted over Leander, then switched to Kyale. He side-stepped and walked on.

Kyale said, "He was looking for one of those stupid uniforms on you."

"I saw that," Leander said. He was also thinking, *He recognized you.*

"Good thing these splat-brained Marlovens are too busy to harass us, huh?"

Leander didn't answer, but mentally braced to transfer the instant he saw trouble. If he could—if they weren't walking into some kind of trap.

They trod down long halls toward the residence wing; instead of the bare stone Leander had expected, the halls had been plastered over, and someone had made frescos, in subtle shades of gray, highly stylized running horses and raptors in flight.

He winced at every painful step, wondering if Senrid was gone. He could even be 'gone' elsewhere in this vast castle. The place was so big that Leander figured his entire capital city would fit into it. Not that Crestel would qualify as a city anywhere else but in Vasande Leror; anywhere else in the world it was a market town.

Finally a young man just a few years older than Leander sped past, and Leander said loudly, "We're here to see Senrid."

The runner did not pause, or speak, but the way he jinked sideways and darted up a stairway caused Leander to whisper to Kyale, "Let's follow him."

Leander grimaced as they did their best to stay with the runner's swift pace, but at least they didn't have far to go, just up two flights of stairs and down a hall. The runner left them at an open door, and there was Senrid, seated at a desk.

"Yuk," Kyale said, by way of announcing their presence. "Here's the king of creeps himself."

Senrid's head came up quickly. Leander thought in relief, *He didn't even hear Kyale's crack.*

He was wrong, but Senrid had gotten used to ignoring Kyale.

"So Uncle was correct for once," he said cheerily. "I told my people not to see you, so officially, you're not here."

"Huh?" Leander and Kyale said together.

Senrid eyed them. Kyale was a pretty girl—if you liked spoiled brats, which Senrid didn't. As usual, she looked sulky, but he wasn't going to comment on that because she'd helped him regain his kingdom, however reluctantly.

He shifted his attention to Leander, tall for fifteen, lanky, pain in his brow and around his mouth. Oh. He was limping.

Senrid began stacking things on the desk, speaking quickly as he worked. "My esteemed uncle said I had a chance to redeem myself by turning you two over to him."

"I knew it!" Kyale looked around for something to bat Senrid over the head with.

"Kyale. Senrid's not doing it." Leander sighed. "Is it all right if I sit down?"

"I don't trust him," Kyale muttered loud enough to make sure Senrid heard.

Senrid said to Leander, "What happened?"

"Ice." Leander dropped onto one of the chairs.

"A Norsundrian chased us!" Kyale said, arms crossed.

Leander said, "Mara Jinea walked into Crestel with a host and took over. All my magical protections swept away like so many cobwebs." He sighed, thinking of his weeks of hard work.

Senrid grimaced, and Leander knew he recognized the cost—not just of losing all that work, but of walking out and leaving his kingdom to the enemy.

"So we escaped," Leander said. "Like a pair of scuttling spiders—"

"Better than staying just to get captured," Kyale stated in a loud, angry voice.

"Absolutely right," Senrid said, and snorted a laugh at Kyale's blank surprise. He turned to Leander. "Same thing is about to happen here. Detlev sent my uncle, which means the war is magical first."

He was angry, and he looked angry. Even Kyale saw it.

"We can't stand up to Detlev. And I have no allies. Apparently you two don't either, despite your being allies with the so-called all-embracing, mutually supportive lighters." His sardonic tone made Kyale flush in rage.

Leander said in a low voice, "There's more." Then he cast a quick look over at Kyale, who watched him with an expression midway between annoyance and fear. "I transferred Kyale to the border, and went back to spy a little."

Kyale sucked in a breath.

Leander raised a hand. "I didn't tell you because I only wanted to have this argument once."

Kyale's face reddened, but she kept her lips tightly shut.

Leander said to Senrid, "I overheard Mara Jinea talking to your uncle."

"Are you certain of that?" Senrid asked.

Leander's mouth twisted sourly. "I will never forget that voice."

"What did they say?"

"I only heard a bit, until a third one showed up. Mara Jinea made a remark about my cowardice in ducking out, and hoola-loola loo. Your uncle said something about you, and I didn't hear all the next bit, but this I did hear: *when the northern rift is made.*"

"Northern?" Senrid repeated, his gray-blue eyes wide.

"Yes. Then a third one showed up, a man. Laughing voice, faint accent. I don't know what it is. He knew I was in the closet. But no one could have seen me because I transferred straight to it."

Senrid's breath whooshed out. "Detlev. Mindreading. Had to be. But he doesn't have a laughing voice. Like you said, I will never forget that voice. It's low, and calm. Even. And no accent whatsoever."

"This was what the musicians call a tenor voice, a singing voice. Music in it, and laughter." Leander shook his head. "I don't know if it was Detlev or not. The only Norsundrian I've ever seen is Mara Jinea. I've got to warn someone about that rift in the north."

Senrid rubbed his eyes. "You might be the only one who knows about that. What you want to bet Detlev told my uncle to make that offer to me just to make sure I stayed put?"

"Trap all three of us," Leander said.

"Time to get out. Now." Senrid finished stacking his work, closed his eyes, and muttered a short phrase. The air scintillated. Leander felt that dry-wind sense of major magic as the papers and books on Senrid's desk vanished, then Senrid threw open the lid of a trunk beside the desk.

"At least Tdanerend will never find that stuff," Senrid said as he shrugged into a heavy winter tunic. The muted clink of metal indicated pockets filled with coins. The tunic was plain green, not the Marloven military black and tan.

Senrid plucked from the trunk a cape, gloves, as Kyale put her hands on her hips. "But I'm hungry!"

Senrid snorted a laugh. "Want to make a wager my uncle has a grab squad coming up the stairs now?" He pulled one, then two coins from his pockets.

Not coins, Leander saw: shank buttons. Transfer tokens, already loaded with a transfer spell. "Here," he said. "Say 'Iasca West.' These will get you to a Destination near my border."

Kyale opened her mouth to complain, but the sound of running feet on the stone outside the office made her blanch. She clutched her token tight and said the trigger words.

Magic far faster and nastier than Leander's yanked her out of the world and hurled her back in.

She fell onto her knees, gasping for breath. Cold air seared her lungs as she blinked away the blur, and finally struggled to her feet. They stood on an old stone platform, mossy and cracked, atop a hill: a transfer destination. Below them lay a long coastal plain, some of it marshy. The cold air smelled faintly of brine. They could just see the ocean, a distant narrow strip of silver, gleaming coldly in the light of the sinking sun. Kyale shook her head to rid herself of the gray-blue curl in the air, like sideways smoke, in the sky above them. She didn't mind those occasional ribbons of undulating color, but she didn't want them now. Blink: good, gone.

Leander said, "Is this your border?"

Senrid said, "Yes. That's Enneh Rual below us. I'm sure Norsunder has border tracers set up by now. We have to walk across." He pointed toward the ocean. "If we can get to the shore, I can transfer from there. No one can ward the ocean."

Senrid looked at Leander expectantly. He'd discovered that he liked Leander—found him interesting—right before he made Leander an enemy, out of what had seemed dire necessity at the time. He hated remembering that.

"Let's get moving," Leander said.

Senrid understood that as an offer of truce. At least long enough to travel together.

They flailed their way down the hill, Leander and Senrid talking about wards, tracers, and spells.

The snow was fairly dry, but Kyale hated the cold sting worming icy tentacles between her gloves and her sleeves, and on her ankles. She refused to wear riding trousers because she thought they were ugly, and princesses did not have to wear ugly clothing. Now she wished she hadn't been so picky. Except how was she to know Leander would mess everything up and they would have to walk everywhere?

She glowered at the two boys, so superior with all their magic chatter. How dare Leander talk to Senrid as if they were allies, and leave her out!

Well, all right, so she didn't want to learn magic the proper way—it was so boring! But they didn't have to assume she was stupid.

She smiled to herself. It just so happened that she *could* learn magic, and just the way she wanted to. It made so much more sense to learn the spells you *needed*. She had had to promise Leander she would not use the transfer spell or any other dangerous spells, but that promise (so she reasoned) did not extend to anything that wasn't the least bit dangerous. Like a certain spell that was quite handy, especially in a castle where a certain brother refused to hire more servants, so even a princess would get stuck going down to the kitchens to scout out something to eat as if she was a scullery-maid. Huh! The food-transport spell had been easy enough to memorize, and she'd proved she could do it.

And Leander didn't even know.

She sighed, wishing she had seen the smallest crust of bread in that vast, ridiculous castle of Senrid's. The problem was, you had to see the food in place before you could transfer it. It worked fine at home, because she knew what Cook made when, and where it was kept—something no princess should ever have to know.

She fumed over old grievances as she stumped along behind the boys, until Senrid stopped and threw back his head. "Damnation!" he shouted.

Kyale frowned. "Watch your language."

"What is it?" Leander asked, instantly wary.

Neither of the boys had heard Kyale. "It has to be Detlev," Senrid muttered, gloved hands pressed over his eyes. "Tdanerend could never be that fast."

"Do you *have* to use offensive language?" Kyale said more loudly.

Senrid's mouth thinned. Leander spoke quickly, to forestall a squabble, "Your protection wards?"

"Gone. All of it. Except the warning if someone set wards against me." He smiled sourly. "I can't do anything now, no transfers, nothing, without them knowing it."

"So we find a ship. My map shows Mearsies Heili straight west of here.

Clair, the queen, is our age," Leander said to Kyale. "She'll listen, and she studies magic. She'll send us up north. We can trade information, what I overheard for help in wards strong enough to get rid of Mara Jinea. All we need to do is find a ship to take us across the ocean." He turned to Senrid. "Maybe they will help you as well."

Senrid doubted it, but at least they were more likely to know where he could go to find help than he was. "Excellent plan."

Leander stole a look at his sister, who glowered down at her shoes. How to turn the subject without seeming to turn the subject? "About bad language," he said. "We all learn not to ever call anyone an 'eleven'—not unless we want a fight. But what I wonder is, why?"

"Ancient pejorative," Senrid said, kicking snow at every step.

"From?"

Senrid sent both Lerorans a derisive look. "Sure all this nasty talk isn't going to make you feel faint?"

"I'm fainting already," Leander said. "You'll have to carry me. Why is it eleven, anyway? Why not six or twenty?"

Senrid laughed. "I doubt Norsundrians care at all what we call them, but it was meant as a pejorative. It came from them first. From what I can gather, they used the number and the time a long time ago as a kind of symbolic strike against the Old Sartoran Twelve Blessed Things."

"Which no one knows all of anymore," Leander said.

"Because most of 'em were destroyed. Or maybe they had different things in different regions. My long-ago territorial enemies, the Venn, thought so, anyway. Anyhow it also has to do with time. We all grow up used to the idea of the day being divisible into twelve units midnight to noon, and the night twelve as well. That notion came from another world called Earth—"

"CJ of the Mearsieans came from there!" Kyale exclaimed.

"Right. I read that they divide time in twelves. Even in lands where they don't have clocks but candles and bells, most kingdoms in the world divide time by two twelves, or eight sets of three hours each—or four sixes cut into twos. "

Leander nodded, covertly watching Kyale. She was still listening.

"Well, I don't know if it's true but people supposedly believed centuries ago that light magic was diminished at the end of the day, and at midnight, the start of a new day, it would be fresh. Like the day. Whether it's true or not, Norsunder makes the transition easiest from there to the physical world here at eleven at night. One of my ancestors wrote that the notions of magic waning is footle, and that Norsunder chose that time because it's when people are most tired, it's always dark, and they can scare you the most."

"So saying 'eleven' is not really an insult to them," Leander explained, his knee beginning to ache again. "If anything it makes them a little stronger if only in your mind, right?"

"Right."

"I wonder how it got turned around?"

"Because people don't like to hear bad things. Names for bad things become bad words," Kyale said in a lecturing tone. "Llhei taught me that, when my horrible mother was still ruling. She said you can refuse to say something because others don't want to hear it, which is manners, and you can refuse to say something because you're afraid that saying it will make it true, which means you just gave it power over you before it even comes."

Senrid shrugged; Leander let out a quiet sigh of relief.

Chapter Four

Kyale stalked up the dock behind Leander, hands tightened into fists inside her mittens. She was furious with Senrid for having chosen such a disgusting-looking ship to travel on, and with Leander for going along with it.

She did not believe that this was the only one going westward to the coast of Mearsies Heili. There were so many beautiful ships all along the dock, ones that obviously had comfortable quarters fit to stay in, if not appropriate for a princess.

She was sure that Senrid had deliberately chosen the ugliest, smallest, nastiest one, with the meanest captain, just to irritate her. Even Leander had looked stunned when he first saw it, but Senrid had said, under his breath, "Only one who didn't ask questions—and seems to have some kind of hiding spot on board, if I understood right. Probably a smuggler."

A *smuggler!* Princess Kyale Marlonen of Vasande Leror to be traveling with *thieves!* And the worst of it was, that stupid Senrid had given that creepy captain all the rest of their money, so they were stuck. They wouldn't have a single copper-bit when they landed at the other shore.

The captain and some of his scruffy crew stood about in a knot on the dock, watching as Kyale followed the two boys up the ramp. He'd said to board just at dawn, and it was dawn. A more bleak, bitter dawn was impossible to recall. Leander had woken Kyale up while it was still dark out. She had insisted on her own room in the small, cramped inn Senrid had found. About all she could say for *that* place was that it had been near the docks, so the boys could go up and down for the long, dreary two days they'd waited in the harbor, before they could find something. Senrid, that is; he had the Universal Language spell on him, and Leander hadn't.

Kyale huffed her breath out, watching it cloud. The water smelled of salt, and old fish, and she was certain she would loathe this journey, especially the way that captain and his repulsive-looking minions stopped what they were doing, turned around and eyed them.

The captain didn't speak. He just watched their approach out of pouchy old eyes, his gray beard blowing in the wind. When they reached the group, Senrid said something in some language, and the captain spat over the side, a rudeness that made Kyale shudder. Why didn't he use the Waste Spell? Because he wanted to insult them, of course.

She muttered to Leander, "He's going to kill us and dump us over the side, I just know it."

Senrid said under his breath, "If you don't shut up, *I'm* going to dump you over the side. And I know you can't swim."

Kyale's chin came up. She clapped a hand to her arm where she still wore the magical armband she'd been given the summer before, when (through Senrid's fault) they'd been hurled through a world gate to another world. She drew in a breath to blast him, but Leander nudged her with his elbow.

"Don't." He mouthed the word.

She scowled. Obviously the boys were not going to change their minds, the idiots. And maybe she shouldn't mention her armband, because what if that horrid Senrid tried to take it away and sell it, or something?

"This way." A tall one-eyed man said in accented Leroran, beckoning for them to follow. The crew, who looked every bit as old and mean as their captain watched them as they followed the man up the ramp onto the ship. Kyale held her nose. The undulating, jerking ramp and the smell of salted fish made her stomach churn.

Leander studied the lashed-down cargo covered with blackweave rain-cloths. No magic here. Good. Senrid's expression was impossible to interpret as he glanced here and there.

All three regretted the absence of cabins on the weather deck, as many capital ships and traders had. They climbed one by one down the ladder, and along a narrow passage. The air was stuffy, and smelled of rope and oil and fish. It was lit by swinging lamps. Kyale crooked her elbow over her nose.

"Here."

The tall man unlatched a small door.

Senrid glanced beyond, and held up his hand. "We paid for a light-port."

The man snorted, ducked in, and a moment later a small opening in the hull-planking let in light. Senrid ducked inside.

Kyale waited until Leander had gone in, and followed reluctantly. She moved so slowly that the hatch caught her on her shoulders as it slammed. She fell between the boys onto a pile of smelly, mildewed old sail. The tiny cabin was obviously a storage space. One end curved sharply, and overhead the bowsprit cut upward at an angle; they were in the forepeak of the ship.

Behind the hatch they heard rumblings: crewmembers rolling barrels up to store, blocking off access to the forepeak.

"We'll be locked in until we leave harbor," Senrid said. "That's all right with me. Customs officials scare them, which is good. We don't want any inspectors seeing us and memorizing our faces. We're well served by the smugglers' caution."

Kyale snarled, "So what's to prevent them from just locking us in here until the journey is over, and Disappearing our corpses at the other end? You *gave* them *all* our money."

"But I promised them three times the amount when we get to Mearsies Heili. I'm gambling on the fact that someone at the other end will understand the importance of our mission and come up with the gold."

"Oh, and they'll let all three of us go?" Kyale asked with corrosive scorn.

Senrid said, "Of course they won't. One of us will have to stay behind."

"I'll do the waiting." Leander sighed, and stretched out his legs on the warped wooden flooring, easing his bad knee, which throbbed anew. It was still swollen. "I won't be very fast until this heals. How'd you explain our presence?"

"Runaway prentices, with wealthy overseas connections."

"Ah." Leander nodded. "That sounds reasonable to me."

"When do we get to eat? Or get to breathe some air?" Kyale snarled, angry with her brother for cooperating with Senrid without an argument. "Or didn't you bother with that part."

"We're to be fed once a day, and if no one is in sight, we are supposed to be able to go on the deck and get some exercise."

Kyale looked around. "No cleaning frames?"

"No." Senrid shrugged. "But no magic aids at all means they won't draw the attention of any Norsundrian searchers."

"Yeuch." Kyale folded her skirts beneath her, shuddering as she looked about. "So what are we to do in the meantime?"

Senrid pulled from his pocket a set of handsomely painted playing cards, and brandished them.

Leander snorted a laugh. "And what do we use for wagers?"

"Our kingdoms, of course."

❧

So it was. Leander played cards'n'shards with Senrid during the long hours of daylight.

Kyale felt sick that first couple of days, and the illness did not improve her temperament. If Senrid and Leander began a conversation about history, or magic, Kyale got angry at being closed out. Senrid fell silent, his expression sardonic. Leander exerted himself to think of things to keep Kyale entertained, or at least occupied.

There wasn't much. She slept until she adjusted to the motion of the ship. After that she was continually hungry. The food, when it came, was never enough, and she refused to eat portions that had other bits of food in them. It was obvious that they were getting the scrapings from the crew's plates, the idea of which made Kyale shudder in revulsion. She couldn't make herself eat anything but the stale biscuits, she just couldn't.

The boys forced it down, each fighting grim thoughts about the future, and about the kingdoms they had left behind.

For a long, miserable week Kyale endured the utter boredom as the ship made its way northward—boredom interspersed with periods of misery when they sailed through rain squalls, and the ship's working leaked cold water through the seams. Two more stops, then at last they headed west. The air through the light-port was cold, but if they wanted light, they had to prop it open; it wasn't lined with glass, but instead was a watertight wooden piece that fit snugly to the hull. Leander had pointed out that it was probably invisible to the eye from outside when closed.

Once the ship was out of sight of land, the three were let out, as promised.

The deck was cramped, the wind icy. They had to watch out for crew members, who didn't watch out for them. Already Kyale had been knocked staggering by a man carrying a barrel. She'd expected him to let her by first, because she was a paying passenger. He hadn't spoken, just thrust the barrel against her, ramming her out of his way.

It happened again at the end of the week. Something hard thumped into her back, knocking her sprawling. Kyale glanced up, furious, to see a sailor smirking as he hefted a bulky roll of canvas.

"He did that on purpose!" she yelled.

"Keep your voice down!" Leander whispered.

Kyale gulped on an angry sob that shredded in the raw wind. "He knocked me down on purpose! And you won't do anything!"

Leander sighed. "Kitty. Please. We have an important mission—"

"Yes, we do! So why not tell this awful captain? I think Senrid's fear about Norsundrians coming after us isn't *real*." She glared around the ship. "*This* horrible ship is real." Her voice rose. "Disgusting people, and treatment, and food!"

Two crew-members nearby stopped pulling ropes and looked their way.

"Kitty. Please? Remember, his uncle knew we were on our way to Marloven Hess. Anyone can figure out that Senrid is with us, and whatever tracers they set up to detect any magic he does are probably set up against me as well."

"Why should there be spells against *him*? He thinks he's so important, so superior, but he ran out just like we did. Faster! Leander, why are you on his side? Don't you *care* how *I* feel?" Her voice rose to a wail.

One of the crew guffawed. Leander felt the attention of every crewman on deck. He muttered, "At least stop whining until we're back down below."

He regretted it the moment he'd spoken.

Kyale whirled around and marched to the hatch. One of the men said something to her, which she ignored with her nose in the air. She looked more like an outraged princess than ever. As she clambered down the hatchway, the men laughed and joked in some other language, derisiveness making their voices harsh.

Leander hunched into his cloak and trudged after, wishing he'd controlled himself. He knew what Kyale was like. She'd been so badly raised by her horrible mother. If only she wasn't twelve...

He wondered if it had been wrong to give her the anti-aging spell. Except he knew that age did not confer wisdom. Tdanerend and Mara Jinea had been proof of that. And how much better would she be at thirteen?

Humor and patience. Those were the ways to calm Kyale, get her to see reason. Humor and flattery, and appeals to her imagination. Now he'd have to spend a day being ignored; he felt treacherous at the small spurt of relief caused by this thought.

No. He was all she had in the world.

He put a foot on the first step of the hatchway ladder. One of the crew addressed him. "You. Girl." The language they spoke in was probably Rualese—which had some words in common with Marloven. "Little duchess, yes?"

Leander shrugged, trying hard to look apologetic. He rubbed his gut. "Stomach-ache," he said.

They laughed, and one of them said something rude that Leander was just as glad not to understand. He sighed, and climbed below.

Senrid had watched it all from the other side of the ship. He didn't hear everything, but he didn't have to know that Kyale had been complaining, and Leander tried to placate her, using the good sense and that endless patience that roused both Senrid's admiration and his contempt.

He liked Leander, who was smart and knew his history. And you had to admit he was loyal to that tiresome girl who wasn't even any blood relation, just the horrible result of her mother's ambitious marriage to Leander's father.

Senrid had only himself to blame for Kyale's presence. He could have transferred out and left them to the Norsundrians. Now the three of them had to live together in a tiny compartment until they reached Mearsies Heili. They couldn't talk about anything interesting, much less important. Even if Kyale dropped into sleep, she slept so lightly that whispers brought her awake and demanding to know what they were talking about, and no, they were *really* talking about *her*.

Senrid gripped a worn, scarred rail, gazing out over the gray-green horizon, and up to the unbroken wall of blue-gray clouds that meant hard weather. He wished he could transfer the entire ship. He wished he dared any kind of magic. This thing was so slow, and he ached to be home, to know what Tdanerend—or rather Detlev—was doing to his kingdom. He wondered if this determination to warn the lighter mages was an utter waste of time.

No. Not with a rift, maybe a secret one. The lighter mages were the only ones to stop it. Good tactical sense dictated you warned those who could defend best, if you couldn't defend yourself.

He squinted against the frigid air, peering at the horizon for the least sight of land.

If only ships weren't so slow.

Kyale woke to find snowflakes on her eyelashes.

She sat up, her face so cold it hurt. Leander and Senrid were barely visible in the weak gray light filtering through the open hole, each wrapped entirely in his cloak. Kyale could feel freezing air flowing down.

She sat up, and her anger from the night before rushed back, heating her from the inside. How *dare* Leander turn against her! It had to be Senrid's fault. Leander was never mean to her at home.

Well, one thing for certain. She was going to eat hot food, and good food, and maybe—if he apologized—she'd share it with Leander. Senrid could stick with the nasty scrapings from the crew. Exactly as he deserved. And since *she* would do the magic, it wouldn't disturb any tracers on Leander or that stupid Senrid.

But as she struggled to sit up without letting any cold air get at her, she thought, glaring in his direction, *If he does get caught, well, that's also exactly what he deserves.*

She said nothing when the boys woke. Leander kept casting her worried looks. She turned away, hoping he'd feel even worse. As soon as they got their walk on the deck, of course she'd talk to him again—for one thing, being silent was boring. But for now it felt good to let him worry. 'Whining!' How dare he!

The boys got out their cards, and she sat, trying hard to pretend she was at home with her cats all around her. Time dripped with all the speed of a melting icicle.

Eventually they heard the thumping footsteps that meant their food was coming. Kyale drank her share of the water, and didn't look at the food. She didn't want to feel sick. Leander muttered about ice being a new kind of herb that hid flavors. Senrid snorted a laugh.

Finally it was time to take their walk on deck. The corridor outside their horrid cell smelled of baked savory pie. It smelled like chicken. Kyale slowed as they passed the galley, and paused to glance in. As soon as they were up on deck, Kyale glanced at the fierce blue of the sky, and huddled further into her cloak. The wind actually hurt.

But then Leander said, in an urgent, low voice, "Kitty, I'm sorry I snapped at you yesterday. It was my fault. I won't do it again. I promise."

"Well." Kyale felt an urge to spin it out longer, but he looked so tired, and the little frown between his dark brows meant his head ached. Her anger melted away. "All right," she said. And tried a smile, though her lips cracked. "Would you like a nice, hot meal? Hot little chicken-pies, and greens, and a big piece of cheese?"

"Would I," Leander exclaimed. "And why not a fine apple-tart to finish it?"

He thought she was just playing an imagination game! Well, why not? It would make the surprise even better.

"Let's go below," she said. "It's too cold up here. And we can talk, you and me, before that stupid Senrid crowds back in."

"All right. Go ahead. I'll tell him to take his time getting exercise." He turned away as Kyale dashed below. Relieved, he joined Senrid at the weather-side, where the wind was worst, but the crew got angry if they stood on the more sheltered lee. "I apologize," he said abruptly.

And though he didn't say what for, Senrid knew what he meant. He also knew Leander was too honorable to actually mention Kyale's name. He shrugged. "Maybe we'll see land within a couple of days."

Leander nodded. "I hope so." And he chatted on. Nothing important— sailors moving around them, if they wished, only heard chat about winter, riding, and what countries they'd like to see some day. But Senrid felt a little less isolated, and though he knew what Leander was doing, he gave him credit for good intentions.

Meanwhile, Kyale laughed to herself as she ran down below. The one part of her plan she'd worried about was doing the magic so that Leander would be surprised—and here, unplanned for, was her chance!

She bustled by the galley again, spotting the position of the foods she wanted, and then clambered into their cell.

There, she sat down, shut her eyes, pictured her meal in her mind, and carefully performed the spell. A tiny *paff* of displaced air, and there was the food!

When Leander came Kyale looked up proudly. "Surprise!"

"What? How'd you wangle that? We won't have to pay extra, will we?"

"Of course not! It's my other surprise. I learned the spell! See, I told you that learning useful spells would be the best way for me to learn how to do magic, and not those silly, boring basics—" She stopped when she saw Leander wince and put his hand to his head. "What am I going to tell Senrid?" he muttered.

He didn't sound angry, he sounded anguished.

Kyale's pang of guilt swiftly turned into exculpatory anger. "Nothing," she said. "This is for you and me. *He* got us into this disgusting, horrible situation. He can sit up there and freeze."

"Kyale. We both explained to you about the wards."

"No one would ward *me*," she pointed out triumphantly. "They don't know I know a spell. Even if there really are tracer wards on you two. I certainly haven't felt anything, and I've been around magic enough to know what it feels like."

"You don't feel tracer wards, unless you have a—" Leander began. "Oh, why didn't you ask me? I hope they didn't put a tracer on you, but they could, knowing we're together. Nothing easier, in fact."

"Because I knew what kind of stupid answer you'd give. I think you're both idiots, and if you don't want your share, fine. I'll eat it all myself."

Leander sighed. "No. While it's here, let's eat. I think we're going to need it."

"Don't tell Senrid," Kyale said, cradling a hot chicken pie in her hands. But the warmth, the aroma, did her good. "He'll only get nasty, and if nothing happens, then who cares?"

Leander frowned. "If you promise no more spells, no matter how tiny, I won't tell him. But if something happens, then I'll have to."

"I promise," Kyale said. "But in the meantime, admit it will feel good to have a decent meal, just once. Like decent people."

Chapter Five

Leander woke abruptly out of a deep sleep when someone shook his shoulder.

He gulped for air, trying to remember where he was, then somewhere on deck a man screamed, *I never heard of any Marloven prince! Never!* Followed by the reddish flare of a lantern on his eyelids.

Senrid stared down at him, twin lantern-flames in his enormous black pupils making his eyes look bright and ferally angry. "Did you do magic?"

Leander worked his dry mouth. "No. Kyale did."

Kyale sat up, silent, her face blanched. She did not deny it, or even try excuses.

"Food spell. I didn't know she had it, and she really didn't understand about tracer wards—"

Senrid made an impatient movement. "Norsunder knows I'm here. Sounds like the crew is deserting." His mouth thinned to a white line. Then he said flatly, "Make certain the message gets through about the northern rift."

He turned his back, the lantern swinging, pushed through the storeroom hatchway, and slammed it, leaving them in darkness.

Kyale clutched at Leander's arm. "You're not—"

"No," Leander said, hating Norsunder, hating her, hating himself. "I don't dare do the right thing and go up there and surrender myself, because he's right. The message is more important than our worthless lives." He couldn't help the bitterness in his voice.

At least she did not protest.

Leander eased the storeroom door open in time to hear Senrid laughing. "Of course I'm alone," Senrid said—too loudly? "I ditched Leander Tlennen-Hess in the harbor and took his money, the sentimental lighter fool."

A fast exchange in a language Leander had hoped never to hear again was followed by Senrid's derisive laughter. That ended with the sharp smack of a fist against flesh, and a thud against the deck.

Then came the rumble of boots, a few shouts, and finally all Leander heard was his own harsh breathing, and the creaks and groans of the ship's timbers. These noises slowly worsened into crashes and then the crackle and roar of fire.

The terrifying singe of fire brought him up and out into the hold, which was filled with slowly eddying smoke. At the far end, the square hatch blurred with reddish glow.

"They're firing the ship," he breathed. "Kyale, we've got to get out of here!"

She wailed in fright and scrambled out behind him. Her small hand clutched at his arm, trembling when a grinding smash above sent a howling whirlwind of cinders down inside.

"The deck is weakening," he breathed. "Come on!"

They bumped their way into the thick smoke, bending low and coughing. Kyale's wails escalated into screeches when they reached the hatch to see flames shooting high above the upper deck.

"Cloak around your head," he shouted into her face. "We'll run for it! Dive over the side!"

And die in the freezing water, if the crew wouldn't pull them into the life boats—but that would be better than burning to death.

He pulled Kyale up behind him on the ladder. She was struggling with her skirts, which kept getting caught under her feet. At the top, he gave her a push and led the way, dodging fallen spars and snarls of rope on the deck. Flames burned fitfully everywhere.

Timbers groaned and ground without cease, then the mizzen toppled and crashed across the foremast, boiling a fury of hot embers into the darkness.

Kyale was screaming again. Leander whirled around. Sparks had landed on her skirt as she pressed back against the rail, her thin fingers spread in terror.

Leander swung his legs over the side of the rail as the ship canted dangerously. He pulled Kyale up, then thrust her out into the darkness.

She screamed all the way down.

Splash!

He held his breath and jumped, coughing when a gout of smoke singed his lungs. He was just about to gasp again when the icy water knocked his breath out.

Blue stars blinded him; his limbs wouldn't work. The need to breathe forced him upward, kicking against the dragging weight of his cloak. His lungs threatened to burst a heartbeat before he broke the surface. His raw throat burned as he gasped and choked, again and again.

Kyale thrashed around in the bitterly cold water. At first she struggled to hold her breath while the weight of her clothes pulled her down. She screamed Leander's name, or tried—water kept sloshing into her face, her eyes, nose, mouth, making her gag.

She wept in terror and despair when a cold sensation round her arm reminded her of the armband from the water world.

She sobbed in relief, and forced herself to relax. To sink below the surface. Then, frantic with fear, she let a trickle of water into her nose. At once the magic took over.

The bone-aching cold diminished to a pleasant coolness, especially on the parts of her that had been scorched in the fire. She gazed upward past the crystalline bubbles rising to the surface, which glowed a frightening red.

The burning ship! Where was Leander?

She lay underwater, trying to identify the confusion of things floating on the surface, lit up by that sinister goldy-red light that blocked the black sky beyond. The huge shape of the ship began to tilt downward frighteningly near. She kicked away, trying to find a human shape among the floating debris.

On the surface, Leander struggled to keep his limbs from freezing as he scanned for the life boats. There were no life boats. What did that mean—had they rowed away, or what?

He swam toward a tangle of bobbing debris. Where was Kyale? He remembered that she still had on her gold band from the adventure on the water world, and sighed with relief. She would be much safer than he was —he could not longer feel his fingers or toes,

He had to get out of that water, or he'd die.

The jumble of debris included the main yard, onto which he dragged himself, avoiding tangling himself in the snarl of ropes surging just below. He lay along the mast as straight as he could, shivering violently. Heat poured from the sinking ship, but he dared not get too near. He'd read that sinking ships would suck anything floating near down with them. At least he didn't freeze on that side. His other side was numb.

He watched as the last of the ship sank, and the red glow flickered out, leaving him alone under the scattering of night stars glittering coldly overhead. *Remember the rift, Kitty,* he thought tiredly, and dropped his forehead onto his wrists, and his mind slid into a soft darkness.

As the last of the red light diminished, Kyale kicked hard, rose to the surface, and broke free. Icy air hit her again. Swimming below the surface was faster, for then the magic aided her, but she couldn't see much. Swimming on the surface meant the horrible cold, and slowness, and the danger of getting tangled in all those ropes snaking out. She bobbed down and up again, slowly making her way through the mess. Was that? Yes!

A leg dangled in the water, over by that long thing with all the jumble attached.

She thrashed her way grimly under and around the snarls and tangles until she reached that leg, and popped up. "Leander!" she called.

No answer.

Danger flared in her, brighter than the fire earlier. She shoved her way past a thick mass of ropes, wincing when a wood shard jabbed into her shoulder. There was his face, resting on his hands, which looked like ice in the starlight. "Leander? Wake up!"

Nothing. She poked at him, then gripped his arm and shook, but he almost slid off the wooden thing. His skin was so cold! He felt like a marble statue.

Think . . . think . . . would the magic work for two? She ducked down, took a deep breath, then—while still underwater—reached up and touched his ankle, which was still below the surface.

She felt magic flow out of her, and into him. She *felt* it.

She tried a breath—still worked. Maybe it wouldn't if two breathed under water?

No time for that now. It seemed the right thing to do, to just stay where she was, floating in the water, and hold onto his ankle.

Sleepiness prickled at her eyelids. She wound her hand around one of those floating loops of rope, and then around his ankle so they'd stay connected, and she let herself drift into sleep.

Senrid knew it was a mistake to dodge that first blow, but then anything he did was going to be a mistake.

Someone grabbed him from behind. Someone else smacked him across the face, forehand, backhand. His skin was so numb from the wind he barely felt it, though he knew he would later. The Universal Language Spell either did not include Norsundrian, or he was warded against understanding his captors.

One voice snapped orders—he knew that from the tone—and others reported back. A hard hand gripped the back of his neck and transfer magic smashed him out and into the world again, leaving him feeling nauseated and unable to balance.

The hand yanked viciously, and he stumbled into motion, shoved in front of his captor. The smeary black dots across his vision cleared, revealing a stone corridor lit by ensorcelled torches at intervals.

The reminder of the prison at home was an ironic touch. Where were Leander and Kyale? Comforting themselves with the thought that Senrid was now with his own kind?

Stop that. There is no bigger waste than self-pity. He had to observe, listen, and survive.

The Norsundrians shoved him into a small room where an older man sat behind a narrow table. A longish exchange ensued, during which Senrid twice heard the name *Detlev*.

Fear made his mouth dry.

During the exchange, two women came in. A young one gave Senrid a derisive smirk as she asked a question. The man gripping Senrid by the neck of his tunic. The other woman laughed as well, contemptuous and cold.

Abruptly the older man pointed in one direction.

Senrid braced himself to face Detlev. Instead, he was marched down a shadowy corridor, taken through a guarded door, and then down another corridor lined with heavy-wooden doors: cells.

A clank of keys, a shove, and he was left in darkness.

The door shut.

No Detlev, he told himself. That was a good start.

Observe, and survive.

When Kyale woke, the water glowed blue-green around her, and golden shafts lanced downward.

She turned her face up. Blue sky gleamed beyond the translucent light-shifts of the surface.

Popping up above the surface, she discovered that the sun was actually almost warm. Leander's face was splotched with red, whether from sunburn or fire burn she could not tell.

She lifted a hand and splashed water onto him.

Leander jerked awake. He winced as if he had the world's worst headache.

"So it was real," he said in a husky voice.

"Ship's at the bottom," Kyale said.

Leander's green eyes focused on Kyale. "We betrayed Senrid, Kyale. It was nothing but a betrayal."

"But I didn't—"

"I don't want to hear it."

"But you—"

"I don't want to hear it."

He didn't sound angry, just definite.

"Leander, you have to listen—if that stupid—"

"I don't. Want. To hear it." His voice was quiet, his gaze steady and remote.

Kyale felt excuses piling up behind her lips, angry ones, desperate ones, fearful ones. Underneath the fear lay guilt, but she couldn't bear to look at that.

She groaned, saying pleadingly, "At least we're alive."

"Alive, with a job to do. We must carry word of that rift to someone who can do something about it," Leander said.

Kyale was relieved. She'd been afraid he'd give up. "Right," she said. "We can swim the rest of the way."

"Swim." Leander winced again. "How?"

Kyale pointed to her arm, and Leander's face eased slightly. "Yes. That's right. I guess that's why I'm still alive."

"I held onto you," Kyale said quickly. "In the night. I felt the magic go into you. I can breathe still, but I don't know if two can."

"I'll try first," Leander said with a grim tone. "The way I feel, it would serve me right to drown. Hold on."

Before she could protest, he grasped her wrist, slid off the mast, and dropped into the water. Kyale sank down and watched Leander, whose eyes were closed. Tiny bubbles escaped from his nose. Then more, and then he opened his eyes, his hair swirling ridiculously round his head.

He motioned down. She motioned for him to wait. What if she fell asleep, or he did, and one of them let go? She had already lost her cloak.

She yanked at her sash, and when it came loose, she wound it round their hands, binding them together at the wrist. Leander nodded approval. Kicking hard, they swam down, away from the surface, and struck out for the west, and Mearsies Heili.

Chapter Six

North and east of Norsunder's temporal base where Senrid had been taken lies an island called Geranda.

The king of the largest kingdom on the island of Geranda was obsessed with recovering the greatness of his ancient forebears, the Venn. The way to do this of course was to conquer the rest of the island, and then venture out into the sea toward the mainland. But such plans are costly, and his treasury was not equal to his vision—more flowed out to building his army, and his castles, than came in.

He tried twice to conquer his neighbors, but they allied together and beat him back both times, each more costly than the previous.

Then someone from Norsunder came, and suggested a new strategy, beginning with sending out covert teams to kidnap the heirs of the smaller kingdoms on the island.

On the day when the team sent to grab Prince Rai Ame of Setazhia arrived, he was playing in the garden with his two best friends, a dog named Dare, and a cat named Rina.

Rina looked like an ordinary cat, black except for a white spot behind one ear. She was not an ordinary cat, or this particular portion of this chronicle would not need to be written.

For one thing, she liked birds. Not in the way cats have liked birds for untold centuries, on this world and on any others to which cats have roamed—or been taken. Rina never hurt the birds who talked to her.

Instead she talked back to them. She'd been born with the ability to hear thoughts, and (sometimes) to send her own.

This had made her curious about the world. Birds travel far. They showed her things with their swift mental images. This made them interesting and valuable.

Local birds who shared their thoughts had learned to trust Rina. They did not peck or bomb her as they did many of her cat friends.

For their sake, Rina did not eat their cousins who did not talk. She only ate small fish, who did not talk or think enough to recognize much less care for their young. Rina was partial to humans, especially to Rai Ame. He, too, was ordinary to look at: skinny, dun-colored skin, eyes, and hair. But he loved Rina, and Rina loved him.

This particular day Rina crouched under a chair, watching Rai Ame and Dare romp about in the castle garden. The sky was gray, the air wet with impending rain. Not clean, not dirty, just damp.

Dare smelled the strange humans first.

He was an ordinary dog, and Rina liked him also, for dogs have good hearts unless their humans are wicked and distort the dogs into resembling them.

Dare began to bark, sharp and loud, in excitement.

Rina listened with her inner ear, and heard human emotions of excitement, intent, and a relish of force kept under control by command. Her hackles rose, just as the humans burst through the shrubs.

Dare attacked one, and Rina another. She got in one good scratch before a huge hand grabbed her round her middle and tossed her (wriggling and yowling) head first into a sack that stank of old onions.

She curled up, and heard Dare give a sharp yip of pain, and his annoyed bark retreating hastily. Rai Ame shouted something, but his voice was quickly muffled.

Rina's sack was set on something hard. She heard Rai Ame's harsh breathing nearby. His thoughts were very clear. He was confused, afraid, and angry, words streaming from his mind in the form of questions he could not speak.

A jolt and a rolling judder meant they were in a cart, drawn by horses whose thoughts were on food.

Gentle but insistent taps on Rina's bag soon altered into wetness. The rain had begun.

She was thoroughly wet and miserable long before the ride ended. Rai Ame had gone from unconsciousness to jumbled dreams and then to an unhappy wakefulness. As soon as she heard his conscious thoughts—and his question—Rina sent him the sounds and images of what she had heard.

Rai Ame's thoughts winged from question to worry. The anger stayed.

At long last cart halted. Rina's onion sack was pulled free, and she heard Rai Ame pulled out as well, but he was borne off in another direction. Rina curled into a tighter ball and followed him with her thoughts. She'd gotten to be very good at this, especially when the mind she wanted to hear heard her, and willingly completed the contact. Rai Ame called it 'holding hands in the mind.'

Now she saw what he saw, which was a very large stone castle.

Rai Ame was carried down and down into a torch-lit stone passage, and then he was put into a small stone room. The door was closed and locked.

Rina trembled with fear and cold.

She had to pull her awareness back inside herself, which usually took time and effort. The sack opened, and she fell out into fresh air, spreading her claws. She landed on a smooth marble floor.

"Your Majesty, may-you-rule-forever," said the human with the sack. "The Setazhian boy is secure, and this is the boy's cat."

"For Prince Guntur?"

"Yes, Your Majesty, may-you-rule-forever!"

Rina watched the human on the great throne. He was a big one, with cruel thoughts. He wanted Rai Ame's parents dead, because he wanted their land.

His Majesty (may-a-cow-gore-him) nodded complacently. "Take it to his rooms. And do not neglect to tell the brat what happened to his pet."

A big hand gripped Rina under the stomach and lifted her. She decided not to fight at present, until she learned more. The man held her close to his body. His thoughts were neither cruel nor kind. He was intent on promotion, a human thing that Rina found strange. So she stopped listening, and looked about her instead.

This part of the castle was made of a glistening light-colored stone. Rina was taken up many stairs to a room with gold trimmed wooden furnishings. The man knocked at a door inside this room.

"What?"

The man said, in the voice that he'd used to His Majesty (may-a-bird-bomb-him): "Your Noble Highness, I have come with a gift from His Majesty, may-he-rule-forever, which was taken from the Setazhian rebel's son."

"Bring it in, then."

The door opened, and Rina was borne into a huge, airy room that smelled good. She smelled a kind human, and cats, and fish, and . . . cat-herb!

"Is the boy dead?"

"No, Your Noble Highness. He's in the Keep."

"My father's new plan." This boy's voice was bland, but his inside thoughts were angry. Not with Rai Ame or Rina, but with his father.

Rina considered this briefly. Humans were the ones who used language to express their thoughts, yet so often the words and the thoughts contradicted. Many animals who could hear both distrusted humans for this contradiction. The 'snakes with two heads' were what the animals in legendary Helandrias—the animals cursed with human speech—called humans, some birds had told Rina. Birds did not like snakes, as a rule.

Rina had gotten used to this habit of humans. So many, like Rai Ame, were not evil. They were just clumsy with their lives, and with one another. Like newborn kittens. Like puppies, but for far longer.

Prince Guntur said, "Please tell His Majesty, may-he-rule-forever, thank you, from me, his grateful son and heir."

The man set Rina down, bowed, and left. She began cleaning the rotten onion off her fur.

Prince Guntur crouched down nearby to watch. Rina pretended to ignore him, but observed him out of the corner of her eye. He was a tall, well-built human boy, darker of skin, hair, and eyes than Rai Ame, with the smell of many cats on him. She saw herself in his eyes: a small, bedraggled black cat.

He smiled. "Poor cat. I'll order some food for you." He held out his fingers for her to sniff.

She liked his scent, and put her tail up.

He scratched behind her ears, then said, "Can you understand me?"

She looked up into his face.

He knelt in front of her, his hands on his knees.

"One of my animal friends can understand me," Prince Guntur said. "But he's not here. He's in Choree. Your friend is in the Keep, the area reserved for prisoners. I'll be able to go down there in the morning, but I can't now." He frowned slightly. "Do you understand me, little cat? Steel, my dog, talks into my head."

Rina sent her thought: *I can do that*, and with the words she sent an image of Rai Ame and Rina hearing one another.

Rina felt his relief as he said, "That's why I told my father I want the pets of his prisoners. He thinks it's to make the prisoners feel worse. But here's the truth. I've an escape plan, but I need helpers, either animal or human."

Rina listened inside the Prince's head as well as outside, and knew that he told the truth as he saw it.

"So tell your human friend this: if he gets a chance to meet the other people our age down there, to listen to them. It's not a mistake that the Keep is full of people our age. It's not my father's plan, either. It has to do with Norsunder."

Rina's hackles rose. She had heard that word before, carrying ugly images.

Prince Gunter walked to the window. "Go down that roof, and across that wall. The guards are all used to seeing animals, so no one will bother you. In fact, the night commander gets sick if cats are near." Guntur grinned. "If you want to make him sneeze, go right ahead."

He opened the window as he spoke, and Rina hopped up to the sill, pausing to lick the smell and ticking from the sack from her fur before she trotted out onto the tile roof, and down to the nearest wall.

She made her way down to the Keep, a long way down into cold, wet, moldy smelling dank. She sensed many forlorn, isolated humans there. An evil thing, this Keep. Dog leaders always watched out for their packs. A dog would be better for that huge throne than that human, except a dog wouldn't want a throne.

Rina's mood was bleak when at last she found Rai Ame, her fur ruffled and the end of her tail twitching. She joined him by squeezing between the bars in his single window.

"Rina," he said, his mind blooming with welcome.

She jumped down, hating the feeling of damp stone on her paws. Rai Ame sat on the edge of a narrow wooden cot, sneezing at the moldy dust raised when he disturbed the blanket there.

Rina sent him a memory of her interview with Prince Guntur.

When he had understood it, Rai Ame whispered, "If it's true, at least we've got someone on our side, don't we? Except why am I here? Oh. To force my parents into surrender."

Rina curled up in his lap, sending Guntur's image of other prisoners in the keep—allies all, he had said.

"My age? Boys? Boys and girls?" Rai Ame murmured. "Norsunder wants children? I don't understand." And a few moments later, "I hope Dare is all right."

Rina sent her memory of his retreating bark.

"Good. Someone grabbed me round the neck, and I couldn't breathe, and next thing I knew I woke up in that cart between two fellows holding swords." Rai Ame's thoughts were troubled. "This is bad. Norsunder? We've never had any of them on our island, not that I ever heard."

Rina purred, trying to comfort him.

Rai Ame petted her, but his hands were absent in their movements, his thoughts full of worries about his parents and the people of Setazhia. Conflicting with those was his curiosity about Guntur, and he wished to know who else was a prisoner, and why Norsunder wanted heirs gathered.

Presently they both heard the clumping of iron reinforced heels outside the cell, and occasional high voices shouting words that were too muffled to understand. Rina listened to minds: bored humans bringing food, and young humans trying to hear one another though they could not see or be seen in their cells.

She leaped to the window and squeezed out.

Back in Guntur's room again she found food, as he had promised—her very own dish of milky grains. Several other cats had appeared. They were complacent, incurious cats all. Rina touched noses and whiskers, and the other cats ignored her after that. She ate, then returned to sleep with Rai Ame. They kept one another warm.

The next morning Guntur sent for Rai Ame, who was brought by the sword-bearing humans to a big room. Rina trotted along behind, ignored by the guards.

Rai Ame took one look at the tall, strongly built boy his age dressed in dark colors, armed with sword and long knife, and he said softly, "Oh, Rina, I'm about to become a ghost."

The boy made a curt gesture and the guards left, and shut the door.

"Sit down, please," Guntur said in badly accented Setazhian.

Rai Ame sat down on a waiting bench, arms crossed over his stomach, which churned with fear as well as hunger.

"You are—"

"Rai Ame Larsan."

"Rai—ahmee...Lar-san," Guntur repeated carefully.

"If you want to, we can speak Gerandan. My parents made me learn it. Self defense," Rai Ame said.

Guntur smiled, and said in his own tongue, "You win. Though I didn't know this was a competition."

"It isn't," Rai Ame said finally, after a silence in which he counted the rapid bangs of his heart against his ribs. And, because he was by nature fair, and could see that Guntur looked disappointed and even wary, "I'm sorry."

"Well, I'm sorry, too, about your being here. My father will hold your life against your parents' submission, but then he'll kill them anyway. You're the last of the hostages. This is Norsunder's demand."

"Norsunder?" Rai Ame repeated, grimacing. People did not speak the name lightly, unless they were angry. And that was considered bad manners.

"They gave my father magical aid," Guntur said in a tight, grim voice. "And in return, he was to gather boys and girls of our age who were in positions of leadership."

"Heirs?"

"Heirs, leaders of any kind of group. They don't have to be nobles, but they do have to be smart. Leaders. I haven't been able to find out why, but you can wager it's not for any good purpose."

"No," Rai Ame said slowly. "You're exempt?"

"So far." Guntur's smile was sour. "I'm supposedly an obedient, unthinking sort of a son, who lives only for sword practice and marching my honor guard around the court. Since they're searching for smart boys and girls, I've been acting as dull as I can get away with. It's easy enough because my father never liked my reading anyway, and he'd as soon think I am never going to question his orders. He had my uncle axed after an argument, and my cousin Mal Venn was stuck in the stables until he disappeared several years ago." Guntur frowned, his eyes narrowed. "Mal Venn was smart, even though he was only four, and Detlev—he's one of the leaders of Norsunder—came and took him away. That's when I started my pretense. I don't want that to happen to me."

"Four," Rai Ame whispered.

"And he was out in the stables, which has to mean that those Norsundrians have spies around. Others besides my father."

Rai Ame hunched up against a chill. "Is that why they want us?"

"I don't know," Guntur said. "No one's disappeared. Yet. But there's another danger. If you see one of them coming after you with a knife that has a kind of greenish glow on the edge, watch out."

"Poison," Rai Ame said, nodding. "That's been around as long as trees."

Guntur smiled grimly. "Worse. It's a lethal magical enchantment. If they put your name on the spell and kill you, your soul is theirs, whether you want it to happen or not. If they just cut you—all they need is to draw blood—then the magic marks you through your own blood. They can always find you, and at eleven—"

"—the hour before midnight, they can send you nightmares, and torment you until you give in and join them. I've heard those stories. Are they real?" Rai Ame grimaced.

"I don't know. But if the Norsunder people come back, and used those knives, then you might find out."

Rai Ame said slowly, "If they torment you, do they take your will?"

"I overheard my father saying something about sending the heirs back against their families," Guntur admitted, looking away."

Rai Ame said fervently, "We've got to escape."

"Right. And then?"

The boys looked at each other.

Guntur lifted his hands. "And then I don't know. Hide out? Get off the island? We can't fight my father. He's got the army as well as Norsunder's aid."

"Can *we* get magical aid?"

"No one on the island studies magic as far as I know," Guntur said. "And we wouldn't want Norsunder's magic—dark magic." Guntur looked out the barred window. One of his hands traced round and round the hilt of his sword. "It's a temptation—a big one—to get Norsunder's magic and use it once. Fast. Hard. Defeat my father. But there would also be a big price. I don't want to pay it."

Rai Ame nodded slowly.

"In the meantime, there's worse news." Guntur's voice lowered and flattened. "And this is why we have to hide. My father has been complaining that once Norsunder finds whoever it is they are looking for, they might drag him into their plans for the mainland. See, they can't get huge armies over, yet, so they are looking around for ones already here, ones trained and equipped and ready to go."

Rai Ame held up his hand, then said, "Rina just let me know that birds have brought similar news."

Guntur rubbed his chin. Rai Ame reached for Rina, but he couldn't feel any comfort in her warm, purring body. Not when the threat extended beyond his parents and country to the entire world.

Rai Ame said, "I think you're right about hiding. And going to the mainland, to find mages to help against Norsunder."

Guntur said, "Then that's decided. Look, we've been talking long enough. Now remember, when the guards come in, you're the miserable prisoner and I've been gloating. Make it good because they'll report whatever they hear to my father. We'll be able to leave soon, in case I can't get back to you. Be ready whenever the chance comes."

He moved to the door and struck it with his fist. As it opened, he sneered, "Just take that thought with you to your miserable cell, weak and worthless Setazhian!"

Rai Ame hung his head, shuffling out with a disconsolate air.

≈

True to his word, Guntur arranged the escape the day after Rai Ame heard a great commotion in the courtyard beyond his cell. By standing on his bunk and peering out, he'd been able to see large numbers of splendidly armed and mounted warriors lining up in parade order, and then riding out amid trumpetings and the thunder of hooves.

The horses were the best of all, but none as beautiful as the white horse that awaited the boys in a garden at the other end of the nearly deserted palace.

Guntur came to the Keep himself. When Rai Ame heard his cell unlock, and he saw Guntur there, he was surprised. Further surprise attended his seeing two guards snoring.

"Put sleep-weed in today's beer," Guntur said with a triumphant grin, as Rai Ame scooped up Rina. "A *lot*."

As he spoke, he led them to the garden. Rai Ame's breath caught. A number of other horses also waited, but Rai Ame scarcely noticed them.

"From the mainland, up north," Guntur said, indicating the blue-white hair, the intelligent eyes. "They are reputed to be magic creatures from another world, who prefer the horse form. She hears my thoughts, and no one but me can ride her, not without her permission."

Rai Ame tucked Rina securely under his arm.

"Here come our allies," Guntur said.

Rai Ame and Rina watched the group of boys and girls coming from the other end of the garden. A red-haired girl a little older than Rai Ame gave them a shy smile.

"Mira of Landir," Guntur said.

She mounted a roan behind a stringy, mobile-faced boy who said, "I am Jandar of Choree. Let's ride!"

Guntur boosted Rai Ame up onto the white horse's bare back, and they and the still-unnamed others rode from the garden, taking side paths away from King's City and then to southeast, the next day reaching Choree.

Rina listened inside them all as they exchanged stories during the long two day ride. She sniffed and sorted past the fear-uncertain bragging, and the angry competition in describing hardships endured, that life in Choree had been especially terrible in recent years. Not all the problems were due to the Gerandans or the ambitions of their king (who-ever-heard-of-a-king-ruling-forever?).

Rina saw Guntur listening intently to everything. The Choree gang, who had a hideout in the wooded mountains above the main harbor, were wary around him—especially their leader, Jandar. Guntur was bigger and stronger than any of the others, but he behaved circumspectly. Yet even Rai Ame, who had never thought about such things before, understood by the end of that day that Guntur was a natural leader. Rina could smell the sour longing in Jandar for the attention that went naturally Guntur's way.

Perhaps there might eventually have been problems between Guntur and Jandar but there was not enough time.

Guntur had miscalculated his father's reaction; when the King found out that the Prince was missing, His Majesty (may-his-boat-sink-with-him-on-it) halted his intimidation march and ordered a search.

Rina and Rai Ame woke up early the third morning. Jandar's group had insisted on riding through darkness the night before, so they could reach their hideout.

Since they knew the land well, it had not been a difficult ride. Rai Ame —tired and confused by flickering torches—had climbed a rope-ladder, curled up in blankets that were given him, and slept.

He woke to blue light through tree branches, lighting up a kind of platform in a mighty tree. Rina sat nearby in her loaf-of-bread shape, two paws just visible, as the air was chilly. Grinning in wonder, he shed the blanket in order to explore.

Rina purred. She was pleased. She, too, liked the tree house, and she had also met all the animals, including Guntur's dog Steel, who also could talk mind to mind.

They climbed down together, finding Jandar's group busy scouting out breakfast.

Steel was the first to stiffen.

A greenish flicker in the air, and a smell of hot metal, froze everyone as four armed Gerandans appeared in the middle of the clearing, one by one.

In their center was the king, Guntur's father, tall and broad and dark-haired. Beside him stood a slim fair-haired man in civilian clothing.

The thunder of hooves rumbled in the distance as the king's guard galloped toward them from the slope below. Above the grove of trees stretched sheer rock. Nowhere to run.

The white horse vanished in a flicker. The king said, "Where is my son?"

"I am here," Guntur said, ignoring a whispered suggestion to hide. Guntur had seen in a heartbeat there was nowhere to hide.

"You will return home."

"No," Guntur said, crossing his arms. "Not while you're allied with Norsunder."

The man who had come with the king stepped forward.

Steel and Rina both sensed danger, though the man appeared to be less threatening than the king.

Everyone turned his way. He was medium tall, lighter in build than the Gerandans, his features regular, his corn-silk hair a contrast to the mostly dark-haired descendants of the Venn. Though he wore no uniform he had a sword at his side; its grip was old-fashioned and artistic, not heavy and martial.

"There is no need for strife," he said to the king. His light, laughing voice, with a faint trace of accent, contrasted with the king's grating bellow.

His Majesty (may-he-drown-in-his-victims'-tears) looked up, his dark eyes wide and unblinking as they met the light gaze of the man.

"Set the children at liberty," the man suggested, smiling. "None of these are the one I seek. They will cause no harm."

The King fell silent.

"You have a greater task now," the man spoke on, his voice carrying in the silent clearing. Next to Rina, Steel whimpered softly. "I have come to establish peace in the world, and you and your fine warriors are needed to maintain it."

The King said in a flat voice, "We will go where you command."

The man turned to Guntur, and caught his gaze.

Rina's fur ruffled up. The air smelled of lightning just before it struck the ground.

The man said, "Guntur, you and your friends may return peacefully to your homes. I will have something for you to do presently."

The leader of the Choree orphans was next, and then Mira, and last Rai Ame. The man caught their attention, said something to them in his pleasant voice, and afterward they all stood quietly, their faces blank. Their minds were muted, distant. Like trying to see through fog.

The man vanished. The King and his Gerandan warriors met the guards, and all headed peaceably toward home—including Guntur.

Rina put her hackles down. Steel whined, ran around sniffing all the children, then he returned to Rina.

Rina thought, *I listened yesterday. Half of these children have no homes to go to.*

Steel thought, *That man cares nothing.*

Both animals felt a strong urge to do something. But what?

Rina remembered her birds.

The mainland, she thought, picturing a ship. *I must go to the mainland and find the humans who know magic. Or animals like us.*

Steel agreed. *And I will guard them here.*

So Rina, a small cat, began a very long journey.

Chapter Seven

Now it is time to introduce Sartora.

Her name when she was born was Liere, her family name Fer Eider.

Before she could speak she knew she was different. She grew up feeling lonely, and above all, afraid. Alone of her family, she could hear others' emotions—sometimes even their thoughts.

Until that winter morning, the sense of danger she'd also grown up with seemed vague as storm clouds. That morning, as she made the shift from dream-consciousness to real, she sensed that the storm was coming at last.

She opened her eyes, and lay in bed without moving, cataloguing every detail of her surroundings. Lilith the Guardian, the kindly mental "voice" who visited Liere's dreams every so often, had encouraged her to be observant. Liere had heeded all of the Guardian's advice, taking guidance for rules.

She started with the view above the bed she shared with her sister. She knew exactly how many rough-planed boards of old oak formed the ceiling, and how many nails studded each board. She'd followed with her eyes the grain in each plank, contemplating the colors and how they might have been so formed, for there was little opportunity in her circumscribed life, in the little house on the narrow stone street, to learn about how and why trees grew in the wild. She had heard that one could find answers to these questions, and to many other questions, in books.

But her father felt that reading made children disobedient and disinclined to obey their betters.

Liere shifted her attention from the ceiling, and the muted shades and shadows made by the pale winter sun, to the room itself. Each morning she charted the angle and quality of dawn's light in the small, plain room. She contemplated the warps in the wood, the worn places on the floor, a year's accumulation of handprints—to be scrubbed out again come spring —around doors and windows, masking the smooth-worn places where hands had touched over many years. Small finger-smudges at low height, steadying beginning walkers, amid the bumps and nicks and knocks of rowdy games. Bigger spots at medium, evidence of careless grabs while racing round the narrow corners. And higher ones, made by adults who navigated by touch when night-candles flickered or had burned out.

Liere liked the worn places because they made her think about Fer Eiders long ago.

I don't play, Liere thought, looking at the ones at her height. *But I'm not a grownup.*

She watched her inner self consider that. *I don't play, but I'm not sad. I shouldn't be sad.* Sadness was a waste. A weakness. That much she had learned through observing her mother, who from time to time was sad, helplessly so, unable to change whatever it was that made her sad as she worked through each day's house, family, and shop crises. *I can't be weak*, Liere thought.

Especially not today.

She knew she was frightened, and she angrily squashed that emotion.

The bed shook. She turned her head. Her younger sister Marga rolled over, murmuring restlessly. Liere watched her waken, sensing Marga's slow transition from dreams to wakefulness. It always took Marga a long time for her 'self' to find its way to the surface world. So it was with the rest of the family.

Marga sat up and poked her.

For Marga, Liere was in every way an unsatisfactory older sister. She wasn't pretty, she never smiled, never played, and she said boring things. Why couldn't she be like other girls' sisters?

"Come on, lazy, get out," Marga said, hoping for a smile, a tickle fight, something fun.

"Who's the lazy one?" Liere asked, conscious of acting out a role. She sensed Marga's disappointment in her, but how could she be someone other than what she was?

Yet Lilith the Guardian had told her during their very first dream-conversation that it was important to act normal, that is, like the others. "I can never get out when I sleep by the wall, and you always make us late downstairs. You know it, Marga," Liere said, trying to act as if it mattered.

"Huh!" Marga tossed her dark curls back.

Liere slid out of bed, practicing softly to herself: "Huh!" While Marga's nightgown was over her head, she tried tossing her hair back. It felt strange. Awkward. But girls did that kind of thing when they were offended—or pretended to be offended, and wanted attention.

Liere did not want attention. She'd learned very early its dangers.

Marga yawned as she pulled on her trousers and smock. Liere's fingers plaited her straight, fine dust-colored hair into two long neat braids while she observed her sister. Marga's braiding was slower; dark, luxuriant curls kept escaping her fingers.

As soon as they were done they ran downstairs to the bathroom. The big tub was reserved for the adults during the week; the young ones got to use it only on Lastday.

The oldest brother had brought the hot water from the kitchen and poured it in the ceramic basin, one of his daily chores. His siblings crowded round to wash the sleep from their faces. There was—as always—much needless shoving and splashing and laughing, in which Liere was careful to take her part. The cleaning-frame on the edge of the basin kept the water sparkling fresh. Liere liked the tingle on her fingers that told of the presence of magic. None of the others ever seemed to notice.

Then they ran to the table, Liere still conscious of that shoulder-tightening sense of something about to happen. She watched her siblings, wishing she *felt* the laughter, the unconscious fun they all felt as naturally as they breathed, instead of merely hearing it.

Why was she so different?

On the outside she didn't look different. They were all small and bird-light in build, like their mother, coloring unremarkable varieties of brown, their eyes either pale blue or brown. Their hair was either sandy or dark with golden highlights, straight or curly. In Marga one could see the best of the combinations. In the younger two brothers and Liere, the plainest.

Their father walked in, and everyone hastily straightened and fell silent, the latecomers breathless and red-faced.

Les Fer Eider surveyed his family as he pulled at his mustache. He frowned, for he liked order and decorum, and above all, he demanded respect from his family. Most of his attention was reserved for his oldest two boys. Liere had long ago stopped asking questions he deemed inappropriate for children, who ought to confine their attention to their proper sphere, the home and shop But a residue of distrust remained with him. She stood, small, uninteresting, and obedient, just as she ought, so his attention passed on.

He sat down. So did Mother, and Liere with her five siblings. Yes, five! Such large families were rare, but Father Fer Eider wanted help for the shop that did not have to be paid, and Mother Fer Eider tried to surround herself with noise, to drown the unhappy voices inside her.

The clatter of passing dishes was not loud, and soft-voiced talk was confined to requests to pass this or that, and return thanks. Private conversations were not permitted at the table. Everyone always turned toward Father and fell silent if he spoke, or answered his questions with words he liked to hear, for to displease him meant being sent away from the table hungry. Liere was careful to listen to the chatter about the weather, and about the store, in this case, repair work that would have to be made up later, because the entire town had been summoned to the hall for a meeting.

"There will be no complaining," Father stated, in a heavy, irritated voice, as he very much resented this high-handed interruption in a business day. "The messenger from Town Council says this fellow's going straight from here to the capital, which is why this isn't held on Restday, as it ought to have been. His stopping in South End is an honor. His subject is no less than world peace. . ."

Everyone was silent, though one of Liere's brothers surreptitiously rolled his eyes, and Marga tossed her hair again.

Liere's mind turned inward as she considered the news. Town meeting on a work day—that was very rare. They had always been on Restday as long as she could remember.

World peace. World peace sounded good. Peace could have nothing to do with the disturbing, questing mind-touch she'd sensed not long after the Guardian's warning, back in the days when she'd not hidden her differences. And again last night, in the middle of her dreams.

She'd felt that presence as a threatening cloud, and had instantly retired behind the mental brick wall that the Guardian had told her to build every night around her thoughts before she went to sleep. She sometimes forgot, like last night.

That was the sense of specific danger. She hoped the cloud thing hadn't found her before she ducked behind her wall, but she was afraid it had.

Hide your second and third faces, the Guardian had cautioned after the first time Liere sensed that cloud, when she was little.

First-face: the physical self. It had made learning much easier when the Guardian said to Liere's dream-figure, *Think of your physical senses and presence as your first face, your mind and dreams as second face, and your spirit as third face. What we called in the days of Old Sartor dena Yeresbeth means the unity of the three, and that unity is what you must work on. But you must also be careful, because those with dena Yeresbeth can send their minds questing outside their physical selves—just as you will able to do with enough practice—and they will be searching for other minds like yours.*

Like you found me, Liere had said.

I am glad I found you before they did, the Guardian had responded, with a calm inflowing of concern. *And when I can, I will listen for you, and help you. But I cannot always be here, for I am a guardian for all the worlds around Erhal, our sun, and there is trouble in far too many places.*

Liere had learned that that was true. Sometimes she could call the Guardian in mind, but other times she couldn't; the Guardian was too far away to sense. Once it had been half a year before the Guardian returned, and she hadn't stayed very long. *I need to return to a far world,* she'd said sadly. *The enemy is very strong there.*

The first time Liere felt that threatening cloud-presence questing in the realm of dreams, she understood that she had drawn its attention the same way she was drawing attention in their part of South End. She was the little girl who wanted to learn to read, though she was a shopkeeper's child, who asked questions about why clouds formed, and where the wind went; about the history of the ruins outside of town, and did horses speak. Her mother worried, her father got angry that she was trying to show off, to pretend she was too good for her place in life. She choked back her questions.

How it hurt to be labeled a mere showoff, and later, stupid! But she'd set Marga and her friends as a model, not even daring to mimic children her own age, and eventually she'd slid out of town gossip enough to feel safe again. The cloud presence had not come back . . .

Until last night.

Father was still talking. " . . . I was told at Council that he is famous not just in our kingdom, but in those to the north." He smiled as he pushed back his plate.

He. So the Visitor bringing world peace was not the Guardian, who Liere knew was a she.

Liere watched her siblings say what Father wanted to hear, but their thoughts were "Oh, how boring.' The younger ones exchanged elbow digs and private grimaces.

Liere's worry pressed on her spirit.

Why would such an important personage want to come to South End? While the girls cleared away breakfast, the middle boys swept the floor and brought out the good rugs, and the older boys got the family's stolid, middle-aged mare hitched up to the cart. Everyone shrugged into coats and mittens then piled into the cart, spreading rugs around. While everyone in town knew that they made and repaired work rugs, mats, and cushions, Father liked to display their sturdy rugs.

The winter sun was bright and the air warm except in the shadows. Liere wedged herself securely in one corner, ignoring splinters. She made certain no one's attention was on her. The siblings joked and shoved, the parents up on the buckboard talked, and Liere risked a questing mind-finger to poke cautiously ahead.

The Guardian had warned her about wandering in second-face, for the mental realm had no physical boundaries. It was all right to practice focus, and it was important to learn how to make her mental 'questing finger' small in order to better protect her own identity—but if she were to touch with that mental finger any entities who were aware of *her*, it was better to retreat behind her mental wall, and withdraw back into first.

She composed herself, and closed her eyes. To anyone else she'd appear to be asleep. Instead she relaxed her body limb by limb so that when she disengaged mind from body she wouldn't flop over like a stuffed doll.

Then the finger became the little rootlet that curled through the mental realm in quest.

She passed by the tangled light-forest of her neighbors' minds. Their thoughts were a little like bits of dreams, with words chattering through —like birds.

She reached farther, and found five new minds.

With great care she let her rootlet touch them, no communication, just 'listening.' Four were like gray silhouettes, composed of threatening thoughts: *Who is the target?*

When can we cut loose from this boring place?

It would only take half a day to smash our way through these stupid sheep!

Let this be a worthwhile hunt . . .

Liere shied quickly away from these violent thoughts. The three others waited for orders, for permission. They did not have the focus of intent.

The one longing for a worthwhile hunt watched the fifth figure. His focus was clear, so clear that the visual image carried easily to Liere: a man sitting cross-legged on the hardy winter grass atop a little hill overlooking the town. Liere knew the spot. The road curled around its base on the way to her cousins'. The man's blond head was bowed. One of his hands supported his forehead. The other rested on something long and shiny-silver beside him.

She abandoned the surface thoughts of the fourth man and sent her tendril cautiously toward that fifth figure.

The mental image that came was a black silhouette against a weird flat gray sun, like molten lead: a *very* powerful wall, keeping her out.

But it did not keep the other mind from sensing her. At once that shielded mind was aware of her, because though the identity was still hidden behind the silhouette, a ghost 'voice' invited her to make herself known—the effect like the sun popping up from behind the rim of the world and shining in your window directly at you.

Snap! She escaped, just barely. She was afraid one more heartbeat and that sun would have burned right through her wall, shining its terrible light on identity and memory, and burning her tendril to ash.

For a short time all she could do was breathe, and control the dizziness and shudders that such quests often caused, especially if she had to return fast. When she knew she had control in first-face, she opened her eyes. The cart jiggled and jounced through caking mud-ruts, and her family chattered happily, everyone except Father glad to be free of work even if only for half a day. Father was enjoying himself in his own way, composing a complaint to be given to the Town Council if he didn't deem this meeting worth losing a day's work.

She closed out the excited surface thoughts of minds around her. The cart reached the Town Hall, jolting behind a ragged line of conveyances.

"Hai, Les!" The familiar shout was from one of the neighboring fathers.

"Hail, Tham! Good day, Inge! Do you remember so many mild days together in one winter?"

"Means a blizzard soon for certain," was the prompt reply, as the two carts creaked to a stop.

The young of both families leaped out, everyone looking for friends. Liere saw the mother in the other cart staring, lips pursed, at the Fer Eiders. She gave that same attention to vegetables at market.

Liere had heard the two sets of parents once talking about how fine it would be if some of their children would marry into one another's families, and ever since then Inge considered them all as if they were for sale.

Liere's siblings didn't seem to care—if they even noticed—but Liere hated that appraisal, and not just because they were always wrong about her. Inge's thoughts about her were unflattering. Liere saw herself through Inge's eyes: a plain, boring, backward scrap of a child only good for kitchen chores and yard work. Liere didn't care about that. In fact, she wanted them to think her boring and backward, because she hated the idea of marriage—of living the same life as her mother.

She slid into the crowd of children from both families, who were busy organizing a game with any others who seemed interested.

At first Liere only meant to escape the scrutiny of Inge and Tham, but then she saw a group of strange men standing at the side of the entrance to Town Hall. They were studying the mass of children with a close attention that burned alarm through Liere.

She thrust herself into the forming game, playing and shouting like Marga. Though she ran when the others ran, she maneuvered so she could watch the watchers, and not be spotted doing it.

Four of the men wore some kind of uniform, not the gaudy one of the King's Guard, but plain gray winter tunics, long black trousers, and high blackweave riding boots. They all carried weapons. The fifth man wore brown trousers and a white shirt, no jacket or cloak despite the cold air. He also wore a sword. And he had blond hair.

Control. Liere had learned that from the Guardian. When one made the unity one could, when needed, shut out cold. That man had such control over first-face that he had to be the mind behind the silhouette-wall.

The children screamed and surged in one direction, and Liere followed, running in the midst of the crowd. *Why does he seek me?* she thought. *What am I supposed to do?*

For now, she had this one advantage: she knew what he looked like, but he did not, as yet, know how to identify her.

Chapter Eight

Davernak loved the hunt.

On some worlds people hunted animals for sport. Davernak had tried it, and found it boring. Where was the fun in running down and destroying a stupid animal whose efforts to save itself were nothing but instinct?

The pleasure was worthwhile when the contest was equal, or nearly so —when the quarry could provide a chase worthy of one's exertion. When there might even be some risk, which made the capture, and the clash of wills, so much more exquisite. It was that sense of loss in the victim's eyes—when he had to acknowledge your power as the greater—that was even more satisfying than the actual kill. Though he enjoyed the kill.

There couldn't possibly be anyone worth the hunt in this tiny town called South End in the northeast region of Imar, a kingdom once great, but through several generations of indifferent government had dwindled to backwardness. The evidence was the empty, tumbled remains of once-thriving cities, on the edges of which small trade towns like South End had sprouted, built from the brick and tiles of the ruins. North End had been even more boring.

Davernak stood on the dilapidated porch of the Town Hall building and looked in disgust at the scrambling mass of children. Children! When he'd first been told that Siamis had somehow sniffed someone out who had those mysterious mind powers shared by the Old Sartorans, Davernak had anticipated a worthy hunt.

Time had narrowed the possibilities not to kings or even war-leaders, but to children, in shambling little towns scarcely worth burning. Even worse, he'd been told just now they were scouting for a little girl! Disgust and boredom made him impatient, and he turned away.

Watched covertly by Liere.

Parents emerged on the terrace before Town Hall, and began calling for their offspring. Liere stopped running when the others did, and she positioned herself in the center of the scramble of siblings and Inga's children. Now she was glad that the families always sat together at special events. She felt safer in the large group. She knew as long as she did nothing to bring attention to herself, none of those sinister people in the gray and black would look twice at a plain, undersized ten-year-old.

The children shuffled glumly inside, Liere in the middle, imitating posture and voice. For the parents, the interesting part of the day was just beginning. For the children, it was over. Town Meetings too often featured some pompous rich noble who issued decrees or made long, dull, and on one memorable occasion confused speeches. (That time being when the shoemaker's son had found the speech and mixed all the pages up, and the fellow never noticed because his wife had written it.)

This time the speaker was a young man and he had no papers, which meant he knew exactly what he was going to say. And he was wearing a sword! The boys looked at him with interest, and so did the young women, for he was tall, and though slender he was well-made, grace and strength in his movements, his fair hair waving back from a broad brow, his eyes light-colored and intelligent, his smile kind and gentle.

"I greet you, citizens of South End," he said, and his voice was like song, his accent reminding them of the ancient chants of the morvende and the dawnsingers. "My name is Siamis, and I am traveling through Imar, visiting every town of importance, on my mission to bring peace to troubled lands."

Siamis! Liere thought back. Had she heard the name before? If so, she hadn't known it for a name, but had thought it yet another of the mysterious terms she didn't understand from the Guardian's shared memories of the days of Old Sartor.

It's an ugly name, she decided, remembering that shadow on the hill. No, an *evil* name.

"Imar has been troubled," he said, and many adults nodded, looking at one another and then nodding again.

There was something for everyone in his talk, for young and old, male and female, poor and rich. He spoke well, sometimes making people laugh by unflattering comparisons to unpopular rulers or buffoons of recent history. He even referenced local gossip, causing gasps of gratification and intense curiosity. How could he know? Who had been talking?

Liere's apprehension intensified.

"What I want," Siamis said, "is for everyone in this country to regain the peace and prosperity your ancestors once enjoyed in the long-ago days of Ancient Sartor."

Ancient Sartor! The words riffled through the room in a susurrus of surprise and anticipation.

Siamis then described, in vivid detail, what life had been like in Ancient Sartor.

At first about half the adults actually listened and the others thought about personal concerns, or about what troubles the government caused when they interfered with local trade, and was it really a wise idea to speak up and ask for change? What power did he have, after all, if the government hadn't sent him?

The children had become bored, shifting and whispering and playing hand games, but one by one they, like the adults, found themselves caught by a compelling image, or a turn of the harmonious voice, as compelling as a once-loved melody.

As Siamis talked about the power and wealth and grandeur of the Old Sartorans, the people of South End seemed to see them, hear them. Know them, as if they were real memories.

But they weren't memories. The Guardian had willingly shared certain of her own memories—some from her childhood, which Liere treasured—and others from later. These Liere had pondered often, for dena Yeresbeth enabled one to revisit memories with the clarity of the first occurrence. The Guardian had promised that understanding would come with age and experience.

These things he talked about were not true memories, they were stories.

The people in them were not real, yet they were all so vivid—

Oh—oh—oh—

They were *illusions*.

Alarm burned through Liere. With an effort she shut out the pleasing tenor voice. The world felt cold and bleak and dreary, with her alone in it, while her mind yearned to return to that vision of a world of beautiful things, of continuous music, where art and life were inseparable.

She forced herself to look, and not to listen. Her family, Inge's family, the baker's family—all so different—wore exactly the same expression, as if they were under a spell.

Illusions were false images made by magic. That much Liere had learned from the Guardian. If people consented to see illusions, like at the great plays in the capital, then they were harmless, for the people knew they witnessed illusions. When the illusion captured the attention, when it pretended to be real, then magic was being used falsely.

Liere closed her eyes, still careful to imitate the posture of those around her, and touched her mental finger to the minds of her family.

Each walked mentally among Siamis's images, in a dream world of illusion. Every one of them. And not just her family, but Inge's as well. And the others were also enraptured.

It's not just an illusion. It's a spell of some kind.

A spell to do what? Wary, too amazed by her discoveries yet to be frightened, Liere sent out another tendril, resisting the images as she reached for the meaning that must lie behind the words, the intent of the spell.

"How do I know so much?" His voice altered from coaxing to commanding. "Because I was there!"

Everyone's attention shifted from the pretty images to the man himself. He regarded them with wide eyes that reflected tiny pinpoints of light from the windows, and his brief smile, his soft laugh expressed victory and enticement. "I was born more than four thousand years ago, and now I am back in the stream of time. I can assure you, if we all work together, we shall regain everything that once was lost."

Liere pressed her knuckles against her teeth. Again she checked the minds around her, and again she found each person thinking about Siamis, agreeing happily to work together—each and every mind waiting for his commands.

Everyone except Liere.

What am I supposed to do? she thought. *O Guardian Lilith, where are you?*

Liere understood that she alone was able to choose, for all the people around her, from Marga sitting quietly beside Liere to the Mayor, big and pompous in the front row, had willingly surrendered—something—in order to wait for Siamis's orders.

"I want you to go home and live in peace with one another," he said.

That sounded very fine, didn't it?

"I will show you the way to regain the lost power and prestige of Old Sartor."

Power. Prestige. Were they wrong? Not if . . .

She struggled with so many new thoughts it felt like trying to capture and hold the dancing sun reflections on water.

Power, prestige, were not wrong as such, only if—

Oh. Oh! She saw the difference, then: in his descriptions he had avoided mention of any of the great magical accomplishments, the harmony between humans, animals, and the other life forms on the world, the awareness of place among all living things celebrated by the Processions between the cities, and other aspects of the Blessed Twelve. The Guardian had shown her these things. All he'd shown them so vividly were skills the Old Sartorans had once had in creating material things. And now he promised personal power, the ability of the stronger mind to impose order on the weak—

"I appeal to your sense of reason," Siamis said. "All of you, regardless of status or age. I appeal in particular to one who is among you, one of exceptional gifts. The potential you show will be trained. You will become a leader if you will come forward and learn from me."

He paused, his gaze moving across the faces before him.

Liere, with her mind well hidden behind her strong brick wall, held her breath, her heart thumping against her ribs. Everyone in South End might think (if they still could think) he meant them, but she knew Siamis was referring to her.

She looked at her lap, not daring to meet his eyes.

Except . . . she should stand up to this man, if he really was evil. She should break that illusion, for it was equally evil of her to cower here on her seat and permit him to ensorcel her family, her town.

"I command you to live in harmony with one another. If the day comes when we must rise against the foes of peace and plenty, then I will call on you. Will you follow me, and become like your ancestors, the Old Sartorans?"

The entire town's voices raised in a single shout of assent.

Now she had it. That was the command to be feared—he would order them to make war on other people, and they all assented together, as if their minds had all been bound into a single will! Not theirs, *his!*

Shaking with fright, with determination, she stood up and called, "No! Wait!"

Her voice sounded embarrassingly shrill in her own ears, but she forced herself to speak on—to try to break that spell. "Who took away the good life from Old Sartor?"

Everyone stared at her with blank eyes.

"Norsunder," Siamis answered, smiling.

Liere gripped tightly on the wooden chair back in front of her. "And . . . where are you from?" she demanded.

Now Siamis looked at her with astonishment. She knew it was false, for she could still see amusement crinkling his eyelids, but her family, her townspeople, all turned to stare at her in shock and astonishment.

Liere gazed back at them in dismay. It was too late. They hadn't betrayed her. They were now under enchantment. She'd betrayed herself —and them—by waiting, by being weak, by being too slow and too timid until it was too late.

Whispers of indignation hissed from all corners of the room. Her own family looked ashamed.

Liere wrenched her hands away from the chair back and stumbled past all the feet in her row. Then she ran down the center aisle and out of the building, tears blurring her vision. She heard her father's voice apologizing, and Siamis reassuring him with kindly laughter. "What can you expect from a confused little child?" was the last thing she heard.

The confused little child dashed across the terrace, but before she could jump down the stairs and go (where?) a hand caught her arm above the elbow. She stumbled against the plain wooden wall and blinked up at one of the gray-tunicked men.

He didn't speak, just gripped her arm firmly and guided her around the side of the building to the back. Another of the warriors opened the door to what looked like a storeroom, and the first one gave her a little push inside, and thrust her down onto a three-legged stool.

The door shut behind her, and she heard the thump of a body against the door—one of the men leaning against it. Through a dirty window Liere made out the gray of another tunic. She looked around at the jumble of boxes, tables, and two dusty mirrors. It seemed to be a sort of dressing room, probably for the players that sometimes came to town. There was nothing sinister or forbidding about the little room, but fear gripped her, making her feel sick inside.

Fear. She sat up straight, forcing herself to examine her own emotions. Fear had clouded her judgment. Fear caused trembling, tears. She had to use reason, not emotion. Now especially, for the door creaked and Siamis walked in.

He looked around with that expression of amusement as he pushed aside a box of dusty decorations, hitched a knee over the corner of one of the tables, and perched there. "I'm glad I finally found you." He gave Liere a kindly smile.

"I found *you* first." She was painfully aware of how thin and high her voice sounded. She'd meant to challenge his friendly comment but she suspected she just sounded silly—knew she'd sounded silly from the look on his face. Not that he laughed, like the local bullies. But his eyes crinkled as though he held the laugh back.

Her face heated up and her insides roiled.

"What I'd like to know," Siamis said, hand open, inviting her to speak, "is what you object to in my prospect for peace?"

He waited politely, not looking the least bit sinister.

She took a deep breath. *No fear! Reason.*

"I know you come from Norsunder. So I don't believe you want to help make Imar into a new version of Old Sartor."

"I didn't say that," he answered. "I told them they'd become like their ancestors, which is true enough in the sense I mean." His tone made it clear that he did not think highly of their ancestors—Old Sartorans or not.

Liere looked down at her hands, then up, and met his eyes. She felt a mental contact, and flung up her mental wall.

"You can't bespell *me*," she exclaimed with all the bravado she could muster. "I passed *that* trick when I was a day old."

Again Siamis smiled the way people do when they're trying not to laugh.

Anger melted the icy fear in Liere's middle. "You don't have any interest in helping people," she began. "You can't, if you're from Norsunder."

"You don't know anything about my interests," Siamis retorted, completely without anger. "What I'd like is your help."

"My help?"

"Yes. Until you agree, I'll be happy to sit here and answer any question you put to me."

"That won't work, either." Her voice quivered again. She hated it.

"I don't intend ill will toward anyone."

"I don't believe you!"

"If you need proof that I do come from Old Sartor, well, I have this one artifact." Siamis stood up and unsheathed his sword, laying it across the table with the hilt toward her, the nasty sharp point safely away. Even in the weak, wintry light it gleamed with a silvery glow that scintillated with old magic. It was beautifully made, that she could see, though she knew little about such things. No jewels, and simple in design, but the metal, the style, matched the memories the Guardian had shared with her. The enemies of Old Sartor had not carried such weapons. The Old Sartorans had.

He really did come from Old Sartor, then. Just like the Guardian.

"They don't approve, of course," he said conversationally, as he lifted it, turned it this way and that to catch the light, then sheathed it, and repositioned his baldric so the sword lay across his back. "It was given to me on my twelfth birthday. That was the tradition."

Liere stared up at him, struggling to banish mere emotion, to concentrate on pure reason. Except all the clues were so strange. This man carried a weapon made thousands of years ago, for people on the good side. He did not look or sound like the monsters of her imagination, or even like the cruel figures of whom the Guardian had given her brief memory images. He hadn't denied her accusation. He'd referred to Norsunder as 'they', not 'we'—but not as the enemy, either.

He said, "After a time I joined them willingly enough, once I'd found that we agreed on specific goals. Norsunder might not like idiosyncrasies like this." He touched the hilt of his sword. "But I have a certain amount of autonomy."

She understood that she was now supposed to ask what those goals were, but she couldn't. Fear dried her mouth.

He spoke again. "My confederates ruined Old Sartor, not I. My plan is to accomplish our contiguous goals without needless loss of life."

"But they are still the goals of Norsunder," she managed, furious with herself for not thinking faster, for not being able to *do* anything. "Norsunder wants to control us, to control life, and magic, and everything. Norsunder's leaders are . . ." She thought of the Guardian's warning, and she hated to use profane words—it made them too real. She squashed down her emotions and said, "They are devourers of souls."

"And the alternative isn't? Do you really think you have autonomy after death? That's Norsunder's goal, to maintain freedom of will after the physical life ends."

"I don't believe that," Liere said. "And I don't want to listen." She kept her gaze on the table.

"You're a remarkable child," Siamis said, still in that kindly, warm voice. "Did you know that? Rare in the world. Perhaps the only one, yet, with your unique combination of potentials. Haven't you felt isolated? Lonely, even?"

Liere pressed her lips together to keep from answering, but when she sneaked a quick glance, Siamis smiled as if she'd said *Yes*.

"I could train you to realize those potentials," he said. "And you will not be alone. Ever again."

Compliments from an enemy were a threat. That much she'd learned watching children tease one another. "No," she said.

"I came to this part of Imar because you are here. I think you understand how long it took to track you down. Your instinctive mind-shield is quite effective. Until yesterday, I only knew you were a child. Last night I finally found your proximate location, and this morning I discovered you were among the girls in this little town. You are, as I say, singular. And Norsunder knows about you. If I don't get you, they will."

Terror squeezed Liere's heart, and there was nothing she could do to banish it. She covered her eyes with her hands.

The even, pleasant voice continued. "I will get what I want." His absolute conviction carried all the force of a vow. "Never doubt that, child." His voice sharpened slightly: from vow to threat. "If you run, you will wander alone and distrusted. I'll see to it. I don't want to kill you. My associates will, because they then have you—with your will or not—if they use one of the enchanted knives."

She heard a slight movement and jerked her hands down to see Siamis lay a black-handled dagger on the table, again the point safely away. But the threat was just as terrible as if he'd jabbed it toward her eyes: its steel blade had an ugly sheen to its edges. It was somehow more frightening than the sword because she had seen no evidence of it on his person, and because there was no art, no beauty—even deceptive beauty—in its design. This weapon had a single purpose: to kill.

"All we need do is inflict a wound. The enchantment on it moves directly into your blood, nearly impossible to remove without killing you, and it enables us access to your mind where ever you go. I'd rather not use this kind of thing," he said, still in that friendly tone. "Such methods are by necessity crude, and they tend to destroy initiative along with the will. I'd rather you make the sensible choice with clarity of mind, so that you will be able to realize your potential once I've been able to educate you. I was twelve," Siamis said, still smiling, "and exactly the kind of child you are now when I realized what I really wanted."

She gritted her teeth against the urge to cry out in horror. "I have to think," she managed. Her voice wobbled worse than ever, but she no longer cared. "Yesterday I—I didn't know any of these things you've told me. I need time."

"They gave me years to decide." Siamis's tone was sardonic, and Liere wondered what had happened during those years. No, she didn't. "But I did eventually come around to the inevitable." He was pleasant and friendly again. "I will give you time to do the same."

Liere twitched, fighting the urge to run. She couldn't believe she'd be free in just a moment.

Siamis picked up his knife. "Don't flinch. This blade hasn't your name on it, as we say. The enchantment on it is for someone far away." In a quick, practiced movement, he made it vanish up into a wrist sheath. Then his cuff fell forward, covering his wrist, and there was no sign of any knife.

Liere still backed away a step, but Siamis did not address her again, or make any move toward her. Instead he opened the door and spoke to one of the two men standing outside. The language sounded sinister: she was hearing Norsundrian.

What Siamis said to Davernak was, "This is the one. Now that we've found her, it's time to pick up the tasks I've been forced to postpone. But as you can see, she will slow us down when we need to travel fast."

Davernak listened with a mental shrug. Maybe now they'd have some fun.

Then Siamis said, "Take charge of her. She thinks she's resisting, but her bravado will fade quickly enough after she spends some time with her enchanted family, worrying about the prospect of what comes next. Let her sit in her house and do my work for me. I'll summon you when I have the time for a recalcitrant child."

Davernak was furious when Siamis turned to the brat and said in a kindly voice, "He will take you to your home and make certain that you do not leave it until I send for you."

Davernak wanted to smack the brat when she said, "My father won't have one of his kind in our house."

"Oh, won't he?" Siamis smiled.

Chapter Nine

Liere had lost all her bravado.

As soon as they were out of Siamis's sight, Davernak gave her a shove. The spindly brat sprawled on the gravel. He hauled her up by the scruff of her neck. *Why me? Why not one of the mindless? They're perfect for child tending.*

There was one of the mindless tending the animals. Davernak got an idea.

He threw the brat up into the saddle, mounted behind her, and snapped his fingers at the mindless guard to follow.

Liere hated having this bully squashing her around the ribs in order to keep her on the horse. She could feel his contempt, his wish to knock her down because he was angry at Siamis's orders. But she was afraid of falling. The horse seemed as high as a roof, only shifty.

"Where do you live?" the warrior asked in her own language.

She managed to give directions. The horse plunged. She clutched its mane tightly in her fists, though the warrior had not loosened his grip.

The horse snorted, began to move, its gait and speed soon alarming. Liere closed her eyes and held tightly to the rough horse hair, despite the jerks and heaves of the animal's head and neck.

When they reached her house, the man climbed off and yanked Liere down, setting her more or less on her feet. He left the horse with the other guard, whose mind was like fog, and followed Liere up onto the porch.

Liere opened the door and walked in. The man followed.

Her father came out as she reached the first stair, but he was not angry, nor did he ask any questions. He smiled, an unfamiliar expression that seemed empty of meaning. That, too, was terrifying.

"Siamis wants her kept from leaving," Davernak said, knowing that he had to use Siamis's name, and speak clearly and simply to the enchanted.

"Very well," Liere's father responded agreeably.

Liere's skin crawled. She whirled and ran upstairs, her breath shuddering. Below, her father, still speaking in that dreamy voice so unlike his real self, invited the Norsundrian murderer into their house. She peeked over the rail.

With his own hands, her father set a chair by the door, so the warrior could see the stairs and the doors to the kitchen and parlor.

She retreated into her bedroom, fighting to control the stupid weeping. Crying never did any good! She had to accept the fact that everyone in South End—everyone except her—was under this spell.

Davernak issued clear and simple orders to the mindless one: "Stay here. Sit by the door. Do not let the girl get past you. Keep guard until I return." Davernak knew that Siamis would send a summons by magic, at which time he could return to South End and retrieve the guard and the brat.

Until then he was on his own. He could make better use of his time.

Up in the room Liere shared with Marga, she thought back over Siamis's threats. She suspected he could do everything he said he could. She remembered his casual handling of the sword and the knife, such a contrast to three of her brothers' sporadic attempts at martial tricks with the kitchen carving knives; their clumsiness, which usually resulted in a cut hand or a nicked knife, had caused their parents to forbid such games.

Liere had never handled a knife at all, for her mother thought her too absent-minded to learn vegetable peeling yet. Siamis could have cut her throat with either sword or knife and she could not have stopped him. Even that warrior downstairs, who had lifted her so easily from the horse, how could she attack him and expect to win?

She wasn't strong enough to fight any Norsundrian. Certainly not in first, and she wasn't sure about second. Not Siamis, anyway.

So what *could* she do?

Sick with fright, she moved to the window and looked into the busy street. Marga and the other little ones were not playing. Instead, they worked at chores. Others moved about their business, but without idling or gossiping like always.

The spell was real, but no one knew. No one except Liere.

I can't fight Siamis, she thought. *But I have to find a way to break that spell.*

Conviction gripped her. She wasn't supposed to fight. Her job was to find a way to break Siamis's spell.

How?

She knew so little about magic! She had to learn, and soon.

But first she had to get away from that warrior downstairs—from Siamis—from South End. Then she could try to call Lilith the Guardian. If she could escape, it wouldn't matter how long it took for the Guardian to hear her.

She couldn't climb out the window as the walls were flat and bare. Her father did not like the messiness of trees or shrubs. She'd be seen by a neighbor, who would surely report it to the Norsundrians.

The only way out was down the stairs—past the warrior.

But not as herself.

Siamis hadn't even asked her name. The warrior had needed directions to her home. The Norsundrians—as yet—knew nothing about her family, but that could change at any moment.

That man in charge thinks I'm a weak, silly, boring little girl. Good!

So . . . to get away, she had to not be a girl. And the one she looked most like was the youngest of her brothers—people had thought them twins, until lately when he'd begun growing like a weed.

She whirled to the battered chest that she shared with Marga. Their sewing basket was neatly laid on top of the two piles of folded clothes. She took out her scissors, looked at her braids, and hesitated.

Angry with herself for that hesitation, she crept out of her room and peeked over the stair rail. The fog-minded warrior sat in a chair by the door, staring straight ahead.

Where was the other one? Maybe he was only going to get some lunch, but one thing she knew: she had better be fast.

She sped to her brothers' room, and opened the trunk the two youngest boys shared. Sifting down through their everyday clothes, she discovered at the bottom their old, worn winter clothes. First, a sturdy pair of wide-legged drawstring trousers that had been passed down through the four brothers, loose enough to fit all. A warm tunic, a very battered pair of shoes that had been handed down, like the clothes, by all the brothers in turn. The shoes were much too wide, but extra stockings would take care of that.

She repacked the trunk, closed it, and crept out again, pausing next to the wall. Using her mental 'finger' she touched the minds of her family, checking their locations. Her father and mother and the two eldest were eating lunch. They would go to the store soon. The younger ones were still out doing chores.

She must act now, before they returned.

In her room she took off her smock and the loose trousers girls wore, and packed them at the bottom of the trunk she shared with Marga. Then she pulled on her brother's clothes, the tunic shorter, the trousers heavy and straight legged, sturdily made. They fit pretty much like her own, but then there was essentially no difference in the shapes of their bodies.

She picked up the scissors and cut her braids off right behind her ears, hating herself for the regret that suffused her at each grind of the scissors. She cut the back by feel, parted her hair down the center like the boys did, pushing the longer top part back behind her ears.

She replaced scissors and basket, then hid the hair under the trunk—using all her strength to tip it back—and last, she pulled from under the mattress the little bag of coins that she had been saving ever since she was very small, to buy books when she got old enough.

The coins vanished into the pocket of the trousers. She walked back and forth, getting used to the shoes, until she heard creaking on the stairs. Her second oldest brother walked up, not running with his usual thundering clatter, but slow and deliberate, like Father. She waited, her heart thumping harder. She touched his mind. Knowing people had always made thoughts easier to touch, in fact sometimes it was like they pushed their thoughts at her, like her mother had, without knowing. But he seemed far away, his thoughts all smeary—like seeing through a fog. He trod at that same strange, deliberate pace to their room and changed into his work shirt.

He walked downstairs without a backward look. Matching his steps, she followed, the horrible shoes clattering as they half slipped off. Her brother did not notice.

She walked past the warrior without looking at him, the same way her brother did. She sent a tendril, observing his scrutiny of her older brother, then he glanced at her, and she saw herself in his foggy mind: a scrawny, smaller version of the big boy now going through the kitchen door.

And he permitted her to pass.

She walked outside, into the street. The air was cold on her neck.

Ducking between two houses, she took a circuitous route to Market Street, and there she moved swiftly from shop to shop, using her store of coins. Everyone seemed to think she was her brother, but no one asked questions. They were all foggily polite and incurious.

The coins did not go very far. She bought a second-hand basket, plain but sturdy, not even having to provide her lie about what had happened to the family baskets. She bought a blanket, a second-hand cup, a candle and sparker, at three succeeding shops. In the old days, shopkeepers who knew her would have asked friendly questions—going somewhere? What happened to your grandmother's cups, did you break one?

No one asked, no one appeared to care. She filled the basket, a few apples here, a loaf of bread there, a whole quarter of cheese, which used up the last of her coins. No one asked nosy questions. No one chatted, unless it was about business.

There was a steady stream of farm folk leaving on the main road, probably a result of the gathering at Town Hall. Liere slipped in among strangers, and made her way down the road until she reached the overgrown pathway leading to Ther Doleh, the great ruined city, reaching it very late in the afternoon.

Legend had it the ruins were ghost-ridden, but Liere had experimented with long distance sensing, and she'd never found any ghosts.

Liere was tired, and her feet hurt from the shoes, from the long walk. As she picked her way among the ruins in the swiftly falling darkness, she wished there were some ghosts. Even lost spirits would be better than no company at all.

No. She couldn't think like that.

She walked slowly a jumble of weather-worn stones, ducking winter-bare branches of scraggly fruit trees, and sat on a moss-covered block of stone.

She was here because no one would think to search these ruins. Though some people scavenged brick and stone, most people (like her parents) disapproved of that practice. It was a good place, a safe place, to listen from second, to learn, and to wait for the Guardian to answer her mental call.

It might not be tonight. It might take days. But Liere knew she would, and then Liere could tell her what had happened, and ask how she could break Siamis's spell.

Until then she would practice searching, for Siamis had shown her that distance was no drawback in the mental realm. Liere would practice that, and practice her second-face wall, what that horrible Siamis had called her mind-shield. One did not need to be a strong grownup to have a strong shield.

She hefted her basket, making her way to the rubble-choked center of the city. And there, under one of the buildings, she found the old escape tunnel—just like in the stories.

She lit her candle, made her way downward, and found herself in a vast cavern with water dripping forlornly at one end, trickling over a mossy stone trough to a silent stream. The cavern smelled damp, of wet stone, but it was a little less cold than the wintry night above.

She kept moving by the faint light of ancient glowglobes, left over from the days when magicians lived in this part of Imar. Presently she knelt at the stream, removed the little cup she'd bought, dipped it, and drank greedily. The water was so cold her teeth ached, but it tasted good.

She put her candle and basket down on a fallen column, and unpacked the thick wool blanket. She wrapped it around herself and then she sat beside her basket.

The silence was broken only by the tuneless drip of water, faintly echoing.

Homesickness made her eyes burn, but she angrily squelched the emotion. Home had once meant security and safety, but it had also meant pretense and enforced ignorance of the world. The first two were gone, wiped out by Siamis's spell. The second two were also gone, now that she was free.

Free.

She blew out her candle and lay down to sleep, listening to the slow, rhythmic drip of moisture echoing off ancient rock.

This lullaby accompanied her dreams.

Chapter Ten

Norsunder's temporal base, where Senrid was held prisoner, lies south of Sartor's border. In the center of Sartor is the forest called Shendoral.

Its peace was disturbed when the air glittered and a girl named Jenel Sandrial plumped down hard after a long magic transfer. When the magic-transfer dizziness passed off, she stood up shakily and looked around.

This had to be Sartor, and apparently winter had not yet arrived. How was that possible? Yet here was no snow on the springy moss, and the air was cool, not cold, and smelled of wood and water and loam. Birds chirped and sang, their songs unfamiliar. Looking at moss-covered trunks and long spreading leaves, Jenel wondered if these trees were cousins to those at home, just like the people were. The forest was different from that in Everon's midlands, but it was beautiful.

She brushed herself off, then shook out her heavy woolen robe. *I'm really here*, she thought, looking up at darkwood branches, the crinkly five-fingered leaves of amber, rust, and gold. *I am in Sartor!* She—an upper housemaid from the royal palace in Everon—was really, truly, in Sartor, center of so many old songs and stories.

But she had to save her best friend Cassandra! Every moment she looked around was a waste of time, and so she began to walk, choosing a gentle downhill slope as she gazed at light-shafts and grottos and unfamiliar blossoms growing peacefully in sunny places. Unseen birds sang, and the rustle of hedges and berry-heavy plants indicated the presence of small animals. How Cassandra would love this place!

A flicker of color caused her to touch her sash, where she'd carefully set Cassandra's magic-silver hatpin. It kept its shape, so there was no danger.

A moment later a girl her own age stepped around a dark green shrub with tiny bell-shaped blossoms and smiled a welcome. She had blue-tinged skin and very long curling fair hair that hung well below the ragged hem of her knee-length cotton tunic.

She's not human, Jenel thought. *Or maybe not quite.*

"Welcome," the blue girl said. "Who are you?"

Jenel said proudly, "Jenel Sandrial, from Everon. Ah, what language am I speaking?" For she said her words in Fer Sartoran, but they came out sounding differently; the two languages seemed to slide together in her mind—painlessly, easily—and become one.

"Sartoran."

"Magic," Jenel breathed. "Who are you?"

"Aroel Merewen. But you can call me Linet. My friends do."

"Friends?" Jenel repeated.

Linet danced a step or two, laughing soundlessly. "I have many, when I am in my human form. So. How can I help you?"

"Please," Jenel said anxiously. "My best friend got taken to that Norsunder place and I'm here to free her, if I can. Those from Norsunder were after her, or maybe they were after *this.*" She touched the silver pin in her sash, its head carved to look like a feather or leaf. *The Guardian's* hatpin. It's magic—it grows into a sword if they come near. Anyway, we ran, but eventually that terrible Detlev caught up with us, and they took Cassandra away."

"He left that behind by accident?" Linet pointed at the hatpin. She made a face. "Doesn't sound like Detlev."

"No, he made her drop it, and then he kicked snow over it. I was there, you see, but hiding. After they disappeared I found it and took it away, in case they planned to come back for it."

Linet frowned. "There's probably magic on your hatpin that causes grief to Norsundrians if they touch it. I've heard of such things being made, back in ancient days. But why did they take your friend, if they only wanted to prevent her from using the Guardian's hatpin?"

Jenel wrung her fingers together. "Why indeed? It makes no sense! Cassandra doesn't know anything."

"Ah. If there was no specific reason," Linet said seriously, "then it has to be the same reason they've been harassing boys and girls all over the world. The reason is yet unclear to anyone. They seem to be looking for someone particular, and maybe your Cassandra is it. Did they see you?"

"No. I hid. How could I stop a whole gang of them?"

Linet waved a small hand, her fingers reminding Jenel of a bird. "Stop Detlev? Of course not! You did right, and so your friend will say when she's free. What matters right now is that you're doing what you *can* do."

Jenel nodded soberly. "You mean, not waiting for someone else to help." Inside, she braced herself: she was terrified at the idea of making her way to the Norsunder base to search for Cassandra on her own, but what other way was there?

Linet smiled. "Too many people in the world have gotten into the habit of waiting for the magicians to rescue them from their messes." She added when Jenel looked frightened, "But that doesn't mean that one shouldn't ask for help when it's needed."

"I need to know how to get into the Norsunder place," Jenel said firmly, hoping she didn't sound as afraid as she felt. "Can you tell me?"

Linet shook her head. "You can't get in and out of the Norsunder fortress, even with your magic hatpin. But I'll take you to Eidervaen—that's the capital—and we'll see what the queen says."

Jenel sighed, rubbing her hands with nervous anticipation.

Linet said, "Since we've got a bit of a walk ahead of us, why don't you tell me more about Cassandra, and how the two of your managed to catch the notice of a monster like Detlev?"

Jenel drew in a shuddery breath of relief. "Cassandra is half dawnsinger, and she's on Detlev's enemy list because she helped break his enchantment over Everon. See, she was put in place of the real princess—that's Hatahra—when she was little, and I was the upper housemaid in the palace, and assigned to Cassandra. The Sandrials are at least as old a family as the Delieths, and we've always taken care of the palace . . ."

The story that unfolded as they walked through the forest was a typical piece of twisted knavery—characteristic of Detlev, Linet thought. Why did he always do horrible things to royal families, especially ones with children? Why torture them with ugly magical 'experiments' instead of outright war? Obviously because he found it much more entertaining than the predictability of general slaughter.

Jenel talked with more and more freedom as their walk led them along old, sun-splashed paths. Linet began to see the people involved, perhaps not as Jenel wanted them to be perceived. Jenel's loyalty was that of the generous-hearted: unquestioning, devoted, active even to the cost of her own life. She obviously admired the Delieth heirs, and she had become the friend of Cassandra, who was for so long the putative princess instead of living with her wandering relatives in Everon's forestland.

Yet after the twentieth "Cassandra says," Linet formed an image of a difficult, moody girl who'd done well enough with judicious help from the Guardian, but who was unlikely to escape from Norsunder's base on her own. Why Detlev would want someone like that was impossible to guess.

The Loi, who watched ceaselessly toward the south where the Norsundrian temporal Base lay, had overheard some patrollers gossiping about guard duty, and a troublesome boy they couldn't get rid of because he was Detlev's personal prisoner. Even Norsundrian rankers wondered: *What does Detlev want with kids?*

Linet led Jenel to a little pool for a drink, then said, "I will take you to Atan, that is, the queen of Sartor."

The queen of Sartor! Jenel braced for the vertigo of transfer magic, but didn't feel it at all this time. A mild swooping sensation shivered through her, blurring her vision, then she found herself in a small, pretty room.

Jenel wondered if they were in the ancient palace in the center of Eidervaen, probably the oldest still lived-in building in the entire world, so famous that every child who listened to any history knew something about it. She looked about her with a fascinated gaze, expertly assessing and approving what she saw, from the well-cared-for ancient furnishings, murals, and art pieces, to the newer ones, all chosen to complement the old. Aged parquet floors in the residence wing had been buffed smooth over many centuries. Rugs with patterns favored by ancestors had been patiently rewoven by expert hands.

A well-ordered palace, in her view, signified orderly rule. There had been neglect during the ugly days of the enchantment at home in Everon. People like Detlev had to live in squalor and gloom, and probably—for some weird reason—preferred it. Or why would he be a Norsundrian? Nobody who liked order could be evil, surely. And just as surely, evil would treasure squalor and chaos, and hate beauty.

"I'll take you to her favorite morning chamber," Linet said. "It's the most comfortable—and private." So saying she led Jenel into a small but well-proportioned room, sunny and airy. Armchairs waited. Jenel admired the rolled arms, the curves of the back that would accommodate wide skirts.

She sat nervously on the very edge of a satin cushion, aware that her heavy winter-gown was dusty and mud-splattered.

A white-haired figure entered without ceremony. Jenel tried not to stare at the milk-colored skin that showed the blue of veins beneath, the talon-like fingernails and toenails, the blue-white drifting hair. She looked away; she'd never been this close to a morvende. The cave dwellers seldom came to the world's surface, and most of those she had glimpsed kept their cave-pale skin covered up, and their feet and hands hidden in the complicated folds of their clothing.

The morvende boy grinned at Jenel as he jumped up to sit on a carved cabinet, his bare legs swinging below the edge of his exquisitely woven tunic. He picked up a book. His lips moved slowly: he was learning to read.

A tall girl of about fifteen or sixteen entered. She had long brown hair and a face—the slightly protruding, droopy under-lidded eyes especially—that bore a distinct resemblance to King Berthold and Princess Tahra. Her gown was midnight blue velvet. Jenel realized she was in the presence of Yustnesveas, the queen of Sartor, and she bounced to her feet.

Linet introduced everyone with a lack of formality that Jenel found both reassuring and intimidating. She was so horrified at the idea of calling the Queen of Sartor 'Atan' that the other two dropped it. Her anxiety nerved her to meet Yustnesveas' kind and friendly gaze, and she relaxed enough to tell her story again.

Linet perched on the arm of one of the chairs. When Jenel paused, looking in appeal from one to the other, Linet said, "Hinder."

The morvende boy set aside his book. It seemed entirely natural that one of the mysterious morvende would be a casual friend to the queen of Sartor.

"Do you think your people could extend tunnels as close to the Norsunder Base as possible?"

"Probably," Hinder said, grimacing. "But why?"

"To effect a rescue."

He shrugged. "I have to ask the elders, of course, but supposing they say yes. The tunnel we can make, but the rescue? We're not strong enough against an army of Norsundrians."

Linet pursed her lips. "By the time you have a tunnel ready, I think a plan will be as well. We can work on that at our end."

Atan turned to Jenel. "We'll do our best to rescue your friend. Would you like to stay with us until it's done?"

"If it's not an imposition," Jenel said fervently.

Atan laughed. "The place is big enough to house half of Eidervaen, and most of it is empty, for we, too, are recently free from Detlev's plots. You have only to choose the room you like and settle in."

And so, for a time, Jenel Sandrial became one of the guests at Sartor's ancient royal palace. Most of the grand rooms were indeed empty, and had been for years and years.

Jenel walked through a series of shadowy anterooms, their gilt, stylized painting high on the walls now softened with age. The portraits along the walls had darkened, some so much that only old faces stared palely from shadowy backgrounds with those same heavy-lidded, droopy eyes, some more protuberant than others. Some of the portraits retained the glitter along the frame that promised a magical capture from the subject's life; most of the frames were dark, indicating that the magic had dissipated over the centuries.

The accumulated authority of all that history, evidenced in her protuberant, droopy eyes, imbued Atan with gravitas, even though her manners were not at all formal, nor did she require any kind of royal protocol. She seemed just as happy to entertain a housemaid as a duchess.

Much as Jenel appreciated being accepted for herself, she found this attitude unsettling. The other guests were an equally disparate group. Social status wasn't even mentioned, so there was no deference. It was nice, but . . . awkward.

If I wanted to be treated like a princess, Jenel thought, finger-tracing the fine acorn carving on an ancient chair, *it would be wonderful. But I don't. I like the old ways, and I wish these rooms would be lit again, and see masquerades, and be filled with music.*

Atan enjoyed Jenel's earnestness. Her own life had been so thoroughly smashed when she was just an infant that she was still learning what normal life was supposed to be. She was always a little afraid that Detlev and his minions were waiting for her to acquire a taste for normalcy so they could have the fun of smashing it all again.

It was easier, in some ways, to live in this huge monument to Sartor's past as if any day she'd have to go back to her hermit's hut high in the border mountains.

One day, Jenel dared to express some of her thoughts. Atan listened as she always did, head tilted, her expression considering. But then she surprised Jenel by saying, "I have to admit that I prefer freedom from social rules. I respect status that is earned, not just conferred at birth, because I was educated by a mage."

Jenel's lips rounded. "I know Sartor was closed away from the world for a century. Like Everon was closed away. But . . ."

"But you thought I sprang forth from my closet, gowned and crowned?" Atan grinned. "No. I was hidden as a babe. Fifteen years ago, the spell over Sartor had receded enough that my guardian was freed, and she took me to Sarandon's border mountains. So though I was born a century ago, I've only lived fifteen years."

Atan glanced out the window, considering her words. Tough as it was for Sartor to re-enter the world, she knew that Sartor's history made reintegration easier. Though the rest of the world had changed, goods a hundred years out of fashion were instantly treasured, just because they were from Sartor.

Atan leaned forward, elbows on her closed book. "But here's something to consider about protocol. A princess doesn't always have the freedom of her farm-girl friend. She knows that her words might affect not just her own life, but many. Her good manners help her to control her tongue, and to move about without peril."

Jenel cautiously assented.

"As for the pretty clothes and rooms, they *are* pretty. But they can also be used as a kind of social weapon."

Seeming harmony, Jenel thought. "I've been learning about that, how words can be a weapon. That's why I like looking and not doing."

Atan said, "My tutor, a great mage who's lived a long time, taught me that we humans tend to organize into categories. If we are put into a place by tradition, those who want change badly enough seem to find a way to do it."

Jenel thought of Cassandra, forced to be a false princess. "I just wish everyone could find her right place and be happy there."

"I think," Atan said slowly, "what's the right place in one person's mind isn't always right for the next person. It's good to find happiness if we can without taking it away from others. First," she said grimly, "has to come safety."

Jenel sighed. "Yes." She, too, glanced out the window, and Atan understood that Jenel was as restless as she was; she worried every day that her friend was imprisoned.

If she was still alive.

So she said, "Before my morning interviews today, Hinder's cousin Sinder brought me word that the morvende have been working to extend their tunnel deep into Norsundrian territory. They say there will probably only be this one chance, but they will take it for the sake of children."

Jenel lifted her gaze away from admiring the fine porcelain cup of deep midnight blue edged with a pattern of gold leaves, from which she drank her chocolate. The underlying message that separated morvende off from sunsider politics and invisible boundaries passed her by. Her attention caught on the word 'Norsunder.' The peaceful room seemed as fragile as the cup in her hand—which had, she noticed, been expertly mended once by clever but unknown fingers.

"When will it all be ready for me to go?"

Atan could have laughed at the valiant but unsuccessful attempt Jenel made to school her expression into gratitude, but the tension around Jenel's eyes revealed her fear.

Atan smiled. "I don't know, but it doesn't concern you, since they won't permit you to attempt the rescue."

"But I—"

"Linet's part Loi. Space and time are different for the Loi, who live in and guard Shendoral. They dream things, or hear things—somehow—not just here in Sartor but that affect the entire world, even though they seldom leave Shendoral. Anyway, you can't go because if you get caught, the entire morvende geliath would be endangered. You have to realize how old the geliaths are here in Sartor. Hundreds and hundreds of years at least. Don't think of them as mere caves, but as cities underground."

"So they're making a new one?" Jenel asked.

"Not a geliath, but a tunnel. However, tunnels do connect, and they have to plan for—"

Atan broke off as a bluish flicker resolved into Linet.

"Guess what I have," Linet began in a triumphant voice—but her surprise was spoiled when the small black thing in her arms leaped lightly down onto the table, where it began lapping at the cream.

"Well it certainly is a hungry thing," Jenel exclaimed.

They laughed. The cat looked up at them, then resumed its delicate lapping.

"This cat," Linet pointed, "is going to free your friend."

Atan and Jenel studied the cat in surprise. She looked very ordinary—black with one white spot behind an ear. Linet smiled down at the cat, head to one side.

"Yes," she said, "she is. We had a, oh, a fascinating exchange last night. I learned that dena Yeresbeth—the mysterious unity that permitted our ancestors to talk mind to mind—is not completely dead in the world, as we'd so long believed, and neither is it confined to upright beings. Animals have their own version. According to Rina, some are willing to ally with humans against the threat of Norsunder. Just think what this alliance could mean to our world, were we to get rid of the likes of Detlev?"

Linet paused, looked at Jenel's tear-glistening eyes, and decided she could air her favorite theories some other day. "So," she said briskly. "To the problem at hand. . ."

Chapter Eleven

Senrid Montredaun-An and Cassandra Muria were the only two prisoners in that particular wing of the fortress at the Norsunder Base. Though they were housed next to one another for the convenience of their jailors, the stone walls were thick and the grating in the doors very small. They were scarcely aware of the other's presence.

Senrid heard Cassandra screaming a couple of times.

Cassandra became aware of Senrid when she tried pressing her face to the rusty iron grating in a vain effort to see even a tiny scrap of sunlight. There was only the ugly reddish glare of magic-perpetuated torchlight. While she searched for any evidence of a window, she became aware of guards clattering up the corridor. She froze in fear, terrified that they were coming for her, but they stopped at the next cell down, unlocked the door, and hauled out a short blond boy, and thrust him down the corridor in the other direction. She remembered that she'd heard some comings and goings from that cell, but she was too miserable to wonder who he was, or why he was there.

Of the two, she was the most miserable, though her sojourn had been much less lengthy and less violent than Senrid's.

She'd only had one visit with Detlev, who'd asked her a lot of questions that didn't make any sense to her. Once he seemed to realize that she wasn't the one he wanted, he never bothered with her again.

But she was so scared of a second visit that for a while the guards entertained themselves with mentioning his name and describing detailed tortures. It was so easy to reduce her to terrified screams and then weeping, whereupon those inclined for such recreation would slap her into silence.

Poor Cassandra! Take a dawnsinger out of the sunshine and freedom of the native forest, and she (or he) will be unhappy; put her in Norsunder, and she'll be very unhappy. Add the proximity of her worst-feared enemy, double that for a youngster, and you get a perfect picture of woe.

She was far too sunk in her well of gloom to note that the boy next door was subjected to more bully visits than she, and they lasted a lot longer.

Senrid had no illusions to lose. Having spent his life so far in a martial environment, he knew what to expect—and because prison guards are not picked for brains, he gave as good as he got.

At least verbally.

Once he'd realized that Detlev had been specific in his orders—alive, and no permanent damage—Senrid couldn't bring himself to back off on the comments. It was too much like surrender. He felt no compunctions about lying or faking unconsciousness when he'd been knocked down, so he could listen to any conversations the Norsundrians held; they didn't always remember to switch back to Norsundrian.

Most of what he overheard wasn't worth hearing, but he did learn a few things while he endured uncountable days, waiting for that dreaded interview with Detlev.

He finally met Detlev, unexpectedly. It was the same day he managed an escape, though he only made it as far as the inner door to the prison wing of the fortress before he was missed and hunted down.

Since Detlev happened to be at the Base that day, the goons muscled Senrid directly along to him.

"Escape attempt," one of them reported, giving Senrid a shove so he landed on the stone floor at Detlev's feet, and hoping for the kill order. What fun they'd have! The mouthy brat had been far too much trouble.

Somehow Senrid now understood their lingo. (Threat? Probably, he decided.)

Senrid rolled over, blinking dizzily. Gray-green eyes looked down at him with cold amusement. "I shall have time for this one presently," Detlev said. "See to it he's there—and in one piece—when I want him."

He stepped over Senrid and walked on.

The disappointed guard snapped out an expletive. A big mitt gripped Senrid's disintegrating shirt collar, and hauled him to his feet.

Back in his cell, the guards he'd evaded put a very liberal interpretation on 'in one piece.'

&

At last Linet's expected hero showed up.

She transferred to Rive Dian and said to Atan, "The morvende tunnel is finished. What they waited on was someone big enough to disguise as an eleven, who can go in with Rina."

Atan frowned in perplexity. Because she did not know that Linet already had someone in mind, she cast her mind over likely candidates. She knew if she asked directly, her city and palace guards would never refuse, whether they were capable or not. So many of her enthusiastic guards were young—not much older than she—and almost all were orphans, as she was.

And they were mostly still untried. The war that had decimated their parents' generation over a century ago in enchanted time lay barely within the young people's memories.

A day later, a messenger came in from the city guards to report having spotted a familiar figure on the North Road. "It's Rel the traveler, back!"

Relief and joy lit Atan's whole being. "Thank you," was all she said to her messenger, and to her Steward, "Prepare Rel's room, please?"

Probably, Atan reflected as she ordered dinner, the world-roaming Rel would be astonished to discover how popular he was in Sartor's capital. He'd been back twice since he first showed up in the middle of the final struggle for freedom and took up their cause with the matter-of-fact casualness that others would use to take up eating utensils to join a meal.

He arrived before sunset, after stopping by the guardhouse to catch up on news of the friends he'd made during the freedom fight.

Atan discovered she couldn't concentrate on any of her usual tasks; she turtled around her favorite sitting room, picking things up and putting them down again just so, until at last she heard Rel's quick tread. She flung open the door and exclaimed, "It's good to see you in Sartor again."

Rel's strong-boned face, his dark eyes and hair gave him a formidable countenance, an impression augmented by his height and breadth of shoulder. He looked like a grownup until he smiled, which was a rare event. Then he looked like the not-quite nineteen-year-old that he was.

"Was on my way south," he said. "Prodded in an otherwise forgettable dream by blue people, a week or so ago. Decided to pick up my pace." His eyes narrowed as he added, "Know any reason why?"

"The Loi. Dinner's ready. Come. We can talk in the dining room."

Rel sat at her ancient table with the same matter-of-fact ease with which he'd sit cross-legged on the ground at a crude campfire with a rough gang of border riders, or with a party of tradespeople.

"We could use your help," Atan said, looking as anxious as she felt. "But have some dinner first, then I'll explain."

She'd been delighted at the report that he'd been seen on the road, and of course he would help. But now that he was here, face to face, her emotions veered to worry. Of course he'd help—but going into the Norsunder Base? It was so dangerous! And, did she have any right to even ask him?

Jenel Sandrial stood by, looking even more worried and ambivalent. From the first glance, she was intimidated by the tall, handsome Rel, which wasn't helped when one of Atan's young noble courtiers whispered self-importantly, "That's Rel the Hero from our Battle for Freedom. I'll wager that the queen sent for him, and he'll be going to rescue your friend."

That a total stranger would go deliberately into danger on Jenel's behalf rendered her speechless, both with gratitude and with fears for Cassandra, for the unknown Hero, and for the morvende who had made the tunnel and risked their geliath.

As for Rel, he would do anything Atan asked.

Linet appeared at noon the next day to report, "Detlev is gone from the Base. The time to act is now."

Everyone knew that Detlev could read minds from halfway around the world, and even kill you with a thought. There was no defending yourself against that kind of skill, no matter how much sword fighting practice you'd had.

Rel said, "How do you know? Did someone see him leave?"

Atan turned his way. "We dare not watch. Not even the morvende."

Linet said calmly, "The Loi listen in the dream realm for his absence."

Rel accepted that. Now that action was imminent, he was aware of his heightened heartbeat, the itch to be moving. "Let's go, then."

Atan had magic transfer tokens ready. They used those and were wrenched by magic to a Destination inside the morvende goliath near Sartor's southern border, where they found Linet and Hinder waiting.

"Here is your clothing," Linet said to Rel, holding out a bundle. "The uniform is left over from the old days, but the boots we fashioned. They look like the others, but they will be easier to move over rough ground in, for they are not capped with iron. Loi magic won't alert the Norsundrians the way light magic might, if warded."

Rel didn't ask what a ward was; it didn't really matter, as talk of magic was beyond him. Atan, who had studied magic all her life, suspected that it had to do with the nature of Loi magic, which was integral to the structure of the world in a way that the mirror-image "light" and "dark" magics were not.

He nodded his thanks and ducked into an adjacent cavern to change.

Hinder followed him. "I wish I could go," he said longingly.

Rel gave his head a shake, recognizing the longing from his own early boyhood. It was not a taste for bloodshed so much as a craving for action, for the chance to have a part in righting wrongs. "I'd like to have you at my back," Rel said. "And we may come to it yet, if all this talk about Norsunder's future plans is true. But today, can't be done. They catch a glimpse of that white head and pale face, they'll start digging until they find your tunnels."

Hinder grimaced, dashing back the drifting snow-colored hair from his brow. "The elders said when they decided to risk building this tunnel that it was only Norsunder's arrogance that would protect us. They won't think any lighter allies have the courage to attempt that fortress."

Rel lifted a hand in agreement, then finished straightening the plain black uniform. He laid aside his sword *Daelender* with a careful hand, remembering the day Atan had given it to him. He smiled inwardly at his own awkwardness; his mumbled thanks—said in Mearsiean—had been taken for a new name for the heirloom blade, and so ever after he wandered about with a weapon called "thank you very much."

What it might symbolize, he didn't trouble himself to parse. This is what he knew: that day, awkward as it was—he feeling stupid at the Sartoran love of ritual, and Atan in her rumpled, dusty gown, her voice quavering with nerves as she struggled to emulate some inner image of her famed Landis ancestors—was one of his most treasured memories.

"Watch *Daelender* for me?" he asked Hinder.

The boy's pale skin flushed, but Rel pretended not to see.

"I will," Hinder promised, and Rel knew if fire and disaster suddenly visited the ancient tunnels, Hinder would stay with his charge.

Rel hefted the plain-hafted Norsundrian blade also left over, like the uniform, from the freedom skirmish. Who'd secreted these things and why? Probably someone against just such an occasion, he decided as he buckled the sword belt on. Sartorans did seem to be packrats. At least Atan's ancestors certainly were, for the palace was crammed with rooms of stuff dating back many centuries. He and Atan had investigated some of it, during his visit last spring.

Last, he slipped a dagger into his boot, and into his pocket a lock-picking device that he'd mastered early in his travels.

"Done." He looked down at the little black cat sitting near the archway. He turned to Hinder, whose thin shoulders and tense fingers betrayed his anxiety. "Keeping me out of trouble is her job. Any sign, and I'll retreat. I know how important it is to protect this tunnel from discovery."

Hinder's chin lifted. "We'll be waiting."

Atan stood at the tunnel entrance. As soon as Rel appeared, she held out her hand.

Surprised, he lifted his own hand, and she laid on his palm a plain ring set with a milky-white gem. He looked at it closely, detecting faint carving at the sides, where it was least worn. It was a lady's ring, and quite old.

"Another of the many ancient Landis heirlooms," Atan said, striving for lightness. "I'm so glad my family was never much for throwing anything away. It ought to work there, for it was made by dark magic."

He suspected an interesting story (Sartoran history was a long, tangled skein of interesting stories) but he could ask about that later.

Instead he held up his hand and waggled his fingers. "Lady's ring. I'm afraid it won't fit."

"It will," she said. "That's one of its virtues—though we don't have this kind of magic anymore. Its primary virtue is light. *Strong* light. Here are the commands you'll need," and she repeated them.

He committed the magic words to memory, slid the ring onto his finger and watched it blur, making his flesh tingle, as it thinned and expanded to fit. He bent to pick up Rina, and was ready to go.

He looked at Atan, who stood in the archway of this new tunnel, her arms crossed tightly. "Can I have that story when I get back?"

She nodded, smiling a little, but her gaze was troubled.

Rel followed two morvende men down the tunnel to the actual portal. The two carried small glowglobes that emitted just enough of the white light of sorcery to enable them to see their way along the tunnel.

Unlike the older tunnels, this new one was rough, with a low ceiling, the flooring uneven. The shadows on rocky contours shifted at each step the guides made. Rel stepped with care, Rina tucked safely in the crook of his elbow. Before long he felt the fur lifting along her back, and the cold breezes drifting down through cleverly disguised vents smelled faintly stale—of dust and smoke and long dried vegetation.

They had to be under the Base, or nearly; Rel was used to geliaths by now. Morvende had their own forms of communication. When he was near geliaths—and aiding those whose causes morvende favored—unexpected escape routes would be opened to him, accesses that he was careful to remember, and to guard against discovery.

The two morvende were so quiet that Rel could hear the click of their talons on the stone, for they all preferred going barefoot. Rel kept silence also, mindful of vents and stray noises.

He'd noticed Rina listening as well, her great cat eyes flicking between each speaker. He hoped Linet was correct about how much of human converse the cat followed. If anything at all went amiss, this mission called not for action but for a rapid retreat.

The morvende stopped, and made signs for a steep climb and a sharp turn at the top. Then they extinguished their glowglobes, becoming pale wraiths in the nearly total dark.

Rel set Rina down, and felt his way upward.

The opening was narrow, cleverly concealed in the deep crevasse between great slabs of stone. Rel squeezed out, careful not to rip the Norsundrian uniform, then looked cautiously about. In the starlit night landscape the entire immediate area seemed to be made up of broken rock. He'd never make it back on his own. He looked down at the cat, who was no more than a shadow.

She flicked her tail up and trotted confidently toward a black shape forming a martial silhouette against the horizon: the fortress. Faint points of baleful orange glowed, like inimical eyes, along the top of the fortress: some stationary, some moving, probably borne by sentries. Above Rel the faint starlight cast just enough glow for him to make out the shapes and shadows of the rock around him, but he had to place his feet carefully, for the ground was uneven in the inky shadows.

Rina hopped from rock to rock, pausing sometimes to sniff the air, then she continued on at a quick pace. Rel had to scramble to follow. He was glad of the black clothing. He couldn't see any outer perimeter sentries, but he assumed there were some. At least they were unlikely to see him, and he worked hard to keep his steps noiseless.

They were close to the fortress when the cat stopped and put her paws against Rel's shin.

All right, that was clear: he was to wait. Linet had said that the cat would probably scout ahead on her own. And who'd notice a black cat at night?

Rel sat down in the lee of a sheared stone, and composed himself to wait.

Impossible to guess how long he waited, but eventually a silent shadow emerged from the darkness and hopped across his leg, tail brushing his chin.

It was time to move.

He rose, following, glad that the boots the Loi had given him were a lot more pliable than they looked. For this kind of work, he preferred mocs, but Norsundrians didn't wear mocs—or at least not in their stronghold, apparently.

The rough ground abruptly gave way to slabs of stone. Rel stepped on the outsides of his feet, toe-heel, the way he'd been taught for covert moving, his tread soundless.

They entered a narrow archway. The cold, lightless air smelled of stone and old smoke. He put out his hands, his fingertips brushing dank stone, then the air of passages heading off in either direction. The cat waited patiently until Rel found her by feeling about. He stayed crouched over, his fingertips touching her tail, while she paced in a third direction, one he hadn't detected.

Walking bent over was uncomfortable for about three steps. By the fourth his muscles began to pull and cramp. He kept at it in the total darkness, working to keep his breathing from hissing.

Rina's tail flicked his fingers once. What now? He straightened up, digging his fists into his lower back, until he made out a red flicker in the distance, and the tromp of boots: a patrol.

He bent again, crouch-running as Rina rounded a corner, and froze against the rough, dry stone wall. Far off to the right, dim, ruddy torchlight beat, highlighting the roughness of the stone.

Tramp, tramp, tramp: the footsteps passed down the adjacent corridor and faded into the distance, along with the light, leaving Rel and Rina again in darkness.

Rina pressed against Rel's ankle. Once again, he bent into a back-aching crouch as he followed the little cat.

It seemed a year later when they halted before a door with a reddish line glowing beneath. Rel opened the door onto a torch-lit stone hallway, shutting the door quietly against the rhythmic tramp of another approaching patrol.

At least now they'd reached the area with torches placed at intervals. They moved faster now, with three stops to hide corridors until patrols had passed.

They reached the prison wing. A single guard paced a long stone hallway with a single door. Keys jangled faintly at each step. Really? This door was really locked?

Three—four—trips back and forth, and Rel had the man's routine counted out. As soon as the guard passed the fifth time he crossed the hall in quick strides, lockpick out. The mechanism was as ancient as he hoped, easy to handle. The biggest danger was noise. He tried to time the click of the tumbler to the steps moving away. The latch gave, and Rel yanked the door open and eased inside two steps before the guard reached the far end and turned to come back.

He leaned against the shut door, his body cold with sweat.

Torchlight revealed a row of doors, each with a tiny grill set in it.

Now the iron doors had grills in them. As Rina ran from door to door, sniffing at each, Rel wondered who had done the labor to build this enormous prison. Norsunder probably had forced prisoners to construct their own cells.

Rina stopped at last. She looked up expectantly.

Rel unpocketed the lock-picking tool again, and soon the door swung wide. The torchlight in the hall sent in a thin slice of firelight. All he made out was a kid-sized form sitting on the bare stone floor.

"Cassandra Muria?" he murmured.

"You're off one," a kid said, and laughed.

The attempt at a laugh was empty bravado, and so young-sounding that Rel found it pathetic. So there wasn't just one prisoner, but two.

"Want to get out?" he asked—knowing that Rina had not made a mistake.

Rel heard a shaky breath, then, "Be happy to." As if he'd expected Rel to shut the door again and go on. "But they've got me in a bind," the kid added, his voice husky with the effort it took to keep his voice from trembling.

Rel ignored the pun and cursed under his breath at this obvious example of pointless cruelty. Did they really think a half-sized kid could break free of this place? He drew his knife, cut the ropes binding skinny wrists, then hauled the kid to his feet.

Rina promptly trotted out of the cell, tail high, and paused at the next cell.

Rel unlocked it. "Cassandra?"

"Who else could it be?" came a sullen whine.

"Someone else try to break you out of here?"

Cassandra gasped.

"Come on," he said, gripping her skinny arm. She let him take her weight. Thus burdened, he followed Rina back up the hallway to the iron door.

This time he paused long enough for the guard to step past, then he slipped out and clubbed the man behind the ear with the hilt of his dagger. He caught the guard under the armpits, dragged him back inside, and dropped him in one of the open cells, then straightened up. He couldn't bring himself to kill an unconscious man, so he shut the cell door, listened for the click of the lock, and hustled back to the prison wing door.

His two charges waited where he'd left them, the girl hunched down in a small ball, her eyes listlessly watching the torch. The other, a round-faced boy with filthy blond hair hanging in his eyes, watched Rel, his expression (as much as one could read past the distortion of torchlight, dirt, and bruises) wary.

"We have to get as far as we can before he wakes up and starts yelling," Rel said, once again gripping their arms.

"Ow," the girl whined fretfully. "That hurts."

"I can walk," the boy muttered.

"Quiet, both of you."

They obeyed.

The trio made it all the way to the outer door before the alarm rose. They'd scarcely begun picking their way into the rocky waste when a sentry shouted on the wall.

Rel didn't understand the words, but he knew they'd been spotted. He dropped the kids' arms, said Atan's magic words and aimed the ring toward the sentries on the tower, and closed his eyes.

A blinding white light, more glaring even than lightning, flared so brightly he could see the tiny veins in his eyelids. From the wall came shouts, curses, and commands.

He said the word to end the light. "Come on," he whispered. "We've got to get away from this position before they get their sight back."

He grabbed the two skinny arms again and walked as fast as they could move. He hoped that the broken stone made organized mount-and-search drills a low priority. Foot teams would not be any faster than he was.

Rina made a more roundabout journey back, keeping them under cover of great stone shards. Someone placed brilliant glowglobes on the walls. Rel and his charges had to move from shadow to shadow, which made the journey so much harder.

And it was already hard. Neither child had any strength. Cassandra whimpered softly, her body a dead weight. The boy's breathing was harsh with pain, but he stubbornly tried to bear his own weight, so finally Rel dropped Senrid's arm and picked up Cassandra.

Shortly thereafter, Rel felt five fingers gripping his tunic for support.

Flaring lights, voices, and clatter behind and to either side a major effort rapidly covering the area in widening circles.

Tension tightened Rel's neck. They pursuit was nearing faster than he and the boy could move.

Then Rina stopped. The tunnel opened. A quick, hard last struggle, and they were in, a sheared stone set directly behind them, almost on their heels. Glowglobes lit, revealing the tense faces of the waiting morvende.

"You're safe," Rel said to the boy, who sank down like a folded chair, his head on his arms, hiding his face.

Chapter Twelve

Rel set Cassandra down and helped the morvende thoroughly block the tunnel entrance. When the last big stone was in place, Rel picked Cassandra up again, and made the long journey back down the tunnel to where Atan and her company waited.

"Cassandra!" Jenel cried.

Cassandra gave a long sigh as Rel put her on her feet.

Jenel held out a shiny silver pin, as Linet whispered to Senrid, "I'm glad he found you."

"Here's your magic pin back, Cassandra. Now you can use it against Detlev," Jenel said.

Cassandra took it weakly, felt for a sash to put it in, realized her grubby dress had no sash, then handed it back. "You keep it for now," she whispered.

Jenel's eyes gleamed with tears. "You have to rest."

"I need to see the sun again." Cassandra's voice was no longer a whine, just weary. "Then I can rest."

"The sun will be rising very soon. Let's go to where you can see it," Linet said with brisk cheer.

Atan gave Rel and Jenel transfer tokens, and they vanished. Linet touched Rina, Cassandra, and Senrid in turn, and they were shifted by the much easier, and rarer, Loi magic, which didn't require a Destination.

As soon she found herself in Atan's big building that smelled of humans, cleaning polish, and mildew, Rina trotted through the door and vanished.

When the transfer vertigo dissipated, Atan spoke. "Jenel, why don't you take Cassandra to the room next to yours? It faces east. She can watch the dawn from the comfort of a nice bed."

Atan' kind voice roused Jenel from her fog of worry and relief. She clutched Cassandra's thin hand and led her out of the Destination chamber, her brimming eyes expressive with gratitude.

As soon as the two girls were gone, Atan turned to Senrid. "We have plenty of space. Would you like to rest?"

Senrid shrugged. It took all his strength and concentration to stay on his feet, so he didn't notice Linet watching him carefully. "There a room near them?" he asked, a thumb indicating the departed girls.

"There is indeed," Atan said.

Senrid made it out the door in time to see Jenel and Cassandra go up a stairway. He followed then up and then along a hall, choosing a room directly across from theirs.

The room was clean and pleasantly decorated, but he scarcely gave it a glance. Instead, he leaned tiredly against the wall directly next to the open door, listening to the murmur of the girls' voices beyond.

"I thank you, Jenel," Cassandra said. "For returning the hatpin, though it's no joy for me to see it again. It is a weapon, and it warns of dangers that I'd rather avoid. I had time to think, in that horrible place. I don't want adventure. I haven't the ability to do anything but sing and dance. I have to find a way to give back the hatpin . . . Oh, I am so tired! Tell me what happened to you?"

Jenel's voice was a low mutter. Senrid's mind hazed into a kind of slumber, until his knees buckled. He swayed, then jerked upright, shock jolting him awake.

The room was full of light. When had that happened? The wetness of drool at the side of his mouth made it clear that he had fallen asleep standing up. He wiped his face on his filthy sleeve. Disgusting.

He cast a longing glance at the bed. No. If this Yustnesveas Landis of Sartor discovered she was harboring an evil Marloven, she'd probably have her tame morvende hustle him right back down the tunnel and push him outside again for his "allies" to find.

Norsundrians weren't his allies. They were his uncle's allies. But he wouldn't beg or plead, trying to convince any self-righteous lighters of that.

Senrid pushed away from the wall, and slipped out.

Cassandra's door was not locked. He eased inside. A brief glance at the quilt-mound in the bed: Cassandra was already deeply asleep, and the other girl was gone.

On the nightstand lay a long silver pin. He remembered that pin. He'd seen it once before. While he was a prisoner he'd heard the Norsundrians complaining about the hatpin that turned into a sword, one that burned like deep-winter ice when it cut anyone warded by Norsunder's magic.

If it really hearkened back to the days of Old Sartor, that would mean it was an artifact of rare, complicated enchantment. According to what Hibern had told him about Old Sartoran artifacts, the magic on them was so intense that that artifacts could be used to counter equally intense magic.

Like, say, a rift, according to some ancient sources he'd dug up.

Tired and achy as he was, Senrid grinned, his chest filling with a fierce joy. That would be one in Detlev's eye, wouldn't it, if Senrid could shut down that northern rift? *The only way to get my kingdom back is to totally smash Norsunder's plans.* And shutting a rift would do it.

Senrid stretched out his hand—and stilled.

The sound was slight, but the air in the room stirred. Senrid whipped his head around and staggered dizzily.

Linet nodded toward the hall.

Senrid picked up the hatpin and withdrew from the room. As soon as the door was shut he said, "Who was the fellow in the uniform?"

"He's called Rel the Traveler. I don't know much about him, but he's a friend of the queen," Linet said, readily enough.

"Look—" Senrid began.

"Linet," she supplied, smiling.

"Linet. Those girls are going to stay around here for weeks, maybe months. This pin thing works against Norsundrians. So I figured I could use it. I'll get it back to them when they need it. Or—" He gave her a derisive smile, remembering how soon he was likely to be identified as a Wicked and Evil Marloven. "—you can come after me with your magic and get it yourself."

Linet already knew who he was, as the Loi had identified him along with Cassandra. One of the elders had also said, *Be very careful with Senrid Montredaun-An. He trusts no one, especially those he was taught to think of as an enemy.*

All she said was, "Cassandra wished to relinquish it, so we can discuss it later. You didn't touch the bed. You would rather be somewhere else?"

"Good guess." Tense gray-blue eyes regarded her warily.

"I know where you can rest undisturbed," she said, and before he could do or say anything, she transferred him to Shendoral.

Alone in a pleasant glade of whispering cypress, with no icy breath of winter, he stretched out on the grass and slept.

Back in the Destination chamber, Atan invited Rel to come upstairs to her parlor.

He accepted, but once they were there, he off the ring, which blurred weirdly in his fingers, and dropped it onto Atan's hand.

"The dawnsingers are inviting you to a celebration," she said, trying hard for an easy tone. The intensity of his dark gaze disturbed her, and she felt foolish. "For rescuing Cassandra."

"It was easy enough, with the cat and the ring. Rina seems to be gone," he observed. It didn't lighten the atmosphere any, so he tried a weak joke. "Looks like yon cat feels the same as I do about parties." He saw Atan's gaze moving sightlessly about the little room, as though looking for Rina. "Make a fuss over those two I pulled out of the cells," Rel suggested, feeling an intense urge to touch her hand, but he resisted it. "They probably need it. The cat did all the real work back there, not me. I think I'll just take off."

Rel never thought in terms of reputation, or bravery, or any of the stuff of legends. In his own mind he was simply Raneseh's ward, son of someone who had for some reason fostered him out, and his adventures were just that: adventures. When he won, it was fun, and when he lost he did his best to survive, and to learn how to do better.

He was tolerated by Sartor's formidable court and mages, he knew, for his help in the bad days when Sartor first emerged from the long enchantment and fought off the occupying Norsunder company. But he was also aware how very much Atan's noble guardians would distrust him if they knew how much he cherished her friendship. They had royal plans for Sartor's single surviving Landis, daughter of the oldest ruling family in the world.

Therefore, he was always careful to keep his visits short.

Atan bit her lip. She said in her calmest voice, "I wish you could stay longer. I could hunt up the history behind that ring, and show you some other interesting things in the archives."

"I'd like that very much, but I should probably be going while the weather holds," Rel answered. "I'll be back. I have an idea things are going to get hot up north. I might be able to use this again." He indicated the uniform.

Atan's brow cleared. Of course he'd want to use the uniform as a ruse to help others who might be in the same plight.

"You've been up all night," Atan said, a last try. "At least stay until tomorrow? I do owe you that story."

"I'd like to hear it, but can it wait until next time?" Rel indicated the north. "I hadn't known Norsunder sent some of their people into the world. From what I overheard from the morvende on the way back from the far tunnel, they're up to something. Can't be good. I'd like to go take a look. I'll send a message if I find anything."

Atan put her hands together. There was no keeping him, then. He wouldn't even take a magical notecase—he'd said he'd lose such a precious item, if it wasn't outright stolen. But he could always find a scribe desk to send a message.

She forced a smile, struggling to accept what he could offer. Sartorans loved celebrations, but the mere prospect of being smothered by overthankment was hastening Rel on his way. She had learned, after dealing with her wayward little cousin Julian, not to hold those who would not be held.

She would content herself with looking forward to his next visit.

He said, "I think I'll change before someone takes a pot at me." He mimed shooting an arrow.

She left to arrange for fresh food to be put into his pack—and under it, where he might not find it until he was well away—a bag of coins.

Rel had crossed the northern border of Sartor and was holed up snug in an inn, avoiding a sleet-storm, when Senrid felt recovered enough to find out where he was, and plan what to do next.

He had slept contentedly on the mossy turf, lulled by the whisper of the wind in the trees over head and the soft chuckle and plash of a nearby stream. He'd woken once to find a cloak lying nearby. Beyond questioning, he wrapped up in it. He soon discovered that it was ensorcelled against rain.

He woke up again, ravenously hungry, to find fresh bread and a hunk of cheese and a spray of grapes waiting. He was recovered enough to be on the move, and so he ought to be.

He ate all the food, then picked up and shook out the cloak.

Cassandra's hatpin lay on a flat rock. He bent to pick it up, and paused when he saw a blue flash.

He straightened up and faced Linet. "I take it Cassandra wants it back—"

"Wrong," Linet interrupted calmly. She hunkered down, the shadows of leaves dappling her bluish skin as she gazed at Senrid. "She said 'fare well' and you can get it back to her some day, unless you meet the Guardian first. It was not given her. It was only a loan. She wants to go home, and I believe Norsunder has no further interest in her. I take it you have a specific plan for it?"

"Yes," he said, and to test his status, "But first to the reason I left my kingdom. Do your lighter allies know about the rift being made up north?"

"We just found out," Linet said. "But the northern mages all seem to think that was pretend, to get our mages running around in the north looking for something not there. The Norsundrians are all here in the south."

If Norsundrians are seen all over the south, then that's what they want you to see.

Senrid didn't want to say that. After his experience with Kyale, and CJ of Mearsies Heili, and a few other lighters, he knew the next question would be something like, *If you understand Norsunder so well, you must be their ally.* And then they'd parade all over the moral high ground with *I've always heard that about you Marlovens. . .*

"About the pin." He hesitated.

"Go on. About the pin?"

Her gaze made him uncomfortable. He said to the dirt by his hand, "I heard some of the guards talking about off-worlders having being brought to this world. You know anything about that?"

"I do," Linet said, still with that steady gaze. "Eight people came through the world gate, four because of an explosion in their domicile, and four after an earthquake. And no, no one seems to know who sent them, or why. Except that it wasn't Norsunder, or they would not be free to go where they will."

"Does anyone know where they are?"

"The Loi speak to the Geres, the snow folk. According to them, four— the ones your age—are making their way southward down the continent of Drael toward the Fereledria. Back," said Linet calmly, "to your use for this magical artifact." She pointed at the pin Senrid had stuck in his cuff.

Senrid eyed her. She was no physical threat. They were both about the same size, and though Senrid hardly had the strength to get to the water to drink and then back, he knew he was good for a shortish spurt. Enough to get away.

Linet's biggest threat was her magical knowledge. The few glimpses Senrid had had so far had impressed him.

He said slowly, watching her for reactions, "I've read a lot of history."

"Yes," she said.

"Especially that written about events in kingdoms where dark magic is used."

"I thought you might have," she said.

He wished she would get out the threat so he'd know where he stood. But of course lighters wouldn't be straightforward with their threats. Not if they wanted to pretend they worked for Good and Right. Whatever that was.

So he considered his words. When he was little, his uncle the regent had permitted him two hobbies, reading and drawing. Senrid had figured early on that he was encouraged in those as a way of dissuading him from wanting to attend the academy to be trained in command, as he should have. Uncle Tdanerend had always pretended that he was training Senrid to become king, but by the time Senrid was ten or so he'd figured his uncle was doing everything he could to keep Senrid from learning how to be a king, while using him for his talent at magic. Tdanerend had been a terrible mage.

"In one of those histories I read," Senrid said, "I learned something about rifts. How to make them. How to close them."

Linet's eyes narrowed; maybe it was just the light, but they seemed to glow a deep blue, like the summer sky just after the sun sets. Meeting that glow made Senrid's head buzz.

Linet said, "I have heard the mages talk about what dark magic can accomplish by sacrificing a life. Is this what you seek, their lives to use?"

"No." Senrid let his breath out in a trickle. Linet was nothing like his expectation of a lighter. "People born outside the world are not bound by certain magics that bind the rest of us."

"I don't perceive magic as bindings, but go on."

"If someone were to find them, and get one of them to use an ensorcelled magical object, like this pin, to close the rift?" Senrid asked.

Linet smiled. The blue glow around her sparkled like light on water. "It would. But aren't you forgetting something?"

He shrugged. *Here comes the lighter speech about gratitude and obligation.* "Am I?" he asked, in the voice adults found most goading.

She walked with a quick, light step to the water's edge, and leaned down to point. "Looked at your reflection?"

Senrid glanced down, for the first time, at his torn, blood-splattered, filthy clothes, and grimaced.

"I've magic," he began.

"Not here. And besides—"

He remembered. "Right." The Norsundrians had him warded against using dark magic, or he would have been out of Norsunder as fast as he was taken there. *That* was binding magic.

Linet smiled. "So what'll it be?"

He indicated the road. She brought the warm clothes, a bespelled carryall, and a clean cloak that she had collected while he was asleep, and then vanished before he could say a word.

A week later he was on board a riverboat, earning his way slowly northward against the cold winter winds.

Chapter Thirteen

Davernak was irritated to discover on his return to South End that the brat was missing. He couldn't even take it out on the guard as he was already effectively dead, and anyway, he'd done what he was told: sit there and watch for the girl.

It wasn't his fault the girl was smart enough to get out of the house by using a window, or the chimney, or whatever she'd done.

So he summoned more of the mindblank guards who wouldn't question orders, or talk about them unless directly questioned. He needed to find the brat before Siamis sent for her.

Convinced it would be simple enough to find a spindly shopkeeper's brat, he sent a squad on a house-to-house search. When that turned up nothing, he had no choice but to issue commands for the roving patrols through that region to stop and question any girls on the road who answered to Liere's description. The enchanted people were told to report any lone girls sighted outside of South End.

That ought to do it.

Trusting Siamis to remain busy on his world tour for a while, Davernak set out to do some spying on his own. He did not stay to run the search himself—he wouldn't even call it a hunt, not when the target was ten years old and obviously frightened at her own shadow. The entire search was, in his opinion, stupidly useless. What possible damage could a ten-year-old shopkeeper's brat possibly do all alone?

As winter deepened, Siamis continued to move swiftly. Yet word travels faster than the fastest conqueror, and there were some who sought to resist the enchantment.

In Sartor—catching word, somehow, that Siamis was coming—the Loi tried to draw Atan to safety, but she refused to hide away and leave her people to the enemy.

So she called for her army of orphans, and they assembled as fast as they could. They and the few city guards deployed along the main road outside the eastern gate, nervous hands gripping weapons—or garden and work implements when weapons weren't to be had— when, a tall, blond visitor transferred to one of the courtyards of Rive Dian, and walked into the palace alone to visit the queen, who was trying to get her council to put out a call for volunteer defenders.

No one paid him any attention to a lone man strolling the ancient halls. All attention focused on the road, braced for the terrifying sight of another great army dressed in gray and black, and loaded with weaponry.

Siamis found Atan, and said, "I have a question."

She turned his way, polite as always . . . and never heard the question.

A short time later he and Atan came out into the main square together, and sent the would-be defenders home. The enchantment spread among them and outward, faster than a summer wind. The defenders began to shift from foot to foot, wondering vaguely why they were standing about holding sharp implements when there were chores to be done.

They dispersed, walking peacefully home to their dinners.

Watching from a distance, Linet grieved to see Atan transformed to a sleepwalker, as were her people, but there was nothing to be done right now except keep ceaseless watch over them—and listen for far-off news.

Siamis left Sartor to its dream existence and moved on.

Were there any who resisted the spell?

One of those who resisted the enchantment had heard suspicious rumors. She might be just short of her tenth birthday, but she had enough recent experience to doubt this news of a grownup who traveled around with Norsundrian warriors while talking of peace.

Devon, now of Imar, tried to express her doubts to Russy and Karia, the young rulers of the country, but to no avail. Her royal friends had changed for the better since the adventures they'd shared together not so long ago—but they were still rulers, and tended to be a little quick to judge, not to mention stubborn.

She remained in her room when the man came to have his interview. Devon looked out at those warriors in the courtyard, and knew she was right to worry. She recognized those uniforms, all right.

She watched from behind her curtains until the Norsundrians were rejoined by a tall, blond man who was not dressed like them.

She ran down to the royal receiving room. Russy and Karia were still there, tall, dark-haired kids with thin, vivid faces. Russy tended to be sarcastic, and Karia pouty, but they were smart and eager to bring Imar out of its centuries-long slump.

But when Devon walked in, they looked like . . . like they were asleep on their feet. Karia idly pleated the fringe on one of her elaborate, brocaded gowns, and Russy ran his hand back and forth, back and forth, along the edge of a table while staring out the window.

"Who was that man?" Devon asked.

Karia looked up. "Hmmm?"

Russy said, "Who, Siamis? He wants peace. Says we'll be as great in Imar as we once were. Greater."

"He had elevens with him," Devon pointed out. "Swords, knives, those jackets—everything. Right in your courtyard."

Russy and Karia looked blank.

"Elevens?" Karia repeated, as if she had never before heard the word.

"We have commanded the Royal Heralds to issue a peace proclamation," Russy said.

Devon scudded back to her room.

Half an hour later she rode out of the capital on her little gray pony Kondaria. No one tried to stop her—no one even noticed her.

Nearly two weeks later Devon reached the ruins of Ther Doleh in the north, for her idea had been to ride for help from the rulers of Everon, who had children. Maybe an adult might not listen to her, but she was confident that any prince or princess would.

She'd gotten used to sleeping in the open again, wrapped in the magic cloak that she'd been given when she left Mearsies Heili. It kept out the cold.

As she rode, she noticed that everyone in Imar acted like they were sleepwalking. She was careful to say or do nothing to draw attention. She bought food for herself and Kondaria, sleeping outside except when it snowed. For her pony's sake she found good, snug barns. No one ever caught her. It seemed that the people who owned the barns sort of blinked out, like lights, as long as no one talked to them.

Three times she was stopped by Norsundrians. Each time they looked at her carefully, and she forced herself to act blank, to answer in that dreamy voice other people used.

"Where are you going?"

"Home."

"Why are you out traveling?"

"My mother sent me to my aunt. My aunt is sending me home."

Another stare at her face, their attitudes impatient, disgusted, for no spoken importance had been attached to this search for small girls. The Norsundrians figured that the orders to hunt down a skinny little brat with light brown eyes and braids concerned some hostage situation. Nobody wanted to be stuck tending a hostage, particularly if she was the wrong one. And this brat didn't have light brown eyes.

So she was let go.

They are looking for a girl, she thought. *Whoever she is, I must look a little like her, but not enough to make them grab me.* Devon silently wished the unknown girl a safe journey, as Kondaria plodded steadily northward.

As she traveled, she had time to think.

First, about what to do. After she warned Everon's rulers, she would ask them to send her to CJ and the girls in Mearsies Heili.

And then . . .

And then . . .

She sighed. The right thing was to find a way to break the spell on Russy and Karia. And if she couldn't?

That was where her thoughts always stopped and her feelings took over.

The *real* truth was, she would love to stay in Mearsies Heili forever. How she loved the girls' underground hideout, and Clair and CJ and the other girls! But Karia was her first friend on this world, and prickly as she was, she seemed to need Devon.

And the Mearsiean girls had all seemed to think that Devon should stay with Karia, because they hadn't offered to let her stay.

So Devon had gone to Imar to live with Russy and Karia, promising herself that when they didn't need her any more, she'd be free to go to Mearsies Heili—or somewhere just as good.

Had that time come?

Honesty said no.

She was deep in thought she didn't notice the sun sinking into the west. She stirred only when Kondaria stopped at the beginning of a bridge, shook her mane, and nickered.

"What's wrong?" Devon asked, jiggling the reins.

Kondaria tossed her head.

Devon looked around hastily, her shoulders hunched. Maybe the pony sensed danger.

All Devon saw in the gathering darkness were ruins.

"It's me," said another voice—a child's voice.

It was Liere, who had been listening to all the minds that passed along the road. Until now she had stayed hidden, for nearly everyone who passed was enchanted. The rest had been Norsundrians riding back and forth on searches.

Devon's thoughts, free and clear, had been so welcome that Liere was out of her hiding place and running by the time the little mare had plodded halfway along the old road through the ruins.

Liere shivered, so glad to at least be talking to a real, unenchanted person.

"Who are you?" Devon cried.

"Don't worry, I'm a friend," Liere responded. "I'm in this tunnel over here . . . a moment . . . Ugh! I keep tripping over things."

Liere concentrated on keeping her voice friendly, steady, conversational. Devon relaxed unconsciously.

"I'm Liere," she said, walking up to Kondaria. Devon looked down at a skinny figure not much taller than she.

"I'm Devon, and that's Kondaria."

Liere petted the pony's nose. Kondaria sniffed at her, then whuffed on her cheek and Liere stood still until the pony was satisfied. In this way she apologized for having entered the animal's mind and commanded it to stop.

"What're you doing in the tunnel?" Devon asked. And she took a risk, "Hiding from elevens?"

"Yes," Liere said promptly. "And thinking."

"All day?"

"More like three weeks or so. I'm not sure. Until I ran out of food."

"Must have been uncomfortable," Devon said. She was used to oddballs. "What did you have to think about?"

"The world," Liere said vaguely. "What brings you here?"

"My mare." And when Liere laughed, Devon said, "Really! I just pointed her toward Everon and here's where we ended up. See, my friends Russy and Karia fell for some creepy Norsunder spell, and so I left."

"Russy and—you mean the new king and queen?" Liere asked cautiously.

Devon's discomfort at being thought snobbish was reassuring to Liere.

"They're my friends," Devon said. "Where I first came from, there are no such things as royalty. But this man came, and they changed—"

"It sounds like Siamis got to them."

"Siamis?" Devon repeated.

"Man who walks around with a bunch of elevens." Liere made a sudden jerky movement. "Pale hair. Wears a very fancy sword, Old Sartoran."

"That's the one! Uh, is something wrong with your head?"

"No—it's that I don't like hair in my eyes. Suffering from a very bad job of cutting my hair. No. Not suffering. Regretting the action. Uh! My vocabulary is poor, and I didn't even know it. Now I do. How to use what I have, but be precise."

Liere spoke in a quick voice, as if to herself. Devon thought about spending three weeks all alone in a tunnel, and said in her own most comforting tone, "Well, I don't have any scissors, but I'm sure we can find some. Is it dry in there? Can I camp safely for the night in that tunnel? I'm tired."

"There's lots of room underground," Liere said. "I can show you where I've been staying. There's water, and it's dry. If you don't mind my company."

"Mind?" Devon repeated. "I'm always glad to make a friend."

Liere caught the wash of loneliness that accompanied the words—a feeling with which she had a lifelong familiarity.

The mare walked into the tunnel after a good sniff around, then went to the stream to drink. After that, she wandered off to explore as the two girls sat side by side, exchanging names and a little talk. Liere sensed how tired Devon was, and suggested a sleep.

Devon curls up and dropped off, as Liere sat beside her, glad to have another human nearby.

Presently she curls up near Devon, and slept, too.

Before dawn, Liere moved to the mouth of the tunnel to watch the sunrise. When the pearly light slanted into the east0facing tunnel, touching Devon's form, she began to stir. She woke up slowly, reminding Liere of her sister Marga: stretch, yawn, look around while a sleepy mind got itself in order for the day.

Liere wondered if she'd ever been so unconscious, and decided she hadn't. The emotional reaction that resulted from that observation was regret, and loneliness—and apprehension.

But those were familiar ghosts, and she dismissed them with the ease of habit.

When she glanced again at Devon, it was to meet a curious gaze from serious, ringed gray eyes. Devon smiled tentatively, her thin, plain face easy to read even without mind touch.

"You look kinda like a boy," Devon observed, a slight question in her voice. It was also clear that it didn't matter if she actually was.

"I'm not," Liere said. "Disguised myself. Siamis's elevens would be looking for a girl, so I cut off my hair and took my brother's clothes."

"They *are* looking for a girl," Devon acknowledged. "Anyway, you sound kind of like a girl, but you don't look like one. Um, did I say something wrong?"

Liere had been thinking that the two of them looked more alike than not—both skinny and plain with thin light-brown hair—but one had gray eyes and the other light brown. And Devon's face was triangular, Liere's round. "Nothing," she said, "that requires action at the moment.

"Huh?"

"Nothing important. Sorry." Liere had intended to ask for a day's ride. But the more they spoke, the more Liere kept thinking of Devon not just as a ride, but as a possible ally.

Devon poked a finger in the air. "If you want to sound like a boy, you might try talking a little . . . oh, loud. You have a very soft, high voice. And you should also use more slang, to sound like other kids. You sound, well, *old* sometimes."

"Kids?"

"Us, boys and girls. It's slang from another world."

"Oh. I don't want to sound old," Liere said quickly. "Yet I must express myself precisely, when I'm not copying my sister or brothers, but I don't want to sound . . ." She hesitated, not wanting to explain her dread of standing out and garnering attention, as she had when she was small. Somehow it seemed she either had to pretend to be someone else, or stick out and get into trouble. That hurt.

Still, she was trying to escape Norsunder. "Remind me if I sound too old?"

"Sure," Devon said, smiling.

Liere realized at the same moment that Devon did that they each had begun to assume that they would travel together. Liere hugged her arms tightly around herself, fighting against both guilt and glee.

"Want some nice wenses?" Devon offered, digging in her pack. "Slightly stale, but still good."

She shared out a traveler's cake for each, and they ate in silence.

Devon reflected on the fact that she seemed to have fallen into another adventure. She accepted without question that elevens might be after Liere for some reason; in her experience, age was no barrier to villains and their plans. *That* she'd learned in Mearsies Heili.

As for Liere, she appreciated Devon at once, the way (she soon saw through listening to the stream of Devon's surface thoughts) that the girls in faraway, unknown Mearsies Heili had done. It was those memories of the laughing, playing gang in Mearsies Heili that made Devon wistful, and Liere, seeing those memories so clearly, felt the same emotion.

Then she squashed it as inappropriate.

" . . . comb your hair?"

Devon held out her comb. Liere took it, watching as Devon parted her long, thin curtain of hair and began to finger it into braids. Another, stronger pang of regret lanced through Liere, and this time she dismissed it angrily, vowing that if she missed something as inconsequential as long hair, she'd keep it short until such worthless emotion vanished.

She ran the comb through her hair with a couple swift, tangle-ripping strokes, parted it, and put the long part behind her ear, boy-style. Blinking watery eyes, she handed the comb back, and Devon threw it into her pack.

"What's next?" Devon asked.

"I am going to break Siamis's spell." It was the first time Liere had said it aloud to someone besides the Guardian, and she braced herself, feeling that now she was committed.

Devon accepted this with the same unquestioning attitude as before. Clair and the girls had defeated villains, so of course this girl could, too. "How can I help?"

"Ever hear of Lilith the Guardian?" Liere countered.

"Sure. She's mentioned in some of Russy and Karia's history books. Are we going to her?"

"I wish we could," Liere said, rubbing her hands up her arms. How safe she'd felt when the Guardian at last came to her! Even though she'd not stayed very long, while she was there she'd filled the cavern with light, and warmth, and good food—for Liere had not bought enough in South End. And they'd talked, mostly about magic, for a long time.

"She doesn't just help here," Liere said finally. "And there are worse villains than Siamis, and they are active, too. But when I told her that I had to—that my duty—what I meant to do, she helped me learn some things, and told me how I might accomplish breaking Siamis's spell."

"Oh, good!"

"It's a long journey to the north, and if Siamis finds out, there will be danger."

"Are you telling me about danger to get rid of me?"

"No," Liere said, and it didn't take mind-reading to comprehend that Devon was both honest and serious. "To be fair to you."

"Then let's go," Devon said. "Kondaria can carry two easily."

Devon watched as Liere's face blanked, her gaze going distant, and then Liere smiled, a sudden, happy-sad smile.

"You're right," she said. "Kondaria can."

Devon didn't ask how she knew. She accepted this assurance just as she accepted the fact that this girl must break the villain's enchantment, and the Guardian couldn't.

In Devon's experience oddballs needed watching out for just as much as anyone else, and Devon liked watching out for people.

Kondaria had not wandered far. Devon fed her several of the traveler's cakes. Those added to the grass outside that the mare had been cropping contented the mare.

The girls climbed onto her broad, bare back and began their long journey northward toward Roth Drael.

Chapter Fourteen

Leander and Kyale climbed slowly out of the water onto the coast of Mearsies Heili.

It was a rocky coast, rising from a long, gradual shelf overgrown with fantastical shapes of coral, which inspired those waters to be named the Sea of Rose—or, as Kyale told Leander as they climbed shivering out, the Mearsiean girls called, it the Pink Sea.

The magic on Kyale's armband began to fade as soon as they breathed air, but at least it took the water from their clothes. Not the salt. Leander was happy to be dry. He'd been afraid they would freeze to death before they could reach civilization.

As they began walking inland, it became apparent that civilization was not going to be easy to find. The coast of Mearsies Heili had no harbors or ports, and there was no building in sight, just flat land, covered with old snow.

The sun began to sink, and the wind got colder. Kyale was trying to figure out a way to bring up magic transfer without reminding Leander of what had happened on the ship when a bird cawed above, and dove down out of the sky.

Leander and Kyale watched, curious and a little wary, as the bird vanished behind a jumble of rocks. They were both surprised when a boy appeared, barefoot, wearing only a long shirt and sturdy trousers. He was small, skinny, an ordinary boy brown of hair and skin, with a pair of owlish eyes.

"Hi," he said. "I'm Ben. Who are you?"

"Who are you?" Kyale demanded.

"Clair's helper," the boy said.

"Take us to Clair at once," Kyale said. "We have desperately important news."

Ben opened his hands apologetically. "I don't know any magic except what's already on me as a shapechanger, and even if I did, Norsunder has wards all over this kingdom." He grinned. "But I can lead you to where Clair and the girls are hiding out."

꧁

As they tramped, Ben told them about himself—an outcast shapechanger adopted by Clair into her gang of misfits—and about the state of the kingdom.

"Siamis came here first," Ben said, his snub face souring. "He seemed to be searching for underage leaders. When Clair turned out not to be the one he wanted, he enchanted her and left her on the throne. The entire kingdom was enchanted, except for those of us with other kinds of magic on us," Ben added, looking grim as he kicked his way through sodden leaves under a melted patch of snow.

Kyale was already bored. She liked tales of adventure, which meant girls defeating villains. Everything about this 'Siamis' person was somehow scary and yet boring: he didn't do anything except talk, then suddenly everyone walked in a dream world.

"We managed to break the spell over Clair. It took some doing," he said, and paused, then when no one asked for details, added, "a lot, actually."

Leander opened his mouth to ask, but Kyale said, "I'm glad she got out of it! Where is she now?"

"She's hiding at her Aunt Murial's. Her aunt is a mage. A hermit. But she let Clair and the girls move in. Except Clair goes into the towns to make sure people are all right. They're trying to act like the enchanted, because otherwise the Norsundrians take people away, and twice burned homes as an example . . ."

Leander's inner vision of a safe refuge with people who would promptly send him to some powerful mage who could solve all his problems vanished like the melting snow as Ben described the petty cruelties and bullyings of what sounded like a very bored occupation commander.

When the light began to face, he led them to a deep grove among old, close-growing trees, and said, "You can sleep here. I'll bring you some food and a quilt to share."

He ran off, and presently they heard the flap of great wings beating rapidly away.

It was dark when he returned, bearing a basket of cold rolls, a hunk of cheese, some limp greens, and a horse blanket. "I stole it from a Chwahir patrol," he said. "Sorry I couldn't get more."

Kyale opened her mouth to complain, but Leander quickly thanked Ben, who said, "I'll be back at dawn."

"At least he could bring water to wash in," Kyale muttered.

"There's a stream not fifty paces away," Leander answered in the flat voice that warned her he wasn't feeling any less tired than she.

Neither of them spoke as they curled up back to back under the blanket.

Ben was back as promised, and so began another day of walking and talking.

Kyale watched more than listened. Ordinarily she didn't like being distracted by the glowing ribbons slowly twisting in the air, that no one else every saw, but there were so many around Ben that she finally asked, "What's it like being a shapechanger?"

"It's fun. Now," Ben said, waving a hand, and she watched the glow-ribbon burst into a hundred little ribbons then slowly reform into one again. "I used to live on another world, where people like me were—well, that's over and done. Until the Norsunder warriors came, I used to watch out for the Chwahir in the outpost under the cloud city. The Chwahir are ancient enemies of the Mearsieans. They want this land. Some of them and the Norsundrians have had some scraps," he added.

He then asked about them, and Kyale brightened as she described her adventures in Marloven Hess, everything of course centered around herself.

That finished the second day. By the third both were filthy and footsore. They couldn't bathe in the shocking cold streams, but at least the snow held off until late the third day. Ben said, "We're almost there . . ." at least three times.

Kyale was going to snap at him to shut up until they got there when they reached the welcome lights of the cottage at last, as flakes began falling.

The door opened, and there was Clair herself, white-haired, square-faced, smiling a genuine welcome. "Ben told us you were coming. We have a feast waiting, and you can tell us all about your adventures."

Kyale brightened at once.

His guide job done, Ben turned into his favorite condor and flashed through the still, cold forest, circling through the trees to scout out any roaming patrols before soaring up in a spiral high into the sky, far above the reach of arrows, as the Norsundrians regarded birds as target practice.

Then he drifted down, hoping his gray feathers would keep him more or less invisible against the falling snow and the gray clouds as he approached the little city on the cloud, dominated by the tall pearl-colored palace with the spires of different heights.

For he had heard that Siamis was expected.

Ben did not like taking the shape of anything smaller than a bird, for the danger of being squished was greater, and he felt this weird sense of pressure that was hard to define: he was somehow more aware of part of his body squeezed into some other space. It also had to do with odd forms of eyes, and making sense of what he saw.

But for spying on Norsundrians, he didn't trust any form larger than a spider.

Forcing his faceted eyes to give him a single, coherent image would punish him with a colossal headache later, but for now he was glad to be in his vantage spot in the carving on an old sideboard in the parlor the Norsundrians had adopted as their HQ.

The Norsundrians didn't trust the palace made of weird moon-colored stone. They only used the austere, vault-ceilinged throne room when handing out threats and rules to the lighters. The parlor had been completely reorganized, useless furnishings shoved into the corners, and the two tables put together in the middle of the room.

On that double table lay the map someone had put together, depicting Mearsies Heili, the Chwahir Shadowland, and bordering countries in detail. Spying on this map had enabled Ben to keep Clair and her Aunt Murial informed on all searches.

"I don't know how these idiots are getting word ahead. I don't like your teams finding empty buildings each time I want an example set. From now on, every empty building you find, I want it burned."

"But Commander," a young Norsundrian said. "Most of these are stone."

"Not the furnishings. Or the roofs."

"Tile."

The Command turned on the speaker, and scowled. "I said *burn them*," he enunciated. "I don't want to be stuck here watching over farmers and sheep herders another day. Don't you want in on the action?"

"Yes," everybody said.

"Then we're starting a new strategy—"

The door opened, and a long-nosed hound face poked in. "He's here."

The commander straightened up, and stepped to the commanding position at the head of the table as Siamis walked in, soft-footed as always, and dressed as a civilian. Ben wondered why he didn't wear the Norsundrian uniform.

"Here's your report," the commander said in the sort of voice men use when they want it clear that they are the important person in the room, and waved at his second-in-command, who handed Siamis papers as he walked to the side of the table.

Siamis glanced through the pages, turned his head sideways to glance down at the map, then he raised his gaze to the commander, whose bony, heavy-browed face was even more smug than usual.

Siamis tossed the pages down onto the map. "All light and no heat?" he asked. His tone made the commander scowl.

Siamis said, "What you appear to be trying to cover up is that the locals are predicting your every move." He glanced around. Ben made himself small as the blond head lifted and the observant gaze swept past his corner.

The commander blustered, "If they are, isn't that not evidence that the brat you're seeking is this Mearsiean girl with the white hair? If you'll look at—" He reached for the reports.

"I did. The brat I was looking for is not Mearsiean," Siamis cut in. "I established that before I left. All it shows is that this girl—or more likely her mysterious aunt—has got a good spy system that you're too slow to catch."

"There's no one in this building but us," the commander said. "We got rid of the servants." His voice sharpened.

"Then the walls do the listening," Siamis retorted, without any anger at all. "You will cease to entertain them." He said something softly, then snapped his fingers, and the commander vanished. "He can propound his theories to Detlev, who might find them interesting. In the meantime, listen up."

This to the second in command. Promotion so suddenly could be just as dangerous for the new commander as for the old, and the tension in the room made it clear all were aware.

"My 'brat' turned up in Imar. Speaking of which, where is Davernak? I sent orders for him to transfer the child here."

"Arrived last night," said the new commander, and he nodded to the guard at the door. "Alone."

Siamis said gently, "Alone?"

Ben couldn't hear any threat in that word, or see any threat in the fair-haired man standing below, but his legs drew in protectively around his body. The new commander rubbed his jaw, as though already worried that he could vanish like his predecessor, and snapped his fingers at the door guard. "Find him."

Siamis said, "My plans require a settled, obedient populace, not a kingdom-wide monument to dead heroes. You will cease the petty reprisals. You will also cease baiting the Chwahir, though if they try any more territorial expansions you're free to play with them to your heart's content. I will shortly have a word with Prince Kwenz Sonscarna. That should suffice."

The new commander signified that he understood with a curt gesture. He edged a step away; Ben didn't blame him. He could feel the mental force of Siamis's irritation from his spot on the ceiling.

"You will confine your searches to locating Murial of Mearsies Heili, or even better, her spy network. The evidence so far is clear that she can outthink all of you." He gave the reports a dismissive flick with his fingers.

Movement at the door brought the door guards escorting another Norsundrian, a tall, bony-faced man Ben had never seen before.

"Davernak," Siamis said. "Where is Liere Fer Eider?"

The room felt colder than the wintry air outside. All the Norsundrians gave one another shifty looks, some fingering weapons. Alone, Siamis stood at ease.

Davernak licked his lips. It seemed to take him a moment or two to find his voice. The silence stretched out at torturous length, before he said, "She vanished. Angelar and I personally conducted searches house to house through South End, and afterward issued her description to everyone, with instructions to report her presence," Davernak said.

Siamis shut his eyes, then opened them. "I do not hear her," he said. "You underestimated her, Davernak."

The Norsundrians shifted. Ben could see that the listeners found that observation, and the verb 'hear,' more disturbing than mere threats.

Siamis went on, "And the citizenry? Did they cooperate?"

"No problem—except in over-exertion," Davernak said. "They obediently report every single brat with braids any color that could remotely be termed brown. It takes time, checking their identities."

"That is the nature of the magic keeping them quiet and content, so do nothing when they bring the wrong child. I don't want to risk anyone startled out of the enchantment, which is only a superficial layer at this point. Worrying about reprisals if they are wrong might be enough for some."

The Norsundrians tried not to show their uneasiness. Ben knew from his listening that most of them thoroughly hated the weird magic that Siamis wielded—there was no way to fight against it.

Siamis continued, "My precocious little friend is hiding. Just as well, as I do not have the time right now for tutoring. But if she does re-emerge, I want the populace to turn her in—and you are to let me know right away." He smiled at Davernak, who stepped back involuntarily. "You have yet to inform me what you were doing when this desperate criminal made her daring escape," he said. "You will have time to tell me when I have leisure." His pleasant voice dropped a single note, and every Norsundrian in the room tightened up.

Siamis seemed to be unaware of the reaction to his threat. "So. I have the rest of this continent to visit—I ride out tonight. Produce this child before I do have leisure, and the interview will proceed differently."

He made a gesture, and vanished.

As Ben scuttled to the window-crack, he heard the new commander say to Davernak, "'Before I have leisure'—that means before Detlev finds her first."

"Yes," said Davernak, who forced a laugh, then mopped his sweaty face.

Ben reached the window, got out, and changed to his condor form. He dove down again, whizzing through the snowy air to the great dark-stone castle wherein resided Kwenz of the Chwahir.

He paused long enough to change to his crow form before arrowing through the upper reaches of the castle.

He glided down the cold, slow-moving air currents to the throne room, knowing that Prince Kwenz seldom left there. Ben saw Jilo, Kwenz' skinny, slouch-shouldered apprentice and heir, lurking in the shadowy alcove beyond the throne. Though CJ scorned any such idea, Ben's own private opinion was that the heir saw a lot more than anyone thought he did, and Ben took care to come to roost out of Jilo's line of sight, high above the glow of the red torches.

All he could see was the top of Kwenz' dull white hair, and Siamis' own hair, wheat-colored in the torchlight.

" . . . but I am not interested in your plans," Siamis was saying. "Regard yourself as an ally if you wish, but you'll not expand here. This region is mine. I may also have use for your army further south, in areas long divided by factional warfare. Until I have time to visit every fool who sets up as a leader I may have to have the areas contained and held by military force. That means until we get the rifts established, I will need extra forces. Detlev won't release his."

"Why not?"

"He's waiting to see me fail." Siamis seemed to find this idea amusing. "Any questions?"

Kwenz shook his head.

"Carry on," Siamis said, and vanished.

Ben waited.

Kwenz wheezed for a few moments, gnarled fingers stroking his long, tangled beard, and then he said to Jilo, "I must consult with my brother."

Apprehension zinged through Ben, and he saw a corresponding reaction in Jilo, far below. Wan-Edhe, powerful sorcerer-king of the Land of the Chwahir lying far to the east, loathed Jilo. He also scorned his brother in his little outpost for his lack of success in annihilating the Mearsieans and creating a Chwahir colony.

Jilo's voice echoed against the barren stone, "Want me here?"

"Listen." Kwenz's wheeze dropped a note or two, sounding wry. "Stay unobtrusive."

"Of course," Jilo said. It was impossible to tell from his flat voice what he thought, or if he had any feelings at all.

Kwenz performed a spell.

Moments later Wan-Edhe of the Chwahir appeared, tall, old, black-robed, his voice harsh and angry. His people found him so terrifying he was only known as 'The King'—*Wan-Edhe* in Chwahir, and never his name, lest he somehow hear and swoop in to smite them. "What is it?"

"Brother," Kwenz said. "I just received a visit from this young Siamis."

Wan-Edhe interrupted. "He's one of these soul-rotted Old Ones." And he added an epithet of little grace.

"I don't like the look of him," Kwenz muttered querulously. "Looks like an ally of the lighters. Silver sword."

"Affectation." Wan-Edhe cursed again, more violently. Then, "What did he say?"

Kwenz gave an accurate report.

At the end Wan-Edhe cursed a third time, adding, "Arrogant fool. One pleasant thought: he won't last. That other one, Detlev, will crush him."

"Detlev." Kwenz pronounced the name with intense loathing.

Wan-Edhe said, "This fool Siamis hasn't dared to face me in Narad yet. I suggest you withdraw to the homeland with me. We'll wait it out. No one commands my army but me!"

Ben didn't wait for the end of what was beginning to sound like one of Wan-Edhe's rants.

He glided round a corner and zapped straight for the outside, then west to Murial's house deep in the southwest portion of the forest to deliver his report.

❧

For a woman who did not like the company of human beings, Murial was managing. Her small cottage was full of kids, and had been for weeks, broken only when her niece, Clair, led spy trips or rescue forays into the rest of the country.

It helped that the little house had open windows and doors, through which Murial's animal friends could pass freely. These windows, magic-warded against the cold, gave the inmates the illusion of space. It also helped that—with one exception—the most restless of the human refugees staying with her volunteered the most frequently, and were gone the longest.

The exception was Kyale Marlonen, who in one day managed to make it clear that she disliked cold, dirt, chases, and Norsundrians worse than she disliked small rude houses with no servants. She did not know how to clean or cook, and had no plans to learn. To keep the peace, the Mearsiean girls quietly worked around her.

Kyale considered it only right. It was their country, after all, and she was the guest. It did bother her a little to see CJ dunking and drying dishes or sweeping, but the other girls were not princesses, so it was only right for them to serve.

Clair had not only her gang, but other stranded guests as well.

The most restless was Dtheldevor, pirate's daughter and privateer, temporarily stuck shipless in Mearsies Heili. Clair found her endlessly interesting. Dtheldevor had done the Child Spell uncounted decades ago, so she looked about fourteen. She was loud, mannerless, almost illiterate, her language full of boisterous curses, but she was loyal to her friends, she was generous in her own peculiar way, and Clair's gang found her fun and funny. Adept with rapier and knife after years of adventure, she was also perfectly happy to help with chores. After all, chores were a part of shipboard life.

She was just very loud and noisy, and her language frequently had Kyale sniffing in disapproval.

It was as well that Murial had a sense of humor.

She also had a sense of purpose.

Though she was by choice a recluse, she knew a great deal more about outside events than most, though as yet she'd said little to her guests. For now, she was content to get to know the niece she'd only been aware of from a distance. She'd left her unhappy family in order to study magic in Bereth Ferian, after which she made her home in the old, wild, almost impenetrable moss fir and cedar forestland along the northeastern flank of the most forbidding of Mearsies Heili's Arusian Mountains. Now, after years of isolation, she had with her not only almost all of the next generation, but a previous, in her child-bespelled grandmother Mearsieanne, who had existed as Detlev's prisoner in Wnelder Vee during its century of enchantment.

Poor Mearsieanne needed peace and healing more than any of them, for it was no pleasant thing to wake up from a century-long nightmare and find your world drastically changed. Murial and Mearsieanne spent a great deal of time walking along ancient animal paths and talking, where no one could hear them.

They were all there when Ben arrived later that night.

The warm glow of fire on the hearth, the smells of cinnamon and spice-baked bread, were welcoming, but friendship was still so new that what Ben noticed was how the other youngsters looked at him and smiled a welcome. At *him*.

The Mearsiean girls played Cards'n'Shards with Kyale. Also playing were Christoph and Clair's cousin Puddlenose, a tall, genial fifteen-year-old who made Ben glad at least he'd been given a name, and not a collection of epithets. Probably Puddlenose had had a real name once, but he'd been stolen from his parents too young to know it, and he'd spent his early years among the Chwahir, where Wan-Edhe kept him as a hostage. 'Puddlenose' was one of the most frequent epithets directed at a sobbing, miserable child, but in escaping Chwahirsland Puddlenose claimed the name as a badge.

"Hey, Ben," Puddlenose called, waving a hand. "Wanna join in next round?"

"Sure."

Clair asked, "News?"

Ben reported everything that he'd heard and seen.

The group listened in silence, then tall, quiet Seshe, the oldest of the girls, emerged from the kitchen and handed Ben some hot chocolate and a fresh-baked bun.

"Where can Wan-Edhe hide?" CJ asked, her blue eyes narrowed, mouth pruned with disgust. CJ's thoughts were always clear on her expressive face. "I can't see the King of Stinkers and Brother Dear sitting knee-to-knee in a cottage like this one, picking spiders out of each other's beards!"

The girls snickered.

"Picking out old meals, you mean," Falinneh asked, tossing back a bright, frizzy red braid.

Sherry blinked, her light blue eyes contemplative as she happily pursued the topic to the most ridiculous possible conclusion. "What would Wan-Edhe consider a good meal? Snail-slime pie? Creamed cactus?"

"Treebark soup!" Falinneh said promptly.

"Yam-cherry-bean cake!" Sherry shot back.

This exchange, Ben knew from long experience, would go on forever—especially if the other girls jumped in, and from the intent looks on Irenne's and Dhana's faces, they were trying to think up better nasty combinations. The Mearsian girls loved their private jokes so much they thought everyone else was just as entertained.

"Anyway." Ben lifted his voice, hoping to stem the flow.

Puddlenose cut in with the ease of old habit. "Oh, Wan-Edhe and Kwenz'll go back to Chwahirsland and hole up in the Sonscarna fortress up in the western mountains." He held his nose. "And if you think his place in Narad is bad, you should see that one."

"Disgusting?" Irenne asked, obviously hoping to hear the worst.

"Nasty is a compliment," Puddlenose said forebodingly.

Murial spoke up. "We can assume at least for now that the Chwahir are little threat, Ben, is that it?"

Ben nodded.

Murial's brows contracted as she brushed back a wisp of her graying dark hair, escaped from its accustomed long braid. "More serious is this news about the Norsundrians."

"Well, but didn't Ben just say that Siamis creep is going somewhere else?" CJ asked.

"Enchanting people," Clair said, her arms crossed tightly. "Which there is nothing we can do to prevent."

CJ sighed, short and sharp.

Murial said, "It can't be helped. Yet. At least we know that it does not hurt. It's something like being lost in a dream. And we knew he would be back eventually."

"I hate the thought of him going around my country," Clair muttered, looking down at the bare wooden floorboards. "He's probably doing it right at this moment."

No one spoke for a time.

Then CJ said firmly, "Well, if he put a new splat-face in charge, and said he can't attack people, maybe the worst is over."

"Here, perhaps," Murial said. "You must remember what Siamis said. He has plans. Do you think that those plans will be good for anyone but him?"

Mearsieanne said, in a low, angry voice, "He and Detlev ought to be killed."

"*Especially* Siamis," Kyale spoke up, from the only armchair in the room. Her pretty silvery eyes were narrow with anger. "Conquering whole kingdoms just by *talking* to people. That is so *creepy!*"

"He's using a combination of mind control and magic," Murial said.

"How is that possible?" CJ burst out. "I remember when I was stuck in that horrible Marloven Hess, and all that about disgusting Tdanerend and his trying to find spells to control Senrid's mind. There weren't any such spells."

"It's not so much magic as innate abilities, with magic extending those," Murial said. At the shock on all the surrounding faces, she decided it was time to share the burden of knowledge at last. "Siamis, like Detlev, is a leftover from Old Sartor."

Chapter Fifteen

Stunned silence greeted this news.

Falinneh broke it, her usual ebullience momentarily subdued. "Eeeeuw."

"I thought people in those ancient days were all good," Sherry whispered. "They went around spouting poetry and being. . ." She flapped her fingers skyward. "You know. Heroic and high-minded and advanced."

"Our ancestors were not some kind of miracle-civilization," Leander Tlennen-Hess spoke up from the window seat, where he'd been studying one of Murial's magic books. "Remember, they got blasted in The Fall. Where do you think Norsundrians came from in the first place?"

"Norsunder isn't unified," Murial said. "Except in that they share a common goal—the acquisition of power—but that's at one another's expense as well as ours."

Leander looked sardonic. "Senrid heard that Norsunder doesn't promote people on merit," he said. "Makes sense they prey on one another as well as on us."

"Just like Marlovens," Kyale muttered, with a sour glance upward at her brother.

Leander shook his head, and moved away. Kyale sighed, crossing her arms.

"To return to the subject of Siamis," Murial said. "The reports coming back to me make it clear he is not just enchanting the world, kingdom by kingdom, but he's also seeking anyone who has the beginnings of what used to be called dena Yeresbeth."

"What's dena Yeresbeth?" Kyale asked, twirling some of her long silvery hair around a finger. She was angry with her brother, who was defending that stupid Senrid just to blame her for that stupid fire on that stupid ship.

"One of what used to be called in Old Sartoran days the Blessed Twelve," Murial said. "Thought gone forever. Unity of body, mind, and spirit is the definition, but what that means exactly is harder to define. We know our ancestors talked from mind to mind, and controlled the aging process." She smiled. "You young ones using the Child Spell to stay the onset of puberty is a kind of far-off echo of those days, when people grew up as slowly as they needed to."

"'Needed' to grow up," CJ muttered, rolling her eyes. "That would be never."

"Hear hear," Kyale pronounced, still with her arms crossed. "Grownups are disgusting."

"Some, maybe," Clair temporized, smiling up at her aunt, who shook her head a little, and returned her smile.

Murial said, "Concerning the old Blessings coming back. Has it ever seemed strange to you that you—so many children—have found yourselves caught up in world affairs? That you had to find or even steal magic to control aging while you learned?"

"Played," Gwen whispered to Sherry, and both girls grinned.

Clair looked thoughtful.

"You say it's not coincidence?" Leander asked, dropping into in one of the window seats.

"It's not," Murial said calmly. "Some mages believe that dena Yeresbeth is awakening again, in your generation, and Norsunder was caught unprepared. At the same time that various Norsundrians are trying their conquering plans, the two Old Ones, Siamis and Detlev, are apparently competing to find—and secure—the first ones to make their unity. They are the only ones who know what it is. And how to find it."

"So that's why we've had so many problems with elevens?" Clair asked.

"Yes."

"And that's what Siamis was doing when he was here before," CJ exclaimed, snapping her fingers. "It didn't make any sense! Of course, they're too glue-brained to make sense *most* of the time," she hastened to add, lest her words be thought to impute anything even vaguely complimentary to an enemy. "When he said that Clair wasn't the one he was looking for."

"Here's what I recently learned through my own sources," Murial continued. "Which now makes sense, after what Ben just overheard. At least one child, apparently a girl, has made her unity. Siamis can listen in some way." She tapped her head.

"That would be the one Siamis talked about," Ben said.

"They musta thought poor ole Cassandra was it when they figgered Clair wasn't," Dtheldevor spoke up from where she sat backward in her chair, her chin on her crossed forearms, her dark, slanted eyes serious for once. "Which is why they chased her all over. What a load o' soul-sucking horse-dropping!" she exclaimed.

Murial said, "Only it would seem—if Siamis wasn't lying during the interview Ben overheard—he has a name, but as yet not the person."

"What c'n we do?" Dtheldevor asked. Pounding the chair back with a fist.

"What is it they *want*?" CJ burst out.

"We just assume they want to grab kingdoms for the fun of grabbing," Clair said. "But there has to be more behind it."

"Of course," Murial said. "The Norsundrians in control, that is the authors of Norsunder itself, well, not much is known about them, but the oldest records are clear in agreement on one thing: they really do consume your soul, your identity, and it appears to make them stronger."

Leander looked around. The reactions were characteristic: Clair somber, translating the news into evolving strategies for protecting her kingdom; CJ fierce; Dtheldevor laughing sarcastically, her desire to take action overtly expressed in her clenched fist; the Mearsiean girls looking mostly to Clair for clues on a subject which they felt was way beyond their experience; Kyale mulish. Puddlenose's expression like his cousin Clair's, and his quiet traveling friend Christoph looked uneasy.

"Did your animal friends tell you all this?" Kyale asked doubtfully.

Murial smiled. "They bring me messages from other magicians I've come to know from a distance."

Leander looked up from gouging his thumbnail in the window sill. He tried to hide the nightmarish regret he still felt over Senrid's having been captured. Especially after Clair and Murial had listened to his news, but said that there was little they could do besides pass it on. Communication had become as dangerous as travel.

Murial said, "The world is changing. No longer can people blithely go about their business and leave it to magicians to ward Norsunder. We are too few, and not always successful. People must begin to be self-reliant. With the possible rebirth of the Twelve, after so long, we might just prevail."

"Who is this girl the creeps are hunting?" Dhana asked, her thin face wary. She and Falinneh were the only non-humans in human form among the kids.

"Ben, what was that name again?" Murial asked.

"Leer? Lee-*air*-ee? No, was it Lee-*air*-ah? Foreign-sounding," Ben said, embarrassed.

"No matter. You did well," Murial said. "Apparently not just Siamis, but others are aware of her. She's got a nickname already, maybe to protect her true identity."

"And that is?" CJ prompted.

"Sartora."

"Named after Sartor's first queen?" Clair asked. "I like that!"

"So what's she doing to help?" CJ asked.

"According to the latest report, she's in hiding."

"Oh, great," CJ groaned in disgust. "So much for *her*. I think *we* need to figure out a way to get rid of Siamis."

"That's it," Dtheldevor exclaimed. "That's the kind o' action I can understand. We go after this soul-eater an' kick his pimpled butt to the middle of the ocean."

Murial winced slightly, and Mearsieanne—who belonged to a generation whose manners had been more circumscribed—frowned.

"It's one plan that might work." Murial gave them a sad smile. "But who will volunteer to execute it?"

No one was surprised when Dtheldevor said. "I will!" She laughed her pirate laugh. "Fer that, I'd even get me a pair o' boots!" She waved one broad foot and wiggled the toes; the others had heard (often) that for shipboard life she preferred bare feet.

Several were startled when Leander looked up from his place at the window and said, "And I'll help."

"*You* can't go," Kyale snapped.

"Why not?"

"You'll get killed!"

Dtheldevor guffawed. "'s awright for *me* to get killed, eh, little princess?"

Kyale glared at her, then turned to Leander. "You can't face that . . . that . . ."

"Groanboil," CJ offered. ever ready with suitable terms for enemies.

Kyale ignored her. "Let someone else go."

"And if everyone says that?" Leander shot back, not without humor. "Look, Kitty. We did what we came to do. One thing I am good at, because of the first fourteen years of my life, is survival in woodlands, and avoiding being hunted. I can turn that around to the hunt, now that it's up to others to get the word out about that northern rift."

Murial nodded calmly. He breathed out. The prospect of a challenge, of a purpose, cleared away the sickening sense of guilt that harrowed him night and day.

"Of course I can't defeat him alone, but maybe two of us can do the deed," Leander said to Dtheldevor.

"Let's move," Dtheldevor said, slapping her square, capable-looking brown hands on her baggy-kneed trousers. "It feels good to have a plan o' action. I been grounded too damn-blasted long!"

Kyale made a show of shuddering at Dtheldevor's language.

"Wait until morning?" Murial asked pleasantly. "It's snowing out, and we'll want to prepare you some food."

"Thanks. Would appreciate that last," Leander said, "but if we're going to go, it seems to me best to go under cover of darkness."

"Good idee," Dtheldevor said genially. "Someone borry me some woodland mocs? Even I ain't tough enough to go bare-toed inta the snow!"

Seshe, the oldest of Clair's gang, got up to oversee the preparation of the food, and Puddlenose beckoned to Dtheldevor, sure that either he or Christoph had a pair of shoes she might fit.

"Now," Murial said. "Something very important. You," she turned her attention to Leander, "have already picked up the trick of the Language."

Her emphasis on the word made it clear to Leander that she meant the language that enabled humans to talk to some animals—a very simplified form of Sartoran. He nodded. One of the ways she'd tried to help him combat that terrible guilt about Senrid's betrayal had been her offer to teach him the limited vocabulary.

"Remember," she said, "that certain among the animals of this world are willing to ally with humans against the greater danger. Do not be afraid to call on them for help."

"Be fun," Dtheldevor put in, grinning, as she stomped around testing Christoph's worn travel-mocs.

Mearsieanne touched Kyale, who had been glaring the while, and whispered to her. Kyale whispered back, fierce hissings that the others ignored.

"The animals, in turn, are the longtime allies of the morvende, dawnsingers, and some of the hidden races." Murial covertly glanced Dhana's way. The girl gave a slight, wary nod.

Leander drew a breath of sheer pleasure. It seemed strange that his intention of ending another's life would bring him into contact with those he admired most in all the world. But then he didn't want to kill Siamis just to be killing. It seemed to be the only way to halt one seriously evil threat.

"I'm glad to tell you," Murial said. "I think—though the times seem very dark indeed—that the world is on the verge of great things, and this alliance is one."

"The greatest," Seshe murmured from the kitchen door.

At the fervency in her usually quiet voice everyone glanced at her, tall and slim, her ash-blond hair bound in locks hanging against her blue gown. Seshe looked like an old-fashioned girl in some tapestry. She was the peace-maker of the group, and the most spiritually akin to animals and birds.

"But do keep in mind," Murial said, as she lifted a young pup from Diana's lap, "that you treat them with respect. They are not minions to be spent." She set the pup in Dtheldevor's lap.

The pirate girl's face was a study in confusion. "Hey," she protested, her hands stiff at either side of the dog, who sniffed happily at her tunic. "I ain't gonna do no Norsunder-blasted insults, but how—"

"A pat is fine," Murial said, laughing. "Did you think he'd prefer to shake paws?"

"I dunno if it's respectful," Dtheldevor said, grinning. "I got no idee what that is, not having need o' it on the seas and fightin' villains."

"Animals are tactile creatures," Murial said. "And though their form of sentience is not like ours, they are always truthful. They like a friendly touch, and show it. Their way of seeing the world varies. Some have no interest in humans. You probably won't see those."

Dtheldevor ruffled the pup's ears, gave him a smacking kiss atop his head, then set him carefully down, where he promptly tried to leap back up into her lap.

"I'll put together packs of travel food," Seshe said. "Sherry, give me a hand?"

"Sure."

"Put in coins, in case," Murial called. "You will find some coinage in the cracked sugar holder."

CJ added comfortingly, "Chasing after a villain? I wouldn't be you two insanitics for anything!"

At CJ's exclamation, Kyale no longer pretended to ignore her brother. She exclaimed in horror, "You aren't—you can't be actually going *now*?"

"Looks like." Leander shrugged into his coat.

Kyale wailed, "What about *me*?"

"You'll be safe enough here," Leander said, with the extraordinary patience that all of the others had noticed.

"But how am I to get *home* again? And what about *our* people? What if Detlev decided to send Senrid after our kingdom again? They're probably best friends by now!"

Leander's face smoothed into blankness, and CJ grimaced. She felt ambivalent about Senrid and Kyale for completely different reasons: the first she had liked, then learned to distrust, and disliked having liked him. The second she kind of felt she *should* like, the loyalty of kids to kids on the side of good.

Murial said, "Kyale, we will find you a task worthy of your strengths and spirit. Leave Leander to his. Remember, they will find allies."

Kyale looked around. There was no support in any of the faces, so she confined herself to warnings that—as Leander moved about, swiftly assembling a few camping items, an extra set of clothes, and a knife— began to sound more and more like scolding. He didn't hear it. He had a goal now, and for the first time in days, felt good.

Seshe set two packs by the door.

Dtheldevor picked up one. "Bye," she said, and strode out into the snow.

"We'll see you at the celebrations," Leander added, and closed the door.

Murial caught Clair's eye, and glanced Kyale's way.

The girl stood there in the middle of the room, her fear for her brother's safety obvious in her stricken expression.

CJ stood up. "C'mon, Kitty. Ol' Algae-eyes is gonna be okay. You know only good kiddies die young. We're all too rotten for that, and boys are twice as rotten."

"Hey," Puddlenose said. "I heard that."

"Me too," Christoph said. Puddlenose's friend Christoph was always looking ahead to the next adventure—or joke. "When it comes to rotten . . ."

"I'll tell you what's rotten," Falinneh announced. "I'm an expect on rotten—"

"That's for sure!"

"Yes!"

"Admits it at last!"

She nodded regally at this chorus of insults from her friends as a queen acknowledges allegiance from her vassals, and continued, "— because I have been granted a glimpse of the Villains' Code of Rottenness. Now, your new villain must, if he wants to be taken seriously, acquire a warty nose, a gloomy castle—"

The others joined in, distracting Kyale with a long string of ridiculousness. She liked being the center of attention, and she adored the silly jokes; she calmed, as it happened, long before Leander did.

Chapter Sixteen

While Liere and her new companion made their quiet way northward to escape Siamis, and Leander and Dtheldevor began to chase Siamis, most of the rest of the world was either oblivious, full of flying rumor, or enchanted.

Rel and Senrid, without being aware of the other, made their way northward away from Sartor. Senrid traveled as straight to the north as he could. Rel bent eastward, toward the home where he'd grown up.

It was scarcely three weeks from the time Rel left Sartor when the enchantment spread around him.

He felt nothing, but he saw the effect when a crowded, crooked street not far from the river dock, full of cart vendors, delivery people, storekeepers, shoppers, loungers, and thieves stopped arguing, bargaining, gossiping, and lounging around. Small children stopped running about, playing, yelling, singing, shouting, laughing. A gangling red-haired wagon-driver about Rel's own age, had been flirting with the young man unloading the barrels, until the silence swept over them. The driver straightened up, gazing between the horse's ears, and the unloader worked efficiently, without a sound.

Everywhere Rel looked it was the same. People went about their business without haggling or chatting. The children separated off, apprentices vanishing inside shops. Everything extraordinarily peaceful and unnervingly orderly. Rel's skin crawled. It was an unnatural order—

occasional voices were direct, without emotion. Question, answer. Go on about one's day.

He lengthened his stride when he caught sight of the river beyond a dilapidated inn. When a richly dressed, grizzled man galloped through town, peering around as if he expected a slavering hunt, the orderly people stopped what they were doing, tracking him with identical gazes.

It almost looked as if someone, or some*thing*, peered through those gazes to mark the man's direction.

The urge to run tightened Rel's shoulder blades, but he made himself walk at a normal pace lest those gazes lock onto him.

He paced downhill toward the river dock, his primary motivation now to get away before whatever had happened spread to him. Two riverboats lay tied up, the crews moving at a snail's pace. He hesitated, wondering what would happen if he went to either, but then his eye caught on a low barge laden with straw-packed ceramics. Instinct pulled his gaze to the left, to meet a squinting, assessing gaze from a gray-haired, stout woman. She stood beside the ramp, arms crossed.

He was going to turn away when she looked quickly to the right and left, then without unfolding her arms, flickered gnarled fingers in an unmistakable beckon.

Rel trod the rest of the way down the mossy, worn stone stair to the dockside and stopped a couple of paces away. Scarcely moving her lips, she said, "You didn't get caught by the glass-eye spell neither."

It wasn't quite a question.

Rel said, "Do you what's happening?"

She gave her head a slight shake. "I seen it in Loss Arkendan, upriver. I saw it happen on a quarry barge we passed, they were dancing on the foredeck, making merry, then of a sudden they stop, and go about checking things, then sat down like someone emptied out their heads. I saw it with these two eyes." She opened one eye wide and squinted the other, then cast a furtive glance around to see if anyone was watching. "But soon's we passed the border, people were normal."

"Why did you escape it?" *Why did I?*

"Dunno." She leaned toward Rel and muttered, "This here is some magic spell. Can't fight against magic. Back at Tiger's Paw Dock, someone said there's Norsunder-kind in charge, and the glass-eyes tattle on anyone that sticks out to them, and the Nightlanders come after them."

"Sticks out," Rel repeated.

She inclined her head in the direction of the dust still hanging in the air on the road the wealthy-looking man had gone. "Like that." She indicated her barge. "I'm moving on come dark, before it sticks to me. Want a ride?"

Rel lifted his head. This river flowed westward, directly to the Sartoran Sea, back in the direction he'd come. "I'd better ride on. Warn my family. They're up north."

She shrugged. "Don't let the glass-eyes see ya. From what a scribe said at Tiger's Paw, any Norsunder-kind can tell 'em what to do, and they do it. No question. No argue. It's . . . obscene." She turned her head and spat into the water.

Rel agreed, and mindful of what she'd said, he walked back up to the inn, which had an enormous stable full of horses to hire. He got one, moving slowly, his face wooden. It was difficult to believe any of what he'd heard, except here all around him was the evidence of something weird going on. Only how did it spread? Why did it not affect him?

Did they know about it in Sartor? He had to find a scribe to write to Atan, and then his foster family in Tser Mearsies, to warn them . . . what, exactly? To leave home and flee? Is so, where to? He knew his foster-father wouldn't abandon his Holding.

One thing at a time. Beginning with staying out of the magical net.

Senrid's uncle had permitted him two hobbies.

One, as he'd told Linet, was reading history. He'd told his uncle that he was reading about boys of the past, which had sounded sufficiently dull that Tdanerend had never bothered to monitor what he'd actually read.

The second hobby, drawing, Senrid had confined to map-making. He'd been very careful to avoid making military maps, once Keriam had taught him how to read them. Instead, he'd drawn elaborate maps with fine lettering, and neat little representations of castles and towns, every building stylized, sometimes right down to fences alongside roads, and blue-painted rivers and lakes.

When Senrid had completed the most detailed of these maps—the one of Marloven Hess that hung in his bedroom—he'd turned to making maps of other countries. Tdanerend had despised this exercise in prettiness as useless, but suitable for a boy-king whom he intended to suffer a terminal accident the moment he felt his grip on the kingdom was sufficient.

He'd never stopped to consider that all that map making would give Senrid a formidably clear internal map of the kingdom—indeed, of the world.

When Senrid's riverboat neared the harbor on the Elgar Strait, Senrid's efforts to remain unnoticed got tougher, for not everyone was enchanted, most especially those who moved about on the seas, loyal to no one but their ship, or their cargo.

He'd worked quietly and well at the tedious job of recording trade items loaded and unloaded at each stop along the river journey. Twice, people went silent and weird as the riverboat passed through, but then they reached normalcy again. Everyone speculated on the cause, but of course no one knew anything.

Senrid kept his head down, and his attention on his job.

&

For a time Rel was preoccupied with staying out of sight, but his thoughts kept coming back to what the barge captain had said. When he stopped to water the horse, he decided to try an experiment. He was alone on a stream bank, shaded by winter-bare trees. Bracing against the cold, he changed into the Norsunder uniform, and then rode on.

When the stream widened, joining a river, he spied a small town at the ford. He spotted escape routes as he approached. The first people he saw, all enchanted, turned toward him expectantly. His heart thundered as he lifted his voice. "Go back to your true selves."

They stood still, blinking, betraying no sign that they'd heard.

He tried again. "Go back to what you were doing."

His voice cracked—he'd done the Child Spell as his voice had begun to change—but no one laughed. They turned as one and went about their daily habits in a mechanical way that gnawed at his gut.

He continued on, wearing the uniform, but anxious that he'd run into other Norsundrians.

He saw none, but from time to time as he traveled he had the sense that he was being watched. Careful scans showed no inimical eyes. As he approached the border, he figured that sense, so vague and brief, was little more than instinct reminding him to be alert.

When he reached a small town, he rode in, wearing the uniform, and as before, told the silent, waiting crowd to go back to what they were doing.

His guts clenched at their lack of will. He found his way to what turned out to be a sizable scribe building on a square at the crossroad to three major routes.

He went inside. The scribes all sat on their mats, at low desks, hands quiet. They stared into the distance.

Heart hammering, Rel walked up to the oldest, figuring the man was in charge. "What is the latest report?"

It had been a guess. To his surprise, the man answered. "All roaming patrols to report daily. Monitoring only. Entertainment disallowed, see Omerenth."

Rel said, "What's Omerenth?"

"Trade center, north-central Goerael," came the flat, emotionless words, as if reading something in a language one could pronounce, but not comprehend. "Former captains Venada and Suh ordered some locals to walk off a cliff," the man said, flat-toned, his green eyes blank. "The first died, the others broke the spell, causing a panic. Siamis had to restore the spell household by household. Suh and Venada are now soul-bound, and their patrol dispersed to stable work."

'Siamis'? Rel bit back a question, *Who is he?* He feared that even under enchantment, these people might have orders to report suspicious questions as well as people.

"Why is there no entertainment allowed?" Rel asked, figuring anyone joining Norsunder had to favor cruelty and mayhem.

The man said, "We are spread too thin. Most are needed to round up the free-floaters."

"Free-floaters?"

"Those with no allegiance but to themselves. Patrols must keep moving: only capital sites get a stationary patrol until the rift is successful and we can bring over the occupation force."

"Rift," Rel repeated, not certain what that was. It suggested a tear in the world, if the bringing of occupation forces meant Norsunder Beyond Time. "When is that happening?" And where could he go to stop it?

"When the enchantment is complete. Siamis found the child he sought. Now he is free to see to the second level of the plan, completing the enchantment."

"And what is the third level?"

The man stirred slightly, blinked, then demanded flatly, "What is your name and orders?"

Rel froze, then, desperately, said, "Go back to what you were doing."

The man sat back, his gaze moving to the neat stack on paper on his desk, the dry pen, the capped ink. His fingers began to crawl toward the pen like a spider, and Rel walked out fast, hoping that the man wasn't about to write a report of some kind.

It seemed too easy, getting the ensorcelled to speak just at the sight of the uniform. At the same time, it was dangerous. These enchanted people had been turned into spies for the enemy who controlled them.

'The Child.' That had to be whoever Norsunder had been looking for when they grabbed the girl and boy he'd rescued. *I should have asked who the child was*, he thought.

But first he had to get over the border to the first unenchanted place he could find, get to a scribe, and tell them to write what he'd learned and send it to the royal scribes in every kingdom they could.

Another hard snow left clean powder. He rode under the cover of woods until at last he crossed the border river, which had iced over.

He'd discovered on his travels that you could learn a lot about local governments and how things worked by how information was given out— if there were heralds, where they made announcements, or if they did. In Chwahirsland, you found out about the king's latest horrific decrees usually after executions. In Colend, you had to get up early, because to the Colendi, the only civilized time for news dissemination was at the Hour of the Bird.

Here, relatively close to Colend, the herald stood on a bench outside the shop that houses scribes and book traders. The herald appeared to be even taller than Rel, a pale-haired, freckle-faced young man with a loud, if unmusical voice. " . . . for the last time, all we know is that some foreign scribe desks answer, some don't. As yet, we're not certain if those not answering are under orders from their guild not to respond until we have first-hand information. We don't repeat rumor, you all know that. When we hear more, I'll say more. No questions—I told you what I know."

He jumped down from his bench, and was promptly mobbed with questioners.

Rel tried to peer over heads, gave up, and began elbowing his way through the crowd, this being one of those times his size and strength were a real advantage, though he left sour comments and even curses in his wake.

That stopped when he confronted the herald and said, "I have some first-hand information."

The young man's eyes widened. "Come inside." He towed Rel into the building, where three scribes crowded around a desk, obviously a family, from grandfather to a bristle-haired girl apprentice.

"First-hand witness," the herald said, indicating Rel as he shut the door firmly on those who all thought that their question was the exception.

The grandfather said, "Wait till we all set up a desk, so the news can go out faster."

"You've got to write to the scribes closest to rulers," Rel said. "This enchantment spreads from rulers outward to the border, worked by someone named Siamis, from Norsunder."

The gray-haired man shook his head. "You must begin at the beginning, establishing your source, where, when, how, *then* what."

Rel hesitated, wondering if he ought to admit to the Norsunder uniform. As he was formulating his words, a peculiar sensation gripped the back of his neck. He looked up, startled, to face four utterly blank faces. Staring eyes.

Staring eyes . . . and the older man's hand crept toward his pen, the exact same way the enchanted man had done back in that other town.

Rel backed away two steps, three, and shut the door behind him. He looked around the square, to find it empty, except for hundreds of mushy footprints.

That was far too close, he thought. When it came to Norsunder, he didn't believe in coincidences.

And so he mounted his horse once again. Colend was the closest kingdom. He would go directly to their king.

❧

As the river widened to estuary and the air began to smell of the sea, the captain offered Senrid a permanent job. He got around her by another lie.

The port of Hanbria was a busy place. Senrid spent a day walking about in the brisk sea-salt wind, watching the noise and bustle and listening.

He had to get across the Elgar Strait, but there was a patrol of Norsundrians prominently riding back and forth along the harbor concourse, questioning every ship that came in.

Senrid watched this happen three or four times, wondering if he could risk a stop-and-search. How much did Detlev really want him? He was a king, yes, but only for a month, already deposed, without a single follower.

And yet Detlev had wanted him for a second interview . . . and Senrid had found himself able to understand the Norsundrian language. What little he knew about Detlev did not lead him to think the commander was ever careless.

Senrid sat on a stool in an old dockside inn, eating fried fish with his fingers, and thought: It's never good to be careless.

Four long days Senrid spent along the docks used by the smaller short-haul ships. He skipped the big ones, noting that some even had Norsundrians aboard.

On the fourth day he found a smallish, old ship taking wine northwards to Imar, Everon, and beyond. The captain, a grizzled, suspicious old cuss, did not want passengers.

This captain—shifty-eyed, angry and fearful, probably running just as far outside the law as he dared—brought vividly to mind the disastrous journey with Leander and Kyale. There was no help for it. This seemed to be the only type of person who'd deal with him.

"Passengers mean trouble," the captain said, spitting over the rail, a deliberate insult, but Senrid did not react. "I got me a crew, an' *Sea Star* don't want no trouble. Trouble costs."

"I'll pay," Senrid said, smiling his sunniest smile. "I'll pay and work both."

"You a runaway?" the captain demanded, squinting down at Senrid.

"Oh, no. Would a runaway have coins?"

"A thief would." The captain spat again, into the choppy green sea.

Senrid kept his face bland. "You can ask Captain Mallec of the river trawler *Diamond*. She offered me a year's employ—"

"So why ain't you there?"

"Because as I said, I'm homesick. My uncle brought me south to learn to be a scribe, and I did learn, but I want to go home to Numa Har." He named a land well north of the Fereledria.

The captain hesitated.

"I have good handwriting, I don't mind work. I can lay aloft and reef, don't mind standing a watch. And I'll pay. You can have my whole winter's wages. I won't need them at home." Senrid shook his bag of coins. "I just want to get back there."

The captain took the golden bait, and put him to work at the grunt tasks that no one else wanted.

Senrid kept his smile, and his temper. When the tide ebbed, he was scrubbing down the worn, warped deck of the *Sea Star*. But when the Norsundrian came aboard, Senrid was there on the crew list. Senrid watched Hanbria's busy port slid away, the Norsunder patrol riding away in column along the docks.

The first rain of spring soaked Rel and obliterated his trail as he rode hard for Alsais. He kept looking back as, once again, he sensed that he was being watched.

And yet nothing terrible happened. He was very adept at hiding, and fast travel, but that did not explain how inward prods of instinct—sometimes benign, other times not--kept bringing him to places where he could get horses, or food, questions unasked. These were the times when the prod seemed benign. The *run, danger* prods kept him moving fast.

He'd decided to avoid scribes, after twice watching glass-eyed scribes crawl fingers toward pens, while watching him. He was afraid that the Norsunder mages—this mysterious Siamis—was somehow watching scribe desks, impossible as that seemed. He would warn the king of Colend himself, and if he was successful, kings had ways of communicating with other rulers.

Every sign of Colendi frivolity as the snows began to melt lifted Rel's heart: so far, the normal noise of people going about their lives had not diminished into the glassy-eyed dream-silence.

He recognized the beautiful tile roofs of Alsais gleaming in the sun of a recent rain, and grimaced, his memory of his previous visit a bad one. Here he was again, only it wasn't the Chwahir invading, but a Norsundrian mage. And the sense that he was being watched, or tracked, intensified. He kept peering around, uneasy at the apparent peace of orchards, gardens, pretty windowed houses. He trusted his instincts, which usually furnished a clue: a subliminal sound, a shadow out of place, a faint scent on the air.

As he rode into the city, he strained to find some physical clue to the increasing sense of urgency and danger

He forced himself to slow to the rate of moving traffic when he entered the city. There were few broad streets on which one could ride; most people used the canals to get about, or walked the narrow brick-patterned or tiled streets. As he looked about at the colorful clothing and the many gardens, even on some roofs, he thought back to that terrible previous visit. Puddlenose had said, *I learned the hard way that even a Chwahir invasion won't stop them from ignoring you if you go in the wrong gate. All the gates have meanings, some at different times of the day . . .*

So which gate was the right one?

Rel gazed at passers-by, and spotted a girl around his age in a soft blue over robe. Blue usually meant mages or scribes, depending on the color. "My pardon," he said as he slid off his horse, and she stopped. He had no idea how handsome he was as he said, "I'm a courier from Sartor. This is my first important run, and I have an urgent message for the king. Where should I go to get it to him?"

She put her palms together, wondering why, if the message was so urgent, the Queen of Sartor didn't write to the royal scribes. But everyone knew Sartor was odd, recently back in the world, and anyway, she would never be impolite, especially to someone so tall and beautifully made. "The Gate of Pecan Blossoms, down past that canal there, will bring you to someone who can help," she said, smiling.

He remembered that putting your hands together was called 'the peace' and the Colendi did it as a politeness. He clapped his hands together and bowed. She laughed at his charming awkwardness, and they parted, he to lead the horse along a narrow lane bordered by flowers, and she to meet her friends for the midday meal . . . which would end in silence.

He reached the Gate of Pecan Blossoms, which wasn't really a gate at all. Pecan trees lined a walkway flagged in star patterns of warm peachy stone and pale cream; before the horse had plodded eight steps, two people in shades of pale rose and gray glided from behind a flowering trellis, one going to the horse, and the other, the taller, to Rel.

A sharp a sense of urgency prodded rel. He whirled around, startling the weedy young servant in the fine linen robe.

Neither Rel nor the servant saw anything amiss, but the startled servant took a step back, thin mouth opening into a triangle of surprise and regarded Rel warily.

Rel said, "I need to warn your king that there's a Norsundrian mage taking down kings."

"You say you came from Sartor?"

Rel knew that he could borrow Atan's name for a good cause. "The queen herself."

The servant frowned to the side, then said, "It's just that the seniors say that Sartor has gone silent. But I'll take you to the chief scribe."

Gone silent? Did that mean *Sartor* was enchanted? For the first few steps, Rel followed blindly, sick with regret and then anger. He should have been there . . . but what could he have done?

Another, sharper prod caused him to whirl around a third time. His danger sense tightened the back of his neck as he followed the servant through a discreet door half-hidden by a carefully tended tangle of flowered vines in three shades of goldenrod. Here, the servant thankfully handed off responsibility to the next up in rank.

Two servants later, Rel was conducted to a marble-floored space that had to belong to the king. Now a new worry began. It was widely rumored that the king of Colend was insane for long periods, and even during his lucid moments was difficult. Puddlenose had talked long and bitterly about that.

Rel wondered if he was going to meet the madman or the supercilious snob. Which would be worse? He thought as he was handed off to yet another beautifully robed servant, who noiselessly led him inside a chamber with a bank of windows that overlooked a wild garden, a canal gleaming peaceful and blue beyond.

The man who turned to face them was startlingly handsome, light of skin and hair, dressed in the deepest royal blue. The servant pressed his hands together and bowed deeply over them. Rel bowed.

"What's this?" Carlael Lirendi said, in no inviting tone.

But judging by the relief that the servant couldn't hide, Rel figured the king wasn't insane at this moment. He had composed his report on the way in, and gave it quickly.

The king listened in silence, his smooth, beautifully proportioned face unchanging as marble. When Rel finished, the king said to the servant, "Send my son to Skya, with a triple guard."

Son?

The king glanced off to the right, saying, "Ring the carillon for Circumspection."

Rel didn't see whom the king spoke to, but he heard the soft rustle of cloth from behind a handsome four-fold screen depicting starlings mid-swoop.

"Now repeat it again," King Carlael said.

Rel did, but he hadn't gotten far before the king stopped him with an upraised hand. "I must question my own people as to why I wasn't warned by our diplomatic connections . . ." He paused, gazing out the bank of windows.

Rel turned his head to see four Norsunder riders astride beautifully saddled horses. None of the horses were happy. They kept tossing their heads, eyes rolling, plunging and kicking.

"How did they get past the herald-guards?" the king whispered, then he dashed into one of the side rooms screened off, and returned with a sword with a gold-chased hilt. He glanced down at the smooth tiled floor, and said, "This is terrible for fighting. If they're after me, I want better ground."

Rel wore his own sword across his back. He pulled it free as the king ran off, calling names of people Rel assumed were guards.

No one came. Carlael and Rel ran down broad stairs in the beautiful palace, which, Rel noted distractedly, was militarily impossible to defend, and out another garden way. Two Norsundrians were trampling flowers as they ran into view from another direction. They turned their heads at the same moment, and charged.

One was young, one old. The old one was a better fighter, but Rel had been training since he was ten. He took out the knee on the young one and stabbed his sword arm, leaving him groaning in a flowerbed. Rel turned to the other, and saw what the king realized at the same moment: that the man wasn't trying to kill or capture the king. He was trying to get past the king to Rel.

Carlael sent Rel a startled look, as Rel distracted the man by kicking up soil into his face, then both Carlael and Rel stabbed him, one high, one low. The man fell to one knee, and Rel used his hilt to club him hard across the back of his head.

"They're after *you*," Carlael said, breathless. He'd been trained to duel, but Rel guessed he hadn't practiced much in a while. "You led them here?"

"No," Rel said as they ran. Then amended, "At least, not that I'm aware. My report was true."

The noise had attracted the four riders, who tore through the garden on their plunging, kicking mounts.

"There he is," one shouted, pointing at Rel.

At that moment, his horse reared above three snakes weaving their heads in the air on the path. The rider fell heels over head. The other horses shied, necks sweating as their riders fought viciously for control, but then a weird rushing sound startled everyone, and a dark cloud arrowed over the roof, diving down toward the riders.

All three Norsundrians threw themselves off the horses as the roiling cloud resolved into three different types of bird flying tight-packed, their wings drumming the air.

They swooped down, driving the Norsundrians back. Carlael turned and dashed past grapevines, Rel right behind him. "Why aren't the bells ringing?" the king asked the air. "Where are my herald-guards?"

He kept running, until the four former riders caught up, and Rel charged them, stumbling to a stop when the birds thundered out of the sky again. Carlael ran, calling summonses, then it was his turn to stumble to a stop, staring as servants and herald-guards alike walked about on their tasks serenely, glass-eyed and blank. The herald-guards were always supposed to be in earshot of the king could not hear him.

"What happened?" the king whispered. And ran again. This time he stopped at one of the gates that overlooked a broad canal. On the other side, pretty buildings rose, people gliding along in silence. "What?" the king said more softly, lowering his sword.

Rel watched in all directions, urgency gripping him. "Siamis. Or someone. Must have gone around to your guild leaders, and your stewards, to spread the enchantment. Your people aren't ignoring you. They're enchanted."

"I can't fight this kind of war," Carlael whispered. "I can't. Better he should kill me now."

Rel said, "You can hide."

"No." Carlael turned on him fast, no madness in his gaze, or supercilious privilege. Just grief. The tension went out of him and he flung down his sword, which rang on the pretty brick path. He pressed his hands over his face, then dropped them. "I must do what honor requires, and face the enemy, whoever it is. But some of them were chasing you. Go —you brought your message. You can do nothing here."

Rel bowed and took off up a path parallel to the canal. In a coincidence that he was beginning to believe was no coincidence at all, two of the saddled horses waited for him, ears twitching, and he rode out of Alsais, and for the border. Sick with defeat, he wondered what he should do now. He wanted to help, but so far had failed at everything.

First, stay free. Clearly someone had been dispatched on his trail.

That uncanny sense of urgency pushed him for a day or two, then faded. He rode back westward, wondering what he should do now.

He hadn't traveled more than half a morning before that inward prod drove him in one direction, where he discovered more people hiding from the glass-eyes.

They were trying to contact others, and Rel offered to carry their message.

This time he didn't fail, and discovered that his instincts about where the rare Norsundrians might be patrolling—or for that matter, where to find hidden resistors—were always right. Not just right, but *strong*, almost like a wordless urge or message.

He'd always had a knack for finding trouble in which he could lend a hand, but the precision of his knowledge was a new thing. He shrugged it off as incomprehensible; maybe it was no more than an unexpected side effect of everyone else around him being under enchantment.

Figuring he would help as long as he found people to help, he kept traveling, scarcely aware of his small black shadow.

The trader ship's captain ignored Senrid at first.

Senrid was unsurprised at discovering that the captain was not popular with his crew, but he was steady, successful, paid what he owed, and he sucked up shamelessly to harbormasters, local lords, and Norsundrians—anyone who could interfere with his trade. It seemed that those who made him afraid made him honest, and he was very afraid of the Norsundrians.

So Senrid did what he was told, watching the slow progress of the old, round-hulled ship and spending his scanty free time running calculations on when the cowardly, wily captain would stop hopping from small harbor to small harbor along the strait and cross at last to Drael.

At last the winter winds began to die, switching around in all directions as spring rains alternated with the last snow. Ahead of a sudden storm spiraling from the south, the captain took alarm at some fleet he saw, and crossed at last, diving between the treacherous rock formations called The Fangs, and heading for Imar's enormous Jaro Harbor, which was so empty that they were signaled immediately to a dock, rare for an old trader. And the *Sea Star* was boarded by a tall, gaunt woman in Norsunder gray.

Senrid had already tried to find a way to nose out what was said during private interviews in the captain's cabin, but the suspicious old geezer had thick walls and a good stout door framing his cabin aft under the flush deck.

So Senrid lurked around the 'tween-decks, sedulously scrubbing the rowboats—and was surprised when the captain appeared suddenly and jerked his thumb at Senrid.

The Captain poked his finger in Senrid's chest. "Get out of sight," he whispered hoarsely. "Bunk. Sick."

Senrid slipped down the ladder to the crew deck, swathed himself in his cloak and lay in his hammock with his face turned away from the ladder, and the flickering lantern nearby.

Not long after, he heard the sounds of heavy boots climbing down. The captain's voice came: "Ship's boy. Got the gut-grippe. Had him for two years."

No one spoke. After a moment came the sounds of ascent.

Senrid counted to fifty, then ran up and forward to the mates' quarters to peer out a scuttle. He glimpsed the Norsunder inspector marching down the ramp to the dock, where a patrol waited, sunlight glinting off their sword and knife hilts. She rejoined the mounted patrol waiting on the dock, while the captain bowed and smirked. That search had been cursory indeed, Senrid thought. Interesting. A fast, scanty search indicated too many done in a day; Siamis still had his forces spread too thin. Hmmm.

He sighed, wondering what sort of lie he could concoct now, because it was inevitable he'd been sent for and jawed at. *Something* had scared the old buzzard of a captain.

In a very short time the captain himself appeared in the narrow forepeak, his hands shaking, his weather-beaten face dark red with fury.

"Just goin' home." His voice was a strangled croak, as he poked Senrid painfully in the chest.

Senrid made himself take it. He knew the man's anger masked fear, and it was that fear that his lies would have to assuage.

"They have a list, some of 'em younguns, and head of that list is Prince Senrid Montredaun-An. And the descriptions was detailed right down to the color of your eyes." The captain seized Senrid's chin and forced his head back, toward the light coming through the scuttle. "Damnation!" His voice scaled up to a squeaky whisper. "It *is* you!"

So much for trying to stick it out. Senrid snapped his forearm up to knock the captain's hand away, then started down to the crew deck, followed closely by the captain, whose voice was hoarse with strain. "I would've turned you in except I don't want to end up in jail for leavin' Hanbria with you. *Should you see any on this list detain them and report to us at once. To refrain is a capital offense.* If I see your face by the watch-bell, I'll do just that."

Senrid had his pack slung over his shoulder before the captain stopped speaking. By the time the captain finished his curse-punctuated expostulation about how he was going to *keep your money against your lies, you little shit*, Senrid'd already gotten his cape and was halfway up the hatch. Two breaths later he trotted down the ramp, scanning quickly for the patrol, and plunged into the crowd of busy dockworkers, carts, horses, and barking dogs.

When the crowd thinned at the other end of the harbor, he dropped onto a pile of boxes to figure out what to do next.

'Prince Senrid.' He kicked at a coil of rope, thoroughly disgusted. Obviously Uncle Tdanerend was still on Marloven Hess's throne.

He thought of the captain's fear of prison. Prison! Senrid's lip curled. Unwanted memory blocked out the harbor noise; he was a small boy again, standing before the assembled palace guard to endure his first beating. *Kings don't fall off horses,* Uncle Tdanerend had said, but that wasn't the lesson the seven-year-old Senrid had taken. Even though he was supposed to be the king, he'd learned who held the power—and what holding power meant.

The Norsundrians held power over people such as that captain just by simple threats.

A shadow crossed Senrid's line of sight. Senrid tensed for flight or fight.

"Senrid," a man said quietly.

Senrid jerked his head up, squinting at a tall silhouette of a man, with the strong spring sun shining directly over his shoulder. Senrid flung up one hand to shade his eyes, his other hand drifting near his hidden knife. "Who are you?"

"You're on a capital list," the man said, in Imaran. His accent was Mearsiean. "My first mate saw you running down the quay just now."

Senrid tensed to run if the man made a move.

"You were once on board my ship, the *Tzasilia*?"

The man shifted slightly, and Senrid took in the regular features, the tied-back brown hair and the traditional green captain's coat.

"Captain Heraford," Senrid said, thinking fast. What lies had he told when he was on the ship last summer, with Clair's cousin Puddlenose of Mearsies Heili? He said, testing, "You know who I am?"

"Yes," Captain Heraford said. "You're from Marloven Hess, about which I've heard plenty during port visits along the Rualese coast. But I like to make up my own mind about people. And if you're on a wanted list, then you can't be allied with Norsunder."

Senrid let his breath out in a whoosh. "My last captain didn't feel that way."

"Got your gear?"

Senrid picked up his pack.

As they walked, Heraford said in Mearsiean, "They've already searched us once. But that might not suffice, these days. We'll get you aboard in a roundabout way."

Senrid assented, amazed and wary both. Nothing had ever been so easy, in his experience. He'd liked Heraford and his privateers. Even so he half-expected a trap. Just half. Not enough to refuse when Heraford led him to a noisy inn.

Heraford said, "Don't look at me. Just follow. Head down. Act like the enchanted. You were drawing too much attention, running as you did."

Senrid grimaced as he slipped behind the man, and followed his broad back through the common area to the kitchen, and through a concealed door to a dank, briny-smelling storeroom down some steps.

There he had to crouch down in a box labeled GLASS, its slats rough with space between them.

Glasses were loaded in with him, and he was told to let them clink together during the transfer. He was hammered in, which caused his heart to beat in panic.

But he arrived on board the *Tzasilia* with no mishap, and when he was at last freed from his box, it was to find that the streamlined little three-master sailing out on the tide.

"Here you go, young'un," a skinny old sailor said cheerily. "Cap'n' is waitin' in his cabin."

By which Senrid understood that his blond hair, gray-blue eyes, and accurately reported height and build weren't to be seen on deck just yet.

He made his way from the ship's hold to Captain Heraford's familiar cabin. There on the bulkheads were the beautifully made old maps. Senrid found those reassuring, though he couldn't have defined why. Senrid shifted his attention from them to the captain, who sat near the open stern windows, from which he could hear the calls of his navigator and pilot.

"Sign the ship's book?" Heraford asked, and as Senrid hesitated, he added, "The elevens will never find it. I've a magical hidey if we get boarded."

Senrid looked down at his first name, his print neat and bland, with no family name or country. Nor far above he saw CJ's bold hand: *Cherene Jennet Sherwood of Mearsies Heili.*

And a little ways above that, he saw a strong masculine hand: *Rel from Tser Mearsies,* and he wondered if it was the same fellow who'd pulled him out of the Base.

Senrid dipped the pen and sign with a proud flourish:

Senrid Indevan Montredaun-An of Marloven Hess.

There, it was a part of the record, and it felt absurdly gratifying just to be himself. Let the consequences come.

"Thanks," Captain Heraford said, closing the book, and stowing it away in a cabinet. "Now. You're a new top hand, night watch, so you may as well claim a bunk and get some sleep. But before you leave the cabin, you're going to wear this."

He tossed Senrid a bright purple knit cap with a long tassel.

"That is what our enchanted passengers will remember, if anyone asks about our ship's boys."

"Enchanted?" Senrid felt that horrible sense of a trap closing.

Heraford raised a hand. "We're all enchanted, they think. You just go about your business without chatter, without curiosity. I've carried post for years, as well as trade. I have three couriers carrying business post."

"Got it." Senrid swallowed, and pulled on the cap, making certain his hair was completely hidden.

"Behave as though you're asleep on your feet. Anything that disturbs the truly enchanted can bring Norsundrian mages to inspect. I don't know how. I've never seen anything like this in all my life."

The man looked out the stern window at the rippling wake, a muscle in his jaw jumping. He said finally, "We don't know how to fight it. But someone will."

He waved a hand in dismissal.

❧

When Rel finally reached the coast, he lurked around the busy port at Hanbria for a month, listening to what rumor said about events, and lending a hand to the small group of non-enchanted resistors he found, who had set up a HQ under a dilapidated old inn.

Spring came with a glorious flowering of green, trading rainy days for heat, promising a hot summer. He was able to get a job as a deckhand aboard a small trading vessel. He kept his own counsel and worked hard. One morning, he glimpsed a little black cat among the ship's felines. It reminded him of the one he'd shared the adventure with in Sartor.

Weird, that.

He paused in scrubbing the deck and studied the cat. She really did look like that one in Sartor as she sat there on the capstan, front paws neatly together, still as a carving.

He smiled, and returned to his chore. Black cats did look alike, after all.

❧

For Senrid the days stretched into weeks. Gradually the sharp, cold winds from the north and west lost their bitter force.

The work of a ship was constant, but Senrid liked the precision of sail and rigging, and the endlessly changing sea and sky. On land, weather was a matter of logistics.

He worked hard, and regained strength and stamina.

He also had time to think while sitting high above the deck through the nights. If he was on a capital list, it might be because he'd escaped, but it was also possible that some elevener higher up—someone like Detlev—had somehow found out that Senrid had the hatpin. Of course Detlev had to know about the same weaknesses in spell-structure that Senrid did, with respect to rift creation and off-worlders.

If Detlev knew about the off-worlders, he would have put Norsundrians on their trail. If they were still on the continent of Drael, Senrid had only to find search parties, and listen somewhere for the description of their target.

One night, as he took a break from worming and parceling a new shroud for the standing rigging and stared out at the moonlit shore of Drael, he decided it was time to leave the next time they touched land.

Chapter Seventeen

Leander crouched in a crockery closet, his sleeve stuffed in his mouth to keep any noise from escaping, and shook with laughter.

Peering between stacks of clay-colored crockery, he watched Dtheldevor hanging upside down, her legs and arms wrapped round an old, iron wheel chandelier.

Her heavy dark braid dangled a bare arm's length over the heads of a couple of Norsundrians who stood at the cookpot, gazing morosely into it.

One of them poked at the soup with the ladle, then snorted.

Leander closed his eyes and held his breath.

The candles in the chandelier had not been replaced, much less lit, or Dtheldevor never would have gotten away with it. Yet he wasn't so sure she wouldn't have tried it even so. The only light in the kitchen came from the fireplace and from a candle in one of the Norsundrians' hands.

The Norsundrians continued to look down into the big pot, commenting in their language. Leander's back ached, and his legs felt like someone had stuck a hundred sewing needles into them, but he dared not move.

As the Norsundrian would-be cooks puzzled over the mysterious smell of their soup, Leander fought against the panicky laughter in his chest by thinking about other things. Like where they'd been. Yes. It had been such a strange winter!

When he first departed from Mearsies Heili, his foremost worry had been how he'd be able to bear killing someone, even a Norsundrian—but within a couple of weeks that had metamorphosed into a worry about *finding* the man.

They'd managed to make contact with some wild horses and rode hard southward through Teldenor, southern neighbor to Mearsies Heili. Some winter jays squawked and scolded them into the capital and thence to a certain inn. There they met a group of outlaws who had escaped the spell, and—delighted to help someone who actually meant to do something about this mysterious Siamis—loaded them with mounts, stolen coins, and good advice on traversing the southern trails.

From there they chased down the Toaran continent, sometimes on horseback, once flying over snowy peaks on gryph-back, a few times on water vessels. The canoe down the mountain stream would always be a particularly vivid memory.

And they'd had help. Murial's promise was no light thing. Everywhere they traveled they found animals willing to aid them, from small ones that spied out the location of the nearest Norsundrians to birds that carried messages or spotted patrols. Big animals bore them willingly much faster than human legs could ever progress.

Yet even with this help, he and Dtheldevor still never managed to catch up. Siamis moved fast, and he seemed to be tireless.

Clink! One of the Norsundrians opened a spice jar, and rather gingerly poured some of the contents into the pot. The sweet smell of loethe tickled Leander's nose, and he bit his lips—hard. Nice enough in puddings on its own or with shaved vanillin, loethe would be truly disastrous combined with pepper.

He forced his mind away. Think about something sobering . . .

Like Senrid.

Leander had discovered that even action did not entirely assuage guilt.

He shifted minutely as the Norsundrians muttered, then one of them decided to throw some flour into the soup. Above them, Dtheldevor clung, silent, still, her face turned toward Leander, her slashing grin just visible.

Leander closed his eyes and continued his mental review.

His thoughts often returned to Senrid; guilt would ride him until Senrid was free. He opened his eyes, and the laughter was back at the sight of Dtheldevor hanging ridiculously upside down.

Like Kyale, Dtheldevor never bothered hiding her emotions. In just about every other way they were as unlike as two people could be.

Leander would never permit himself to compare them, for Kyale was in a sense his family, and very definitely his responsibility, but he had to admit it was fun to travel with someone who could move as fast as he, who cared nothing for cold, or wet, or strange foods, who never once—that he ever saw—glanced into a mirror any more than he did, who thought it a very great joke if her clothes got ripped or dirty. She had little fear of risk, and her quick wits and deft fingers more than once got them to hot meals and away from danger. She always kept an eye out for an unclaimed rope, which she'd wind round her waist until she needed one. "Faster'n twistin' 'em," she said cheerfully—though she was amazingly fast at that, too.

It wasn't always easy. Dtheldevor had a habit of issuing orders, and her table manners were nonexistent. If Leander had something interesting on his plate, out would come her knife and she'd help herself. She also drank wine—when she could get it—and though she didn't get drunk, she always snored afterward. Though she'd never released the child spell, and so had never developed as an adult, she had lived many years. The fine lines beside her eyes and nose, plain in sunlight, testified to those.

She didn't think like any adult Leander had ever known, but she had far more experience than a youth.

She was the one who'd thought up this game. Each Norsundrian-occupied place they came to, if they had to wait for Siamis, the enemy would get a visitation from them. 'Visitations,' Leander discovered, were to Dtheldevor what sabotage was to the rest of the world. The game was a contest. Whoever made the other laugh the hardest would win.

The prospect of fun kept them going as they took ship—working as crew slubs—to avoid the long, arduous (and dangerous) land bridge from Toar to Leander's own subcontinent, Halia. Whether they found a barracks or an encampment, they found some way to make their mark.

He'd had private misgivings about having to visit his own homeland, several days' fast ride to the north. He did not want to see his own people enchanted.

But he didn't have to. While he and Dtheldevor shivered outside a small temporary Norsundrian outpost in Perideth, they found out that Siamis had already been through the kingdoms to the north. In his wake, small units of Norsundrians were to cover the countryside looking for pockets of resistance.

So he and Dtheldevor turned to the east—after Dtheldevor used two of her spare ropes and a block-and-tackle to rig a mud-filled horse trough over the door to surprise the Norsundrians when they returned from their rounds.

At first they traded off on their wager. False alarms—fires, spooked horses, clanging bells at dawn—were their most frequent ploys, but once or twice inspiration caused them to work together. Their most spectacular success was the diversion of an ice-cold stream in Naidhiahi's heights, which flooded a huge Norsundrian encampment below.

The funniest so far was this one. If they survived their attack on Siamis, who was due at any moment, it was going to make a great story.

Noises outside the kitchen had sent Leander racing behind the crockery and Dtheldevor, lacking a better place, vaulting onto the prep table and to the chandelier just three breaths ahead of the entry of some enchanted Norsunder flunkies obviously stuck with kitchen duty.

Leander couldn't understand Norsundrian, but he knew they were discussing what the peculiar smell could be.

Finally one of them made a decision, and as Leander watched, his sleeve still stuffed in his mouth, they slopped the soup into waiting bowls and then bore the trays back through the door.

Dtheldevor dropped down, snorting and sniggering, her face purple.

"C'mon," Leander breathed.

"Wait. . . I wanna . . . hear their screams when . . .they . . . taste that mess. . ." She clutched at the table.

Leander grabbed her tunic collar and hauled her backward. "Imagine it," he muttered.

Just as they rounded down the worn stairs to the wine cellar, they heard the Norsundrians open the kitchen doors again—and howls of rage and disgust wafted down.

Leander's knees almost buckled, he was gulping and wheezing in an effort not to bray with laughter. Dtheldevor now had to hold him up. Together they made it through the secret door that a friendly cat had shown them, and out into the night.

Two, three buildings away they made it before they collapsed into mud.

"Pepper! All—the—pepper!"

"Sourberries! Salt!" Leander thought of his own additions, and his stomach hurt with his efforts to breathe. "The—the jug of pickling-s-s-s-yrup . . ."

"The loethe!"

"Loethe and—and—and—puh—puh—puh—pepper!"

"The . . . the curses! The curses! *How* they c-cursed!"

"Ow, my gut hurts!"

"Wa—wa—wah . . ." She finally gave up.

"You . . . win . . ." He couldn't talk any more.

Slowly the laughs died to snickers, and then to panting.

Dtheldevor rolled onto her back in the mud, rain beating in her face, her black eyes open, reflecting the light from a nearby window. Then she got up and pounded away, her steps sloshing.

Leander held his breath. He'd managed to give himself hiccups.

Dtheldevor reappeared fast, cursing softly. She hunkered down and punched Leander in the arm. "Fart fire! I overhead the orders. He was already *here*. They had their meetin' in the stable while us and everybody was waitin' on 'im in the inn! Time t'hit the road."

They did—but when they reached their next destination he was gone.

Senrid exerted himself to stay out of sight of the civilian population of Everon. He hoped his trail had gone cold as he tried to make sense of the search patterns. They had to be after some powerful leader because he saw more Norsundrians here than he had in all the rest of his journey since leaving Sartor. They rode about constantly, stopping in every town, every village, clearly searching for someone.

He discovered that the knapsack Linet had given him no longer produced warm nutbread from somewhere. Either the spell had worn off, or else he was beyond the reach of Loi magic's influence. So he stole horses and food from strangely heedless people, and racked his way cross-country northwards, where the searches seemed to be coalescing.

He rode steadily, changing mounts when he could find a new. One day he dozed in the saddle, to discover to his amazement when he jerked awake, his neck aching and mouth dry, that the animal had not turned around and made its way back home, but was still going north.

No time to puzzle that out, not with the sound of hoof beats in pursuit. He kneed his mount. The horse jumped into a gallop. The hoof beats altered in rhythm, and there was the sound of a human voice, an exclamation. They'd spotted his mount's fresh prints.

He kneed the horse again. The hunt remained the same distance behind, still not visible—the trail was far too windy for that.

By the time that horse tired, he had reached wild, dark, old oak and hickory forestland. He watched carefully, and when he was safely round a curve with a drop down one side he flung his leg over and jumped.

He landed on his feet, slipped on rubble, and tumbled headlong into the gulley, smashing through bracken until he landed with a splash in the mud at the side of a stream. He flung his head up, whooping for breath, then slogged deeper into the water, wading downstream a ways before he dared to emerge, dripping, cold, but at least the mud had been washed away.

So had his faked-up knife sheath. He scrabbled around. Gone. He'd bought the knife on the river, but hadn't found a decent sheath, not like they made at home.

His body trembled as he jerked the knapsack straight. He reached inside and felt the inner seam. The hatpin was still there, pinned firmly.

He splashed to the other side of the stream until he spied a goat trail, and took that.

The shadows had hardly changed before he had to slow. Searchers galloped along unseen paths, once northward, another time westward. Either they'd called all the locals out, or there were two or three patrols circling around in increasingly tighter perimeters.

Night fell. The noise of the search ceased. He wove himself into a thick brush and slept, then continued on the next day, plodding steadily though he had no more than a couple sips from a stream to fill his gut.

That day he counted seven patrols.

The following day he only had to hide twice. There was no sense of triumph. The difficulty the Norsundrians had in finding him mocked him with the inescapable truth that he was just as likely to miss the off-worlders.

From a distance, it had seemed so simple: move along the main highways, and watch for kids who didn't act like the enchanted. As he zigzagged between all the major north-south routes, tramping along mossy paths or wading through thick, leafy undergrowth that had gone undisturbed for ages, he wondered if he'd pass within shouting distance of the off-worlders and never find out.

Finally, the terrain opened into rolling, gentle hills, brush land and meadow dotted by farms and divided by hedgerows. Senrid tramped along the roads in the summer light, and found himself wishing for the cool shads of the oak forest again.

The weather continued to alternate between hot days and sudden thunderstorms. He used the stormy episodes to sit quietly in what looked like they'd once been well-frequented inns, so that he could listen to the talk.

Nothing happened. No one paid him any attention. No one followed him.

No one talked, except about their immediate business.

The third time a storm-line towered on the western horizon, he was near a small town. He made straight for the first inn he saw, and walked in just behind several travelers as big drops of rain splattered down and thunder grumbled in the distance.

On the pretext of watching the lightning, he moved about the crowded common room, which still carried the summer heat and smells of cookery. People exchanged occasional, dispassionate words about the day's business. There was no laughter, or gossip, or music, even. No rowdy drunks, no older teens flirting, no little kids chasing about, or big ones playing games.

When the storm had passed, Senrid trudged by the innkeeper, who polished her pans with methodical movements, her eyes absent.

"I'm looking for my cousins who are traveling south from Flendere," he said in a flat voice. "They are my age. They might not speak the language."

"I have not seen any foreign children who cannot speak the language," she murmured, raising her eyes. They were dark eyes, their focus unnervingly fixed.

'Foreign children.' It might be a restatement of his lie, but there was something too smooth about her words, too much like a phrase from a remembered order, such as *Report any foreign children who cannot speak the language.*

Senrid departed with a muttered "Thanks."

No one followed him, though his shoulder blades crawled. He circled around and helped himself to a horse from the stable, as the stable hand sat mending a harness with slow, methodical movements.

At another inn, the next night, he tried a different approach. He was now on the outskirts of a good-sized town. Not everyone would know everyone else.

He slid into the kitchen through the back way, and found a young kitchen helper chopping potatoes. "Me and the apprentices have been assigned a task," he droned. "To count how many foreign travelers under the age of twenty seen in one month. You noticed any?"

The girl looked up at him, her blue eyes narrowed and unblinking. "I have not seen any foreign children who do not speak the language."

He backed away from that narrow gaze, nerves tingling. He'd deliberately left out anything about language.

Time to get lost.

The next afternoon he was walking eastward as fast as he could across the hilly country when he heard horse hooves behind him. He looked around the open countryside. The next cover of hedges and trees was too far ahead. He doubled back and dove down behind a thicket of tall grass surmounted by a flourishing wild lemon bush.

A big patrol rode by. Senrid peered between shiny green lemon-leaves at the grim, heat-flushed faces watching the road. The smell of horse-sweat and dust was permeated ridiculously with the fresh, astringent scent of lemons.

When they were well out of earshot Senrid emerged cautiously. The chances were slim that someone would put that much muscle on *his* trail, but he wasn't going to make any easy assumptions. He'd proceed as if he were the target, though he'd probably blundered into whatever other search was going on.

He dusted himself off, and set out on the road, but he'd not gone twenty paces when again he heard the drum of hooves on the road behind.

He made it back to his lemon bush just in time, and threw himself down, sweat stinging his eyes.

Into view rode four men: two young, one middle-aged, one old. They were dressed like civs, but there was no mistaking their military bearing.

He knew he hadn't left a trail because the road was too hard, too furrowed. When he saw them all scanning, two low, two tree-level, either side, he knew it was a search. He sensed that these were not allies of Norsunder. Nor were they enchanted; their gazes were direct.

He'd read about Everon and its famous guardians, called the Knights of Dei. He was pretty sure he knew who these riders were.

His heart slammed against his ribs as he stepped out.

"Hey," he called—not loud.

But loud enough. The four reined in, and surrounded him.

"Where are you going?" the oldest one asked.

"North," Senrid said, pointing, though he was on an east road. "Ah, eventually."

Another said, "You are the one who's been asking about child travelers."

And the leader added, "The Accursed Ones are hunting you."

So much for his careful ruses.

Still, he had to test them. He pulled Cassandra's hatpin from the inner seam of his knapsack were he'd carefully pinned it. The silver flashed in the sunlight, but did not lengthen into a sword.

The sight of the pin caused them to react with surprise. Senrid's insides tightened when the leader said, "I recognize that artifact."

"Cassandra Muria lent it to me," Senrid stated, and again saw subtle signs of recognition when he spoke her name. Oh yes, she'd come from this area. Instinct urged him not to lie to these Knights. "She was a fellow prisoner down south at the Norsunder Base. When we were rescued, she said I could use it. She stayed in Sartor to recover."

"And you are seeking these foreign children that the Norsundrians also seek?"

Since he'd gone this far, there was no point in holding anything back. "They're not just foreigners, they're from off-world. I know a way that they could close the Norsundrian access rift using this—" He held up the hatpin.

The young Knights looked to their leader as one's horse whuffed. Another animal shifted its weight, hooves clopping on the hard ground.

The leader, a middle-aged man with thinning gray hair, had bowed his head. His scalp gleamed in the sun. He looked up. "It is a worthy goal."

There was no overt change in their expressions or manner, but Senrid sensed approval. They four rode the white-coated horses famed here in the north. Having grown up around horses, Senrid appreciated how these animals were as well-behaved as their honey-colored cousins from the Nelkereth plains near Marloven Hess. Senrid felt their focus, too, another instinctive reaction that he didn't quite know what to make of.

"You must proceed warily," the leader said, as he fingered his short gray beard. Then his hand dropped to stroke his mount's neck. "If you are a prince from a foreign land, you too are being sought. We will take you to our border."

He nodded to one of the young ones, who extended a hand and pulled Senrid up behind him. Senrid barely had time to thrust the hatpin through his cuff before they took off across the field to the north.

Chapter Eighteen

Much as I'd like to believe otherwise, Senrid thought the next morning, *this Siamis is not an idiot. If he thinks I'm after his secret rift, he's going to sic an entire wing on me.*

He'd learned what the Knights knew about the enchantment brought to the world by a young man from Old Sartor four thousand years ago. They told him everything they knew about Siamis, except what he looked like. Apparently you didn't survive meeting him with your mind intact.

He also learned that asking questions of the enchanted populace made him a target. He'd have to do his listening covertly—if he could find a hint of civilization.

After a day or two of walking through denser oak-and-fir forestland, he began to wish that learning woodcraft had been one of the 'safe' subjects allowed by his uncle. He'd picked up a few basic rules during his brief acquaintanceship with Leander Tlennen-Hess, but not enough: he knew that a good tracker would easily find him.

Add to that the need for food. He still carried his knapsack, in hopes that he'd enter some area within Lois magic's reach again. He had no idea where they lived outside of Sartor.

He tried to content himself with water, for there was very little wild fruit in this forest. Lots of berries, and an astonishing variety of nuts, but he didn't dare eat any that he did not recognize.

It was also frustrating to have the wrong weapons. He was excellent with a bow, and could throw a knife with deadly accuracy—

both skills he could secretly practice on his own, without his uncle knowing. He'd also gotten lessons in contact fighting from Commander Keriam. He was very good at that, too, at least as good as anybody could be at his size. He had no illusions about his ability to take on trained adults.

But his uncle had forbidden anyone on pain of death to teach Senrid sword fighting, and here he was, his only weapon this hatpin. Even if he was bad at handling a sword, at least it was a weapon. He decided that it was stupid to keep it buried in the knapsack where it would take precious time to get it free. He kept it in the cuff of his shirt, against the inside of his wrist.

Then began the long trudge northward in search of a road. Twice he came across paths, but when one wandered off to the west he abandoned it. Another ended at a riverbank. By the time he found a relatively safe place in which to cross the river, he'd lost the path.

Nightfall comes fast in deep forest.

In a vile mood, Senrid wrapped himself up in his cloak, picked a mossy spot under a huge tree, and tried to sleep.

His dreams were even more vile: revisits to his days in Norsunder's Base.

I have time for this one now, Detlev said, and laughed.

The laughter shrieked on, and on, harsh, high, insane . . . and Senrid woke up in a clammy sweat to find a chipmunk sitting on his chest, chattering away. The idea of Detlev sounding like a chipmunk made laughter bubble inside Senrid's chest, but the bubble of hilarity popped. The memory of those direct gray eyes with their little flecks of green was much too vivid, the atmosphere too tense.

Senrid had dismissed all the foolishness about the eleventh hour as lighter hyperbole . . . but now he wondered what time it was.

He rose on his elbows and blinked. Moonlight shone in the little creature's round, dark eyes, and Senrid could have sworn he saw not just fear but urgency.

"Are you warning me?" he addressed the chipmunk, and he felt stupid for talking to a woodland animal.

It stopped chattering, its head alert, as though listening. For a heartbeat it sat like that, utterly still, then flick! It was gone, with only a faint rustle of leaves indicating its direction.

"Any enemy of yours is probably an enemy of mine," Senrid muttered under his breath.

He swung to his feet, reached for the nearest branch, and pulled himself into a tree. The urge to take action—fast—drove him upward until he perched precariously on a not-very-sturdy branch.

He reached for another, and froze at the slow thud of horse hooves.

Flaring torchlight sent reddish shards of light up into the trees. Branch shadows flickered like skeletal fingers. Senrid closed his eyes against vertigo. He felt very exposed, and hugged himself against the frail top-branches of his tree.

The horse hooves neared. He heard the creak of saddles, and animal and human breathing. Torchlight glowed steadily on his eyelids. He opened his eyes, and looked down. They had stopped right below.

He gritted his teeth. It couldn't be coincidence, it couldn't—

No. It wasn't coincidence, it was rank stupidity.

He had left his pack on the ground.

Why not just leave a signpost? he thought bitterly, furious with himself.

"Come down from the tree," a voice commanded—in Marloven.

He waited, looking around desperately for some hope of escape, some miracle. Would they think he'd left? No. He looked down. Reddish torchlight lapped up to his shin.

"Now."

He started down as slowly as he could, still looking about for some—any—way out, no matter how desperate. Lie? They probably wouldn't give him the chance to open his mouth.

As he felt with his foot for another branch, his mind careened, making random observations: moths dancing about in mesmerizing circles, gold-lit above the torches, and there, lower, in one of the Norsundrians' hands, the cold-fire gleam of torchlight on the edge of a drawn blade.

Blade?

He remembered the hatpin still stuck in his cuff. Catching hold of the last branch, he swung back and forth, assessing position of the enemy. The Norsundrians efficiently circled him, close enough to easily stop a target on foot if he tried to dart between their horses.

He dropped, and clamped his hand on his cuff. He did not expect to win this battle, but he would not go back meekly.

He pulled the hatpin free. A flash of bright blue-silver light sparked and made him blink, and the found a glowing white blade in his hand, its hilt perfectly fitted to his palm.

"Hah!"

The dark figures retreated a pace or two; he swung the blade, and light streamed, brighter than their torches, coruscating in every drop of dew on leaf or blade of grass. The Norsundrian horses sidled, plunging, and the ring widened.

When the brilliance began to fade, two green glows remained, close to the ground, just beyond the Norsundrians' horses.

The green things shifted, and a sinuous silhouette swarmed under horses' legs. From behind the Norsundrians came a deep growl, and from another direction the hideous, shrieking yowl of a big predator cat.

More feline shapes burst from the bushes, growling, claws raking. The horses circled, desperate to get away, and the circle broke as the Norsundrians fought to control their mounts and to strike the cats.

Senrid felt a flat, triangular head butt against the back of his knees. A muzzle thrust itself insistently between them.

Surprised, he lifted a leg—and found himself seated on a muscular back.

He barely had time to grab the sides of the strong cat-neck before he was in motion, a flowing run that made balance difficult. He bent his knees, tucking his feet under the lean ribcage as the great cat ran silently through the trees. His ankles ached. The sword shimmered down to a hatpin, which he jabbed in his cuff.

The run lasted a long time, during which he crouched awkwardly on the animal's back, half lying to keep from dragging his toes on the ground.

When the cat stopped he slid off, stunned and grateful, but before he could figure out if he should speak (and what would he say?) the cat had vanished.

He stepped forward, and almost tripped. He reached down, and his hand felt the familiar strap of his knapsack, damp from the cat's teeth.

"Amazing," he said softly, and started walking.

Sleep was a lost hope after that episode.

Blue moonlight made silhouettes of trees, rocks, and shrubs. The oak had given way slowly to pine forest, tall, whispering, tangy of scent. When he emerged on a hilltop clearing, he saw dark mountaintops etched against the slowly purpling sky: that had to be the Fereledria, the mysterious mountains that girdled the land masses on the world.

His direction sense adjusted itself, placing him much farther north than he would have gone, had he been left on his own. By now he was certain that none of the strange things that had been happening to him were happenstance. He looked up thinking, *if I've been put here, straight north is where I should go.* He'd given up planning. Either he'd find his off-worlders, or he wouldn't. His strategy had narrowed to staying out of Norsunder's hands, and moving as fast as he could.

It took a day to wind his way along the forested hills, each one higher and rockier than the last. By nightfall he was in the mountains.

He camped under a sheared rock, and at dawn drank from a trickling fall nearby. Then up the narrow animal trail that he'd been following.

The path leading upward was steep, sometimes treacherous. Senrid rejoiced in every narrowing, every fall of rock or tricky turn, because each of them lessened the chances of a mounted patrol hunting him down.

As he climbed, the air turned cool in the shadows, and he pulled his cloak from his knapsack. When he reached the first snows, hunger made him lightheaded, and at first he thought it also made him weak, for the knapsack felt heavy.

He was ready to fling the thing away and walk free, but when he unslung it the weight shifted.

He opened it, and found wen-cakes, cheese, and bread. Loi magic back again? He remembered Linet talking about some other magic race. Geres, wasn't that it? He sat down on a rock and ate until he was stuffed. Presently the light-headedness faded.

He'd always been taught to distrust the elusive indigenous races. He knew there was tremendous power in the world, available to humans and non-humans. What he did not believe in was any power the lighters claimed was Good or True. There were only factions.

When he was done eating, he pictured hot coffee with cream—and when he reached in, there was a warm green-weave flagon from which escaped the enticing whiff of fresh-ground and scalded coffee. Drinking that, he continued up the mountainside with considerably more vigor.

That night a freezing wind scoured down from the peaks, but his cloak had also regained its warming virtue. He holed up in the lee of a great, color-striated rock, and slept deeply.

Next morning, he found himself on one of the peaks. Though he was still wedged against a rock, surrounded by mountains, the details were different. He eyed the unfamiliar peaks, and suspected that somehow he was farther into the mountains than he had any right to be. So this, too, was true: time and distances were relative in the Fereledria, just as they were reputed to be in Norsunder-Beyond.

He began walking, his feet crunching through pristine snow.

At about noon he saw that he was no longer alone.

Four figures loitered along the white-boundaried path in the middle distance. Four kid-sized figures. Right here, on his trail, though weeks of desolate mountain trails surrounded him.

Surprise lasted a heartbeat. Wariness lingered. He'd been chivvied here. In his experience, that only happened when you were of use to someone.

He squashed down the defensive anger and surveyed the off-worlder kids, who appeared to be three girls and a boy. As Linet had said, they were more or less his age. Two of the girls had identical pointed chins and long brown braids: twins. The other girl didn't look at all like them, with round pale face and blond hair. The boy was stocky and swarthy.

The four stopped talking, and eyed the first newcomer they'd seen since the Guardian sent them on their mission.

To them, Senrid was an oddity as well as a surprise: alone, their own age, on a path that until now had been completely empty of other humans.

"Uh oh," Peridot said in English, instantly wary. She held out a hand to halt her twin. "That sure doesn't look like any girl."

Gloriel muttered, "The Guardian did say we were supposed to look for a girl, didn't she? I didn't dream that, right? Right?"

Nobody answered as the five surveyed each other.

"Who are you?" Peridot demanded, arms crossed.

"Someone looking for off-worlders," Senrid said.

"That's us," said Frederic, the stocky boy. "Who are you?"

"You don't look like any Lee-air-uh Something Something," Deirdre said. "So who are you?"

"Senrid," he supplied, waiting interestedly for a reaction.

"He's got to be the other kid," Gloriel exclaimed. "We did it!" She threw her arms wide, accidentally bonking her twin in the arm, and promptly got poked back by Peridot.

Senrid said, "Did someone tell you about me?"

"Well, not *you*. Kids. *Watch for kids*, the Guardian said, when we got blasted here to this world," Gloriel said earnestly, as her sister continued to glare warily over tightly crossed arms.

Deirdre, the pale. quiet one, said, "She would have sent us somewhere safe, but we all want to find the friends we made before, so we're traveling south. But while we do, we've been watching for this girl, named Liere, who seems to have disappeared, and everybody seems to be looking for her."

"Everybody on both sides," Frederic said.

"I just came from the south," Senrid said slowly. "There are hundreds of Norsundrians all over the place. If that girl is there, which I doubt, there's no chance you'll find her first."

"I *thought* this was stupid," Peridot muttered in English. She didn't know that Senrid understood it via the Universal Language Spell. "Let's go find Dtheldevor, and take sail again. We can fight Norsunder with Dtheldevor, can't we?" Her tone turned pleading.

Senrid said, "If you really want to help, you should go north to where the rift is being established."

"North? We just spent an eternity coming south!" Peridot wailed.

"Well, won't a reverse of our direction fake out the bad guys?" Frederic pointed out.

Gloriel sidled a look at her twin. "Yes, and anyway we agreed to help out, so we may's well shut our flaps, go along, and like it. I mean, isn't a trip back and forth better than being stuck at school breathing smog and memorizing spelling words?"

As all three off-worlders agreed with a vehemence that made Senrid curious about Earth, she added, "I'm Gloriel Warren. Pleased to meet you, and so on and so on."

"I'm Senrid Montredaun-An. Most delighted, and so on."

"I'm Deirdre Weiss, gladda yadda yadda," said the blond girl, with a rare, quick smile.

"Yadda," Senrid said graciously.

"And I'm Peridot, also yadda." Peridot flourished her hands about grandly.

"So on." Senrid bowed, a gesture he found ridiculous, but he knew it was done in polite circles outside of Marloven Hess.

"And I'm Frederic. Yadda, so on, and et cetera." Frederic bowed even deeper, waving his arms more extravagantly than had Peridot.

"Most et ceteraed," Senrid replied, pronouncing the foreign words correctly.

The off-worlders grinned.

"Wow, wouldn't the grownups have a fit if they heard that," Peridot stated in a rather smug tone—as if she'd gotten away with something.

"Nevertheless, we carried it off most skillfully," Frederic drawled, his snub nose in the air. Then he said in his normal voice, "Why d'ya think the Guardian had us come all this way if we just have to go back again?"

"Because of the girl," Peridot exclaimed impatiently. "Don't forget the other kid in need of help."

Senrid said, "I'm pretty sure there wasn't any wandering kid down south. Whoever they were searching for has to have gone. Or is tucked up tight somewhere, because the kingdom is swarming with an army of searchers."

"Then we won't find her either," Gloriel said, her brow puckered. "I hope she's okay."

"If she's here in the mountains," Senrid said, "we may or may not find her, but she's sure to be safe. Norsunder doesn't seem to be able to come here."

Frederic said, "So . . . should we go back?"

Peridot groaned, but her companions ignored her in a way that suggested to Senrid that it had become habit.

Gloriel picked at the split ends on one of her scraggly braids as she frowned around at the mountains. Senrid turned his own gaze northward. Going that way would increase the danger, especially if the Norsundrians managed to pick up his trail once they left the Fereledria.

Pick up his trail? *Why bother*, he thought. Whatever Lilith the Lighter was up to, he knew Detlev had to be prowling around somewhere out there, in between trying to get the rifts established.

That meant Senrid had to be fast, and sneaky. All right. He knew how to be fast. And sneaky.

"Well, kiddies," Gloriel said, "let's beat the bushes back north."

"Beat the bushes?" Senrid repeated. Was it some idiom translated over from their language? To a Marloven, 'beat the bushes' meant a thorough search.

"Not really." Gloriel laughed. "I mean, for one thing, there weren't many bushes just before we hit the mountains. Grass, yes. Before that, though, lots and lots of forest."

"We got sidetracked a few times," Deirdre said.

"Rotten weather, and we were slow because that forest was pretty wild," Frederic added.

"Anyhoo," Gloriel said, "what I meant was, look for a road back. Then hustle. Beat feet."

"Skedaddle, my great-uncle used to say," Frederic put in.

"Scramola," Deirdre added.

Peridot whirled around, her braids flying. "Who cares? Let's just do it, if we have to! I want to get this part over so we can go find Dtheldevor!"

"All right, then, back to Roth Drael," Gloriel said.

"Roth Drael?" Senrid repeated, hiding a surge of rebellion and distrust. There was no need to go to a Lighter center; the rift was supposed to be much farther north.

"That's what the Guardian said." Deirdre spread her hands. "That's where we were to bring the girl if we found her."

Senrid said, "But you don't have the girl."

Frederic shrugged. "We have you. And if you're the other one we were supposed to find . . . maybe we should go there."

Senrid thought, *Why does light magic load itself down with all these extra wards, safeguards, tentative steps, so that every Norsundrian in the world will have plenty of time to figure out what's going on, and strike?*

"There's another way," Senrid said, lying cheerfully. After all, what would it hurt? Nothing. His plans were contiguous with Lighter plans . . . to a degree. "We go straight up the coast, fast as we can."

The off-worlders looked at one another.

"That way's faster?" Peridot asked.

"Yep," Senrid said. "Has to be. You yourself said the North Forest is wild. We'd be walking up the coast. Lots easier."

He watched the others, who exchanged uncertain looks. Only Peridot looked impatient. She'd decided. And not because she was on his side. He sensed antagonism—not just to him, but to anyone who might conceive themselves in authority.

Like the Guardian.

To test his theory, Senrid said, "It does mean danger, because Norsunder will be on the watch for us."

Peridot glared at him, her lip curled. "So you think we're chicken? If your way is faster, I vote for that, and let the Norsunder turds watch out for themselves!"

"But the Guardian said Roth Drael," Deirdre murmured, looking doubtful. "And I remember that was way, way inland."

"Oh, who cares?" Peridot exploded. "Why isn't the Guardian with us now, if this is so important? I say we take the easiest way, since we're doing *her* boring job and she's too busy to help out, and if she doesn't like that, she can send us a magical message with directions."

Nobody answered.

Senrid said, "If we start up the coast, which is faster, remember, maybe she'll catch up."

Deirdre's brow cleared. "Good thinking. Okay."

"So north it is," Senrid said, and laughed inside.

Detlev, even if it costs my life, you're going to be very sorry you ever messed with Marloven Hess.

Chapter Nineteen

S enrid and his new companions walked northward, passing through
snowstorms that scintillated with color at the edge of one's vision.
Senrid sensed such powerful magic that their sense of time and
place was not to be trusted.

They walked for a full day, Senrid watching the clouds and the
landscape. Occasionally snow veiled the latter, but not enough to hide
how it would change. He couldn't catch the transition, nor could he
feel it.

At first he assumed that the others didn't notice. Peridot kept asking
him questions or making statements in a goading tone. "Did you go to
school?"

"No."

"No? How did you learn to read, or didn't you?"

"Tutors."

"Tutors! Are you some rich kid, then? Where are your servants and
coach and eight horses?"

"Lost them," Senrid said. "Where is your school?"

"Blown up, I hope," Peridot said angrily. She was even angrier than
Kyale. He tried to shift the focus by turning to Gloriel, "Did you go to
school?"

"Yes. Our schools are different from yours. At least," Gloriel said, "we
never actually saw any here. But they can't possibly be as stupid as

schools where we come from." For a moment she scowled as fiercely as her twin.

When Senrid kicked at a clump of snow without offering any observations about schools, Peridot, who couldn't figure if this kid was stupid or just sort of bland, said, "So what's the worst word in your language?"

Treachery, Senrid thought, and grimaced. It sounded too much like his uncle.

"Whatsa matter," Peridot goaded. "Too prissy to talk about cusswords?"

"No," Senrid said. "I was remembering someone I hate. What do you mean, worst word, as in worst thing you can call someone, or a word for something vile?"

Peridot said, "Words that get you into trouble if you say them around adults. Like . . ." She unloaded a string of English swearwords and obscenities, watching Senrid closely.

Senrid blinked—and there was a new cliff face. It couldn't be the same peak he'd seen before. Deirdre squinted up at the same cliff, then whispered to Frederic, who slewed around, hand over his eyes as if that could sharpen his focus.

Senrid masked his impatience as he said, "What I'm hearing through the translation magic is just sex, sex, private parts, sex, and human waste."

Peridot put her hands on her hips. "Don't you have any cusswords?"

"Sure. But not about sex. We do about waste, though."

"You don't have sex?"

"I don't," Senrid said, hiding his disgust at the idea of permitting anyone such close proximity. He knew that if he released the aging spell, he'd reach the threshold of adulthood within a couple of years or so. But he didn't want that to happen until Detlev was defeated. And if he did release it, he wasn't going to relax his guard like his father had. Ever.

He was also not going to entertain Peridot with his private thoughts. So he said, "Adults have sex. I'm not an adult."

"Even talking about it gets you into trouble at home," Peridot said. "Disgusting as it sounds."

The other kids sidled glances Senrid's way, and he wondered what he was missing. Except that the subject was so boring, he didn't really want to know. "Sex is sex," he said. "It's not a bad thing, it's just a thing. When you get old enough, if you want it, you have it." He shrugged. "What's to talk about?"

Peridot's brows lifted; Frederic smothered a laugh, then hastily turned it into a cough so Peridot wouldn't start yelling at him.

"I *know* that mountain changed," Deirdre said low-voiced. "It happens every time we see the rainbow thingies." She twiddled her fingers at the edges of her vision.

A crunch just behind her caused her to look over her shoulder. There was Senrid, obviously listening in.

She'd noticed the way he was constantly scanning the landscape, and wondered what it meant. Maybe it's just that since he'd picked the direction, he felt that he should be on the watch. But he seemed so tense. At first she thought it was because of Peridot, but even when Peridot ran ahead and started talking to her sister ("sex words" floated back) the quick way Senrid turned his head, the tense way he raised his forearm when they passed a tree and an old branch fell with a 'crack' made her uneasy.

Frederic shrugged. He obviously didn't much care about magic, except as a thing that did other things. Like thinking about electricity, back on earth. Deirdre had always wondered what made it, and how this invisible thing could cause lights to work and machines to run. Frederic would rather read an adventure book. Deirdre loved adventure books, too (that was how they met, in the fourth grade), but she liked knowing how things *worked*.

There was definitely something magic at work here. From the looks of those mountains it should take months to walk, but the kids' trail never got arduous. It felt kind of like being on a train—when you walk from car to car, your steps are slow, but outside the windows, the countryside slides by.

Next day (after a warm night in a kind of protected cave) they started down a trail winding northward. Before long they glimpsed the coast between snowy cliffs and palisades, and by nightfall they'd reached the hilly lowlands. A warm breeze caressed their faces—warm compared to the heights, for though in this hemisphere the season was early winter, the current weather was quite mild.

"Well," Peridot said with satisfaction, "that wasn't so bad, and I hate snow. Now that we're back in some kind of civilization, shall we spend some of our coins, or try to get a free night?"

"Neither," Senrid said.

Frederic exchanged glances with Deirdre. They dropped back a little—easy, as Senrid walked fast.

"This guy expects trouble," he muttered to her in English.

Senrid topped a little rise, and looked sharply about with a narrow-eyed expression.

"Yep," Deirdre whispered.

"You want to ask him?"

"You," Deirdre whispered. "You're a boy."

"So?" Frederic shrugged. "Like that makes a difference?"

Deirdre knew it didn't. But she didn't want to say that Senrid's tension bothered her. It seemed kind of mean, when he was not only polite, but he put up with Peridot's crabby moods and showing off.

He didn't look afraid, exactly, but like somebody waiting for a thunderstorm, or for bullies to come around the corner back at the school cafeteria. Only Senrid didn't look like the type to run. More like he'd face whatever was coming. Ready, that was it. Alert and ready.

Senrid kept his thoughts to himself.

He didn't relax until they found a secluded grove near the bend in a slow river. Night birds chirped cheerily overhead, and Deirdre gladly breathed in the clean scents of water and grass. Peridot and Gloriel flopped right down on a grassy spot and curled up to sleep, and after a time Frederic's breathing slowed. The last thing Deirdre was aware of was Senrid sitting with his back to a tree, his form shadowy in the starlight. He was fingering something in the cuff of his sleeve that gleamed with faint silver highlights.

❧

"There's the beach!" Peridot yelled a day later.

"Barefoot time!" Gloriel crowed.

The two kids ran down the last hill and when they reached the sand, they danced about, turning cartwheels and kicking sand into the lapping waves.

The others followed at a fast walk. Plugging along behind, Deirdre thought about how much she hated moving fast in hot weather. But when Senrid reached the Warren twins, he looked over his shoulder at Peridot and said, "You're slow." He gave her a challenging, toothy grin that would have goaded a rock. "Are all girls that slow?"

The race was on!

Deirdre thumped along grimly in last place, watching Senrid pacing Peridot. Though the Warren girl was a little taller, Deirdre was willing to bet he was the better runner—at least, the more determined. He ran easily, whereas Peridot was crimson-faced, feet pounding churning up the sand until her breath gave out.

Rather than admit she wasn't the winner, Peridot veered toward the waves and splashed into the water. Deirdre panted up behind, glad at least they could run on wet sand. She caught her breath while Peridot and Gloriel splashed water at each other, their laughing voices sounding a lot like the cry of gulls.

Senrid watched, his arms folded. On impulse, Deirdre strayed up to him. "You're not going to do that the whole way, are you?" she asked.

He cut a glance her way, his forehead tense. "I think we need to move as fast as we can."

"Why? We had no problems coming south," Deirdre said. "I think the elevens lost interest in us."

"They know you're in this world. I found out by hearing gossip in—"

He made an impatient, flat-handed gesture, as though smacking something away. "They're going to put us together eventually, and from there even the soul-bound ones could guess what we're planning to do. I'm hoping they're figuring on our going to Roth Drael, and their trackers are strung through the North Forest. It won't last forever, but it'll give us time, since your friend Lilith the Guardian seems to be too busy guarding someone else."

"You believe it's that desperate?" Frederic asked, coming up on the other side.

Senrid had spent enough time around the four kids to figure out who were the smart ones. Not that the twins were stupid, it was just that Peridot let her feelings lead her, and Gloriel tended to follow her sister.

So Senrid explained quickly about rifts, and about how off-worlders could close them if they sacrificed a sufficiently powerful magical implement.

"If we close the rift they're making—or maybe have made, but I don't think they've finished it yet—it ends access between our world and Norsunder-beyond," Senrid finished. "The little rift gates are easier enough to make, but they can only transfer through one person at a time, like a Destination between points in the world. All of these can burn out fast. Moving whole armies through takes extremely powerful magic."

"Why do they have to make it way up north? Why can't they just make one anywhere?"

"It has to be where the old rifts were, the ancient ones. I've read about them. Those weakened the world permanently, and they still lie there, like scars. And it has to be in open area, where nothing living is about. If something live gets into the space of something else live, both things kill one another as they cross the rift. Norsunder isn't going to want to waste all their warriors bumping into a herd of cows or people in a trade town, or even trees. I guess grass doesn't create the same problem—seems to be confined to live things that move. Anyway, that leaves out forestland. Mountains are dangerous for transferring through great numbers, because the rift might form over a cliff."

Frederic grimaced. "Okay. Got the idea."

Deirdre nodded soberly. "I don't really understand magic stuff. We don't have it on Earth. But it sounds convincing. Here, I'll go get the Warrens."

Senrid said, "It's not just speed. Even if the magic runs out on your knapsacks—mine is already gone again—we will have to forage. We can't be seen by any other people."

Frederic sighed. "If you think so." His ambivalence was clear.

Senrid said, "And if they do find us, we need to scatter."

Deirdre and Frederic looked at one another. "Okay," she said.

Leader lay flat on a roof above the Norsundrian HQ in Wnelder Vee's capital.

This was Dtheldevor's home kingdom. She'd met up with her beached crew in one of her many hidey-holes. They were busy raising a ruckus all over the city—loosing horses, firing hay, ruining Norsunder's supplies, even setting fire to buildings the Norsundrians had taken over—in hopes of waking up the enchanted people. Leander had chosen to spy instead.

Below, the Norsundrians blabbed in Norsundrian. So it had been all day, making Leander feel that he had to stay just a little longer, and longer again, in spite of the hot sun broiling the back of his neck—long enough to hear *something*.

Two more Norsundrians came in. They and the other two conversed incomprehensibly, and just when Leander felt he was going to go mad from frustration a new one came in, this one speaking Fer Sartoran to someone behind him.

" . . . so we'd better finish with the locals." His accent sounded like Dtheldevor's, meaning he'd originally come from this area.

"What's the difference?" asked another, in the same language. "Part of the playacting?"

The first one shrugged.

Talk more, Leander begged mentally. *What playacting? Who?*

"Who's to be impressed?" asked a fourth, one of the newcomers.

The second retorted, "Who is to be mind-ripped for bucking orders?"

The fourth zapped back with, "Who's going to be ripped for a city full of chaos when he's due in?"

"Shut up." The first one lifted his head, and when the others fell silent, he returned to reading his papers. 'He?' A commander? *Siamis?*

Leander squinted down, wondering if the papers were written in Norsunder as well. He was trying to figure out a way to nab at least one of those papers when more arrivals came through the door.

At first Leander thought the first one a civilian, maybe even a prisoner. He was tall, dressed in plain shirt and trousers, the sleeves of the shirt rolled to his elbows. As the man moved to the center of the room Leander saw that he wore a silver sword—a nifty-looking blade that was very unlike the Norsundrian issue. No prisoner, then.

"What do you have for me?" he asked in Sartoran, holding his hand out for the papers.

The promptitude with which the first one rose and surrendered his stacks of papers made it clear that, at last, Leander was actually seeing Siamis. After a wild chase of half a year, Siamis was right there!

But Leander couldn't reach him. And he remembered that business about mind reading. *You're nothing but a bug on the roof,* he told himself. *A quiet bug . . .*

Siamis leafed rapidly through a bunch of papers, then tossed them on the table. Leander stared down at the blond head. Even if he'd had anything to strike with, could he have managed it at this angle? Senrid probably could, he thought with an inward sigh.

Siamis looked up at the second Norsundrian, smiling pleasantly.

"Your people appear to be preoccupied today."

"It's Dtheldevor," the second one said, adding exactly the same sort of pungent insult that she habitually used about his allies. "Tearing up the city, and disappearing down their old rat-holes."

Siamis waved a hand. "Never mind the details. I'd like very much to meet Dtheldevor."

It was genially said, but Leander saw in the reaction of the second Norsunder —the tight mouth, the tendons showing on the right handing hanging beside his sword—indicating that he didn't hear a comment, or an invitation, but an order, if not a threat.

Siamis turned his head slightly. Five or six heartbeats later another eleven entered. Leander gripped his fingers together. *If he really 'heard' that fellow coming by mind, why doesn't he hear me up here? Or does he 'hear' only the minds he expects to hear?*

"The deaf boy you told us to follow has spoken. Encounter a day's ride south of the lake," the newcomer said. "Our horses went wild. Couldn't control them."

"Not deaf, then." Siamis smiled. "Or a boy. Liere Fer Eider is much more clever than we gave her credit for, eh, Davernak?"

The newcomer said nothing; his gaze was lowered.

Siamis turned to the fourth, who'd waited in silence. "You have people along the north coast, don't you? Any sign of the Marloven boy?"

Leander thought, *Marloven boy? Is it Senrid—did he somehow escape?*

"Yes," the fourth said.

"Excellent." Siamis looked at the third. He pointed at the papers. "Your excuses are entertaining, but I believe we can dispense with them. You will cease playing hide and seek with the Knights of Dei. You will find their leader, and bring him to me in the North Forest. I am very much afraid that we're going to have to take some time out for some riding."

He walked out, followed by the three or four who'd come in with him.

The second one jabbed a finger toward the fourth. "You know Detlev marked that Montredaun-An brat as his."

The fourth switched to Norsundrian for what were obviously curses. He must have been fluent as well as unstinting, for the others grinned.

It's Senrid, Leander thought, agonized. *He must have escaped, but now he's running straight into a trap.*

Chapter Twenty

For Liere Fer Eider, the six months following her meeting with Devon were the most frightening and the most exhilarating of her entire life.

For Devon, life had become interesting, exasperating, scary, wonderful, tiring—and sometimes very lonely. She was used to loneliness, and had never minded it once she discovered that her own thoughts could be good company. Unlike Russy and Karia when they were involved with their noble friends, Liere never shut her out deliberately or thoughtlessly, but she inadvertently shut the entire world out, sometimes for half a day or longer.

Liere found those sessions challenging and endlessly fascinating, during which she inevitably lost all sense of time and place. She had always been adept at listening on the mental plane; she sorted through the unguarded awarenesses surrounding her, sifting through the crazy jumble of images and words that comprised most people's thoughts. She learned to narrow her focus, to listen over great distances, and so she found the Guardian.

Her first lesson concerned Roth Drael, and what she must do there once she reached it. Her second lesson was short, and frightening, for Lilith the Guardian taught her how to identify the dangerous minds who spied on the mental plane.

She did not intend to complain, but the Guardian must have heard her wish that she would come herself, would show the girls the way. Maybe even take them there, for did she not know how to travel by magical means?

The Guardian's thought came sadly, *I must stay here in the south. We are in a constant struggle with Norsunder, who is trying to extend a rift from their temporal base. Every mage who knows this kind of magic is here, yet there are not enough of us. Be strong, Liere! I have tried to send you some companions for your journey.*

Twice Liere sensed Siamis listening in the mental realm. His wordless amusement was clear before she broke contact. Once, at a far greater distance, she sensed another mind, one much more sinister. It deflected her quick, instinctive identity-probe with all the careless strength of an armored hand swatting at a bee. That time she made the shift to first-face so fast she had a headache the rest of the day.

She practiced hiding her own identity asleep and awake.

In the physical plane, their progress was very slow.

At first this was because of winter, and because it was hard to get food. They had Devon's money, but unless they were careful to go to market in big towns, children buying food caused questions, which brought investigating Norsundrians. Every single time they bought food in a small town or village caused an onslaught of patrols riding back and forth, forcing them to hide in barns, or abandoned houses, or once in a child's playhouse, for days at a time.

They had to let Kondaria go free, for she couldn't be hidden, and food for a pony was impossible to find during winter.

Devon wept at that, but Liere listened for the pony for several days after, and was glad to eventually report that she'd made her way to a farm whose family seemed unaware that a new pony had joined their herd wintering on an upper pasture.

Liere ventured out alone, as a boy, keeping keep her gaze down and her words dull, until they ran out of money. Then they had to resort to stealing.

This was hard because neither girl liked the idea of theft. They were also bad at it, so the two, who were thin and frail of build, went without food to a degree that would have been dangerous had they not managed to reach the border of Everon at last—and there they were discovered by the Knights.

The animals had been on the watch, and it was vigilant birds who brought the Knights to the two shivering, starving girls deep in Everon's forest.

Their days took an abrupt turn for the better. The party of Knights delivered them to the dawnsingers of West Everon, one of the oldest enclaves on the deles. There they were made welcome, wreathed from dawn to dusk in song, fed plain but nourishing forest food whose preparation—mostly comprised of a bewildering variety of nuts—had been refined over the centuries into fare that satisfied despite the lack of meats or spices favored by most human palates.

From the dawnsingers Liere first heard the name that they had given her: Sartora. Partly honorific (this embarrassed and frightened her), the name was also intended to hide her true identity. It was this latter aspect that made the nickname bearable.

The dawnsingers loved singing and telling stories, and Liere adored hearing them. Devon did as well, but many was the night when she struggled against sleep, finally dropping off with the sound of sweet, poignant laments—many of them hundreds of years old, and even older— lulling her into dreams of lost lives and times. Her last sight would be the glow of firelight on the ruddy or coin-colored or pale yellow hair of the dawnsingers, and in their midst Liere's straight, thin figure. Above them all laced the sheltering tree branches, and beyond those the canopy of clouds, and sometimes the eternal stars. Devon would curl up gratefully in her cloak, enjoying the gentle swaying of the tree platforms in the breeze. Breathing deeply of ancient forest scents, she often hoped that the visit would never end.

But with spring came incursions of Norsundrians searching—for this was when Liere had that one encounter with the distant mind.

It was after that incident that Liere mastered the identity shield, once she comprehended that that distant mind had in that single heartbeat of contact expertly plucked from her own dreams the cherished memory of a night of song. And their location.

"We have to go," Liere said the next morning, shaking Devon awake.

Liere told their hosts what had happened. The dawnsingers gave the girls a basket of nut-breads, then all departed, leaving the tree platforms empty.

As if the whole world wept, rain slanted through the trees, cold and wet and gloomy. Devon felt sad that the dawnsingers had vanished, leaving their platforms bare; they might return to them in a year or a hundred years, for these trees were exceedingly old, and the platforms made not by them but by their ancestors.

The girls spent several anxious days toiling down tiny animal paths or crouching in thickets while powerful horses and torch-bearing riders thrashed their way back and forth through the forests in searches.

When those were gone, some animal always appeared: a timid, still deer, or a gliding bird, or once a light-tailed squirrel. There'd be that long moment of mental communion that Devon could not share, and then they'd be off, following this new guide.

Spring ripened while they made their way through Wnelder Vee.

Something else was going on, for there were more Norsundrians here than at any other time. Liere sometimes touched the enemies' minds. Most of the time she could not read past the narrow focus on the immediate, or past the blood-lust anticipation (or cruel memories) of some. Once she discovered that she was not the object of that particular search.

When they ran out of food, they figured out a story that they could stick to: they became a brother and sister. The brother (Liere) was deaf, communicating with Devon by vague twitches of fingers and waves of her hands. Liere sent mental pictures to Devon when she actually had to communicate something.

They knew that their presence was reported on—inevitable in places where everyone was enchanted—but Liere, now adept at sifting thoughts, twice found city orphanages and they did their shopping nearby. This left the Norsundrians having to sort through all the local kids, and each time they wasted time interviewing quantities of war-orphans, she and Devon slipped away.

And so the guise held long enough to get them across the country to the Fereledria.

There again their days took a turn for the better. Safe, surrounded by magic, Devon slept deeply.

Liere resented every moment that she had to sleep. That is, until she discovered that high in the magical realm of the Geres, the dream realm was equally safe. The watching Norsundrian minds could not hear her, and again she learned new things.

In the long, mild days of late summer—for now they were in the northern part of the world—they descended the last trail and crossed into the Great Northern Forest.

Three days' walk into their journey they were surprised by a pair of Norsundrian scouts. Liere had been sitting in silent contemplation, as she often did. Devon lay in the new grass, staring up through the trees into the sky.

The Norsundrians came on them suddenly. Terrified, Devon shook Liere hard, just as the horses flanked them.

"What is it?" Liere exclaimed, rubbing her eyes. "Oh."

"Who are you?" One of the Norsundrians demanded.

Devon stared, numb with shock.

Liere gazed intently at the horses, who suddenly reared, nearly throwing their surprised riders.

Then the animals began to plunge and whuff and toss their heads—despite the swearing and kicking of their riders—following which they turned and galloped away.

"I hate taking over their minds," Liere said. "But I'm not the first. Their wills have been almost ruined."

"Let's get out of here," Devon quavered.

"Okay," Liere murmured, having picked up the word from Devon. She sighed. "And don't let me get lost like that anymore. I guess I have to get back into the habit of staying in first-face again."

Devon promised.

They forgot that the Norsundrians had heard the supposed deaf boy speak.

Chapter Twenty-One

S enrid and the four off-worlders soon found the walk up the shoreline hot and sweaty work.

For a couple of days, it was fun to veer and splash in the water whenever they got overheated, but it tired one out faster and clothes that dried stiff and salty got nastier with every dunk.

On the third day, they spotted a small town built around the mouth of a minor river, and turned inland to avoid it. They swam in the river during the early evening, which ridded them of salt and grime. That night they slept long and comfortably on a grassy hill above a feeder stream.

Next day they returned to the beach, chivvied by Senrid, who was adamant about avoiding the main coast road.

Peridot sighed loudly. "Talk about your one crack-mind!"

The others laughed, as usual, and as usual Senrid said, "Can't we walk faster?"

"NO!" Peridot bellowed.

No one argued. They didn't want to move fast during the heat of the day. Once the sun finally disappeared and a breeze flowed off the sea, their vitality slowly returned. When the stars came out, a gorgeous jewel-bright display across the black velvet night, a mood of silliness hit the Warren twins as they walked through the ebbing tidewaters.

"That for Detsie," Gloriel yelled, churning up the shallow foam as she danced about on the wet sand. "And that for every villain in the world!"

"That for every villain in the universe," Peridot retorted. She, too, kicked water high in a cool spray.

"Biggest towns are south of the Fereledria," Frederic was saying to Senrid. "At least, from what the Warrens said to expect. What we saw in the north, there weren't that many people."

"That's because the Guardian put you west of the populated areas," Senrid said. "From what I hear, the Great Northern Forest is not necessarily faster, but it's probably a lot safer. It has to be hard for searchers."

"Definitely not fast," Frederic said with a grin. "But we sure didn't see any people. We were alone for our whole trip. I'd rather be lost in fogs and turned around for a month than risk coming face to face with that stinker Siamis in some town—"

Gloriel, who'd danced near enough to overhear, said, "Stupid, pimple-faced, potbellied, pie-eyed poops!"

"Ugly, smelly, nauseating barf-faced crap-heads," Peridot shouted.

Senrid was tempted to recall some of CJ's more inspired insults. For sheer variety, he'd never heard better. He kept them to himself, but memory made him grin.

"Fatwit dust bunnies," Peridot was going on.

Deirdre sighed. "Won't it be a relief to find this rift thingio and get rid of 'em once and for all?" She walked on Senrid's other side, sliding her toes through the foamy ripples.

"Why do they have to ruin things anyway?" Gloriel asked bitterly. "They gotta have a reason. I mean, nobody wakes up and says, *Hah hah! I think I want to ruin a world! So I'm going to buy me a Norsunder uniform and go out and start murdering every person I see as practice.*"

"Because they're STUPID!" Peridot yelled.

"Because they want power, twit," Senrid said, tired of Peridot's one-note harping.

A man spoke from behind, "And you don't?"

Laughter accompanied it.

The five kids whirled around to discover armed and mounted Norsundrians some twenty paces behind them—the animals' hoof beats muffled by the sand and breeze and the booming of the surf.

Senrid gritted his teeth, knowing that they had to have transferred in somewhere behind and commandeered the horses, then rode just far enough back so the kids didn't hear them. He'd gotten sloppy at checking his surroundings—and now was about to pay for it.

"Ugh!" Peridot bellowed.

"Run," Senrid snapped.

"Everyone for herself! Fade out!" Gloriel shrieked, bending to snatch up handfuls of sand. These she flung at the foremost Norsundrians, then she dashed across the beach toward one of the grassy hills.

The Norsundrians ignored the sand and spurred their horses forward, with practiced ease surrounding the kids. Senrid waited until they'd drawn into a tight ring, then he pulled the hatpin from his cuff and whipped it round in a circle. Sparks of blue-white light streamed along the edges as it flashed into sword length. He slashed right in front of the Norsundrians' mounts' noses. The horses plunged aside, eyes round with fright.

The kids took off in five directions—Senrid going straight for the underbrush.

The last thing he heard (amid the screams, yells, and insults of the off-worlders) was that same man saying loud enough for Senrid to hear, "You two. I want the Marloven."

Senrid dove through a scrubby brush, its wiry branches catching horribly on the straps of his pack. He wrestled violently out of it and thrust himself through the shrubbery. Two horses galloped along either side of the hedgerow, one of the Norsundrians laughing derisively as they reined in.

Then the horses reared, pawing the air as an explosion of blackbirds launched out of the hedge and into their faces.

Senrid gained the firmer dirt, and ran flat out for the thicket, leaving behind the shrill screeching of a thousand birds, human swearing, and a sharp-voiced command to dismount and carry on the chase on foot.

And so began a two day chase.

At night, among the low, scrubby bushes that grew thickly along the coast, the odds of a boy on foot outdistancing two mounted men were evened. Add to that the interference by local birds, and Senrid's surprise at staying free for moments turned into amazement that he was still running the next day, even after the shadows began to shift eastward.

After that the surprise gave way to grim determination.

Senrid gulped down water when he splashed headlong into streams to break his trail. At least that assuaged the agonizing thirst. The only food he got was by accident, when he hid in some kind of berry bush. The berries smelled familiar, so he tried one, and then picked and ate more, as fast as he could with shaking fingers, while a patrol crashed across his path not twenty paces away. When they were gone he changed direction and ran on.

Through the night he continued, and the next day, sometimes running, and when his lungs were on fire and black specks swam before his vision, he slowed to a stagger. By morning he'd blundered deep into woodland, which again gave him somewhat of an advantage. He tried to grab brief rest until he realized that the search had been augmented. If he stayed too long in one place he would be caught.

He knew all about search and defense perimeters. As he ran, the rules governing a successful hunt streamed through his mind, and he put his dwindling energies into confounding the Norsundrians, for speed was their advantage, not his.

He was vaguely aware that animals still aided him. How, he did not know, nor did he care. It was enough that they did. His entire concern was to stay on his feet and keep moving.

The third morning dawned bright, clear, and hot. Blue skies gleamed above the canopy of the trees. Senrid sensed as he topped a gentle hill that his searchers had somehow been sidetracked to the north. "Somehow" because he knew better than to believe it was due to his skills.

When he stumbled over a small rock, he wrenched himself upright, and nearly passed out. Branches whipped his face, but he didn't feel them. He knew only thirst, and the terrible ache through his body that meant he'd reached his limit.

Strength of will had kept him going for almost three days, with only brief rests when he hid. At some point, the mind must surrender to the needs of the body, or risk sundering the tie forever.

His faltering steps brought him to a creek. He fumbled his way down the gentle bank and fell to his knees in the cold water. Cupping shaking hands, he tried to drink, realized he didn't have the strength to hold liquid, and so he dropped his hands onto the smooth rocks visible below the surface and buried his face in the cool, clear, refreshing stream. He gulped water until he had to breathe, lifted his head, and slung his hair out of his eyes.

For two heartbeats, he felt great.

Then he stood up. Reaction hit with the force of a boulder dropping on him.

Three steps, four, five. He made it to the top of the grassy bank, tripped over nothing, and splatted full length.

Shadows crossed his eyelids.

Some remnant of his drive to survive brought him awake, but when he tried to sit up, the world spun, and he fell back, arms outflung. He hadn't even the strength to pull the hatpin from his cuff.

His eyes were still open. A pair of disheveled Norsundrians rode up, their anger after nearly three days of grim toil lighting to triumph.

He winced, made an effort of will, and a whisper came from close by. "Don't. She'll get rid of 'em."

Senrid arched his neck, staring upside down at a scrawny little girl. Beyond surprise, he turned his head—slowly—as another kid walked toward the riders.

The kid was small and skinny, probably his height, but thinner. No weapons. She looked more like a boy than a girl, but if the other said 'she' was a 'she' then so be it.

She stopped half a dozen paces from the Norsundrians, and rocked on her heels. Somewhere birdsong broke the peculiar stillness.

The Norsundrians drew weapons, but this strange girl paid no attention. Her focus was entirely on the horses—who reared and galloped away, their riders cursing in futility as they tried to wrest command over their beasts.

The girl turned away, and approached Senrid. He gained a swift impression of large, serious light-brown eyes in a thin, plain face.

She spoke in Fer Sartoran, with a strong Imaran accent. "They'll stop only when they reach the great river."

Senrid stared at her witlessly.

She put her head to one side. "The old fear of Norsunder, eh?"

Shock zapped through Senrid. Antagonism? Maybe she knew who he was.

"Your posture's too good," the little girl murmured.

"Oh yes. I forgot. Guess I was reveling in my little victory." The boy-girl sounded contrite!

She flopped down cross-legged, and Senrid's assumptions took another spin. Was she insane? If only he didn't have a near-blinding headache!

"Who are you?" the strange one continued.

"Senrid," he said, awaiting a reaction.

"I'm Liere." She added in a cold, remote voice, "Don't hold awe. Anyone with dena Yeresbeth could have sent those poor animals in a panic."

"Oh. Right. Of course," Senrid sneered, a reaction more look than voice, as his voice was nearly gone. "Of course everybody knows what day-nah Ya-blabba-nagga is."

Liere gave him a valedictory smile, got up and moved away. She said over her shoulder, "I have to go somewhere for a time. Listen for any more of them. Be back soon, Devon."

Devon. That was the shorter girl.

Senrid struggled to sit up, grateful for the canopy of foliage that shaded his face from the sun. Hazily he noted the leaves angled to the south, their undersides silvery-brown. The season was late autumn at least, though the air was warm.

"Here," Devon said, holding out some bread and cheese.

Senrid took it and started wolfing it down.

"Don't hate her," Devon said. "It's just that she's really scared of being admired. She's afraid that she might like it, and become like Siamis, or something. I don't quite understand it, really, but the more different she acts, it means the scareder she is."

"Who is she?" Senrid leaned on one elbow, letting his annoyance fade away. It took too much effort.

"Liere Fer Eider, from Ther Doleh region in Imar."

"Some kind of deposed royalty, or—"

"Oh, no! I don't think she's ever seen any royalty."

"She has now," Senrid remarked in Marloven. So this girl didn't fit his evolving theories about Detlev and his messing with royal families.

"I understood that." Devon grinned. "It has to do with her abilities. And this thing she has to do. Soon, I mean. Not right now."

"Ah," Senrid said. "What *is* she doing now? Or does she want to reinforce her image of an everyday kid by stalking off in a shroud of mystery?"

"She'll explain if I ask her to. Always does, though I don't always understand. Right now I think she's listening, with her mind, for more of those Norsunder guys. Has to do with DY."

"DY," Senrid repeated.

"Dena Yeresbeth. You'll have to ask her about that."

Senrid had just finished his sandwich, and was feeling incrementally better, when Liere returned.

She frowned as she came up to them.

"Senrid, were you with some off-worlders a couple of days ago?"

"Why me?" Gloriel muttered as she was herded at sword point to where the main group of Norsundrians waited. "I'm *always* the first one bagged, and just watch, that one will be Siamis." She looked up at the eleven she was being pushed toward.

Well, maybe it wouldn't be so bad after all, for once. This guy wasn't even dressed like an eleven, and he didn't look especially threatening, at least in the starlight.

He reached a hand down. Of course she crossed hers—until a vicious jab in her back nearly pitched her face-first into the side of the man's horse.

So she sighed and held up her sandy, sweaty hand. The man gripped it and pulled her up easily to the saddle before him. She made a mental note to wash villain cooties from her fingers first chance she could get.

Or was he a villain? Maybe one of the zombie-ized enchanted people that Senrid had told them about? She glanced up over her shoulder doubtfully. No uniform, and though he had a sword thrust into a saddle sheath it wasn't in his hand and he wasn't making any sinister speeches. Nor did he look like a zombie.

Gloriel heard Frederic's plaintive "OW!" and an angry yelp from Peridot, as if to underscore the usual procedures of villainy.

Gloriel looked about, counted Deirdre (looking miserable even in the weak light), Peridot, and Frederic. No Senrid.

"Seems one of your number has ditched you," the man observed.

"Well, of course," Gloriel said. "Who wouldn't?"

"Where were you going?"

"That's for me to know and you not to find out," Gloriel said, and then remembering her initial question, she added, "That is, if you are an eleven."

He seemed to be trying not to laugh. "I heard something about closing the rift. We were behind you that long."

"Well, then, why are you asking me?" Gloriel retorted.

"Conversational gambit," the man answered in a pacific tone as he clucked to his horse.

They fell into a line, two by two, and started riding up a trail toward the interior. Gloriel and her rider were first.

"I don't know any more than that," Gloriel said, somewhat smugly. If this guy *was* a villain, he sure wasn't any big threat. She was getting away with a delightful lot of smart-mouthing.

"I'm aware," the man murmured.

Gloriel, testing further, said, "And I hope Senrid gets away."

"He won't," the man responded tranquilly. "But—since he isn't here now—I suspect he's going to give them a worthwhile run."

Gloriel sighed. "I just don't see why destroy such a beautiful world. Maybe Norsundrians should go to Earth. They'd love all the crime and pollution and creepy stuff."

"Who is advocating the destruction of the world?" he countered. "What I want is peace."

"Peace?"

"Yes."

"Are you a prisoner? You don't sound zombie-ized!"

Above her head she heard a soft laugh, so soft it was almost just a breath. "The temptation to mislead you is almost overwhelming. My name is Siamis. And you are . . ."

"Anti-Norsunder," she said, and then felt something almost like dizziness, like seeing with two sets of eyes, only inward, not outward. Or both at the same time.

"Gloriel Warren," Siamis continued.

"How did you do that? Yuk!" Gloriel exclaimed. Not only was she stuck on horseback with the head villain of all of them, he was a mind-reader, too!

Then she realized she was overlooking an opportunity, and she tried to remember all Dtheldevor's choicest anti-Norsunder insults, and think them at him.

But apparently Siamis was done with mind-reading, because he said, "There are some who like war for the sake of war, but few of them are in any position of command for long."

Gloriel snorted so loud her head buzzed. "So you're trying to say that the crumbums—" That word sounded really odd in the middle of a Fer Sartoran sentence, and her voice trembled on an inadvertent snicker. "The mushroom-brained crumbums who control Norsunder all like peace and plenty? Wow, that's a hot one! Unless, of course, you mean *plenty* for *them*."

Siamis said with a quiet laugh, "I only speak for myself. My goal, I assure you, is worldwide peace."

Where's the trick? she thought. "What do you mean by peace? Maybe we have different definitions," she said aloud. "Like some idi—people think that strawberries are a yummy dessert, and I think they are a nasty, cloying mess."

"I like strawberries very much," came the smiling voice.

"Figures."

"But let's talk about peace, then. . ."

By the time they'd finished discussing peace, history, and Old Sartor, she'd forgotten what her initial objection was. She knew only that it was late, and she was tired, and Siamis wasn't going to let her fall off the horse, so she slid into dreamless sleep, her head against his arm.

Riding on the next horse behind Siamis, Frederic heard Gloriel stop talking, and he wondered sourly if the creep had poisoned her, stabbed her, or just strangled her. He couldn't see past Siamis's back; the white shirt gleamed faintly in the starlight, with one of Gloriel's braids looped over the guy's left arm.

Frederic could hear Peridot on the horse behind him, breathing hard with fury. She at least wasn't dead. He'd heard her insulting her Norsunder loudly until she was told to shut up. Twice in fact, and then came the sound of a hefty slap. After that came Peridot's snorty anger-breathing.

Frederic still ached from his own unsuccessful attempt to escape. He'd slid off the horse when they started up a little hill, but the eleven had wheeled the horse immediately and almost rode him down.

Frederic had hoped that some animal would appear and miraculously help him—like that flock of birds when Senrid got away—but either there weren't any extra birds, or there were too many Norsundrians, or maybe it was Siamis's presence that scared the animals off.

He got hauled back up into the saddle, his shoulder wrenched painfully.

"Try that again and I'll pin you to the saddle with my knife," the Norsundrian said. He looked about the age of a high school senior, with the thin, smug grin of a bully.

"That's impossible," Frederic snarled. "Stupidest thing I ever heard."

"Want to try me?" the high school bully retorted, and Frederic heard the metallic scrape of a dagger being pulled from a sheath. "Where there's a will, there's a way," the gloating voice went on. "We can experiment."

Frederic knew he wasn't going to win this contest. "Earwax," he muttered, staring between the horse's ears into the blackness beyond.

And so it went for what seemed like an eternity, until Siamis finally called for a halt to water the horses.

Somewhere up ahead the kids got switched around—Peridot now riding with Siamis—and then they rode on. Frederic kept nodding off and jerking awake, each time more unpleasantly—and more frequently—than the last, until at last they finally stopped in a clearing lit by a ring of torches. Someone had pitched four tents.

He slid off the horse, his entire body a bundle of aches, and almost fell. Hard fingers yanked him upright, and pushed him into one of the tents. A blanket was pitched in after him.

He wrapped it around himself, wondering what the Norsundrians had done with the Guardian's knapsacks. He missed his cloak. Gloriel stumbled into the tent. In the ruddy torchlight streaming in the open tent-flap Frederic saw her yawn.

She shuffled directly to a corner and lay down.

"Gloriel," he whispered. "We gotta escape!" He spoke in English.

"Go t'sleep," she muttered in Fer Sartoran.

Peridot appeared a moment later, and after several minutes Deirdre finally came in. All three girls curled up to sleep. Frederic reluctantly settled down as well. He was too tired not to.

He had rotten dreams. When dawn filtered weak light through the walls of the tent, he was the first one awake.

He got up and poked his head outside the tent. Black-and-gray clad warriors moved about in a businesslike manner, breaking camp. A tall one with a hawk nose glanced his way, and jerked his thumb toward a campfire off to the left.

Frederic hesitated, then decided he had nowhere else to go, so he stepped out.

Two or three Norsundrians sat around the campfire with Siamis, who looked up, smiled, and gestured. "And here is the last of our guests. Good morning, Frederic. Do you like coffee?"

"Disgusting pigswill," Frederic said, adding to himself, *I wouldn't drink it with you anyway*. He glanced about, feeling pleased when he didn't see any sign of Senrid.

"Come. Sit. Pass the time of day while we wait for your companions to waken."

Frederic sat cautiously on a tree stump. The uniformed Norsundrians ignored him, except for the high school bully, who gave him a contemptuous glance and returned to whetting a long knife with a flat stone.

Siamis, on the other hand, looked friendly. Casual, sitting there on the fallen log from Frederic's stump, a coffee mug in his hands. He looked no more dangerous than Frederic's old English teacher from junior high.

"Any questions for me?" Siamis asked.

"Questions? For you?" Frederic repeated, considering and discarding half a dozen sarcastic answers, before choosing the one that meant the most. "How can we get rid of you?"

A couple of the Norsundrians laughed nastily.

Siamis ignored them. "You can't," he said, not smug, not gloating, not nasty. He didn't sound even remotely like his henchminions. "I'm back to stay. Your job right now is to resign yourself to that, and I'm taking the time to help you."

Frederic felt that the schoolyard fit the situation. He flipped the guy off, and added the words, just in case they didn't get the message.

It came out in English.

The meaning zipped right past the Norsundrians, who obviously didn't understand English. Siamis just smiled. There was no annoyance, no impatience in his manner. Instead he started talking about his own youth, and all the questions he had had.

Siamis had a calm, pleasant voice. His accent even reminded Frederic a little of the Guardian's own accent, kind of, sort of. He found himself listening more closely to identify that accent, and when he began to see flashing images—vivid memories—of Siamis at his own age, he found he was interested.

When Siamis lifted the silver sword from the saddle sheath nearby, he offered it to Frederic hilt first.

Frederic took it, staring in amazement. Here, in his hand, was an artifact four thousand years old! Only it had been preserved outside of time and space somehow. Frederic was glad, for it really was a thing of beauty.

"*Emeth*: truth," he muttered, repeating its name as he made an experimental pass in the air. His muscles protested all the way from wrist to shoulder, and the point wobbled. He tried again, secretly impressed that Siamis had been able to handle that thing at a younger age.

He gave it back, and wondered what it was that he'd been worried about?

"There's nothing to worry about," Siamis said. "Why don't you see if your companions are awake? As soon as our friends here get the new mounts saddled, it's time for us to ride."

Frederic turned obediently. As he walked back to the single standing tent, he heard the short, heavy-shouldered guy address the one with the long, somber face. Funny, he understood their lingo now.

"Why do we have to drag these accursed brats about? What game is he playing now? I say we kill them off, and we'll be twice as fast."

Long Face—what was his name? Oh yeah. Davernak. He said, "Because prisoners can always be made dead if you need to, but dead ones can't be made alive—only soul bound. Which would make them worthless for what he's got in mind."

Prisoners? Worthless? Frederic shrugged. Nothing to do with him.

Siamis would take care of him, and the girls. Siamis would watch out for them all.

&

"Yes," Senrid said. "There were four off-worlders."

Liere sighed.

"I take it they were caught?" he asked, his mood grim.

"Siamis has them, and they're under the enchantment."

Senrid swore under his breath. He knew what it meant, even if Liere didn't.

Chapter Twenty-Two

When Senrid woke next, he was surprised to discover Liere and Devon still there. Since the weird one seemed to be able to get rid of Norsundrians at will (mounted ones, anyway) he was just as happy that the girls hadn't taken off.

He sat up, aching in every muscle and joint. He kicked off his boots and forced himself into the stream. The cold shocked the aches into pain, but then his body numbed. He thrashed about, doing his best to divest himself of the grime he'd taken aboard during his run.

When he slogged out of the stream into the sunny clearing, wringing out his socks, he found Devon sitting on the grass. Three portions of some kind of nutty bread lay on broad leaves.

Liere walked through the dappled shadows as Senrid laid his socks in a patch of sunlight and sat down to his portion of bread.

"Where'd the food come from?" Senrid asked.

"Dawnsingers gave it to us a couple of days ago," Devon said. "We've got enough for another day."

"We should meet another group by then, I think." Liere looked upward.

"That what you found out on your spy trip?" Senrid put the question as more of a test than a request for information. Though he wanted that, too.

Liere glanced at him, her gaze remote. "That, and also I found out that Siamis and the off-worlders are riding north."

"To Roth Drael?" Devon asked. She looked worried.

Liere nodded. "We have to get there first."

"You can't," Senrid said. "Unless your magic mind-powers extend to flying. Siamis is mounted, and I don't see any horses. He also has magic, if he really wants to move fast."

"They can't use magic to transfer into Roth Drael," Liere said, then she crammed a bite into her mouth.

"Why not?"

"I don't know," Liere mumbled thickly. "All I know is they can't. Not yet, anyway." She gulped down her bread so fast her eyes watered, but her voice cleared. "We should have help soon, and there are those who will hinder Siamis. But we have to be as quick as we can."

"We," Senrid repeated. "Am I included in this 'we'?"

Liere said, "I hope so. You have that hatpin, which will help warn us of danger if I can't. And it's a kind of defense, isn't it?"

"Not nearly as effective as whatever it is you do," Senrid said with a laugh.

"That's only with animals," Liere said, remote again. Her voice was thin and flat. "And the enemies might figure a way around it."

"If I'm the only hope of defense that you have—" Senrid's expression was caustic "—then you haven't much of a chance. I'm no good with a sword. Not against trained warriors."

"You have to be better than we are." Devon shrugged skinny shoulders. "Anyone is!"

"And the hatpin can warn us." Liere picked off another piece of bread. She appeared to be impatient with having to eat. "We could use your help."

Roth Drael. Senrid did not want to go to Roth Drael, famed center of light magic study and practice, at least a few centuries before. Apparently still in use now.

He didn't know much about light magic, other than that it was so hedged with safeguards it was next to useless. On the other hand, in spite of those safeguards, it could make things like this hatpin. If whatever lay in Roth Drael was more powerful, why not?

It didn't seem to Senrid there was anyone, anyone at all, trying to stop Siamis.

"All right," Senrid said, testing his socks. Damp. But bearable. He yanked them on and shoved his feet into his boots. "Let's get moving."

Liere had been watching Senrid with an odd, tense, unwavering gaze.

When he spoke, she jumped a little, then grabbed up her share of the food and finished it off as they set out northward.

Senrid forced himself to match her pace. Before too long the worst of his aches had worked themselves out, his clothes were dry, and the food helped infuse him with enough strength to keep him moving.

"What else did you find out?" he asked Liere after they'd been walking in silence for a time.

Liere shook her head. "There are watchers."

"Watchers," Senrid repeated. "You don't mean human. Or even one of the magic races. Animals? Birds?"

She nodded. "Some of the animals of Helandrias are guardians there, though few see them."

"So you're the one behind the animals?" Senrid asked. "All along I've been getting last-ditch rescues and warnings, and it can't be a coincidence."

"It isn't my doing," Liere said. "But I can hear them." She tapped her head, then frowned at Senrid, not anger but perplexity. "You probably could, too."

"Oh. *Sure.*"

Her lips thinned as her shoulders hunched. She walked on, staring at the ground.

Senrid tried again. "I've never heard of anyone really talking mind to mind, with either people or animals. Only in old myths about the ancient days, and I think half of that was a lot of poetical shield-thumping on the part of the lighters."

Liere looked up, her brows quirked in relief. When she wasn't withdrawing behind that wall of aloofness, her changing reactions were so clear.

"Dena Yeresbeth is one of the Twelve Blessed Things," she said.

Senrid was about to point out that the whole notion of 'twelve blessed anything' was just more lighter shield-thumping, but he kept his mouth shut. This mind-business was clearly no myth. At least, not any longer—and whether it was 'blessed' or not depended on your point of view, right?

" . . . unity of body, mind, and spirit," she was saying. "When you make your unity, they all work together. It takes focus and control, something I keep trying to learn."

He said casually, "Seems to me you're doing all right, what with hearing all these birds and things."

She tipped her head back, staring up through the tree branches. "So much to learn. And when do learn things . . ." She stopped, staring ahead at an oaken coppice growing on the jumbled bank of a very old riverbed.

Senrid cut a fast glance from Liere to the scenery and back again, wondering if she really noticed what was in front of her. Her problem seemed not to be apprehension of danger, but some inward battle. "Learn?" he prompted.

Her voice was so soft he almost didn't hear her. "I can't let my abilities turn into a wish for more power. Then I'd become like *him*."

"Him? You mean Siamis?" Senrid's memory flickered back to the beach, and he heard his own voice saying to Peridot, *They want power, twit,* followed by Siamis's taunt, *And you don't?*

Liere nodded, taking a swipe at her forehead, which was grimy and sweat-streaked. Though they walked in shade, the air was warm and close. "He must have been good, once. I don't believe people are born to evil—to the desire for power—or suddenly find it their only path. It must be a gradual thing, mustn't it?"

Try telling Kyale that, he thought with an inner laugh, but he said nothing out loud. The terms 'good' and 'evil' themselves were almost meaningless, quite separate from the matter of acquiring power. He was very sure that Uncle Tdanerend thought himself—well, if not 'good', *right*. He certainly held the power in Marloven Hess, even if he couldn't hold it on his own and had to have Norsunder back him up.

Another example? Well, he was quite sure that Detlev would not waste time or breath trying to convince anyone he was good, but he certainly had power.

"You equate power with evil," Senrid said at last.

"Isn't it?" Liere asked. "Wanting to force others to do your will. That's evil."

"Magical power is a separate thing. Political power is just another word for leadership, and people follow leaders," Senrid said. "That much I know is true, whether for lighters or anyone else back in history before the magical, and cultural, distinctions of 'light' and 'dark' happened. I always thought 'good' and 'evil' came down to terms for sides in a power struggle. My side is good, your side is evil—and you say that yours is good, and mine evil."

"Norsunder does not claim to be good," Devon said, skipping a couple of times to catch up.

Liere looked at her. "Except Siamis uses the language of good," she said. "When he talks about peace, and harmony, and prosperity."

Senrid thought, *He doesn't use the language of a conqueror, he just does it.*

Liere looked at him, eyes wide. "You're right! His language and his actions—"

Senrid recoiled.

Liere winced, and stumbled to a stop, hands pressed over her eyes, half-circles of grime under her nails.

When she spoke again, it was in a low, embarrassed mumble. "I can't help it." She added plaintively, "You were sending your thoughts right *at* me, like you *wanted* me to hear."

Senrid's breath whooshed out, and he kicked at a drift of fallen leaves. "I don't suppose there's a way to fix that?"

Liere said quickly, "Actually, there is. Like anything else, a mind-shield takes practice. It's nothing we've ever had to learn before Siamis came—"

"*Mind* hearing," Senrid cut in. "Say, if you can do that, can't you undo whatever it is that Siamis did to the off-worlders?"

"There's magic mixed in," she answered. "And he'd know I was there. Also, two people invading a third's mind—well, I don't know what would happen, but I'm scared it would kill the person."

Senrid whistled. "How long've you been doing this stuff?"

"Hearing thoughts of second-face? All my life. I remember hearing my mother's." Liere looked away, as though fascinated by the sight of Devon picking stickers out of her dirty stockings. "The Guardian says that minds are private things. Trespass is a betrayal, and it can hurt."

She looked back in her own memory, hearing her mother thinking, *What a homely, awkward child*, when looking at Liere—but her emotions had not been bad ones. A strange mixture of astonishment, worry, exasperation, and love. Helpless love. Liere still struggled to try to understand it, but all she could comprehend was how little her mother believed she could actually do, besides day-to-day chores.

Senrid comprehended some of these emotions as he watched Liere's face, which was completely unguarded when she did not withdraw.

She turned his way, her upper lip long, her brow worried, and he wondered if his own reaction had somehow echoed back. She squared her shoulders, and he *felt* her retreat behind some kind of invisible wall. Or was it mere imagination?

"I learned early not to reach to hear those things," she said at last. "In fact, I did it so long I had to relearn to listen."

"Read my mind now," he said. "I just want to know once and for all that it can be done."

"Have I your permission?"

"Go right ahead."

"Think on something safe. I'll know when to stop. Or," she added, "you can try to block me out."

"Got it."

She half-closed her eyes, walking with her hands stiff at her sides, fingers spread. Devon danced ahead of Liere, swishing her skirts back and forth as she watched the trail.

Liere said in Marloven, "Senrid Montredaun-An, Marloven Hess, capital Choreid Dhelerei, boundaries on the east (dismay) I thought I could keep her out—" She stopped.

Senrid laughed, a little embarrassed, but mostly intrigued.

"The shield is something you have to construct in here." Liere tapped her forehead. "I always thought of it as a wall. It was easier to make, that way."

Devon dropped back, now that Liere was done with the mind stuff and she didn't have to watch. She scuffed happily through the autumn leaves. She'd heard all that about mind-shields several times before, and it made little sense, but it was so good to have company, to hear voices! She could listen to them talk without having to talk herself. Instead she could listen to the rustling and crackling of the dry leaves, and sniff the sharp smell of them, and love the sight of orange and yellow and brown and gold and red. How pretty it all was!

The talk sped up. It seemed the boy didn't have any trouble understanding what Liere was talking about as he fired questions at her. Was that because he was a prince?

Devon had been afraid at first, when she understood that he was a prince. Would all her happy peace with Liere be gone, if they had to remember to bow when he rose or sat, and say 'your highness' and serve him first, as Russy demanded?

So far Senrid had made no such demands. Another person, Devon thought, feeling very sophisticated, might not believe him to be a prince, for Russy had insisted that all princes required deference—it was manners, royalty-style. It was respect, *if not for the person* he would add with one of those fake laughs people use, *then for the rank and what it means.*

But Devon remembered the wonderful days with CJ and Clair, neither of whom insisted on titles, or bowing, or any of the rest of it. Though CJ became a princess when Clair adopted her as a sister, Clair had been born into a royal family, just like Russy.

Maybe this Senrid came from a wonderful little country like Mearsies Heili, and that would explain his lack of insistence on royal manners.

Devon put her head back, watching leaves drift down from the trees.

The other two were still talking about mind stuff. She sighed with resignation. Maybe she could ask him about his country later. It would be so much fun if it was nearby, and they had pie fights there, like CJ and the Mearsiean girls.

"I take it your finding me was no accident," Senrid said.

"Your emotions were like a beacon." Liere picked her way among mossy stones half-hidden among great tree roots. "And your trail wasn't hard to find, especially when some forest creatures put us in the right way."

"A blind man could have followed me," Senrid stated with derisive cheer. "The only reason I stayed clear as long as I did before you came to the rescue was because of those animals I mentioned, and because Siamis wasn't along with his minions."

"He was busy with the off-worlders that first night, and then they went north. Looking for me."

"Looking for you," Senrid repeated. "North. Then you lost time protecting me."

Liere shrugged. "I can't let them get someone if I can stop it. And all the creatures I commune with know who you are . . ." She paused and shook her head. "Said you should be protected."

Senrid touched the hatpin. "Because of this thing?"

Liere shrugged again, reaching out to catch hold of a tree branch as they picked their way to the bottom of the gully. "There's lots I still don't understand. Every new thing I learn brings me ten awarenesses of how much I don't know."

A cool breeze had sprung up, fingering its way up the little valley and sending a brilliant fall of leaves drifting and swirling around them.

Autumn rain was on the way. All three sensed it.

"Let's begin with what you do know," Senrid said. "Roth Drael. Siamis needs magic and lives if he's going to make extremely powerful spells, the sort to force rifts open between the real world and Norsunder. There has to be some sort of light magic either pooled there, or some enchanted object of staggering power, or maybe both. Do you know?"

"Some *thing* is there," Liere said. "Something very magical, something Norsunder has wanted for centuries. It's a thing I have to get so I can break his enchantment."

"So it's not just this thing that they're after?" Senrid touched the hatpin in his cuff.

"No, there's something else."

"If they know about it, why didn't they pinch it years ago?"

"Because they didn't know where it was, only that it existed. Still existed. It is an artifact from Old Sartor." Liere looked strained in the filtered, greenish light. "I didn't have a good shield when the Guardian gave me what I needed to learn. Someone else came at the mere mention of the thing. Someone far more dangerous even than Siamis. So we had to stop right then."

Senrid snapped his fingers. "I'll wager you anything you like to stake that that would be Detlev."

"Perhaps. When I tried to find the identity, I got deflected." She clapped her hands. "Like that." Which sent a pair of tiny birds jetting upward from a nearby tree, scolding in song.

"So he can't get into Roth Drael?"

"The Guardian says the city is a web of magical protections. If anyone with dark magic does manage to get in—and it will take lots of work—they'll never find this thing. And they can't transfer in at all."

Senrid gave the trail a sardonic grin. So much for his evolving plan for netting this mystery power object for himself, and using it to go after Uncle Tdanerend—or anyone else who had a hankering for Senrid's throne. He thought, *I'll probably not get in, either. Certainly not by magic.*

But there was no use in worrying about it now.

Instead, he considered the problem objectively, as they started upward alongside the stream. "Ah. So that's where the off-worlders come in, eh? Siamis camps on the perimeter of the city and sends Deirdre, Frederic, and the Warrens in to do the job for him."

Liere looked confused. "I find it so hard to understand these things about magic. So many of the words I just don't know, and they don't always come with clear images."

"And you think you're going to get there first." Senrid called up as accurate a map of the Northern Wilds as he could. There were no political boundaries around Roth Drael, nor to the south, clear down to the Fereledria. That was why Frederic and the others hadn't met any humans on their journey. That area was also reputed to be rife with other sorts of beings, none of whom recognized human political boundaries—except as something to avoid.

"I think so," Liere said, her voice muted. "We shall know for certain very soon."

"So your worry is that we won't make it."

To his surprise Liere shook her head. "We'll make it. I think." Her mouth tightened, and once again she walked stiffly, each step precise, her expression bleak. "But. If—if we are to get there first. And get that object. I will have to, well, declare myself."

"To whom?"

She lifted her hand, indicating the entire forest to the north. "To let them know my quest. To take the consequences."

"Risk of discovery by elevens?"

She shook her head. "We will be protected. But the thing I will get . . . my getting it . . . all will bring me a kind of attention that—thinking—don't want. Ignorance! Ignorance of magic, of learning, of the world, but they will think greatness—"

Devon cut in, her face solemn, "Liere! You're doing *It* again."

Liere's skinny chest heaved. "Thanks, Devon. Sorry! I—here. I think I sense a messenger coming." She jumped across the little stream, whisked herself around a great-grandfather oak, and vanished up the other side of the gully, sending leaves scattering.

Senrid put his hands on his hips. "It?" he asked Devon.

"Leaving out 'I'," Devon explained. "She said it's because she thinks sometimes in the Old Sartoran that the Guardian taught her. The, um, verbs are formed so you don't say words like 'I' 'you' 'he' 'she' and so on."

"Pronouns," Senrid said, amused.

"That's it," Devon said, relieved.

"Several languages are inflected that way."

Devon shrugged. "I guess thinking in Old Sartoran is really, really different. Anyway, she doesn't like it when she does that, or other things, and so I stop her."

Senrid didn't believe the Old Sartoran explanation beyond the time it took Devon to express it. He saw that Liere was trying in some strange way to squeeze herself as a discrete presence outside the coalescing alignments of power that—nevertheless—seemed to have her at the center. Idiocy!

Liere withdrew to put distance between herself and the others. Maybe if they didn't see her they wouldn't think about her, and she could get control of her own emotions.

I hate feelings, she thought. How hard she fought to control them, to not let them muddy her mind! This one thing she could learn from Siamis, who had not displayed any foolish, weak emotions at all.

If someone could learn to control them in order to do bad things, she could learn to control them in order to do good things.

She could. She must.

So do it.

She leaned against a tree, rubbing her hands along the rough bark and inhaling the pungent resiny scent. Roth Drael . . . that was for later.

For now, she needed clear thoughts in order to talk to this boy from Marloven Hess, a place whose images in Senrid's memory frightened her. That didn't matter yet, either. What mattered was that at last, she'd found someone who was close to making his unity. So close, and yet he thought himself an adherent of dark magic.

She sorted through the images, memories, emotions, that he'd sent so strongly—so unheedingly—during their talk, clearer than anyone ever before. Senrid's mind was like a cascade of rushing water down a mountainside.

He repudiated words like 'good' and 'lighter' yet he seemed to reject their opposite.

He was so very alone.

Like she was.

She understood this much from the tumble of his memory images: though he'd been born a prince, a single child, cherished by his parents, and she had been born one of many children to ordinary shopkeepers, both had found themselves alone at an early age. He through assassination, she through the discovery that she was utterly different. What they shared was a sense of duty. They were both driven by that sense of responsibility, something no one seemed able to help with.

Liere at least had had Lilith the Guardian to guide her from a distance.

The only person Senrid had had was some military man named Keriam. Liere shut out the images: to her, 'military' was very close to 'Norsundrian.' If you were born among bad people, would you know badness as badness? Or would it seem normal?

She'd heard Senrid's thought about getting the 'dyr' thing and using it. She'd also heard his resigned expectation at being closed out of Roth Drael.

He was on the verge of making decisions that might change his life, and not just his, so many people's, and she didn't have the vocabulary or the experience to say the right thing.

What if she said the wrong thing, and *he* became the next Siamis?

I can't be a coward, she thought. *No emotions. Don't let them get in the way.*

Senrid's not a coward, and he's lived through the kinds of terrible things I was too afraid to even think about.

Having made this decision, she contacted Devon and discovered that she and Senrid had reached the top of the gully. As she tramped over mossy grasses that had probably not felt a human foot in over a century, she shivered. The breeze had kicked up into a wind.

Autumn was not just coming, it was here. She looked up at the freeshaken leaves skirling through the air. By nightfall there would be rain—and not one of the soft summer rains, but hard and cold.

Devon and Senrid sat under a big oak. Wind fingered through their hair and clothes. Devon's small face, made thinner by its frame of scruffy brown braids, wore its anxious look. Unkempt yellow curls lay across Senrid's forehead, but they did not hide the tension there; his mouth was bland, but the expression around his eyes betrayed wariness.

"Soon we'll get rained on," Liere said. "But I think we better keep going."

"How about some food?" Devon suggested, pulling her small, flat knapsack around.

"I won't turn it down." Senrid grinned.

"Thanks, Devon," Liere answered, and the younger girl divided up three portions, looking doubtfully Senrid's way. But he did not sit back as though expecting to be served, nor did he elbow forward to take his first. He reached out when Liere did, saying nothing about deference, respect, or manners.

They began to eat. No one talked at first. The wind strengthened steadily.

This is an opportunity to learn control, Liere thought, forcing herself not to feel the cold. The problem was, when she did that, she could feel the need for more food.

Presently Devon, who was huddled in her torn cloak, made a remark and a general conversation started, to which Liere paid just enough attention to be polite.

Her true focus was on a mind making its way steadily toward them. Her mouth dried. What awaited her, she knew, was the kind of place and people most only heard stories about, but what it meant was that she was no longer in hiding. She was going to go through with the Guardian's magic, and take up a weapon against Siamis.

There was never again going to be an awkward Fer Eider child hiding in South End.

There was no going back.

Chapter Twenty-Three

"Listen," she said.

Bushes rustled. A small forest-dwelling animal emerged, its dark eyes steady with the kind of awareness that spanned species.

As Liere stepped forward and bent to touch its curly head—facilitating contact—Devon and Senrid watched.

To Devon, this was yet another inexplicable incident, one in a half-year's stream of them.

To Senrid it was . . .

Marloven vocabulary failed him. He watched, waiting for some morally superior, power-wielding lighter-mage to point an accusing finger at him.

But the animal stepped back, its paws silent on the thick humus, and with a flick of its tufted tail it was gone.

Senrid watched Liere wiped her hands slowly down her sides as thought they'd gone clammy. What did she fear?

"They're coming for us," she said. "The morvende."

"That creature reads minds?" Senrid asked, amazed.

Liere's smile flickered, shifting the planes of her grimy face. "Oh, yes. This is the only good to come out of Siamis and his spell, the alliance. A kind of dena Yeresbeth exists among creatures, but normally they live in their part of the world and leave us to ours. Now they ally. Not serve," she added, looking up.

Devon promptly scanned the tossing treetops, but in vain. Moments later, with scarcely a rustle, three white horses emerged from a curtain of ferny leaves.

Two were riderless. Astride the other was a morvende boy, who looked at them with interest from under drifting snow-white hair. The only color about him was the faint blue of veins beneath visible skin, and the pale brown of his eyes—exactly the same shade as Liere's.

This is it, Senrid thought. *Time to turf the evil Marloven.*

"Welcome," said the morvende.

He was dressed in a short-sleeved, knee-length green tunic, his feet bare, his finger and toe talons honed to sharp points. He wore a stone knife at his side. Otherwise he looked like the morvende that Senrid vaguely remembered from the tunnel under the Norsundrian Base.

Liere said, "Thank you," and she made a kind of sign with her hand.

More lighter ritual. Devon looked bemused. The morvende grinned as he mirrored the sign with his long fingers. It looked good when he did it.

"These are for you," the morvende said. "And your companions are welcome as well." He indicated the horses.

Liere clambered up onto a boulder and then scrambled with stiff, awkward movements onto the back of one of the saddleless horses. Senrid took the other, vaulting easily up. Devon was left looking lost. Senrid reached a hand down and hauled her small weight behind him.

Devon clasped a desperate death grip around his waist. As soon as her skinny little hands locked together, Senrid suppressed the urge to shake her off, conscious that this was the first time in long memory that someone had touched him without intent to harm or to subdue.

The morvende clucked. The horses moved smooth-gaited into a canter. Senrid enjoyed the cold wind, the speed, the forest blurring by. Devon shut her eyes and held on.

Liere was also terrified. This was very different from sitting atop placid, plodding Kondaria all those months ago. She was concentrating so hard on keeping her seat that she was totally unaware of the morvende's curious and admiring glances.

Senrid noticed, finding this interaction entertaining.

"So you understand the ancient Sartoran?" the morvende asked, after a short time.

"The basics." Liere sounded as stiff as she looked. "I'm still learning."

"Who taught you?"

"The Guardian. Through memories. I hope your people are safe from Siamis."

"Oh, they will never see us," the morvende said with a laugh. "But they will see mistaken trail markings, and much fog, and so will ride east for a time, thinking it west."

Senrid was very interested in how that was managed, but he knew better than to ask.

The rain began. At first occasional taps and patterings of cold, wet drops rustled through the leaves overhead. As yet they heard more than felt it, for they rode deeper into the tangled thickness of very old forest.

When night fell, they stopped at a dawnsinger enclave, but only for a short time. Senrid watched the forest people gather in a circle around a great bonfire, their faces lit in the ruddy glow.

Space was made for all three kids, which surprised Senrid. He could not see any structures around them. He knew the dawnsingers were purported to live in tree houses. If any such houses were in the branches above them, they were camouflaged extremely well. He felt no rain despite the steady hissing thrum of the storm all around them.

The dawnsingers sang in slow, long melodic lines that echoed in counterpoint sometimes but otherwise never seemed to repeat, harmonies evocative of bright image. There seemed to be no rules governing who sang, who stopped, and when.

The stone-baked nut-and-fruit bread tasted good and was filling.

As the storm passed westward, once again they mounted, riding for a short time into hilly terrain. Senrid lost all sense of direction. Before midnight they rode through an opening in a rocky palisade. Then they dismounted, and were led down old tunnels, deep below the surface, the animals being taken off in another direction.

Old tunnels? Senrid thought. Ancient! The stone was worn smooth all about them, as if polished by countless hands over the centuries. Air flowed constantly from somewhere, cool, fresh, smelling of stone and water.

They wound down and down into a vast cavern with a great dark lake at one end, and Senrid thought he knew where they were: on the edge of one of the great lakes of the Northern Wilds.

The cavern was filled with white-haired people, and a scattering of dawnsingers. Animals as well, and even a few centaurs.

They were led to a place not far from the water's edge where soft-woven rugs had been laid out. Devon plopped down, sighing in gratitude. Senrid threw himself down near Devon, watching everyone and everything. He noted that the lighting was kept central, so that it was difficult to make out the perimeter of the cavern. Still, light did reflect off of faint striations in the rock, and paintings that were not at all symmetrical—like those one would find in a building—but instead followed the natural contours of the stone. He lay propped up on his elbows, staring at the nearest wall, and made out highly stylized birds, interlocked with patterned knotworks of everbloom blossoms and laurel leaves.

Fascinating. Also fascinating that the lighting obscured the tunnels leading off to further caverns. There were none of the legendary sentient jewels in sight. Perhaps those were the lighter hyperbole he kept expecting to encounter.

Liere lingered behind, talking to a group of white-haired figures. She never gave her surroundings a glance in the little while that Senrid watched her.

His attention snapped back when food and drink were brought by quiet morvende adults. The brewed drink tasted of wood and good water and subtle herbs. It cleared all the remaining aches from Senrid's body.

Devon busied herself with her food, yawning more and more frequently. When she was done eating, she curled up on her side, hands tucked under her cheek. Two breaths, and she was asleep.

Senrid lay back, watching through half-closed eyes as Liere was surrounded by various older morvende who were probably leaders. Occasionally their voices rose in song, fast triplets shifting in and out of minor keys, echoing off the stone in timed beats, blending voices and chords in intricate counterpoint. Interesting that the syncopation was all sung, whereas at home, it was drummed, and the ballad melodies sung in chorus as counterpoint.

As his mind began to drift, he figured Liere was being pulled into some kind of lighter ritual. Better her than him . . .

"No," Liere was saying. "I don't want to sleep. I want to listen, and to learn. I want to know your history, and oh, everything."

"Thousands of years of history would take a thousand years to tell," a young morvende assured her, his face earnest, to laughter from the older generation.

"Some day, when time is not pressing, you will return," an old, bearded man said. "And we can share with you all that you wish to hear. For now, we can lighten your burden a little with some celebration."

"We'll sing about those of your sun-siders who have helped ours," a small morvende girl said.

"And those who make peace."

"And those who gift us with their own arts," a third put in.

Liere walked the length of the cave, listening to old laments and joyous songs and ancient chants that referred to names and events of which she had never heard. She felt as if she had wandered into a great story, or perhaps the Story, for this people seemed to have woven together into a long tapestry of song all the history of the world, and here she was, about to embark on a deed to save them.

And they knew it. All the songs were chosen to hearten her.

She looked back once. Senrid and Devon lay sleeping in the great cavern, surrounded by softly singing voices. Perhaps she could find someone wise to talk her into courage, and to show her what to do.

Four morvende her age sang about the first Queen of Sartor. When it was over, the old man who had been walking with her said, "The animals call you Sartora."

Liere got that horrible hot, itchy feeling all over. "It's an honor, but I don't know that the spirit of she I'm named for would accept me." After all those songs, the formal language felt strange—and right.

"She, too, came from humble beginnings," the old man said. "Her gift was the ability to make each comprehend the other, until all felt part of the world's kinship."

One of the white horses came forward, and lowered her head. Liere laid her hand flat on the place between the animal's eyes, and she heard a mental voice so very different from humans, so full of sound and image, with few words: *You are the Sartora. You must ward the Evil One. We have watched for you through two seasons.*

"You who are animals?" Liere asked.

All the living, the horse replied, and the images included water beings, and those of wood and sky.

Then came an impatient growl from a silver timber-wolf near the horse's legs, *Naturally. Who else?* Wolves, it seemed, were impatient of formality.

The old man said, "Do you see what Lilith the Wanderer has done? She has given the world a hero."

"Who?" Liere looked around. "Where?" A hero could give her advice—show her the way!

The man chuckled. "It is you, Sartora."

Liere ducked her head, her chest feeling hollow inside with dread.

"You," the quiet voice went on, "are a symbol of the alliance for freedom. You will also be a hero for children like yourself."

"The others close to dena Yeresbeth?" she asked. "Has anyone done it? Because they can be the hero. Not me. I don't know anything heroic."

"How do you define heroism?" the man replied. "If you confine it to those who wield weapons and destroy others, perhaps you will never be that kind of hero. But if you can use your wits and skills for the task awaiting you in the moonstone city, that is the heroism we celebrate."

She breathed, short and sharp. "I'll try to do what I can against Siamis," she said. "But I'm doing my duty." And in a low voice, almost a whisper, "As for Sartora, it's just a nickname."

Even as she said it, she knew that she was being silly, that it wouldn't matter to them. Two things did matter to her: that she succeed, and that she only stay a symbol. She would *not* seek power.

More songs greeted her, and she fancied that she saw the news being carried from lips to ears through the cavern, and thence out into the Northwest Wilds, and from there into the world. Other kids would hear. . . her family would hear.

Siamis would hear.

I can't let fear stop me, then he defeats me before I take a step, she thought.

Somehow—she never did discern the meaning, the pattern, behind the people who flowed around her—she found herself facing an older white-haired woman.

Like Lilith the Guardian, this woman had kind eyes and a restful manner. As she held out a hand and bade Liere walk with her to the very edge of the dark waters, the others all faded away.

"The people of the Lake will shift you to the northern waters," the woman said. "From there you will have only a day's ride to Roth Drael, and the horses have offered to bear you and your friends."

"Thank you," Liere said. "How much to the Lake people know about what I'm supposed to do?"

"They know more, and less, of our concerns than we are ever able to discern. They guard secrets that only time will reveal." The woman looked down, her profile serene. White hair the color of new snow hung down her back. It was impossible to guess her age.

"So they can't help me prepare?" Liere dared her greatest question, but not her greatest fear.

"With what do you desire help?" the woman asked.

"The magic," Liere whispered. "The Guardian twice showed me Erai-Yanya's book, and I have the sense of it. I think. Ah, I can't read. I don't know if I can hold it all here." She touched her head. "And I know nothing of magic."

The woman raised her hand, palm out. "Though Erai-Yanya of Roth Drael is a prisoner, there are ways for us to communicate with her. She feels that you will be able hold the magic much better than she could even if she were free. The unity is important. She has not made it. She is of the older generation. But she has laid the path carefully for you. Practice what you were taught. It's the way we all learn. Practice on your ride tomorrow, again and again, but within the mental shield that you construct."

Liere repeated, "'Hold the magic.'" And then, in a rush, "I don't even know what that means. Oh, why can't the Guardian be here? She could do this magic. Why must it be me?"

The woman shook her head. "We have not enough allies. That is the nature of the times we live in. I do not know everything, only this: right now—this moment—there is a terrible magical struggle going on along a great line to the south, where Norsunder is trying to force one of their access rifts into our world."

"South? Senrid says it's in the north."

"It seems that the south is where the efforts are being made, and the Guardian leads our mages, who must defend."

Liere understood that she was not the center of the world's struggle. Maybe hers was a very small matter, and here she was, whining the way her father had always despised.

She bit hard on her lip. Again emotions were ruling her mind, and she knew that mind must rule emotions. *I only have this one thing to do. And I have so many allies. I should stop being cowardly, and do it.*

The woman said, "You need rest. Join your companions. Come dawn, the transfer will be made."

Rest. Her eyes ached, and her legs were sore from the unaccustomed riding.

She remembered Devon—and Senrid.

"There's another thing," Liere began, then she stopped. Somehow— she couldn't define why—to discuss Senrid's inner turmoil seemed a betrayal. "No." She squared her shoulders, and straightened her spine. "Never mind. I'll see to it myself if I can."

They reached the woven rugs. On one Devon lay curled up, deeply asleep. At first it seemed Senrid was asleep as well, but when she lay down on the rug set aside for her, she saw a glint under his eyelids. His gaze was not on her, not even on the cave, but a thousand rides and a thousand days away.

She closed her eyes and dropped into sleep.

❧

Senrid was not asleep. His mind had drifted into memory.

What had brought him so far into his past? He'd thought he'd forgotten his mother. "Your mother was weak," Tdanerend had said repeatedly. "A weak-willed lighter who weakened your father when he married her. You will have to work hard to overcome the weakness they bred in you. Believe me, everyone can see it."

Her patient hands, her warmth, gone so suddenly. Why had she left him? *Because she was weak, said my uncle, but that's not true. It was because she trusted him, and he betrayed her. So is trust weak?*

Tdanerend certainly never trusted anyone. Yet Senrid had realized just this last summer that Tdanerend himself was weak, as is a tyrant who can never get enough power because he goes to bed afraid of the knife in the dark. Who permits corruption in his adherents in order to get loyalty in the form of lip service.

Tdanerend trusted no one, and nothing, but force.

So was the use of force a kind of weakness?

That meant . . . that meant . . .

The words wouldn't come. Not yet.

Questions streamed through his mind, until he saw that Liere had returned. She lay nearby, her face relaxed in sleep. Beyond her, little Devon lay curled up in a ball, her side rising and falling in a gentle rhythm.

Senrid closed his eyes, and dreamed.

Chapter Twenty-Four

When they woke, they were still lying on rugs in a huge cavern, and the cavern looked more or less the same—though Senrid noticed that the wall paintings seemed to be stylized lizard and chameleon shapes, not birds, the lizards knotted together with what looked like wheat and wen stalks.

A good breakfast and the gift of rain-repelling, warm green dawnsinger cloaks awaited them, and from the cave they rode on two white horses who needed no guidance. And here they discovered redwoods, rather than the fir, oak, and hickory they'd been riding through before.

The horses took them southeast through huge mist-shrouded redwoods as cold mist grayed the world.

Liere rode alone. From the way she gazed sightlessly ahead, her body stiff and her lips moving, Senrid guessed that she was practicing whatever spells she had to perform. He also guessed that she was feeling the effect of the day before's long ride—feeling it and determinedly ignoring what she couldn't help. When Senrid mounted his horse, his leg muscles had protested for a short time. Despite the months of not riding, old habits made him adjust quickly.

But a glance over his shoulder at poor little Devon made it clear that she, like Liere, was no rider. Terror and pain blanched her narrow face and drew her lips into a thin, white line. Her arms were locked around Senrid's waist again, and she clung with desperate strength.

She reminded him a little of Ndand, his cousin. Tdanerend was a rotten guardian and a bad king, but even worse were his skills as a parent. He hadn't quite dared to try magic experiments on Senrid, but nothing had stopped him from experimenting with magic for mind control on Ndand, which had pretty much made a mess of her. She was also the only companion Senrid had been permitted, and so he'd gotten adept at diverting desperately frightened and unhappy small girls.

"See that rock over there?" he began.

"Yes?" A quick look. "What's wrong?" Devon's voice was high and trembly.

"Hiding behind it I saw a toad-shaped old geezer with six purple noses—"

She gasped, and then giggled. "Six? What do you do with six noses?"

"One's for sniffing, one for snoring, one to stick in the air when visitors come, one to snout into others' business . . ."

"One to honk," Devon whispered. Senrid felt the tremor of laughter in her voice a victory.

"Definitely one to honk, and the other to hang lanterns off, of course."

"How did he get them?"

"Oh, he lost a wager with a very cranky old sorcerer, who . . ." Stories were as easy to spin out as lies—which, of course, they were. Lies had always been stories, little ones lived in briefly, in order to escape from real life if only for a short time.

And so he kept his story going as the horses paced steadily through the blue-green shadows of the woodland. They rode through the entire day, past vast ferny canopies, occasional brilliant splashes of late-season wildflowers lighting the misty green world, for this far north, autumn had set in some time ago. The air was so good that breathing it made a person feel a little drunk. After a time Devon fell asleep again, leaning against Senrid, her death-grip relaxing at last. He had to hold her spindly little wrists to keep her on the horse.

The sky was obscured by the immeasurably tall redwoods, the profound stillness broken only by the horses' progress over the rich ground, and the occasional, startling thrush-songs that ascended upward like jets of light from the hidden birds.

Liere didn't speak until the lengthening shadows had begun to meld into darkness, making the trees nearly indistinguishable. By then the horses walked, but Senrid wasn't sure if they watched for invisible branches that might knock riders clean off their backs, or if their heads were low from tiredness. Horses at home would be tired by now.

When he felt the slap of needles across his face, and saw a branch swat Liere, he said, "I think we'd better camp."

Liere gasped as if he'd poked her. She was nothing more than a black shadow against the blue background now. Only her horse's pale shape marked her out. "Yes," she said, in her flat voice.

"We just crossed a stream," he said. "Maybe we ought to go back there."

Liere fell silent. The horses wheeled about and retraced their steps, splashed across the stream, then headed up a small incline.

"Here," Liere said. "They say this spot is good for humans."

Senrid slid off onto velvet-soft grass, still wet from the rain. He pulled Devon down. The girl snorted and sighed, then staggered as he set her on her feet. "Oh. We're stopping?" she mumbled.

An older kid would have netted a sarcastic answer but to Devon Senrid just said, "There's water over here."

Devon rubbed her eyes, amazed that she had actually fallen asleep on the back of the horse! Then she recovered the vague, comforting feeling of Senrid's strong hands holding her secure, and she thought, sleepily, *He doesn't act like a prince the way Russy says, but more the way you'd expect one to act.* Not that she defined that further, for to whom would she say it? She knew Liere had no interest whatever in the actions of princes, and she was too embarrassed to say anything about the subject to Senrid. But she had accustomed herself, in her short life, to inner dialogues.

Senrid looked doubtfully at the horses, for they had no grooming gear. But the animals shook their manes, and trotted gently away to graze, so he gave up. At least they hadn't been galloped into a lather.

One by one they got drinks, and then Liere shared out the nut cakes that the morvende have given them. They ate in silence. After the meal, Devon wrapped up in her cloak and dropped into deep asleep.

Senrid and Liere both felt tiredness pulling at muscles and joints, but Liere's yammering heartbeat would not permit her to relax. Anticipation made her restless. A whole world's safety depended upon her actions, and she was afraid to fail.

Senrid sat across from her, Devon's small form between them. All Liere could see was a finger of light on his fair hair. All he could see was her bent head, outlined against the pale bulk of a horse who cropped at grass a few paces away, and the faint blue-white gleam of moonlight on the worked silver clasp she'd been given for her cloak.

She looked his way. "Would you mind a question?"

"Go ahead."

"It's about, well, fame. I mean, you're a person of royal birth, so you're used to everyone knowing who you are."

"In Marloven Hess, anyway," he said. He wasn't about to get into the Marlovens' reps in outlying countries—and he wouldn't let her get into it, either.

Liere said, "Do you feel that, if they know you, they have a claim on you? That you might have to . . . you might feel obligated. . .to, well. Live up to their expectations?"

Surprised, he said without thinking, "I do feel that obligation to the people of Marloven Hess. Felt it all my life." He promptly regretted saying that much, but she didn't jump on it.

Instead, she sighed. "How do you know what's the right thing to do?"

He wasn't about to get into *that*, either. Besides, he knew by now that this wasn't the real issue.

"You're having second thoughts about your magical object?"

"It's called a dyr. Die—rrruh." She carefully pronounced the word, squashing the instinct to make two vowel-sounds out of "y" and swallowing her "r", which in Imar was trilled. "I'm still trying to learn what that means. All I know is, we don't have anything like them in modern times, yet they were common enough in Old Sartor. Anyway, not about that. I know that part is right. It's after. I don't want people putting into my hands power . . . responsibility . . . decisions that will affect their lives."

"Who says that has to happen?" Senrid countered. "At least from everything I have read, people don't give power away, they work to keep it. And even if it's different for lighters—which I doubt, despite all the rhetoric—it's only there if you accept it. You can always go back to your home in South End after Siamis gets axed."

"I can't go back," she said quickly.

"Why not?"

"I can't. I can't be what I was. And anything else . . ." She gave a shuddering sigh. "Wouldn't fit."

"Then you go back to those morvende. From where I sat, you'd be plenty welcome, and they're not going to turn you into a figurehead."

"They already have," she whispered.

"So that's what's bothering you."

"Does that sound cowardly?"

"It sounds like you're borrowing trouble when there's plenty right at hand," he said. "Look. Get this dyr thing. Use it for whatever spell Lilith the Ligh—the Guardian told you to perform. Seems to me, that's enough to concentrate on. And maybe by the time that's done you'll know what to do next."

She ducked her head in a quick nod, a movement barely discernible. "You're right. Dyr first."

"Then let's rack up. You're going to need it. Magic takes effort, and when you're tired, you don't have the strength to hold it."

"Yes," she said. "Sleep."

She rolled up in her cloak and lay down, as did he, but a few moments later he heard her voice again. "How do you live with that? Knowing that what you do affects so many lives? Or are you so accustomed to it you don't think about it?"

"Contrary," Senrid said guardedly. "I do think about it."

Liere was silent, and because—so far—she'd been straight with him, he said, "I think about it a lot. I hated having the name and not the power. Things—stupid things—done in my name. I know how I want to rule. When I get home I have to see to it that I can." He heard the fervency in his own voice, and shut up.

Liere sighed again, but not the shivery sigh of suppressed tears. She said slowly, "A different set of problems. But . . . I think . . . we have the same goal."

"Do we?"

The derisive question shut her up.

After a time he slept.

❧

And woke with her hand on his shoulder.

Weak blue light barely illuminated her thin, taut face and exhaustion-marked eyes.

"We have to go now," she said, her voice nearly lost in the hush of the forest around them.

Senrid rolled to his feet, old habit making him alert at once. He breathed deeply, seeing his breath, and feeling that heady sensation, a little like drinking ale, that was a characteristic of the air here. Ale with no stupidity, no headache. Liquors were for those who took safety for granted, and who didn't need to think ahead of everyone else.

He slipped the gift cloak off, and cold hit him. He stepped down mossy rocks to the stream, splashed his face and washed his hands clean. The water was even colder than the air, but it tasted good.

When he climbed back up he saw that the horses, who had vanished sometime during their talk the night before, were back, waiting side by side, their eyes gleaming in the diffuse light from above, their breath clouding faintly.

Devon's cheeks had regained their pink, though she still sat stiffly. She smiled as she divided up some food. They ate in haste, then Senrid boosted Devon up onto one of the mounts and vaulted up himself, still in front, as he didn't want anything between him and a possible fight.

"Shall I show you some ways to make riding easier?" Senrid offered over his shoulder, after a time.

"Is it hard?" Devon whispered.

"Naw. I did this when I was six. It'll be fun! You start by holding onto the horse with your legs. Like you're trying to walk with a barrel between your knees without dropping it."

Devon giggled at the image, and he felt through the horse's subtle muscle contractions how Devon clamped on.

Liere rode in silence, her mind far away, as Senrid coached Devon, one small suggestion at a time.

By afternoon, she tried loosening her grip more and more often, as she concentrated on settling into her seat.

Light slanted through the remote treetops, golden shafts splashing on patches of grass, or moss, or pale-blossomed late-autumn wildflowers. Devon looked around with evident joy, and in an act of bravery, let go with one hand to rummage in her knapsack. The air was clear, and cold, but their cloaks kept them warm.

"Wen stalks?" Devon asked, offering long green stems to Senrid. "Found them growing right near where we slept."

"Good. Thanks," he said, taking one.

They tasted sweet, and killed the craving for food; they'd eat when they reached their destination.

In mid-afternoon they encountered the animals guarding the ruined city. Roth Drael was near. A gazelle leaped across their path, and the horses stopped.

"Isn't that one of the Fens?" he asked. "Aren't they supposed to be able to talk in human speech?"

"Yes, but they hate human speech," Liere whispered. "We won't ask them to speak to us."

Senrid shrugged.

Liere communed silently with the waiting gazelle, who stood still under the girl's touch, only her flanks quivering. Then Liere looked up. "Siamis is still behind us, but no more than a day."

Senrid whistled softly and appreciatively. "He's fast."

Devon made a frightened noise.

Liere said, "I've asked her to tell the Fens not to risk their lives trying to stop him. I think we can finish the magic and get away before he gets here."

Senrid said nothing.

The horses started forward again, and within a short space of time they descended along a riverbank into the ruins.

There was no building standing whole in what was left of Roth Drael, one of the cities of Old Sartor. Great chunks of a glistening white stone lay scattered about, mute evidence of a truly terrible magical battle. What they could see of the architecture hinted at design to maximize light, and air, with commodious rooms. Graceful curves and angles were all the more shocking because they drew and momentarily pleased the eye—and then there'd be the crack, or the jagged wall, testifying to sudden violence, below which lay the scattering of weather-worn stone.

Roth Drael had been long ago reduced to a street lined with broken columns, walls, and rubble. Midway along it stood the remains of a large building. There were two short towers, one broken, and one wing of rooms, one side of which—adjacent to a wide semicircular terrace—was open to the weather, though he detected a faint sheen of magic.

The horses halted at the shallow steps leading up onto the terrace, and the three kids jumped down.

Liere scanned their surroundings, her shoulders hunched, her hands clutching at her elbows. At Senrid's glance she jerked her hands down, obviously hating her own weakness, and she said, "I've got to find my way around. Then there's this spell I have to try first. You can either watch, or else meet me here when I'm ready to free the dyr."

Devon looked from one to the other, then said, "Unless you need me, is it okay if I wait out here?"

Liere looked relieved. Senrid would have been interested to hear the lighter magic, and compare its lumbering form to what he knew, but not if it meant Liere would stutter and fumble with false starts. Better to let her do what she had to do. He could always ask about it later.

Liere walked inside the building.

Senrid sat down on the steps. The sun—hanging low in the south— was hazy, and not very warm, between drifting gray clouds. The horses had gone somewhere else. Devon dropped down beside Senrid, using a forefinger to trace shapes in the fine dirt that had drifted up against the step.

Senrid said, "You know anything about this dyr thing?"

"Only what she told me."

"Which is?"

"Erai-Yanya's family has had care of it for a long, long time. She learned magic from an old mage called Evend in Bereth Ferian, then came back and lived here all alone and studied more. I guess the family hid all their books, so she had plenty to study, because they are all hermits. That's all I really understood."

"Liere's told you everything she knows, hasn't she?"

"Everything I asked. Though sometimes it doesn't make sense."

"You know Norsunder's going to want to get their hands on you."

Devon got up, unslung her knapsack, and began to hopscotch over an imaginary boundary along the first level of steps. "They don't know about me."

"They will if she's successful with what she's about to do. And they will if they get her."

"I'm not too worried," Devon said, shrugging. "Liere's got them all figured out."

"She does, does she?" The idea of this scrawny kid thinking Norsunder was no problem because an eleven-year-old had them 'all figured out' was breathtaking in either arrogance or ignorance. He was sure it was the latter, but that didn't make it any less exasperating.

"You should ask her. Too hard for me to 'splain." Devon went on with her game, her cloak fluttering in the cold wind.

"Right." Senrid kept his voice even. "I will ask her."

Devon shared out a meal, setting aside a portion for Liere, who never came out to get it. As the shadows lengthened, Devon put the food away again in her knapsack, then she sat on the steps with her cloak tented about her. Senrid spun out another story—prompting Devon to add bits when she got ideas—and so they whiled time until the sun vanished in the cloudbank above the western treetops.

Then Liere appeared in the doorway. "Come inside," she said. "If you want," she added in haste.

Devon jumped up and clapped her hands. "Magic," she exclaimed, grinning. "Liere promised she'd let me watch. And she didn't forget!"

She ran across the terrace then peeked in as if expecting to see something strange or frightening. Senrid, following more slowly, and saw only a plain room, the white stone unmarred by any kind of decoration. In the center, fine carved lyre-backed chairs circled a heavy wooden table, near two carved-wood cabinets and a desk. Blue-white glowglobes on brass pedestals lit the room, and the archway beyond.

Beyond, what rooms he could see were completely bare, though one with a faint haze of magic in the doorway suggesting a ward hiding something behind it.

Liere waited by the big table. "I was successful with my first spell," she said, her voice echoing slightly. "These rings are what Erai-Yanya and her people have used when they handled the dyr." She pointed to three silvery objects lying on the otherwise bare table. "I don't know why yet, but I expect we'll find out. Take one. Put it on."

There was a faint tremor in her voice, and a husky edge, as if from tiredness and thirst. She lifted one of the rings and slid it onto her finger.

As soon as the ring was on, Liere's body lightened, like breathing the air the first day of spring when her mother opened the house after the long siege of cold. She laughed, she was strong. She *could* do what must be done.

Devon reached for a ring. Senrid hesitated.

Liere saw his hesitation. "This magic does nothing against your will. The Guardian told me that is the real difference between the two, did you know? Light magic cooperates with the world, and dark magic uses force. That includes its effect on people who use objects of power."

Devon had been admiring her ring before she put it over her thumb.

Senrid made no answer, but held out his hand.

Liere's thin, grimy, ragged-nailed fingers picked up the last one and slid it onto his forefinger. Then she stepped back.

He looked up at the wall, waiting for something to happen. His awareness seemed to intensify subtly, heightening all his senses. He wondered if it was just his habitual wariness, except he did not feel wary. The habitual questions—strength, power, conflicting loyalties—faded into unimportance.

Devon smiled up at Senrid and Liere, feeling safe, and content. The older kids looked around with the kind of inward expression that she was used to seeing in Liere. Devon waited patiently, knowing that whatever was to come next had to be wonderful. Devon thought, *If this is what Liere feels like all the time, I'd like to be an Old Sartoran.*

And she and Senrid were both surprised to hear Liere's thought in return: *What you're feeling is a magic replication of the unity. But only the Guardian and Siamis are Old Sartorans.*

And Detlev, Senrid thought.

And Detlev. Ready?

The question was to both, but Senrid knew it was really for him. He lifted his hand in a 'carry on' sign.

"We'll go in here." Liere pointed to the room with the haze. "It was the library and magic room, but the mages hid the books and things, somehow."

The two followed her through the doorway. Senrid was surprised that the ward, which prickled briefly through flesh and bones, did not stop them. Powerful—but benign. The room looked empty, and there was an enormous crack in the ceiling, open to the sky.

They stopped, and stood in a triangle.

Then Liere began a chant.

Senrid recognized it at once. It had an analog in dark magic. It was a kind of prelude to making an enchantment, which was in essence a great spell binding other spells. The prelude called on all the magical elements to be bound, and it helped the magician shape his or her mental processes in order to hold all the elements together.

Liere had been told that the enchantment she was preparing formed around three abstract concepts, faith, hope, love, a trinity called in Old Sartoran *mrardya defar-yan*. Defar-yan . . . even when she was busy with the words, little thoughts bloomed in her mind, like was that where *Ferian* came from, as in Bereth Ferian? But she couldn't follow the blooms, no matter how lovely, or she'd get lost in a sea of flowers . . .

She concentrated on what she'd been told. *These words are symbols, hiding protection after protection.* As each protection was released, the power of the dyr strengthened, offering Liere a world of gardens.

Liere's voice was steady, but dry with tension. Devon swam in a sensory glory, utterly trusting, unable to contribute.

Senrid found his center—just as he'd always found his center—and once he had balance, he held the magic for Liere. It was unconscious, partly habit, for he'd been disciplined in the use of magic for most of his life. He knew the dangers of losing hold, losing control; with dark magic, if you lost the gathered power it would burn you up fast. In light magic, the danger was simply that the balance would not be achieved and the spell would fall apart, like water splashing from a shattered glass.

It was his holding of a far more benevolent but exceedingly powerful magic that enabled Liere to find her way back to the physical world long enough to make the last sign, and then to reach with her hand into non-space and non-time, and grasp the dyr.

Its presence intensified the sensation of light and being and infinity . . .

A vast chord, no, an endless, infinite harmony sang through the mental realm. One could get lost in it forever, a joy reaching and reaching—

Liere sensed the others' identities dissipating. She'd been warned by he Guardian, and remembered just in time.

Barely, barely, she managed to move, to end her spells, and to remove the rings from the others' hands as well as from her own.

The moment the rings left their hands the other two slid into sleep.

Liere sank down on the floor beside them, closed her hands around the rings and the dyr, and put her head on her knees. Her heart expanded, buoyant with triumph. *I did it, I did it.*

Dawn was barely a paleness in the east when a warning image from one of the horses shot into her consciousness, forcing her tired mind and body to respond.

She performed the spell to hide the rings again.

Then she bent over Devon and touched her shoulder. Devon roused, bony knees and elbows hunched in protectively. Senrid woke up fast, his body instantly tense and alert, his yellow hair sticking up in wild curls all over his head.

Both kids stared at Liere.

"We have to go," she said. "Siamis will be here this morning."

Chapter Twenty-Five

Liere, still sensitive, felt Devon's dismay as an internal blow. "Devon, we knew he was coming, and we got what we came for."

Liere held out her hand. There lay a round, coin-sized object, but thicker, made of a silvery-white material that seemed partly metal and partly the white stone of which the building was made. It fit perfectly into the palm, like a pool of melted starlight.

"The pockets tore on my trousers a long time ago," Liere said. "Will you take it?"

"I don't have any pockets," Devon said, stepping away with her hands behind her back. "And I'm scared it might bounce out of my knapsack and get lost."

Liere offered the dyr to Senrid, who took it wordlessly, considered his own pockets, and how something that small might fall out again. He put it into his shirt pocket. This he pinned closed with the hatpin.

They walked out and found the horses waiting for them. They mounted up, the girls with more ease than before, though Devon winced and tried to stretch the saddle soreness out of her legs. She settled gratefully against Senrid's compact, strong body; he reflexively braced for her small weight.

Liere paid no attention to the complaints of her body. All her attention was on the road ahead.

Liere scarcely saw her surroundings. She never noticed that the Fens paced them steadily through the day, far beyond their own boundaries.

Devon noticed, and felt safe to see sinuous feline shapes flashing over the mossy ground, muscles bunching under sleek fur as they leaped with breathtaking grace over shrubs and boulders and streams. Senrid, too, noticed this flanking escort.

Here is real strength, he thought.

He had been taught that force was a measure of power. And to an extent, it was. But that power required constant exertion on the part of forcer. The moment the exertion halted, the object pushed back.

The kind of strength he witnessed now sustained itself. Each of its components—all of whom alone might be considered weak against the armed and trained soldier who obeyed lest he be flogged at the least and put up against the wall at worst—willingly contributed strength. How much of force's power was consumed by resistance, however secret?

As the horses galloped along paths worn centuries ago, Senrid's mind raced through memories, re-evaluating everything he thought he'd known.

Tdanerend's fear of treachery was so fervent that he'd constrained his strongest men to guard his chambers ceaselessly when he had to sleep, which meant the real power lay with them, not him. If so, then true strength was the ability to go to sleep not fearing the assassin's knife. And not just on behalf of oneself. A strong king also guaranteed that all his people could sleep in peace at night.

Therefore, power had to be the ability to defend his people, and not just his, but those in the neighboring lands. The kind of power he saw in the silent cooperation all around him could be defined as mutual reliance —the ability to fight back to back, trusting one another, which doubled one's strength.

Senrid knew that if Siamis somehow found them right now, there would not be armed men facing three kids, it would be armed men against three kids and a forest of animals that knew how to fight.

This was not just a new definition of power, it was an entire strategy, compelling in its truth.

What did it mean?

The magical ramifications were obvious: it would be absurd to continue his studies of dark magic exclusively, thinking that lighter magic was not worth knowing. His former unexamined contempt had another name: willful ignorance.

He thought back over the times he'd come up against dark magic's limitations. He'd assumed he had to learn more, and yet more again, ascend to a new level of discipline, at which time he'd master the power needed. Which was true, but only so far as his own safety was concerned. It was also true that dark magic was not for the weak-willed or the coward, for it could so easily destroy the mage.

He understood now that the danger was not just to the mage, but to the world.

A life of study, now gone. Worthless.

No. Not worthless. His studies would forever furnish an insight into the methods of those he knew as enemies. That would always be an advantage. And he did know how to study.

But it also meant he was going to have to begin all over again, relearning the basics from the other point of view.

First, of course, he had to get rid of Tdanerend—and his Norsundrian allies. . .

While his mind ran down new trails, the horses ran steadily on, and overhead the sun reached its zenith and then descended toward the west.

Shadows had lengthened and were beginning to gather into blue gloom in hollows and groves when Devon's restless little movements against his back finally penetrated Senrid's self-absorption.

She'd started practicing riding once she re-accustomed herself to being on horseback, but now she was clinging again. He looked back into her face, to see more than just discomfort. Her eyes were narrowed as if against a sizable headache.

"Liere!" he called.

Her head turned sharply, and she swayed, then clutched at her horse's mane.

"Time for a halt." He tipped his head slightly in Devon's direction, and saw the golden eyes shift focus from him to Devon. Then widen.

Liere didn't speak, but her horse began to slow, and so did Senrid's.

The animals' pace was soon a walk, and once again they chose a safe place for the humans to dismount, on soft grasses near a stream.

As soon as they slid off the horses' backs (Devon dropping straight onto the grass) the animals vanished, two ghost-flickers of white in the intense forest darkness.

Senrid's tiredness pulled his body like a mantle of boulders. A residue of the sensitivity afforded by Erai-Yanya's magic rings seemed to linger. He could feel Devon fighting tears as she dug in her little bag for the dense cakes the morvende had given them.

"I'm sorry, Devon," Liere said. "Please. When we go on too long, speak up."

Devon said unsteadily, "I thought it was more important to get away from where Siamis might be. You know he's probably real mad, if he found out we got that dyr-thingie."

"Probably," Liere said. "But I think we'll be all right. That is, we will be if you don't get sick."

Devon hiccupped, bit her quivering lip, then said, "I wish I could go on like you two do, but my legs hurt, and my back, and my head, and I can't." Her voice rose high on the last word, and she looked down, tears of shame bouncing down the grimy front of her gown.

Liere looked up at Senrid, her face drawn with uncertainty. He turned out his hands in a brief gesture: it was up to her to speak.

She said, "I'm sorry, Devon. We shouldn't do it, either. Lilith the Guardian says too much control weakens first-face. I'm glad when you remind us. It's important. Come on, let's eat. Then we'll all sleep."

Devon hiccupped again, but fought valiantly to blink the tears back as she passed out food. Soon after she'd crammed some of her cake into her mouth her face began to relax. Senrid felt an immediate benefit from the food, which tasted of nuts and breads and spices he couldn't name. His appetite was fierce, but the thick, heavy cakes filled him comfortingly, after which he followed Devon down to the stream to drink.

She made her way back up, her movements stiff as she wrapped up in her cloak. The girls' voices murmured, light and almost inaudible over the quiet hush of rustling trees. He splashed water on his face and hands, then climbed up the rocky bank, blinking water from his eyes. The dyr's unfamiliar weight thunked against his ribs as he sat down next to Liere.

She lifted her head. An owl drifted among the high tree branches, and then disappeared.

Devon's breathing deepened.

Senrid said in a low voice, "You told her you've got Norsunder all figured out, and not to worry."

Liere glanced his way. He couldn't see her expression, but he felt her surprise. "She doesn't know anything that could help them. Why would they harass her?"

Senrid said, "Siamis might not. Or Detlev, even. But the underlings—" He thought of the countless petty cruelties he'd endured at the Base, all of which was considered 'entertainment' for the denizens.

Liere drew her breath in. "Yuk."

"There you go again," he said, irritated.

"I can't help it. You're sending."

"'Sending.'"

"You wanted me to see those memories. So you sent them."

"I didn't 'send' anything," he retorted, unsettled and annoyed. He moved away from her.

"You can deny that you made your unity last night, but I don't see why," Liere said flatly.

Senrid snorted.

Now sure of herself, Liere spoke in a firm voice. "You used dena Yeresbeth—the unity—last night during the Twelfth of Never—"

"The what?"

"The Old Sartoran name for that last spell. When we pulled the dyr into the world, from beyond time. It was you who managed the magic, not me. If I'd been on my own, I'd still be back there caught in that lovely dream realm, waiting for Siamis to come in and collect me and the dyr."

Senrid snorted. "So the Guardian abandoned you?"

Liere fell silent, then lifted her head. "No. There was someone. I didn't get identity. On the . . . outskirts . . ."

"Periphery."

"On the periphery. I think, watching over me. But you helped me first. And then that awareness was gone."

"All I remember is confusion," Senrid said. "Anyway, you sidetracked me. So you think you're too tough for Norsunder?"

"Well, for that torture stuff," Liere said. "I could get out of first-face, and stay in second-face, and never notice if they drilled holes through me. I'd just never wake up. A battle of wills . . . I think I can win. I think. I have so far." Yet even as she spoke she remembered that unknown mind swatting her away like a gnat—and how she'd cowered when her mind had encountered Siamis's. She flushed, feeling as if she'd been bragging.

Senrid sat back. Maybe it was true, but he doubted it. She seemed to have a distorted picture of Norsunder. With a mental shrug, he dropped the subject. Maybe *he* had the distorted view. His original point was still important, though. "I think you're wrong to give Devon the impression she's not in danger from Norsunder, unless you can promise her safety."

Liere's head bent. He sensed that his words had troubled her. He sat back, glad to let the drowsiness overtake him at last. It was good not to have to fight it.

Liere ate her food with methodical inattention. What Senrid had said indeed had disturbed her. Had she been arrogant after all? Had her success against Siamis—a grown man from four thousand years ago, an enemy, dedicated to evil—given her a false sense of her own strengths?

What was Siamis doing right now—and would she cower away again if their minds met in the mental realm?

Unconsciously, she reached—

And he was waiting.

At noon, Frederic and the girls had ridden into a weird ruined city, in company still with Siamis and his men.

"'Looks like bleached bones," one of the Norsundrians said.

Another promptly made a comment about bleached bones, a comment nasty, graphic, and predictable. Frederic was used to this type of interchange by now. He knew better than to comment—not that the Norsundrians would listen. If Siamis wasn't around, they'd just smack him for speaking. The only one who didn't slap the kids if they spoke was the silent Davernak, who left the kids strictly alone. The meanest was the young one.

They didn't talk much when they finally did stop, after long, seemingly endless days of hard riding. Rain, clouds of insects flying in their faces, mud, sudden bursts of wild animals from bushes that spooked the horses, thick fogs that somehow got them going the wrong way—it all made for a miserable trip. And that was only the outer stuff. Frederic's legs and butt seemed to hurt worse each day, but he dared not complain, and neither did the girls. Whoever said horseback riding was fun? Some idiot who never did it, obviously.

The Norsundrians complained bitterly whenever Siamis wasn't there to hear, but not about riding. They wanted an honest fight (they said) and not this typically cowardly lighter war of attrition.

But a hard ride was what they got. Of them all, only Siamis seemed tireless, and because he rode every inch of it with them, springing down at the end of a long day as if it had been a casual half-hour's canter.

The food wasn't bad when they finally did stop, and it was fun when Siamis had time to pay them some attention. He really seemed to enjoy hearing all about their previous adventures—especially about the Mearsieans, and Dtheldevor, and their friends who knew magic.

Stories about Dtheldevor made Siamis laugh. Frederic couldn't tell if it was what she'd said or what she'd done, but he smiled with evident inner enjoyment when Gloriel and Peridot bragged about the privateer girl's various exploits, and he even asked questions. The only thing the Warrens couldn't seem to remember was how to get into the island hideout, or what kind of spells protected it.

A couple of times Siamis gave Frederic and Peridot lessons with the sword. Not just any sword, but his sword, the silver rapier *Emeth*. Frederic enjoyed the attention, but it would have been better with only the other girls as audience, because the watching Norsundrians were loud, sarcastic, and unstinting in their comments about his and Peridot's lack of strength, speed, or talent. It *was* better when Siamis organized the Norsundrians into teams to fight one another, for his comments were just as unstinting about their performances.

Best of all was the one time he practiced with the Norsundrians himself, defeating them all. Not just one on one, either, but one against three and even four. A few of them he stung hard with the flat of the blade, and the young one he deliberately nicked over one eye. Siamis was a blur of movement, deft, strong, never out of breath, always just ahead of the others—as if he knew what they were going to do next.

"He does know," Deirdre murmured, firelight reflecting in her eyes as she watched. Deirdre almost never talked.

Frederic was mildly puzzled. He hadn't meant to speak out loud.

He was disappointed when Siamis stopped fighting without letting Davernak have a turn; he saw by their looks that the Norsundrians were also disappointed. They wanted to see Davernak trounced.

Siamis didn't practice again, but the Norsundrians' complaining lessened after that. And the complaining stopped the day they finally reached Roth Drael.

They trotted up a kind of street, the horses skirting white stone rubble.

Siamis murmured, making signs. Magic spells, Frederic thought incuriously.

"Fresh tracks," Davernak said.

"Two horses," someone else pointed out.

Siamis looked around, his eyes half shut. "They were here," he said finally. He dismounted right in front of a big tiled terrace, and tossed the reins to Davernak. "You see to the animals. The rest of you? Occupy yourselves while I do some investigating. I must break the remainder of the wards. There's a web of them."

Frederic and the girls got down, and Davernak took the horses away. The girls poked at the bits of stone on the grassy street. It was boring— but boring was better than hard riding through mud and rain. Frederic was glad to be on his feet, stretching legs that he'd been afraid were going to be forever bent in a barrel shape.

Frederic noted some of the Norsundrians going off to search, carrying bows. He heard snatches of commentary in Norsundrian, wagers being placed on who could nail the first animal or bird that showed muzzle or beak. Not for food—nobody ate mammals on this world, or birds that flew. They wanted target practice. The kill.

Time wore slowly on, shadows moving steadily eastward and lengthening. The searchers returned, reporting to Davernak, who waited silently outside the big building, that there were day-fresh animal tracks a couple hundred paces to the north, and what looked like human tracks.

"Adult size?" Davernak asked.

"No."

"Must belong to either the Fer Eider girl or the Marloven. Put out a full search tomorrow, if we're still here."

He posted guards, and then they passed out bread and cheese. The kids were last to get theirs, as always when Siamis wasn't around. He hadn't emerged from the big building.

Nor did he until after sundown.

When Liere first reacted to the sudden contact with Siamis, jolting as if she'd been kicked, Senrid was alarmed enough to leap to his feet, hand on the hatpin, feet planted in a fighting stance. But the pin remained just that, a silver pin, and no Norsundrian warriors boiled out of the darkness, swords in hand.

Presently Liere looked up, her breathing audible over the rush of the stream.

"What happened?" he asked. "Siamis, I take it?"

"I can't . . . I can't talk about it," she said in a quavery voice, wrapping up in her cloak.

Senrid watched her sit down, her knees drawn up to her chin.

"At least tell me what to be ready for."

"We're going to have to go alone. No, *I* will have to go alone," she declared, her voice thin and high with strain. "He said he will have the dyr at any cost. He said I am the only one they'll keep alive—something I'll regret forever—"

"Never mind the threats," Senrid said, when her voice suspended. "Standard scare-babble."

"Is it? New to me." She gave a shuddering sigh.

Her anxious gaze met hers, and he felt the memories impact her just as if he'd spoken. Her expression changed.

She flinched. Senrid knew what he was talking about. He had lived through just the sort of experiences she dreaded most. She sighed again. *Siamis didn't have to try very hard to scare me, when I did most of the work myself. So much for my brag that I can win a battle of wills!* "And I'm a stupid coward to listen. Fear! I'm letting it defeat me and he's not anywhere near. But he said anyone with me gets the knife. The cursed kind." She gulped in another breath. "I'm going to have to tell our allies to leave me alone."

"Horseshit!" Senrid exclaimed. "That's the oldest trick in the world! He told you that to cut you out from the run. Make it so much easier to hunt you down. You'll do their work for them before they even touch our trail."

"So you're saying I should not warn our allies?"

"Warn 'em all you want, but don't cut free."

She shook her head. "I can't risk others' lives."

"Let them make that choice. Starting with us." His thumb indicated small Devon, and both stood there uncertainly, looking down at the sleeping child.

"Let's sleep," Liere said sharply, and she threw herself down on the mossy ground, her back to Senrid.

But within a very short time she sat up. He was not asleep. He wasn't even lying down, but leaned back against a tree, arms crossed, faint moon and starlight gleaming palely on his shirt.

"Senrid, I don't think you can understand how impossible it is now for me to—"

"So now it's time to fling my background in my teeth, right?" he shot back. "What could a Marloven possibly know of ethics?"

"Senrid, when have I ever said anything about your homeland?" she retorted.

Senrid whuffed a laugh of surprise. And embarrassment. "Never. I ask your pardon," he added. "It must be twice as sickening, my claiming the moral high ground when I harp on about how morals don't really exist."

"Pardon granted," she responded with a quaint, somewhat shy, formality. "But you do have morals," she added, and though he couldn't see her, he felt her regard just the same—steady and honest and true. No pretense whatsoever. "That is, you're finding—I don't know, matching— oh, I wish I had a better vocabulary!"

Senrid was thoroughly unsettled at someone having so much insight into his most private thoughts. His survival had depended on hiding his thoughts. "Yes," he said, experimenting with how the truth sounded out loud. "Yes." He grinned sourly at the dark sky overhead. "But maybe one moral at a time."

And was rewarded at last with her laugh, as faint starlight glinted in the tips of grasses and in loose strands of her hair.

"It's this Sartora thing," she muttered, and it was her turn to feel embarrassed. "It makes me feel a sham, and yet I still think I have to live up to some, oh, some ideal from a great story as if it were real! Because of what it stands for, *that* much is real!"

"So why are you so resistant, if you believe all the fine things they say are true?"

"I just don't want them to say it about *me*. It's the Sartora name. No. Not the name. What it's beginning to mean. Good meaning, but . . . I don't want to be the one wearing a hero-face even to people who will never meet me!"

"Why not?"

"It's, oh, that I can't make mistakes. I get it, why the Guardian told all these people about me. The animals, even. Not only to watch out for us, as they've done. But now they have a kind of symbol, something to give our side courage in a terrible time. So if I make a mistake, then the mistake isn't just mine, it affects everyone. I cannot bear that!"

"You think the Guardian set you up?" Senrid said. "Now, that's interesting. Using myth as a weapon. And . . . it *works*."

He thought back over what he knew of lighter viewpoints on history. He'd already categorized much of lighter celebratory ritual as a poetic way of naming "ins" and "outs"—the ins being our side, and the outs being the enemy. And it did work to hearten the weak, to bind them emotionally to the greater cause. He'd seen it work in Kyale Marlonen, selfless, even heroic gestures from someone who otherwise was the most selfish and narrow-minded person he'd ever met, despite her righteous prating about being on the side of Good.

"Right. Sartora aside, and back to Siamis. One thing we wicked Marlovens know is military stratagems, and I'm telling you that Siamis slipped you that threat in order to prod you into doing just what he wants."

"And I'm telling you that that's the risk *I* have to take," she said.

"Liere, you're being a blockhead."

Silence.

She lay down once again, this time on her side, facing away from him.

He flung himself down on the grass in disgust. Moss tickled his ear, and his back was tired from the posture he'd adopted during the long ride so that Devon could lean against him, but his mind would not cease its whirl of memory, calculations, questions.

He rolled over, and it was his turn to break the silence. "So what do we do? Because I'll tell you now I'm not going to stand by and watch you blunder off alone, leaving me to twiddle my thumbs and wait for the great, sad songs about the late martyred Sartora—"

"I. Am. *Going.*" Her voice was cold, so cold he knew she was as upset as she'd probably ever been—and as usual, had buried her emotions behind a wall. "Fast. As fast as I possibly can. Use the dyr to free people. It's what he doesn't want, so I have to do it. Don't you see? The dyr will break that weird spell he has on people. That's why he makes all those threats. He doesn't want me to use it because he knows it'll work."

"So you get allies to speed you along. Hide your trail."

"No. He will *kill* them. Not just kill them, but bind them to Norsunder. He promised—"

"You believe the promises of a Norsundrian?"

"When it comes to death and murder, I believe them."

Back and forth they argued, too passionate to be angry with one another for long, because they both knew the stakes were horrible.

Neither convinced the other, though they tried until they were too exhausted to keep their eyes open—and dawn was very near. Sometimes he referred to incidents in his past as illustrations, always brief, not really comprehending that the entire memory impacted her just as if they'd shared the experience. That is, he didn't know until he realized that the images he was seeing when she talked about her own limited experiences were not coming in words, but by then he didn't care.

Eventually exhaustion wore them both out, and they slept.

The Norsundrians had started a big fire on the terrace, using gathered wood and some furnishings they'd scouted out of the building and smashed up.

Frederic drifted around the edge of the warmth, occasionally shoved out of the way until he found a spot behind some rubble. He was there, out of sight, when a new Norsundrian appeared. No, not new. He'd been around once or twice; he had a loud, stinging voice. He began many sentences with "But Detlev says . . ."

Siamis came out, standing in the archway. "Well?" he addressed the newcomer.

The man was big, with grizzled gray hair. "Detlev sent me for your report. What do you have?"

Siamis made a summoning gesture. The newcomer and a couple of other Norsundrians crossed the terrace to go inside, boot heels ringing on the white stone. Frederic drifted along behind—ignored, as usual.

The building had been some kind of palace. It was weird because so few of the rooms were whole. Great cracks marred them all. Most had portions of walls or ceiling missing and were opened to the sky, yet the furniture below (that left by the Norsundrians) didn't look weatherworn. Someone had lived quite comfortably here.

Siamis snapped his fingers and blue-white glowglobes lit.

"Liere Fer Eider has indeed been here," Siamis said. "And she managed to successfully find and free the dyr that had been hidden here for centuries."

"Dyr?" One of the Norsundrians muttered, and "Shut up," Davernak muttered back.

"It can be used to undo much of what we've done," Siamis explained. "And we can presume that the same helpful busybody who told her how to free it has provided lessons in how to use it."

The Norsundrians were silent. None of them understood magic, especially the kind that related to Siamis's Old Sartoran background, that much Frederic had perceived. What they saw was a rarity: Siamis was angry.

Anger, now that they understood. Someone was going to catch it hot any moment now, and while they hoped to get an unimpeded view of the entertainment, they didn't want to be blasted by the flames.

Siamis said, "I just finished an enlightening exchange with our young friend. She seems to see herself in the guise of a crusading heroine." He pointed down at a map that lay open on a big round table. "Probably the same sources that transferred her here ahead of us will return the favor come morning, putting her somewhere south of this lake." He smiled gently at Davernak. "You have now your opportunity to make up for your error. You will take your group and follow her to the first town or city she comes to. When she's in the center, you make certain that she doesn't escape."

The newcomer, the loud one with gray hair, said impatiently, "I'll take that order. I'll see it done right."

Siamis shrugged a shoulder. "You may share the command—you settle it between yourselves, as long as you carry out my order."

The Norsundrians, except for Davernak, grinned. Frederic could see that this was the kind of command they liked. The gray haired one gave Davernak a contemptuous glance.

"Whatever damage you cause in carrying out this order, see to it that whoever hid her understands that Liere Fer Eider is at fault because she—encouraged by Lilith the Lighter—refused my offer of peace, and chose war."

"We're to let her through until she reaches a city," Davernak repeated, as the gray-haired one looked impatient. "What about the brats with her?"

"Oh, she'll be alone. I made sure of that. If her 'brats' do manage to follow her, I want the Marloven boy. I have no interest in the other one."

The two Norsundrians left. Frederic followed, as usual comprehending without will or direction, as if in a dream.

He was not the only eavesdropper.

Chapter Twenty-Six

After weeks of chasing after the Norsundrians, Leander and Dtheldevor got close enough to spy Siamis's party riding alongside a stream below the ridge they lay on, and thereby discovered Siamis had captured four off-worlders, two of them old friends of Dtheldevor and her gang.

She pulled out a bottle halfway through the afternoon.

Dtheldevor uncorked the bottle and was just raising it to take a swig when Leander gave in to instinct at last, and kicked it out of her hand.

She looked up, her mouth open, her fingers still curled as if to hold the wine, then her eyes narrowed to slanted black lines of fury and she whipped free her sword.

"Go ahead," Leander said, arms out wide. "I'm no match for you. And if you keep sozzling that swill we're finished anyway."

Dtheldevor flung down her sword, cursing violently. Then she heaved a great sigh. "Yer right. Me dad used to say, anger is like smoke. Hold it in and it burns ye. I been lettin' it burn, and tryin' to put it out by sozzling."

Leander said only, "We're going to have to find some way to ride."

And that was why Dtheldevor liked him. No smugness, no parade.

She snapped her fingers. "Morvende. Sarmonwilda taught me how to find 'em."

She slapped her hand against her leg, picked up her sword, wiped it off, and they were soon on their way; by the next morning they rode side by side.

Now that they were close enough, they discovered why the Norsundrians rode such an erratic course. They were being deflected by forest life, and that meant Leander and Dtheldevor shared the fun.

Fog, diverted streams, mud-sodden paths, and various other disasters kept pursuers and pursuit on the hop. Siamis and his gang pushed hard despite the obstacles.

Leander and Dtheldevor grimly stuck it out until, after two or three days of westward corrections, Leander figured that Siamis had to be headed for Roth Drael, just as he'd originally said. So they headed straight north, and nothing disturbed them.

Dtheldevor shook her head after a disaster-free day of travel. "How do they *know*?" After a long curse, she admitted, "Gives me the butt-chaps in me head, that they can see inside me skull."

Leander grinned. "Maybe Norsundrians smell different to animals. I'm just glad we're out of it."

Early the next morning they rode for the ruined city, stopping on the northernmost border at Leander's insistence.

"They'll search," he said. "I've got to hide our mounts."

"You do that. I'll do some nosin'."

Leander withdrew to care for the horses, and to find shelter. He left markers so she'd know where to look.

About noon, a flock of crying birds alerted him. Before long a lynx slunk out of the forest undergrowth and yowled in the Language: *Evil Ones. In the human dwelling.*

Leander checked his hiding place, a sheltered cave next to a waterfall. Thick growth around the upper level would have protected it from discovery by anyone but a boy who had been survived since early childhood in just this kind of terrain. He sat down, without making a fire, and waited patiently.

Dtheldevor showed up on the ridge well after dark, her hand on that same lynx's back.

"You there?" she whispered. "Dark as Detsie's heart."

"Down here," Leander murmured.

Dtheldevor skidded and slipped her way down, muttering fierce oaths.

As soon as she was on level ground, she said, "No lights. The soulsuckers are stayin' and some o' them are out lookin' for sport. I been on the roof all day. Couldn't move till dark."

"What happened?"

She snorted. "We gotta get in there and bump off that-there fart-face."

She repeated Siamis's orders concerning Liere, punctuated by colorful invective that under other circumstances would have diverted Leander. But that order quenched any impulse to laugh. "They'll kill her," Leander said, sickened.

"An' have fun doin' it, too. You shoulda seen the grin on the one soulsucker. Then I hadda lie there all the blasted day, cause they was swarming all over. The kids, too! My own friends, sittin' there like someone scooped out their heads! It's bad, bad," Dtheldevor said under her breath, too grieved even to curse—for a heartbeat, anyway. "This mind messin' is bad. I know how t'fight some o' it, but it don't always work. In me dad's day, you squared up with sword or knife, and cheats were maybe usin' a chair or a bottle to pitch at yer enemy, or a friend behind to trip up yer foe if you wasn't so good with yer blade. None o' this mind damn-blastation."

Leander remembered her accounts of cruel-sounding experiments that Detlev had played with the royal families of Everon and Wnelder Vee. Not for him senseless slaughter: that had nearly extinguished human life from the world four thousand years ago. Mind games. Distort the leaders, and half your conquering work was done for you, saving effort and affording entertainment for anyone patient enough to watch it.

Apparently the unknown, sinister leaders of Norsunder had just that kind of patience. The world was their puppet, and they hammered their strings through minds. And hearts.

Leander's palms had gone clammy. "So you got out unseen," he prompted.

"Don't worry none." She snorted a laugh. "I ain't good's you in the woods—you know that—but I know plenty about snakin' around buildings. Spotted the patrol routine. Saw they got no blind spots. Leastways not yet. They will, though." She grinned, a brief, fleering grin. "They will. The blank-phizz ones got the outer walk, and they ain't gonna see no one. They'll get careless, so long as Soulsucker Siamis is busy, I bet you anything."

"I won't take that bet." Leander rubbed his eyes. "You kept your mind-shield tight?"

"You bet! So anyhoo, I got me a bird to make a noise in some bushes, and got me carcass on the move soon's they snouted over to see what was what. Took two breaths o' time. Then I wandered about until the big cat found me."

"Then they don't know we're here."

"Nope. Saw yer prints and mine on the northside up there, thought they was Sartora and her pals. I reckon theirs got wiped by rain betwixt their leavin' and Siamis' comin'."

"Sartora," Leander repeated. The dawnsingers down south had called this mysterious girl, whose real name they kept forgetting, by the name Sartora. That was easy to remember.

"Was here yesterday, right enough. Dang! If we'd been faster—"

"Except our job is Siamis," Leander said.

"Yes," Dtheldevor said, grim and cold. "I ain't forgot."

Devon woke first.

When Liere and Senrid opened gritty, tired eyes, it was to find the last of their food shared out, plus some berries and wen stalks that she'd found.

When they finished eating, the horses were there, waiting side by side. Liere walked to them and stood next to one, her head bowed, her skinny hand flat on the front of the animal's face.

Finally she looked up. "They can let the other animals know to stay away," she said in a low voice. "But the horses will carry us. They say they're faster than those of the evil ones." She rubbed her eyes, and sighed. "They aren't horses like our horses. They're descendants from some kind of creature, not of this form, though it is one that they like, and so they mated with native horses. But I can't really understand their true form. All I get is light."

Senrid thought how weird it was that a being with choice wouldn't choose human form. *What is it in the horse view of the world that's better? I guess if you want to move fast, and don't trust speech, then horse would supersede human.* Then he shrugged. "What it means right now is that we ride, so maybe we've got a chance. Until they leave." He leaped onto one's back, and extended a hand to Devon.

Liere pressed her lips together. She ran a few steps, and jumped on a rock and scrambled onto the other horse's back.

Devon looked from Liere to Senrid. Something was wrong. She knew it, but she also knew she couldn't fix it.

Liere continued to stay silent on the ride south, which was relatively short. Senrid entertained Devon with another story, spun out to last all morning, interspersed with riding lessons masked as casual suggestions. The pinched look left her face, and she even laughed out loud.

The horses veered westward and took them up into the rocky hills above the lake, and from there to a morvende geliath. Liere was silent and remote again, angry with herself for the fear that she couldn't quite banish.

Senrid's awareness had developed so gradually—and so completely—that he couldn't remember when it hadn't been that way. He did not know what to say to Liere, since he couldn't understand her willingness to risk her own life on behalf of these nameless others for whom she felt such responsibility. He respected the desperate courage it took, but he didn't understand it.

They arrived at the morvende geliath, again through a difficult access that Senrid knew he'd never remember later. He'd looked hard, and discovered a blurring of physical details around the entrance meant to deceive . . . *him*. Liere and Devon would never think to look for such things.

Once they were in the tunnel Liere blurted to the first morvende she saw, "We mustn't stop. The Norsundrians are after us."

Senrid, feeling the dyr thump against his body every time he moved, offered no more arguments.

"Stay for food," was the answer, and they were led inside.

This time he was aware of the transfer.

It was like no other magic. There was no sense of displacement, none of the wrenching vertigo associated with dark magic transfers. The cave around them flickered, resolving into subtly different lines and colors. Again, the perimeter was shrouded in shadow, the light concentrated toward the center along the water's edge.

He found unnerving the way the morvende in the new cave were silent, and waiting. He could feel their expectancy, and their respect that bordered on awe.

How had they known so fast? His palms prickled. Liere lifted her head, her body straight.

"Thank you," she said, sounding very young, her voice tense. "I thank you for all your help. But I have to go on alone. Any who follow, even to help, will lead the enemies to us all. I have what I came north to get, and if I'm to use it to break Siamis's magic, I must go on alone."

"We will give you travelers' fare," a very old morvende woman said, coming forward. She was barely taller than the kids, but her presence, her tranquility, were calming to the spirit. "Eat, and be at peace."

Liere saw Devon's anxious question and said quickly, "That we'll accept, and gladly."

They were led to a water-carved, round alcove of a cave, where cushions had been set, and a low table with fruit and more of that filling nutbread that was so very different from the heavy travel bread the Marlovens had made for centuries.

They drank water poured from wooden containers, that tasted brewed, somehow. It was delicious, imparting a heady sense of comfort, as in the greater cave, at every level all the way up the striated, carved and painted walls, clusters of people appeared, and sang.

Senrid had thought the earlier music clever counterpoint. It did not prepare him for the shower of sound that echoed back and forth now, a brilliant weaving of counterpoint, voices rising and falling in ravishing chord changes for which he had no name or knowledge, but they somehow scoured the emotions, causing wonder and joy to well up, so sharp it was almost painful, but an exquisite not-quite-pain. Intensity, that was it.

Only two words were sung, over and over: hope and peace.

Liere listened with her head dropped back, her eyes closed, and for a time her hand suspended with a piece of bread between plate and lips. Devon hugged herself, eyes bright with wonder.

Presently one by one, the groups in the alcoves quieted to humming, and then that, too, faded, and they vanished, until all who remained was their guide, who handed a fresh bag on provisions to Devon.

As they walked up the tunnel toward the surface, they had to pass the line of waiting morvende. Young, old, male, female, they were all there, all quiet—hundreds of them. As Liere approached, they put their hands together and bowed their heads over them in the old gesture of peace and respect. Some murmured words of gratitude, of good wishes. Her face burned with embarrassment. At least they didn't say anything.

These were the people she was trying to keep Norsunder from destroying. Hope, and peace, these were the things she was trying to protect. Weakness was a luxury. She had to be strong. She had to succeed, or she would fail not just herself, but every single one of these kindly, faithful, hopeful gazes.

If she failed them, every death would weigh forever on her conscience.

Senrid paced beside her on one side, Devon on the other. After an eternity, she made it to the cave entrance, and out.

There, she turned to Devon and Senrid. Her mouth was dry, but she forced herself to speak. "I think you should leave me now," she said. "I can't put you two in danger."

Senrid unpinned his pocket and closed his fingers around the dyr and the hatpin. "You can take this thing back if it'll make you feel better, and you should take the hatpin, too. It'll keep the dyr safe, and the sword might scare away a Norsundrian horse." He held out his palm with the two objects on it.

"But," he added, "as for your stupid idea of going it on your own . . . you know what I think. And I'm not sticking around here." He jerked his thumb over his shoulder at the morvende cave. He grinned. "I'm sure I'm about as welcome as a fart at a party, though they're putting up with me for your sake."

Devon said firmly, "I won't go." Her eyes were huge, dark gray with her own strain. "I'm in charge of the food. That was what you said, when we were in Imar. We each had an important job. That's mine. And I'll watch out for you if you forget to sleep. You let me help before. I like helping." She stuck out her lip, then added, "If he can go, so can I."

Senrid understood that it had been a mistake to speak first. Devon would only slow Liere down, and she was obviously worn out and terrified, but there was no denying her courage.

"You need my help," Devon pleaded, and Senrid sensed how much she needed to give that help.

Liere nodded slowly. Senrid sensed her relief that she would not be alone after all, though the relief was tangled in guilt and fear and regret.

"Keep them," Liere said, touching the dyr on Senrid's outstretched palm. "I still don't have pockets."

And so the three of them walked out past the rocky entrance, emerging under a cloud-covered sky, to where the—or some—white horses waited. It was impossible for her to tell them apart; Senrid was beginning to, as he'd been raised around horses. These were new ones. Though they all had the white hair, some of them had dun undertones, or roan, or grayish. One had pale, pale spots.

Senrid leaped up onto one, and held his hand down to Devon, who scrambled up behind him, her knapsack—now full—banging against her ribs, a feeling she found comforting.

They rode south.

❧

The forest changed, the northern trees opening into grassy fields that Senrid hailed with relief, at first, because here they could see some distance. Raised to see landscape as military topography, he'd never been a forest lover. He liked being able to see danger coming.

The problem was that as they could see, so could they be seen.

"Let's stay with cover while we can," he finally said.

The horses complied.

Devon watched the yellow grasses flash by beneath the horses' hooves. It made her feel that they were covering more ground, for she was secretly tired of all this traveling. A glance at the horizon made it seem as if they'd never get there.

Late in the afternoon, a cold wind swept down from the distant mountains. Devon huddled into her cloak and gripped Senrid's waist as tightly as she used to when she was scared, because the cold couldn't get between them, and he blocked the wind. Still, she shivered.

Liere's strength was fading. Too many nights had gone by with little sleep. She said, when the horses stopped for water, "I need a rest. Just brief one."

"A brief rest?" Senrid exclaimed in fake shock, looking around appraisingly. They were on a knoll shaded by a cluster of thick oak trees, around which a stream flowed, chuckling over rocks. A good place to rest. "Lazy! Sloth!"

Devon laughed, grateful for the stop, and Liere reluctantly smiled. "Am I being stupid?"

"You're tired," Senrid said. "So am I. And Devon's got to be ready to drop."

Liere's big, haunted eyes rounded in horror. "Devon, you've got to say something!"

But Senrid had made a mistake. Devon's chin lifted as she said grittily, "I'm not tired. I won't slow us down." She bent over her knapsack. "I'll get some food."

The other two sat down, both aware how important it was to Devon to divide up shares and serve them out. They fell on the bread, drank from the stream, and Liere curled up in her cloak. She meant to rest only that hour, but when sunset brought cold rain, the three stayed under the biggest oak, protected by their cloaks. While rain pattered through the last of the autumn leaves overhead they slept long and deep.

Unseen, the animals of the North Forest borderland kept silent vigil.

Chapter Twenty-Seven

It was near noon when they began to waken.

Liere opened gritty, stinging eyes, more tired in mind than in body. She scolded herself for letting her fears rule her as she picked her way down to the stream to get a drink. She *had* to keep them under better control.

Senrid was already up, soaking wet, his face a blotchy mess of white and red, his clothes plastered over his body. He was clean, but from the look of him the bath had been horribly cold.

"Chilly?" she asked, laughing a little. It felt good to laugh. When had she done it last? She couldn't remember.

"Oh, no," he exclaimed with genial sarcasm.

He stamped about barefoot, waving his socks and wringing them by turns. On a rock sat his neatly folded cloak, and on the cloak the hatpin and dyr gleamed like a little pool of starlight.

The girls enjoyed his performance. When he saw that, he spread his socks on a rock and grabbed his butter-colored hair in two handfuls. "Wish we had a knife," he said. "My hair gets any longer, I'll be sitting on it."

"It's hardly past your collar," Devon pointed out, flinging her grimy braids behind her. "That's not long."

"It is for me," Senrid exclaimed, then he puffed out his chest. "We Marlovens are tough! Our hair stays short, not long like some foppish courtier." He stretched out the front part, which, when straight, nearly reached his chin. "A curtain like this is good for hiding an ugly mug, but it sure gets in the way if you're fighting a duel."

Devon snickered as he demonstrated fighting a duel while blinded, lurching, staggering, and tumbling around. Devon laughed happily, and Senrid warmed himself up as his clothes began to dry out.

Liere looked down at herself, aware for the first time of the accumulated grime under her nails, and in the cracks of her knuckles. Grime also darkened the stitched seams of her brother's tunic, which was now too short lengthwise, but was still baggy through the body. The knees of her trousers were shiny with ground-in smears of forest moss. *I probably smell like a dirt pile*, she thought. But then dirt piles didn't smell so bad—not outside, anyway. *Ought I to have asked the morvende if they had a cleaning frame?*

She leaned over and picked up the dyr, passing it from hand to hand as she turned her attention to Devon, whose dress was also grimy at hem and seams. Her hands and neck were shadowed with dirt, but her braids lay neat and straight down her back and her dawnsinger cloak had been lovingly folded and set on a rock while she brought out and divided up their breakfast. Her expression was one of contentment.

Liere reflected that Devon, too, had a quest. It was small in relation to the world, but important to her. She wanted to take care of people.

What was that image the Guardian had shared with her when she was little, when she tried to explain what harmony in the world meant? Liere saw Devon's work as a kind of weaving made of invisible threads, golden in the realm of the spirit, bound to everyone whom she contacted: Liere, Senrid, the animals, the morvende.

Was it so for her own actions? Yes, it was, and for Senrid as well, everything he had done was a kind of weft to her own warp. And so their actions bound to others. In turn, the others' actions wove invisibly out and out, not just their aid in this quest, but their music, their art, the animals through their own actions, weaving with others yet unseen, until the world was covered by a great tapestry made up of kind acts and music and common endeavor and shared life. Art, and the making of food. Dance, and weaving cloth for clothes.

That's what she meant by harmony, Liere thought, watching the silvery, melted-ice glint of the dyr in the sunlight. *The Guardian hears it as all the voices singing together, all the way back through time.*

Liere glanced at Senrid, who sat across from Devon, eating his breakfast. She wouldn't tell him her thoughts, because she was afraid he'd think she was being pompous. But there would be time enough during the days to come.

There'd be time if Norsunder didn't find them.

Urgency squeezed invisible bands around her heart again, ending the brief respite.

She set the dyr down again and forced herself to eat her portion of the food. When she was done, she concentrated and listened for the white horses. They were not far. They seemed restless, though.

She opened her eyes again, and turned her focus to Senrid and Devon. Senrid's clothes looked damp, not soggy, his more-or-less clean hair curling away from his brow and down over his ears and collar. She was conscious of her own grimy, lank hair clumping drearily over her own collar.

Thinking about appearances?

Annoyed with herself for such a pointless waste of time, she said, "Let's go. The horses are uneasy."

Senrid's head lifted quickly and he gave her one of those assessing looks. For once she wasn't reading his emotions or even his thoughts.

She turned away to get her cloak and get a last drink of water while he put on his shoes and socks.

When she returned Senrid was pinning the dyr in his pocket. Then he slung his cloak around Devon, who looked up in surprise. "I want to finish drying out," he said. "And you got cold yesterday. Maybe two cloaks will keep the wind out."

"Okay. Thanks," Devon said, pulling her own on over Senrid's.

Senrid mounted, then lifted Devon up behind. By now it was habit. Devon settled herself, thighs gripping, hands loose.

The weight of the dyr in Senrid's pocket reminded him of the discovery he'd made earlier: that he could, in fact, hear others' thoughts, just as Liere had said.

She had not even thought to shield her reverie, and so he too experienced her image of the great tapestry, but he also saw the utterly unconscious generosity and compassion motivating her view of the world.

Just as well that she hadn't directed her thoughts at him, forcing him to respond, because he had no response. Not yet. He still didn't trust himself, or anyone else, with that kind of discourse.

So he tried constructing one of those mental wall things, and to his surprise discovered that he could shut her out. He could also shut out Devon's small, running stream of busy thoughts.

For a time he maintained it, watching the countryside around them as they progressed ever southward.

The afternoon had lengthened the shadows, turning the light to a mellow gold when Senrid sensed a change in the atmosphere. No danger in sight, but the horses' bodies signaled tension.

Senrid shifted his gaze away from the river valley below. Flat meadowlands greeny-yellow with late summer growth were dotted here and there with dark groves of trees. He scanned from horizon to horizon. Nothing.

So he scanned the sky—and got that shoulder blade crawl of danger.

A huge, dark bird wheeled overhead. Both horses saw it, their heads tossing.

"Liere?"

"You, too?"

They were near one of the clumps of young oak. The horses veered, halting beneath the spreading bare branches. Liere shut her eyes, focusing on the bird as Devon and Senrid watched in silence.

Liere tensed, then she looked up, blinking hazily. "Elevens," she whispered. "It's spying for the elevens. It's a binding spell."

Senrid said, "I wondered when they were going to get the idea of finding animals of their own to use."

"I don't know if it's looking for us," Liere began, then she saw Senrid's sarcastic face, and she summoned her strength and forced herself to make contact again.

She was used to contact with Norsunder horses, and had managed to become—not accustomed—but inured to the twisting of will she'd found, the knots of fear and anger that underlay magic-reinforced obedience.

This bird was something new, but she made contact and gave it a brief, vivid image of two white horses bearing human riders moving away to the east downriver.

The bird gave a shrieking cry and flapped away to the east.

"Let's get out of here," she muttered, struggling against the dizziness caused by the mental dislocation.

The white horses moved again, staying between hills, and zigzagging between groves of trees. Senrid had forgotten his mental wall, and Liere picked up his thoughts, relaying to the horses the idea of sticking to cover.

Clouds piled up overhead, driven by a strong and steady wind. The storm blew out of the east, ending the day's light early.

When the horses slowed again, Senrid said, "Send the next spy-bird to the west, okay? We need to bear east and get back under cover again."

"For now, let's just find a good spot to—"

Liere's voice suspended when one of the horses tossed his head.

The other sidled nervously.

"Elevens," Liere breathed.

All three scanned the sky, seeing nothing but clouds.

Senrid touched the hatpin. It didn't grow, but it gleamed silvery, as if reflecting a light-source that Senrid knew wasn't anywhere near.

He slid off the horse, then looked back at Liere and Devon, who stared down at him with twin expressions of fear.

He handed the hatpin up to Liere. "I'm going to scout around a bit. Take a look over these two hills down-valley. This thing only works if elevens are right nearby." He dug in his pocket and pulled out the dyr. "You better take this, too, because I don't want it bouncing out while I'm running and getting lost in the grass."

Liere said, "But I should—"

Senrid cut in with his old sarcasm, "You want to scout? Sure. You're so well trained."

"Danger," she said, her voice high. "Don't go into—on my behalf—"

"Look. I don't want to ride blind and trust the elevens not to find us. You shut up, keep looking in that direction over there, and if anyone pops up, you keep your hand on that pin. If it turns into a sword, ride out. I'll find you. Horse trails are not hard to follow."

"So what does scouting mean?"

"Nothing dangerous. I'm just going to sneak a quick squint down the road in that direction. If I see anything, we'll know which way to run."

Liere hesitated, looking down into Senrid's face. All she could see was a shadowed blur. She could hear nothing of his thoughts.

What he said sounded sensible, and he also sounded impatient.

"All right," she said.

Their fingers touched briefly as he slapped the dyr and the hatpin onto her palm, then he was gone.

Senrid ran low and fast up the adjacent hill. Liere, watching from between branches, saw only a faint glow on his shirt from the disappearing light, then nothing as he went to cover.

Senrid eased his way up to the crown of the hill, taking care not to create a silhouette or rustle the stiff, prickly autumn growth.

He peered out.

On the next hill a lone rider sat, motionless. Such an arrogant disregard for cover meant only one thing.

They're here! Run!

He sent the command to Liere's mind. Then he closed her off, and made a rapid plan of diversion.

He shouted and pointed away from the girls, "Get away! They're here!"

The eleven on the other hill turned his head sharply, and whistled on a piercing note. Senrid slipped down the side of the hill and began running flat out to the north. From the east came the rest of the Norsundrians, veering to close in.

Senrid lifted that inner wall, reached for Liere, and—ah! She and Devon were now just outside of the search perimeter, and galloping away fast.

Senrid laughed as he ran. Laughed for once not in bitterness, though he had no illusions about what was about to happen. If he could just keep the Norsundrians from getting the girls, he would call it a score against Siamis.

The thunder of hooves on the right made him dodge left, leaping a little stream. He ducked through a thicket, heard cursing behind him; the mounted riders were forced to ride round.

Time. He had to win her time.

Once again he veered, then doubled back and dove through the thicket again, to almost collide with a horse's chest. His face stung where prickly leaves had ripped. He rolled, nearly under the horse's hooves, leaped to his feet, and—

A hard fist clouted the back of his head from behind. He staggered, tripped, and fell with a splat.

The Norsundrians ringed him. The single dismounted one moved in with casual ease, clearly expecting to expend little effort to subdue the short, round-faced kid.

Only to find that the short, round-faced kid, denied training with swords, had been coached by the very best in contact fighting. All his speed, his unvoiced anger, drove him up with all his strength.

Palm-heel to midsection, foot to knee, doubled fists behind the ear, lightning speed and focus.

The Norsunder crashed down, rolling away to the scornful whoops of his fellows.

Senrid made a dash for the man's mount, but a grip on his ankle snapped his head back and he hit the ground hard. A heavy knee thumped down across his spine, and his hands were wrenched excruciatingly behind his back.

Pain shot across his vision. The red mixed with flaring torchlight.

"Slit his throat?" came a hard-breathing voice just behind him.

Senrid's cheek ground against crushed grass and gravel. He smelled sharp herbs, and almost sneezed.

Someone stepped near. Senrid heard the crunch of boots on gravel.

"We'll have a look."

A heave, more pain, and Senrid stood more or less on his feet. Behind him, a pair of big, strong hands held his wrists in a murderous grip. In front a tall man yanked his head back by his hair.

He stared up into a face silhouetted by torchlight.

A voice: "That's Senrid Montredaun-An. Detlev had him on a list—"

Another voice, one of command: "Siamis gave me specific orders. You four, take him back to Roth Drael."

A third: "The girl is riding southeast."

The command voice: "Pace her. But stay out of sight."

Senrid gritted his teeth.

The girls were 'escaping' straight into a trap.

Chapter Twenty-Eight

Thoroughly ashamed of herself, Liere wept as she and Devon rode at the gallop across the wide starlit meadows southward, poor Devon clutching desperately at the horse's mane as she rode alone.

Liere was angry with herself as well as ashamed. She knew that crying did no good at all, yet sobs shook her like rocks slamming her ribs, because Senrid had forgotten his mind-shield when he began to run. She'd seen in his memory that he knew what horror he was going back to yet he still ran deliberately into danger and maybe even death in order to deflect her enemies.

Would this be the first death branded forever on her conscience? The first person killed because she was weak—and the first person she'd ever met who didn't think her boring, or awkward, or incomprehensible. Or some kind of symbol.

He'd talked to *her*. Liere Fer Eider. And their talks had been *interesting*, even though they always ended up arguing. But that hadn't mattered, because she had known from the beginning—even though he hadn't—that their goals were truly the same.

He was not just interesting, he'd become a friend. Two friends in her life, and one insisted on sharing her danger, and the other had possibly thrown away his own life on her behalf.

She couldn't stop crying, hiccupping and nose running, until her chest and throat ached, and her head pounded.

The horses—great-hearts both—at last had to slow.

They'd brought the girls back to the protection of forestland.

We'll go on foot. Liere sent the words to them, along with an image of the girls walking. Even though they descended from creatures not of this world, they were still finite, and she could feel their exhaustion. No more lives would be risked on her behalf. *Thank you. Thank you.*

She slid down, and Devon wordlessly followed. They watched the horses trot away into the darkness, and then Liere, seeing Devon's anxious little face in the moonlight, forced herself to say, "I think we're safe enough from elevens now. Let's sleep."

It was the first time she'd spoken since they lost Senrid. Devon, racked by fear, felt some of her worry unknot from her bones, and she plumped down onto the grass, hugging the two cloaks around her, and the knapsack against her chest. Liere's face had gone remote again, and it was clear to Devon she wouldn't speak—wouldn't tell Devon what had happened.

Devon wasn't sure she wanted to know. Her eyes blurred and stung as she curled up right where she was.

Liere sat on the grass, then opened her right hand. She felt the ridges that the dyr had cut into her palm. The hatpin she could stick in the collar of her tunic, but the dyr she would have to carry. And rightly so, she thought bleakly. Just as she would have to carry the memory of Senrid's last, bitter thoughts as the Norsundrians closed in on him. Then he'd shut her out, and now she couldn't reach him at all.

She slept badly that night, and her mood remained bleak through the next day.

Senrid's absence galled her attempts at control in so many little ways: the sight of Devon's extra cloak; the extra food in the knapsack; the lack of conversation. The lack of someone to ask when Liere wanted to air a question, because Devon did not really comprehend what interested Liere, and would always quietly defer.

Liere worked hard to build a shield against her feelings. She had a job ahead, and she could not fail, or there would be yet more deaths on her conscience.

Halfway through the day more horses showed up, tossing their heads and sidling when Liere tried to warn them away. Devon's unspoken but strongly felt relief when she gave in reminded her that Devon was only just turned ten—Liere's eleventh birthday had passed unnoticed as well—and she'd made a long, hard journey for barely comprehensible reasons.

Devon could ride now, even without reins. Senrid had obviously taught her as they rode south, and Liere hadn't even noticed. Now the sight of Devon's straight back, her legs tight against the horse, was yet another reminder of Senrid, a sickening reminder that forced her to realize she didn't just feel guilty, she missed his company—she who'd never looked back when she left her own family.

The girls rode the rest of the way to the Fereledria, where they spent a couple of days in safety. The snows did not hurt them, and they slept well, always waking to oat-cakes, cheese, and fruits from somewhere far away.

Rainbow figures shimmered at the edges of vision. Liere sensed the dyr resonating in her hand to the sound of faint singing, always nearly inaudible, like the echo in a morvende cavern after the voices have stopped; the boundaries of time and space blurred. The dream realm was nigh. It was also safe, and so she reached for Lilith the Guardian, to tell her she had the dyr. The Guardian was very far away, and Liere suspected from the shortness of the exchange that she was not in a place of safety.

Liere and Devon left the Fereledria with regret, descending to the very western boundary of Wnelder Vee in the deep, green-layered cove forest that had been growing there almost since the world was made. It was wild, beautiful country—morvende and dawnsinger country—and despite the rich tangle of ancient growth those peoples made certain that the next few days' travel were easy ones.

But Liere felt she could not seek or stay with individuals, for they'd become targets, just as she was. She had to make for the cities under the enchantment. Towns. Lots of people. Siamis would never find her there.

Yes, that was a good plan.

And so, on the ninth day, the girls were taken downriver under cover of darkness to the border trade town of Loss Harthadaun.

Rel, surrendering to a sharpened sense of urgency, left his ship when they landed on the coast of Everon. He was granted a day's leave, but he left his pay, which was easier than explanations, and walked inland until he came to woodland.

Near a certain path he left a sign, and by nightfall he was met by three of the Knights of Dei.

Rel knew his foster-father, Raneseh of Tser Mearsies, had had some connection in Everon in his past, and so he'd visited this kingdom after his adventures in Sartor. He'd made friends, had helped against the Norsundrians in small ways, and had found himself invited into the Knights, a rare honor given to few, and none (in so far as he was aware) who were not natives of Everon.

He'd very nearly accepted, except for one thing: he couldn't swear to stay in Everon for the rest of his days. It had probably been the toughest decision of his life so far, something he'd not told anyone.

He sat around a campfire with two young men and a young woman, friends with whom he'd trained during a spring in better times.

"The situation is grim enough," Enthold, the oldest, said. "We're limited in movement since we're targets—"

"People reporting you?" Rel asked.

"On sight," Seiran said, her face somber. "It's a part of the enchantment."

"So we've been relying heavily on allies to find out what's going on."

"Which is?"

"A child, from Ther Doleh just to the south, who reportedly has the means to break Siamis's magic. The very latest news is that she recently escaped Siamis in the northlands and is making her way down toward us."

"Then she'll have to reach Wnelder Vee first," Seiran put in.

"The elevens will be on the watch," Rel said, as the familiar inward prod caused the back of his neck to grip with urgency. Each time he'd acted on it, he'd found someone in need.

This time was the strongest, almost a compulsion to find this girl and aid her. No, not a compulsion. A compulsion would leave him no choice. He felt the need for his intervention with a strength that could be called exigency, but his desire to heed it was very much his own.

Enthold gave his head a shake. "The enemy are not searching, they're waiting."

"Where?" Rel asked.

"On the outskirts of the capital city. Outside some towns. We three are supposed to get into Naer by morning. We shall ride tonight."

Why would the elevens gather outside towns and cities unless preparing for attack? But why attack pacified, enchanted civilians? Again he felt that inner tightening, and he thought of his Norsunder uniform, safely residing at the bottom of his pack.

"What's the girl's name?" he asked.

"They're calling her Sartora."

Rel began to see some connections with earlier rumors, and he said, "They'll hit when she arrives."

"That's what Commander Dei says." Enthold rubbed his jaw. "We don't know where she is. We have our orders in case she bypasses towns in Wnelder Vee and progresses through Everon on her way to her home."

"Where are you strongest?"

"Where the Norsundrians are, along the coast."

Rel nodded. "Any chance of a mount?"

Enthold stared across the fire at Rel. There was no expression in the deep-set dark eyes.

Enthold remembered a conversation with Commander Roderic Dei, after it became known that the commander had invited Rel (with King Berthold's full concurrence) to join the Knights, and that Rel had declined.

The younger Knights had been a little resentful at first. Not surprising, since the group was intensely tightknit, proud, and loyal. Roderic had said: *You are to treat Rel the Traveler as if he were one of us. Teach him the access signals, and always make him welcome, sharing with him as you would a brother or sister Knight. In all true ways he is one of us, and may someday be greater.*

Enthold said, "Seiran and Harn. You two have ridden double before, and we're almost at Naer."

Seiran shrugged, and Harn grinned and looked resigned. They'd expected to be the double since they were youngest and the lightest in build.

"Thanks," Rel said.

"Fare well," was the response, and very soon they all parted.

As soon as he was alone with his new mount—one of the white horses, rare everywhere else in the world but here—Rel said, "Take me to Sartora."

A year ago he might have felt foolish assuming that animals had any interest in the doings of humans, outside of their own immediate connections. But that was before he'd been led successfully in and out of Norsunder's impregnable Base by a little black cat. Though he still didn't understand that, he felt the communication was worth a try.

The horse's ears twitched, and the animal moved westward.

It took Rel a week to cross Everon while bands of heavy rain pounded the countryside, and the Norsundrians watched the roads in and out of every major town or city.

At the end of the week he rode, under cover of a heavy storm, down an ancient and treacherous dawnsinger trail into the border town of Loss Harthadaun, and only then did the sense of urgency loosen its grip.

He still did not know why, or what he was expected to do, but he was definitely where he was supposed to be.

Senrid's second trip north to Roth Drael was a dramatic enough contrast to the first to underscore the difference between lighters' and Norsundrians' attitudes toward their fellow beings.

They moved fast, the Norsundrians dividing night watches two and two; they rode armed at all times, with bows tight and arrows nocked, their eyes constantly sweeping above and below for targets. No animals attempted rescues this journey. Senrid never saw a glimpse of any kind of life except for silent shrubs and trees. He also felt the Norsundrians' disappointment, for they'd looked forward to some target practice against bird or beast or whatever came at them.

The man Senrid dropped during that brief fight obviously felt that a solid week of bullying was hardly enough to even the score. Orders for a live prisoner to be delivered restricted his creativity, but he made up for that by constant petty cruelties.

The weather seemed to conspire against Senrid as well. Autumn was edging into winter, and a long succession of cold, dreary days with intermittent driving rain kept Senrid's teeth chattering and his body shivering.

The ropes round his wrists chafed into infected nastiness, but the Norsundrians had just sufficient respect for a short unarmed kid having decked an armed warrior to keep his hands bound behind him while he rode, and while he slept. Or tried to sleep. The only time they cut him loose was when they remembered to give him a meager portion of their trail food, which was mainly comprised of stale bread, dried-out turkey-jerky, and hard cheese, for there was no one to steal from, and trail food did not get any fresher in blackweave packs. The meals (or Senrid's inclusion in them) were infrequent enough to make him grateful for what he got, but he did think with regret of those music-graced meals among morvende and dawnsingers, and with more regret of peaceful meals sitting under trees with Liere, arguing freely back and forth.

He never spoke. He knew the rules governing the treatment of prisoners: there weren't any, except to deliver the victim more or less alive. Anything he said—anything at all—would only result in more torments. Those were going to happen anyway, for Norsundrians did not sing or tell stories when they camped, but if he was boring the bully sessions were shorter, and orders insured that he'd survive.

He was determined to survive.

When he didn't respond to goads and taunts, the Norsundrians decided that the lighters had enchanted his mind into rocklike stupidity. Tit for tat. Senrid treasured up all his sarcasm for the inevitable interview with their leader.

Eight and a half long days he endured until they rode at last into Roth Drael.

The sun rimmed the eastern horizon when Liere felt the blankets lifted from where she crouched behind a load of barrels. The rain had gone. The air was cold and clean and clear.

The owner of the trade raft silently loaded Liere's and Devon's arms with rolls of cloth, which they carried carefully to the loading area.

When Liere straightened up, the young woman who owned the raft said in a low voice, "Welcome to Loss Harthadaun."

Then she turned away—as Liere had requested.

We cannot aid you in the political lands, Arand the morvende had said to her two days before. *In our lands, so far, Norsunder hasn't the strength to attack, and we will protect you here.*

But I cannot stay. I have to break Siamis's enchantment, and I don't want anyone going into danger with me, Liere had answered. *I must go alone into the city to break the enchantment.*

She gazed at what looked to her inexperienced eyes like a huge city, built along the hills that bordered the lake, and thought: Loss Harthadaun. 'Daun.' It was part of Senrid's name, too.

Her mind sorted through the words in Old Sartoran that the Guardian had given her, and she traced what seemed to be its development: once Venn, the word had come south as 'davan', shortening over centuries to 'daun', always meaning 'dweller'. She gazed up at the mellow golden stone buildings, the reddish timber bridges and upper stories. Pale, almost peachy golden stone. She remembered Senrid's memory-images of Choreid Dhelerei, his capital, so very far away, on another continent. Golden stone there, too. Was there a shared history? Some day, she hoped, she could find out.

She walked silently beside Devon, trying to look like a responsible big brother to any unfriendly eyes that might be watching.

At least—so far—she knew Senrid was alive. The contact had been brief, inadvertent, made on the edge of sleep when she had been thinking about him, and it was very unpleasant. Senrid couldn't maintain it (he might not have even been aware of it) and she didn't dare prolong it. But it had been enough for her to discern that he was angry, and miserable. But alive. A surge of joy bubbled inside her, followed by fear.

Stop that. Emotion is weakness.

She watched her scuffed shoes treading the worn cobblestones leading up into the town. She and Devon had talked about how to walk, to look like the enchanted people. She watched her plodding steps, not meeting anyone's eyes. Her brother's shoes—so large and uncomfortable when she left South End—had molded to her feet, the once-sturdy soles now worn thin.

She'd hacked off her hair again, when the morvende let them stay overnight in a cave. She'd used one of the finely homed morvende knives. She didn't want to know what it looked like. Such things ought not to matter. What did matter was that she and Devon were clean again. It felt good.

"Where now?" Devon whispered.

Liere blinked. Her reverie had carried them up a street. She peered over the roof tops, toward the highest building, with two smallish, rounded brick towers. "That way."

She didn't dare say 'town center' aloud, not in case some enemy—human or animal—was listening.

No one paid them any attention as they made their way past gardens and larger houses to the Guildhall, which their rafter had said was where the Magister lived and worked.

The central square was cobbled with patterns in colored stone, washed clean from the recent rain. Opposite was the tall building with the brick towers, its front decorated with handsome columns and carvings and colored-glass windows contributed by all the guilds.

The sky had partially cleared by the time Rel reached the quiet streets where the artisans lived. He found what he was looking for worked into the wooden carving around the door to a glazier's shop.

He passed inside, and found a gangling youth stacking frames. The youth looked up, his eyes incurious.

"I am a cousin," Rel said.

The boy looked away. Family members were compassed by the enchantment; strangers caused the people to drop their work and seek someone to report to. Rel disliked using people this way, but he would not harm them, and his errand was urgent.

He wondered if they remembered anything from day to day. If they'd remember being enchanted. If they would ever know. Somehow that seemed worse, as if Norsunder had robbed them of a part of their lives.

But then, that was the idea.

Upstairs he found a locked door, and tapped softly, a pattern of three-two-three.

The lock clicked. The door cracked, and an eye peered out. Then the door was flung wide, and the long, heavy-featured face of Roderic Dei, Commander of the Knights, relaxed into pleasure and relief. "Rel. Ah, it's good to see you. Come in."

"Commander Dei, you've got what look like strike troops lining up along the river road into town."

"I know. I saw them. Just came in from the north." The commander indicated his mud-caked boots and dusty clothing.

The other two people in the room, a young morvende and an older woman, exchanged glances.

"Is this girl everyone is looking for here?" Rel asked.

"Sartora," the morvende said. "She is in the city. I just came to tell you," and to Rel, "I arrived moments before you did. She entered just after the sunrise."

"Why is she here? What will she do?" the commander asked, turning to the morvende. "I tell you, my mind misgives me, this making war through children, and through the minds of our leaders."

"She will try to lift the spell, if rumor is right," the woman said. "If the spell is bound to leaders, then she will go to the Magister."

"Can you do anything?" Commander Dei asked.

She lifted her hands. "I have been unable to use magic for nearly a year, that is, magic of any consequence. Each month their control is a little stronger, and there are more traps for us. We do what we can to unravel the minor spells, but the great ward preventing transfer, and other major magics, holds. We're spread too thin, with the battle against the rifts in the south."

The commander said, "I can't raise an enchanted populace to fight."

Rel considered what this meant, and nodded.

"I'd better get over to the Guildhall," Commander Dei said, then paused. "If I have need of you, will you be within contact?"

"I'm here to help," Rel said.

"Then bide until I scout out the situation. We'll plan after."

The commander and the morvende descended the stairs, the morvende's bare feet soundless.

Rel looked around as the woman bent over her magic books, a pen thrust behind her ear. Her gray-streaked brown braid slipped over her shoulder, unnoticed.

"Transfer," the woman muttered. "If there was a way to . . ."

Rel walked out quietly so as not to disturb her concentration. He leaned against a narrow wooden balcony and watched the skinny youth below, who moved methodically about his tasks with unswerving focus.

No one noticed Liere and Devon as they walked inside the Guildhall.

Devon admired the inlaid wood, the great murals celebrating historical moments in bright color, with noble figures and fine details, all surrounded by ivy-leaf gilding.

"I'm trying to make contact," Liere whispered. "It's so horrible. Their minds are like fish, slithering away. But maybe I can catch one long enough to get us to the person I have to find."

Devon watched people stare vaguely, then look away again. It was creepy. Just as creepy was the unseeing way that Liere walked, her feet fumbling blindly for the stairs. Devon took her hand and guided her up the giant curved stair.

At the top Liere sighed, swayed, then she opened her eyes. She moved on and stopped at each of the tall, carved doors along the balcony.

"Here." She laid her hand on a fine brass latch, then pulled from her tunic the little cloth bag that the morvende had given her. She dug the dyr out and opened the door.

A tall, plump old man with a snowy, spreading beard stared out the window.

Liere walked to him, her hand held out. The dyr caught light from the window, looking like melted silver on her palm. When his eyes seemed to focus on it, Liere stumbled hastily through her spell, the words sounding blurred to Devon's ears.

"Did you wish to see me?" the man asked, sounding like all the other enchanted people.

Liere began her spell again, her voice shaking. The man's gaze roamed from Devon to Liere in disinterest, and then to the glinting silver thing on Liere's hand. His brows quirked in puzzlement, and he leaned forward, staring as if from a very long distance. His expression changed from confusion to wonder, and then to a perplexed impatience.

"Hai!" he exclaimed. "What's this? I haven't time for children!"

"The Norsundrians," Liere said.

"What?" The white brows snapped together in a quick frown.

"They're outside the town," Liere said.

The man stood up angrily. "Here? In Loss Harthadaun? We can't have that! Where are the Knights? Lam? Lam! I need to send a message to the King. At once!"

A young scribe ran in, his arms full of papers. "Oh, sir, I—"

The white-bearded man looked past the girls and the scribe, and his expression changed again, to relief. "Roderic Dei," he said. "You are most welcome indeed. This child tells me there are Norsundrians outside our very gates!"

Relief washed through the commander when he saw the two children standing near the magisterial desk. The taller one dressed like a boy watched him through wide eyes, their expression a compound of patience and joy and apprehension, though marked by the dark circles of stress.

"Wait," he said to the girls. "Wait here, please."

"Commander, what is to be done?"

The commander said, "By now I suspect they have ringed us entirely, except perhaps from the water."

"Us? Why?"

"You've been enchanted," Commander Dei explained, lifting a hand to indicate not just the Magister, but the entire city. "That girl over there just freed you. You and all the people who owe you allegiance."

"How? Lam! Do you know aught of this?"

"No, sir." The scribe looked totally bewildered.

"Roderic, are you certain that it is not you who was enchanted? I surely would be aware if—hai! Summon Mistress Hollem."

"She's at work trying to break Norsunder's magic," the commander said. "I just now came from her."

The Guild Magister pressed his lips together, then he said in a less forceful voice, "Why would they line up against us? We have no warriors here. We are a trade town."

"They seek this child, we suspect." The commander pointed back at the silent girl. "They may just be waiting for her to leave Loss Harthadaun. It was not just you who was enchanted. It exists all over the country. The King and Queen. And all over the world. This girl—the morvende call her Sartora—is going to break it."

Liere flinched, and Devon bit her lip.

"Ho. Hai! I think you had better come within my chamber here, for every question you answer raises ten more. Much too akin to the weeds in my garden, when I try to tend my starliss! You, Lam, make this child comfortable—here, where is the boy?"

Liere and Devon had slipped out onto the landing. The commander spotted the scribe standing several paces away, talking with excited gestures to a growing crowd of people. Obviously spreading the word.

Liere's insides quaked with fear. What to do now? Devon clutched her arm, terrified at the crowd of loud, talking, arguing adults.

Enough, the commander decided. He would not issue orders to this child, who was apparently a great mage and whose arrival had occasioned a rare visit from the morvende, but he wanted to see her safe.

"I shall return shortly," he said to the girls, hoping that that was sufficient to keep them in one place until he and the Magister and the local mage could agree on the best course of action.

But plans seemed impossible to make. Gone was the nerveless order of the enchantment days. Every person must be heard. *Celebration!* That was the word he heard most often. By the time he was halfway down the crammed stairs, the Magister's great, booming voice reached over the hubbub: "I proclaim today a holiday—a day of freedom!"

A great cheer rang up the walls and rattled the windows. The commander smiled grimly. That loud voice had had at least as much to do as the man's political acumen in holding onto Guild Magister so long.

The commander spotted the two girls, and fought his way down the surging tide of people. "Sartora," he shouted. "Don't go anywhere until—"

She vanished from view.

"Where is she?" he yelled.

"Guest chamber!" Lam yelled back, jumping up and down to be seen over the heads. "The little one was frightened. Too crowded!"

Good. That kept them safely in one place.

Now to do something about the Norsundrians.

Chapter Twenty-Nine

Senrid looked around as well as he could without moving his head, counting elevens, noting positions and possible escape routes—not that he saw any of the latter. The signs of a more permanent camp indicated that Siamis had augmented his forces, or else he'd called all his searchers in for new orders. Senrid counted tents, estimating their size, and counted sentries at the inner perimeter.

There were a lot of elevens, obviously bored here in the wilderness, where from the slackness of their grip on their weapons, the careless looks at the unchanging forest, they had not only never seen any worthy targets, but did not expect to see any.

Near the two-towered ruin of a palace, Senrid spotted the off-worlders. The Warren girls were playing some kind of game with rocks and twigs, listless and unfocussed. Frederic sat with his legs dangling on a broken column, and Deirdre leaned against it. All four looked up at him, their faces wearing the same exact expression of incurious blankness. It made his skin crawl.

Then one of the Norsundrians pushed Senrid inside, to the room where Liere had performed the magic freeing the rings. Senrid thought of his empty pocket and his lip curled.

The room was different. The few remaining furnishings not broken up for firewood had been shoved back against the white walls. Only the great round table remained in the center of the room. On it was a map dotted with flags and markers.

Senrid looked down at it, rapidly assessing—

"Who is this sorry spectacle?"

All heads turned sharply. The Norsundrians flanking Senrid faded back and Siamis moved around the table, giving Senrid an amused up-and-down. Senrid stared at the Norsundrian commander who had managed to enchant a good part of the world, and was surprised to find someone not all that many years older than he was.

As the leader of his capture party stated who he was and where he'd been found, Senrid looked away, angry and furious. Siamis knew very well who he was. He drew in a breath and held hard onto his mind-shield.

"Your friend Liere," Siamis said pleasantly, "is right about here."

A long finger reached past Senrid and tapped the map at the northwestern corner of Wnelder Vee.

Senrid glanced up over his shoulder. For a moment he and the infamous Siamis studied one another. Siamis smiled faintly, his gaze steady—inviting Senrid to meet it. Senrid turned his back.

Siamis said, "Noliar."

Senrid heard a knife pulled from a sheath, and braced himself. The eleven named Noliar did not grab him by the neck, but by the wrists. A quick saw and Senrid's hands were free. He flexed them, trying not to wince at the ache of lacerated flesh, of muscles too long confined.

So Siamis was in the mood for talk, not blood.

Senrid would rather have postponed this interview. He was ravenously hungry and desperately tired. It took all his fading energy to hold onto that mind-shield. He knew what lay ahead. The four kids outside were plain enough testimony to the efficacy of Siamis's spell.

It was either that or execution.

Siamis waved a hand in casual dismissal, and Senrid heard the ring of heels in the direction of the door.

"Have you any questions for me, Senrid?" Siamis asked.

Senrid said nothing.

"You've been elusive until now. What prompted you to run into a trap?" The amused voice was edged with contempt.

So it would be at home, from anyone who heard.

A year ago, Senrid would have reacted exactly the same.

"Save me a longer trip," he said finally, unlimbering some of his stored-up sarcasm, and hoping to provoke a hint of Siamis's plans.

Siamis cooperatively said, "Your young friend Liere Fer Eider is not going to enjoy the trap she's walking into, I fear. But you figured that out, did you not? Why didn't she listen? The taint of the Marloven taste for war?"

"That and the praiseworthy desire to snap her fingers under your nose," Senrid retorted.

"Irresistible," Siamis agreed, still smiling. He added gently, "But it's going to cost."

The lack of threat was more sinister than the most graphic bully speech would have been. Senrid swallowed convulsively, his cracked lips thinning despite how much it hurt.

Siamis continued, "Detlev maintains that you exhibit possible signs of the family gift for strategic thinking. If that is true, perhaps I can use your gifts myself before I accede to his request to send you along southward. Look here, and tell me what you think."

Family gift? Accede to his request?

Senrid knew he was not being complimented. Almost dizzy with exhaustion, wary, he looked down at the map, where Siamis's long hands swept over familiar continents and political boundaries. "Settled first were physical locations for the old rifts, as well as the new rift we're creating. These sites await only the access spells. . . . "

The voice was warm, pleasant, instructive. Senrid watched the hands, noted the callus-hardened palms. The voice—the voice—

Alarm zapped through Senrid. Tiredness was no excuse for rank stupidity: of course the mind-shield was not enough. He wrenched his gaze from the map, and fixed his attention on the middle button of Siamis's shirt.

" . . . areas of potential military uprisings. . ."

No. Close out the voice. Concentrate on the button. Wooden round hollowed-out shank, little holes at each end, white thread.

" . . . and the final step will be to consolidate all the spells, and at the same time to use that power to force the rift into permanence, and I think you know how it's most effectively achieved. I'm afraid that we've just suffered a setback down south, which is going to cause some realignment on both sides. Since lighters value symbolism, I prefer my original plan, which is to proceed in Bereth Ferian . . ."

The voice had caught him again. Desperately Senrid ground one of his wrists against the edge of the table. Blisters and scabs broke, and hot blood trickled down his palm, but he welcomed the pain. He concentrated —and he felt his mind lock behind that wall of pain.

He could no longer hear the voice. The words, meaningless as rain, fell around his ears.

The triumph did not last long.

A hand grasped his chin and forced it up. His aching head rocked back, and briefly, just briefly, he met Siamis's steady, humorous gaze. "Very good! We'll try again presently," he said. "For the moment I have other business awaiting my attention." And then, in a hard voice, a singular tone that numbed nerves and seized control of Senrid's body from within, Siamis said, "In there. Now."

Senrid's nerves flared white-hot then cold. His body jerked around and plunged through an arched doorway, into the empty room where he and Liere and Devon had freed the dyr. Then he abruptly collapsed on the floor.

That wasn't the enchantment, it was a voice of command, of control so calculated it got between your own mind and your physical self. *I will learn that voice,* Senrid vowed to himself. *I will learn it, and no one else will ever use it on me again.*

He forced himself to his feet, wincing against aching skull and joints. Though every muscle, nerve, and bone throbbed, he forced himself to pace back and forth, back and forth. He essayed the arched doorway, but backed up hastily when his bones and teeth hummed and he perceived the dark sheen of a vicious ward. Not the protective ward he'd previously sensed, but something new, strong, and made by lethal dark magic.

He looked up. The broken ceiling was at least the height of three men overhead. Smooth walls, no way to reach that promising hole.

No windows.

No escape.

He could not sleep, he dared not, for he knew he would wake up like those kids poking around outside.

As the light disappeared Siamis worked, steadily, and then at last, haloed in the light of a glowglobe, Siamis sat down and put his head on his hand in a posture that reminded Senrid of Liere when she'd done long distance contacts.

Senrid swayed, forced himself upright, and watched.

Chapter Thirty

In the glazier's shop, the apprentice, a boy a couple years younger than Rel, abruptly looked up. Blinked. Then he threw down his etching tool and bounded to the door to gaze up at the sky.

When he turned back, he put his hands on his hips and surveyed the shop. His lips were pursed, his brow furrowed. As if he'd lost or forgotten something.

Then he glanced up at Rel. Friendly brown eyes rounded in surprise. "Hey! Who're you?"

"I'm Rel, a traveler."

For the first time in weeks, Rel received a normal response—curiosity, even excitement. " . . . you're big enough. Are you going for a Knight?" the boy demanded. "My sister did, and I want to someday, if I can just get better with my archery and my . . ."

Rel listened to the boy babble on, letting the incoherent family history wash over him. It was almost as if a year's worth of conversation, of reaction, of activity had to free itself all at once from some corner of his mind.

Rel was released when the boy spotted a friend through the window, and ran off to talk to him. "Mind watching the shop?" the boy asked over his shoulder as he disappeared out the door. "Tell any custom to come back later!"

Rel lifted a hand in assent and walked slowly downstairs. He wished he'd been able to keep the white horse as he leaned on the counter, studying the glazier's tools with mild interest. So far, he'd never posed as a glassmaker.

He was examining glass containers of intensely colored liquids when the front door opened and Commander Dei entered, looking grim. "Not out celebrating?" he asked.

"Celebrating?" Rel repeated.

"You're the only one who isn't. It's like they've all turned into children again."

"I've just been put in charge of this shop." Rel gestured.

"There's no controlling them. The Magister is going to post notice that no one can leave town. I hope that will be sufficient to keep those warriors out there at bay."

"Think they're waiting for Sartora to come out?"

"What else can it be? Watching not just the roads but the countryside. But why? There's no tactical advantage to attacking a market town full of civilians who aren't going anywhere, just as there's no need for hundreds to grab one child."

Rel, thinking of the number of those strike troops, said reluctantly, as if speaking might make the horror of his speculation into reality, "There's an emotional advantage."

The commander paused two steps up the stairs, and looked back, his mouth grim. "This Siamis does tend to use that, doesn't he? But it wouldn't be a war, it would be—"

"A slaughter," Rel said. "And a warning."

Commander Dei bounded up the stairs. "Mistress Hollem!"

Senrid kept up his pacing, but felt the increasing weight of weariness in all his joints and muscles, and especially in his mind. It was a weariness so deep that surrender was not a choice, it was inevitable: his body was going to give out.

Siamis sat motionless, alone, in the big room. None of the Norsundrians were in sight.

The door shimmered with ward-magic.

. . .at the same time to use that power to force the rift into permanence, and I think you know how it's most effectively achieved.

Gripped by the sick anger of helplessness, Senrid stared at the ward-magic, wondering if whatever the ward did to those who tried to cross it was less horrible than the end Siamis intended for him. *Coward! Do it fast—*

He was nerving himself when he heard a soft "Psst!"

Had to be one of the Norsundrians tormenting him.

"Senrid." A whisper.

A boy's whisper.

"Don't think on us."

A familiar voice—in the Leroran language.

The desperation in the voice convinced him, though he admitted to himself he was ready to believe anything, risk anything, for he had nothing more to lose.

So he obligingly pretended that he was going to be rescued. Of course it was totally fake, but why not pretend? So he pretended to look up at the jagged ceiling, and lo, a rope made of woven vines was descending.

A rope. From familiar hands. And beyond the hole, a familiar face: squarish, framed by overlong black hair, and spring green eyes.

All pretense! Pretense.

I'm daydreaming. Leander Tlennen-Hess is not really here. Just pretend, that's it.

Now he was going to imagine jumping up and climbing hand over hand up the rope. Oh, he imagined his hands hurt, but he'd done this kind of rope climbing every morning at home ever since he was six, and anyway if his hands gave out he'd use his teeth, his toes, anything that got him up, and away, where Siamis could not enchant away his brains and his will, and force him to end his own life by using his magical knowledge to open the rift for Norsunder to pour into the world.

Two very different hands would now reach down and grasp his arms, hauling him up onto the roof, where slanting rain instantly wetted him to the skin. Rain? Why didn't it reach the room below? Well, that was part of the daydream!

And here, sure enough, was his old enemy, Leander Tlennen-Hess.

Pretense! Hold onto it! *Leander is not real, and neither is what's happening . .*
.

And so Senrid wound himself deeper into the daydream, into the sense of unreality that paralyzed mind and thought, as Leander and a tall, strong girl with heavy dark braids helped him down a broken wall and then—by degrees—into the blackness of a forest.

Mistress Hollem shoved, elbowed, and hip-bumped her way straight to the Magister.

Once she reached him, a few words convinced him to rescind his holiday and declare an emergency, but no one stayed around to hear it.

She came back to report, "You cannot pour the wine back into the bottle when it's been spilled. We'll have to go out and talk to people face to face."

The commander said tiredly, "I don't think many will listen. Especially those already half drunk."

"They probably won't," Mistress Hollem said, "but children will."

They separated off, Roderic to the houses, Rel along the city streets, and Mistress Hollem to the town's small school and to the guild training building—everywhere there were prentices. They ordered the children to go to the old tunnels behind the quarry, as they'd been trained.

All the rest of the day the three worked, talking to everyone they could, and asking them to spread the word to friends, relatives, neighbors: Get out of town! *Now.* By the water, or through the old tunnels behind the quarry, which opened onto rough country.

As the sun sank westward, its light washed into gray by another brief storm, Rel began to feel the futility of his efforts. For every person he convinced to stop celebrating and leave town, five laughed him off, or offered him food or drink and turned away to resume dancing in the streets.

But he kept at it until long after dark, until no one would even listen. People were too triumphant, too angry, too determined to show those soulsuckers outside the city just what celebration meant. Too drunk to listen.

He stopped when a sozzled baker handed him a freshly baked chicken pie. No one was giving him the chance to finish a sentence. It was time to give up, and find those children. Make sure they were safe.

As he ate his pie, he wove through the crowd. He heard Commander Dei shouted down by a carpenter who roared, "Whadder ya worried about? That little girl mage'll wave her hands and winkle away any damned elevens who dare to poke their noses inside the town walls!"

A few jutted their chins, and took up martial stances as they yelled variations on, "Let 'em come. I'll show 'em enchantment."

Darkness shrouded the sky, stars gleaming into existence above, as below, in windows and open doors, candles glowed with golden color. The light spread as bonfires flamed up in the streets. The cool, rain-washed air carried happy voices taking up old songs, or laughing and clapping to the beat. Silhouettes danced around the fires.

The eleventh hour was nigh. The urgent sense that Rel must find Sartora was so strong he could not stop walking, looking, listening.

He started across one of the streets leading to the town square. The dancers and singers limned in torchlight reminded him King Carlael of Colend—usually urbane, elegant, chillingly remote—staring, his eyes so wide Rel could see the sun reflected in his black pupils. *I can't fight this kind of war.*

Leander tried to shake off the shock caused by his first glimpse of Senrid. He had to get Senrid safely away while Siamis was busy doing whatever it was he did when he sat like that.

He and Dtheldevor had gotten pretty good at concentrating on a stone or a tree or a blade of grass when they moved in and out between the steadily less vigilant sentries for spy trips. Siamis was either surrounded by Norsundrians, or else inaccessible in the room beyond the magic ward. They could see him, they could hear him, but they couldn't—yet—get at him.

Leander led the way back to their new hideout. They'd had to let the horses go, for they were too hard to keep hidden, and bored Norsundrians often tramped through the forest hoping for target practice. They'd found so few they hadn't yet figured out they only got targets when a diversion was needed, and those targets knew how to evade attackers, drawing them deep into the worst, thorniest thickets where a bow could hardly be drawn.

Leander's new camp was the best yet, a real cave. Here they could risk a fire, at least while the storm was bad. The inevitable search once Senrid was discovered missing would be slow while the rain lasted.

They tramped inside and Dtheldevor whooshed in relief. "I know I need a bath, but blast their souls! Not by rain, and not until I get me some soup!"

She looked at the short blond boy with interest. He was in terrible shape, so it didn't surprise her that the boy just stared stupidly at the ground.

Dtheldevor waited while Leander skillfully started the fire, which he'd laid out before they left. She appreciated how he'd thought up their rescue, planning the rope thing out in his head while they moved through the forest. She hadn't seen him get all the vines. Suddenly he just had them, coiled round his arm: it was she who bound them into a sturdy rope, something anybody on shipboard was skilled at.

After Siamis put the boy in the room, Dtheldevor would have been all for attacking from the front, despite all those blasted warriors, even though she knew the likelihood of winning was just about zero. *No. Wait. I know a better way,* Leander had said. Same way he insisted they not attack Siamis when he was sitting in the room all alone, his eyes closed. Easy target that he looked, he was protected by wards. Dtheldevor could see their shimmer.

Now Leander studied the boy as if he didn't know what to do next.

Dtheldevor peered into Senrid's vacant face. "Well," she said. "He's lookin' like some of 'em used to look at home. He have any smarts?"

"Yes," said Leander.

"Then let's try this." Dtheldevor opened her hand, and dealt Senrid a ringing slap across the face.

"Don't—" Leander began.

"Too late," Dtheldevor said cheerfully.

Senrid staggered backwards, arms wheeling, and hit the ground. Then he looked up, his eyes wide and mouth tight with anger. "Who did that?"

Dtheldevor smiled with satisfaction. "I did." And when he tensed, she added, "Wanta make something of it?"

"Don't try," Leander cut in, almost laughing. "You could dice him easy enough with your sword, but you'll be sorry if you tangle with his hands."

"Uh?" Dtheldevor said doubtfully, eyeing Senrid.

"He's small but he's quick, and a lot stronger than you'd think," Leander said. "He nearly drowned me once, and you can see how much taller I am. Speaking of water. Where's our pan? I want to brew up some of that summer-leaf while the storm lasts."

Dtheldevor cast an eye over Senrid's scrawny body, then shrugged. She'd learned long ago not to underestimate anyone. "Maybe so," she said, to see how Senrid responded. "But I could give him a mighty good thumping first."

Senrid said, "I don't doubt it, judging from the example you just bestowed upon my handsome visage—" He had to stop here because Dtheldevor snorted loudly. "And when I think how close I came to . . ." He realized then that he was babbling. Waves of tiredness wrung down his body, making him dizzy.

Leander held out a cup of water. Senrid took it gratefully, sucked it down, then he dropped back flat on the dirt, closed his eyes, and dropped promptly into sleep.

"Ho," Dtheldevor said, watching Senrid snore. "I couldn'ta done that."

"Nope." Leander stuck his finger in the pan of water. "One thing for sure, he'll wake up hungry. I don't know how long he was a prisoner, but they obviously didn't stand him to any banquets." He rubbed his chin as he looked down at Senrid's open mouth. "He's changed. Last summer he would have tried to murder you, tired as he was."

"You changed, too." Dtheldevor leaned against a moldering hunk of gnarled tree branch, her hands in her pockets. "In that country we was in, what, Mearsies Heili? Anyhow you was a rule hound. Order. Didn't think I could stick travelin' wi'ye."

"Feeling was mutual. Opposite reason."

"Then how come yer still here?" Dtheldevor grinned wickedly. "I been around too long to change."

"Because I changed," Leander said, laughing. "Come on, let's scout out some grub before the search is on."

Dtheldevor moved to the entrance to the cave. "Tell ye what. I'm a-goin' back to see ol' Siamis's mug when he discovers our boy is up an' missin'. No action, just nosin'."

"See about some extra eats while you're at it," Leander said.

"At me home port, the question in tough times was, who'll we snaffle it from. Here it's where," Dtheldevor observed, then disappeared into the rainy night.

Liere jerked awake.

"Fire! Town's on fire!"

The voice was powered by a psychic load of terror that clove through Liere's head like an invisible sword.

On the mental plane she sensed a jumble of terrified sleepers wakening, then caught someone's shock-stilled sight of ordered groups of Norsundrians riding with deliberate intent toward the Guildhall.

It's me they're after.

She flung off the quilt and landed barefoot. Where were her clothes? Tiredness confused her. She'd had a bath, but someone had taken her clothes away, saying they'd be mended by morning.

Move, move. Get out, save lives. They are after YOU. Her inner voice chattered.

Her dyr bag thumped against her ribs, and chill made her flesh go bumpy as she dug feverishly through the trunk in the room.

You can have my grandson's room, the Magister had said. *He's away in Ferdrian, studying at the scribe school.*

A boy. Liere did not want to deal with gowns, after a year of trousers. She found clean clothing and wrestled into it with shaking fingers. Then she dashed into Devon's room.

The girl sat up in bed, her eyes huge with fear and tiredness.

"They're after me," Liere said, voice quavering. "Get dressed. We've got to get out right now—"

Devon sprang out of bed and pulled on a pretty blue dress that someone had laid out for her the night before. Liere saw it, felt a pang, then squashed it angrily. No fancy clothes for her. No heroics. Deeds, not the person—

My deed is to bring death—

Devon was crying as she thrust her arms into the sleeves of the dress, a noiseless, shuddering weeping that scared Liere even more.

"Come on," Liere urged. She pushed Devon out the door, and they clambered down a staircase. Elsewhere in the great house Liere heard shouts, and an adult wailing angrily.

"The doorways are all blocked! I *can't* get out!" a man cried.

No emotions—think! What would Senrid do? He'd go out the—

"Window." Liere pulled Devon to one of the side rooms. Norsundrians ran by, swords reflecting redly off distant fires.

The window opened with an easy latch. She and Devon climbed out, and dropped directly into a thick flower-shrub a heartbeat before more Norsundrians appeared, moving slowly; the ones at either end stuck swords in each bush they passed.

The girls flattened to the ground, Devon still weeping soundlessly. Liere threw her arm over Devon's skinny shoulders in hopes Devon would hold back the scream Liere could sense wanting to tear its way out. *Slish, hiss!* The sword jabbed above them, then withdrew. Liere held her breath until the Norsundrians had tramped past.

Smoke stung their noses, eyes, and lungs, and Devon coughed, but the sound was swallowed in the escalating noise. Liere crooked one elbow over her nose, grabbed Devon's hand and pulled her into the street.

Panicking people ran past, some pulling carts. Liere and Devon dodged, Devon stumbling over the hem of her new dress. She grabbed her skirts with her free hand.

Liere scanned the intersection. A formation of torch-bearing riders approached from one direction, and four mounted riders from the other. Liere pulled Devon back into someone's ornamental shrub.

Liere heard them on the mental plane: "Search first for brats!" from the leader of the torch bearers.

The leader of the four riders said, "We haven't seen any brats!" And he thought in disgust: *Tell that snake Davernak he can kill all the brats he wants. We're looking for a fight.*

The four passed on, and as the girls watched in horror, the Norsundrians cut down everyone fleeing from the Guildhall. Chase, chivvy, laugh, they sported with them if they took a desperate stance, fighting either with a sword or some other implement they'd grabbed up.

The leader pointed. Two riders with streaming torches separated off. One paused across the street from the hiding girls, cocked his arm back, then flung the torch high. Fire arced upward, looping in a cartwheel, then splintered a window. Two heartbeats, three, and flames licked up draperies.

Another torch *whooshed* up, and smashed a window directly above the girls. Shards tinkled down around the girls' shrub. Devon trembled, pressing herself against Liere.

The Norsundrians passed slowly on, leaving the buildings in flame. Devon's breath came in soft whimpers, but Liere kept her hand on the girl's wrist, her gaze on the perimeter of warriors who watched the Guildhall burn.

A cluster of Norsundrians stood in the streets admiring their bonfire, whose brightness reduced the rest of the street to impenetrable shadow.

Liere whispered, "Now."

The girls crept out, and dashed into drifting smoke; the Norsundrians were too busy talking and laughing at every crash of burning timber and gout of upward- spiraling sparks to gaze into the shadows.

From all around, the cries of terrorized minds barraged Liere. The impact on inner as well as outer senses made her head ache fiercely, but she forced herself to run, for she had to save Devon and the dyr. How? Everything around was flame, death, smoke, crashing and screaming and burning—terror, anger, desperation, savage laughter—and here and there, *Find that brat!* And *But there aren't any brats in sight!*

Liere didn't see any children, or hear them on the mental plane, but there was far too much terror all around her for any vestige of relief.

Through the mental chaos came a quiet, determined thought: *Sartora. How can I find her before they do?* The emotion and flicker of mental image made it clear that this person wanted to save her.

She sent a tendril to find that mind. There was no mental shield. The thoughts belonged to fellow somewhat older than Senrid, in whose mind there was an echo of another mind, an animal. A cat!

She sent a thought directly to both minds: *We are here.*

She and Devon began to cross a square, but out of an adjacent street came the clop of hooves. Another patrol! Half-hidden by wreathing smoke.

She withdrew her tendril, staggered dizzily, and looked about for somewhere to hide. Nothing but smoke, flames, and the fallen—

"Down," she breathed. "We're dead."

She and Devon dropped besides the motionless form of a man. Liere heard nothing from this man; his mind had fled. Liere squeezed her eyes shut. Devon's thin body trembled but she did not move, even when the horse hooves clopped within a palm's breadth of her head. The horse leaped over her.

The Norsundrians passed. The growing fires were a reddish smear in the smoking gloom.

Sartora?

Here.

The silhouette was a Norsundrian on horseback. Liere desperately reached again for the mind, and saw herself through his eyes. The echo made her so giddy she staggered. When she shut her eyes, she understood what she was seeing: the fellow was in disguise.

"Get her up," she cried hoarsely, pushing Devon to the young man's nervous horse.

Their rescuer pulled Devon over the saddle front. Then Liere felt a strong hand close on her arm. She was hoisted up.

"Lie flat," a voice said to Devon. "You, act like a prisoner."

Devon curled around the saddle horn, her legs hanging awkwardly.

Torchlight danced at the edge of Liere's vision: guards, looking at everyone passing.

Pretend, Liere shot the thought into Devon's mind, her face bumping against the smooth, warm side of the horse. *Pretend he killed somebody . . . he killed your mother.*

"Let me go!" Devon screeched, her voice shrill with real fear. "Let me go! You killed my mother! Let me go!"

"Not till you tell me where your family keeps their gold," their rescuer snarled. "You won't need it anymore!"

Harsh laughter, and someone shouted, "Turn the brat over to Davernak!"

"When I've got their gold," Liere's rescuer responded, his voice harsh with his anger and disgust. "Then he can have their corpses."

The Norsundrians did not understand his anger or disgust was aimed at them.

More laughter as more horses clopped by. Another ugly voice yelled something unintelligible, to which their rescuer replied in a hard voice, "*I found 'em, I kill 'em.*"

Liere was beyond question. The voices of the dying still echoed in her head, endless and agonizing.

Her eyes blurred with smoke and tears. More torches, angry laughter, sudden plunges of the horse. A Norsunder horse. Liere sensed its fear and desperation, the training through pain. *Run away*, she sent the thought, as its rider dismounted to chase someone. *Run free.*

Gradually the air got sweeter, cooler. The rescuer said, "You can sit up now. We're outside the perimeter."

Devon just clung tighter. Liere was held on the horse by a relentlessly strong grip on her belt.

Up, up. Liere coughed, briefly smelled pine.

"We're safe enough," the rescuer said, and let go his grip. Liere slid down the horse's side to the ground.

"Loose the horse—" Liere croaked, but he was already doing that.

He set Devon on her feet, unsaddled the horse, freed it from bit and bridle, then slapped the animal's rump. As it galloped off into the darkness away from the drifting smoke, he shifted a knapsack over one shoulder. In the ruddy glow of the burning city below he looked unsettlingly like one of Siamis's Norsundrian guards.

Devon swayed, then crumpled to the muddy ground.

The rescuer picked her up, and set her on a broad, low tree branch.

Liere climbed up into the tree and looked down at the city, clutching the dyr in both hands. How could she help? How—

She sensed the dying, those whose firsts were pain-bound, seconds frantic with terror or anger. They slipped into third like vanishing stars—those who were not consumed by a vast, horrible mental awareness, one that was so powerful she quailed away, the horror unbearable.

Was that Siamis? No, it was someone even worse: she knew Siamis's signature on the mental plane, and powerful as it was, this one was far, far stronger. Older. Like a blackness in the night sky that swallowed suns.

She closed herself within her own pain, letting the dyr in its bag drop against her breastbone. She wrapped her arms around her middle and rocked with grief.

She was too inexperienced to identify the watchers who darted skillfully in, easing the passage of as many as they could.

Chapter Thirty-One

In Senrid's dream, Liere tried to call to him. She stood on a hillside above a smoking city, but he couldn't hear her voice. He could see her face, and had no defense against her terror and grief. But when he tried to call to her, he seemed to fall through a storm of sound and light—

—and he woke to the smell of roasting potatoes.

He sat up, grimacing against headache and pain in his wrists, arms, and shoulders. Leander Tlennen-Hess sat over an almost smokeless campfire, cooking fresh-caught fish, chopped potatoes, carrots, and scallops. From the smell, he'd found olives somewhere and had crushed them into the pan. Olives, and sweet pepper, and garlic.

Senrid's stomach yawned emptily all the way down to his toes.

He was not aware of making a noise, but Leander glanced up. "Awake? Steeped listerblossom there." He tipped his head toward a pan lying on a flat rock. "It's a little old," he added apologetically. "I made it a while ago."

Senrid took the pan and slurped the listerblossom tea. It was barely warm, and so strong his nose stung, but it felt good going down. Some of his aches lessened.

"Hungry?" Leander asked.

"Ravenous."

"Be ready soon. It's all we got left, but I'm hoping Dtheldevor will come back with something. Usually does." Leander grinned. "I got the carrots while you were hibernating. Here are some nuts for dessert."

The outside area was dim and blue-lit, rain hissing steadily. It was good not to have to think. Senrid watched Leander efficiently chop up carrots and add them to the sizzling foods in the flat pan.

The dark-haired girl from the night before appeared. She was shivering, but her grin was triumphant over the bag clasped in her arms. "Couple o' sparrows helped me out," she said. "Led me right to 'em." And out of the bag tumbled three sizable shapes that Senrid recognized gratefully as the dense, tasty morvende cakes. "Hey! Looks like you found some eats as well."

"Squirrel led me to the spuds, chameleon to the rest, believe it or nuts," Leander murmured.

Senrid choked on his lukewarm drink, but as usual the pun was too subtle for Dtheldevor.

"Also found me all these-yere grapes. Wild vines up yonder b'hind the city. Someone a bunch o' generations back musta growed their own drinkin's," she added.

"Any news?" Leander asked. "I take it you were there for Siamis to discover Senrid's absence, since you were gone all night."

"Yep. Was a damn-blasted bust." Dtheldevor sounded righteously disgusted. "You'd think if we're gonna go to all the trouble t'pinch a prisoner, that soulsucker could at least get burned! Stomp around a little. Cuss an' fume. Nah. He just did that thing all night." She mimed sitting, head in hands. "I know—I fell asleep up on top—magic makes that roof warm, you know—and when I woke he was still at it. Nearly missed it. One o' his stench-faces comes in an' lets out a squawk. Siamis looks up like it's been just a moment and not all night, and he takes an eyeball inta the room, and says, 'Our guest has decamped, I see. You may content yourself with a search, but I suspect that our shadows got ambitious.'" Her attempt at Siamis's voice was surprisingly accurate, making both boys laugh. Then she made a face. "Whaddaya think that means?"

Senrid frowned. "First thought was, he knows you're here."

Leander shook his head. "That can't be right, or they'd be combing the wood for us, not sitting around waiting for something."

Dtheldevor added, "We never left a print, outside o' the first day. Leander taught me that."

Senrid remembered how very good Leander was in the woods, and accepted that. "The Guardian and her morvende allies must have someone tracking Siamis. He has to think I'm with them."

Leander looked up quickly. "Being careful means we haven't been able to get at him, which was our original intent. Do you think at least we can get those Earth kids away? I mean, I know he's got magic wards, but how bad are they?"

Senrid shook his head. "Unless you know more magic than you did last summer, forget it. Dead on my feet as I was yesterday, I felt traps all over the place, ones I couldn't break, as they were crawling with tracers and traps. He's destroyed the lighter protections. Go on," he added to Dtheldevor.

"That's it." She shrugged. "Whatever he was doin' all night, unless he sleeps that way—"

"That's not sleeping," Senrid cut in. "It's long distance contact, scouting others' minds over a distance. Have you seen him asleep?"

"Nope," Leander said. "He doesn't use any of the other rooms, but he does come and go by magic. He's been gone a lot. He was gone all the day before yesterday, and came back just before you showed up. How'd you know what he's doing? Were you really with Sartora?"

Senrid lifted a shoulder. "For a time."

Leander grimaced. "We heard the orders he gave. About the first city she reaches."

"Shit."

Dtheldevor grinned.

"That's probably what he was doing, then, listening in," Senrid said, and shut his eyes. "Liere must have reached that lake town he pointed at yesterday. On the border. Ah, I can't recall the name."

"We'll hear the name soon enough, I'm afraid, if the elevens really smash their way in to find Sartora," Leander said grimly, watching Senrid's brows draw in, and anger tighten his face. "Here, food's ready."

He divided the meal into three portions, two going onto camp plates and one staying in the pan, which he kept for himself. He gave the biggest portion to Senrid, gaining a nod of approval from Dtheldevor.

"If they do catch up with Sartora, why not just have his bullyboys knife her quick-like?" Dtheldevor asked. "Why do in a whole town?"

"Make sure she won't become a heroic martyr," Senrid said, his food sitting unnoticed beside him. Liere. Unknown distant town. His brain had woken, and his thoughts rushed headlong, leaving hunger behind. "If his plan works, she gets smeared as she goes down." He got to his feet and paced across the back of the little cave, quick restless steps. "But what I don't get is, he's *here*. So why doesn't he transfer to that city and do it himself? Or at least watch from a tower or hill?" He paused again, and rubbed his forehead. "I think, though—I *think* it's over. And that she's alive. I saw her, just before I woke up, in my dream, but it was a strange kind of dream. I mean, not like a dream at all. In any case, what is Siamis doing *here*?"

Leander sighed. "I don't know much about Norsunder, or this kind of thing, but the answer that seems obvious to me is—"

Senrid stopped, his wide eyes brightly reflecting the fire. "That there's something else going on, something even more important."

Leander had not been about to say that, but he dismissed his own surmise with a mental shrug. "What, then?" he asked. "We've spied, but we sure haven't gotten anything."

"Has to be the southern rift," Senrid said, snapping his fingers. "And what he said about realignment . . . If the lighters closed the south rift, then some Norsundrian mage's going to pay for it. They don't like failures there. That much I know."

Leander said, "Be nice if the one who paid would be Detlev."

Senrid didn't seem to hear him. He muttered in that same quick, absent voice, "Siamis is holding this place for a reason. Maybe just a good, isolated spot to keep those off-worlders. Maybe he's not hiding them from the lighters so much as from Detlev, or one of the other big blades. That would explain the heavy backup troops just to guard four enchanted kids. Whoever makes the new rift is going to control it . . ." He sighed. "I need to know where Liere is. If she's safe. I need to know what's *happening*."

Leander and Dtheldevor exchanged looks.

Leander said, "Well, we can always go back and take a listen after we get some chow into us. Here. Sit down. Eat. You still don't look too good."

Senrid plumped down abruptly. "I don't feel good," he admitted.

Dtheldevor made a few pungent observations about elevens and their habits, then said, "So what's Sar—uh, Liere like?"

Senrid shrugged as he put his plate on his lap. "Call her Sartora if you want. Everyone else does."

"Does she act like a kid Siamis? Seem like a grownup?" Dtheldevor asked.

"No to both."

"Weird. A kid doin' that mind stuff. Can't get it straight in me own head." Dtheldevor 's greasy fingers held a bite of food in the air. "She do it to everyone? The mind stuff, I mean."

"No," Senrid said. "Not if she can help it."

His patience and politeness convinced Leander that Senrid was beginning to wish himself elsewhere, rescue notwithstanding. "Let him eat," he said. "Bet you haven't had this much food in a week."

"You win the bet." Senrid's smile was sour. "Ow! It's hot." He wrung his fingers (since silverware was not part of the supplies), then picked up a potato piece more carefully, blowing fiercely on it. He then popped it into his mouth. "Hey, that's good." And, in a tone of discovery, "I'm starving."

He began shoveling it in as fast as he could eat.

Dtheldevor finished first, gave a vast yawn, and ambled to the back of the cave to change into her dry outfit, after which she curled up and zonked out.

When she was asleep, Senrid tipped his head in her direction. "Who's she, and what happened to you?"

"Dtheldevor of Dthel Rendm."

"Pirate girl?" Senrid frowned slightly. "Not the same one from, um, Wnelder Vee?"

"That's the one."

"Huh. I've heard a few stories about her. And you found her. . ."

"In Mearsies Heili. Nothing much to tell." He gave a brief report, feeling awkward. Apology was never easy. "I'm glad you sidestepped Norsunder. I've felt like a betrayer ever since we got you taken, and I am sorry for our part in it."

Senrid shrugged, feeling even more awkward than Leander did. He knew as well as Leander did that Leander was not at fault, and he couldn't show how much the apology meant to him. It was strange enough to realize that it did mean something. "Escape wasn't mine," he said. "Some fellow got me and Cassandra out—"

"Cassandra is free?" Leander interrupted. "Dtheldevor will want to know. She all right?"

"Yes. I came north to try to close the rift. Fell in with Liere. Unlike you, I accomplished nothing." The corners of his mouth tightened, and his eyes were wide and angry. He looked very much like the Senrid of old as he added, "But I really believe I know where Siamis is going next."

Rel looked in dismay at the putative world-savior early the next morning. She'd just come down from the tree branch she'd wedged herself during the night. There, in the sensible light of morning, he saw a small, spindly scrap with raggedly hacked hair, her tear-stained face streaked with smoke-grit.

She bent over Devon, who lay still and quiet on her broad branch, her chest rising and falling slowly in deep sleep. Sartora touched Devon's hand, which stayed limp, then checked her mind. Devon's mind was so deep she was below dreams.

She straightened up to face Rel, who'd gotten rid of his Norsunder clothes. Good. She couldn't bear to look at them.

"Is Devon all right?" he asked. "Do we need to try to get her help?"

"I don't know. Who are you?"

"Rel. And you are Sartora?"

She sighed. "I guess so." Another wave of nausea made her press her arms against her stomach. *Sartora the 'hero' who caused a whole town to burn.*

"You sure she's all right?" Rel frowned.

"Am." She was too tired to explain.

He pointed to the bag hanging against her clothing, and the silver artifact glinting there. "Is that Cassandra's hatpin?"

"Yes. How did you know about it?"

"Saw it in Sartor during winter. What happened to the boy who was carrying it?"

"Senrid? Elevens got him." Grief wracked her ribs, and her breath shuddered. She squeezed her eyes shut, held her breath, and got control. Barely. "He might be back with Siamis, but I don't think so." Yes, Senrid was free, at least. *Think about that, and not . . .* "I just tried to check. His mind is his. But someone was listening and I ended the contact."

"Check? You have messengers?" Rel looked around for animals.

"No." Liere gave a bitter laugh. "I'm alone. I'm going to stay alone. I check by mind."

Rel grunted, feeling the same helplessness that Commander Dei had expressed about this mind-magic business.

Then Liere stilled, and he watched in silence.

She felt a contact: a small being, very definite, very nonhuman, but very clear.

A small black cat appeared.

Rel frowned in perplexity as the cat approached, delicately setting each paw down. When she got close enough for him to see the white spot behind one ear, he exclaimed, "It is! It *is* the same cat!"

"What?"

"This cat helped me in Sartor. Her," he amended, remembering Linet's introduction. "Rina, her name was."

Liere sorted through the jumble of words and images sent by the cat, then she looked up at Rel in wonderment. "It was you who rescued Senrid and Cassandra. You didn't tell me that."

He shrugged. Liere's eyes were already blank again, then she almost smiled. That is, her tense young face relaxed a little, the corners of her mouth lifting minutely. "Rina has been with you ever since, trying to help you." She tapped her head. "Here."

Rel thought about the cat he'd seen on shipboard, the occasional glimpses of what he'd assumed had been local black cats, and snorted a laugh. "I suspect I know now why I came after you. And how I found you." Not to mention his other adventures. He smiled in self-mockery. He'd never really believed that he'd suddenly gained miraculous instincts about where to find both rescuees and enemies. Though he didn't much care for the idea. "If the cat really was controlling my mind in some way, why didn't she just tell me what to do, and save us both time?"

"It doesn't work that way," Liere said, sighing again as she tried to rub the grit from her eyes. That made them itch worse. "Rina offered you contact, but you didn't seem to believe it, or her, yet some of the images she offered seemed to match with your own . . ." She waved a hand as if seeking a word.

"Instincts? Intentions?" Rel offered.

"That's it." Liere nodded absently. Her gaze was on the shrubbery where the cat had vanished, her hands white-knuckled as they gripped the bag so tightly that its cord dug into the flesh of her skinny neck.

Rel contemplated this new aspect of events. It made sense—if you accepted what seemed to be happening, that minds could communicate with other minds without benefit of voice or sign. And the idea that he'd been somehow controlled quickly vanished. He did remember brief moments of confusing images, some that he rejected, others that matched his own perceptions. He also knew he'd chosen his paths, that no one had compelled him.

All right. Dena Yeresbeth was possible. "Humph."

Liere blinked her burning eyes and said, "There has to be another way."

"To . . .?" Rel prompted.

Liere sighed raggedly, still gripping the bag. A year ago she would have scorned her own temerity in even thinking about world events. After days of talking with Senrid as though anything was possible, including two kids making a difference, no, knowing *how* to make a difference. Thinking in terms of world movement had become another responsibility. "Evend of Bereth Ferian. Closing the rift." Liere frowned, glowering downward, her stringy hair curtaining her thin face, then she looked up. "Rina says that the light magicians recently smashed the big rift down south, the one the Guardian has been working to destroy. But now, Rina says, the great birds of the north all maintain that the elevens're making an even bigger one, and have been all along, up north."

Rel frowned. "This is news indeed. Can it be trusted?"

"Rina is certain that the false one was the south one. Apparently, there is a place all along a coast in the north, a new place. Animals don't use human names for places, but there's some area no creature wants to go, because the magic in the air is like lightning about to happen."

She paused, glancing at Rel with an expression he successfully interpreted as tiredness, leftover headache, and the need to be listened to. Believed.

"Go on," he said.

"Well, also, the animals—the mages—*someone* thinks Evend is going to do something desperate."

"Something desperate?" Rel asked.

Liere twisted the bag around her neck, jerking it from side to side so the skin above her skinny collar bones turned red from chafing. "I wish I knew more about magic. I wish I knew *more*. This rift that Norsunder is making. I took this part from Senrid's mind, before he knew I could, because he wouldn't tell me. One sure way to destroy it is to put the enchantment on yourself, and then die, taking the bad spells with you. Dark magic workers can do that to others, but a lighter mage could do it to himself. If they are ready to die." Her face under the grime had blanched, and her voice was urgent. "Oh, oh, I hope that isn't what Evend is thinking! Have you paper?"

"Knapsack," Rel said, indicating with a thumb where it hung from Devon's tree. He felt strange, listening to this strange child who communed so silently with the little cat, but he believed them both.

"You'll have to help me." Liere got up, her hands stiff with tension. "I have to write a letter, but I don't know how to."

Very soon they came up with a letter, dictated by Liere, then signed with slow, painstaking letters.

Rel folded it.

Liere said, "Rina, please take that to Evend in Bereth Ferian. It's desperately important."

The cat put her paws on Liere's leg.

Rel watched as the girl bent and respectfully offered the folded paper. Rina bit down on it, and disappeared with a flick of her tail.

Leaves rustled, and Devon joined them. Despite her grubby dress and smoke-smeared face, she looked rested as she smiled happily. "Is that Rel?"

Rel nodded. "Good to see you again."

Devon turned to Liere. "He was there on my first adventure. In Mearsies Heili."

"You got a good sleep?"

"Yes. The smoke made me sick, but I'm all right now." Devon scratched her scalp vigorously. "We'll feel better when we find a stream and get another bath."

Liere was relieved that Devon had not really comprehended the horror of Loss Harthadaun. Liere did not want to burden her with the knowledge, either. What would be the point? But it made her determined about her own vow.

"I'm glad you two know each other," she said. "Devon, why don't you go with Rel? You see what happens to people around me." She stopped as sorrow crashed through her fragile control yet again. She forced the words out: "I'll be fine on my own."

"So you are going to continue on?" Rel asked.

Liere's lips trembled. Her eyes were squeezed shut, but tears leaked through, running down her smoke-grimed face. Her chest heaved and her fists clenched. The other two could feel her struggle to get control.

When she opened her eyes, her voice was flat. "I *have* to. I just have to be faster, so I won't . . . it's my fault, because we stayed . . . I . . ."

"Liere," Rel said, implacable as a mountain. "What happened yesterday is not your fault. You did not give those orders. Siamis did. Do not put yourself in his place."

Her eyes widened. "Is that what I'm doing?"

"Yes." He saw the effect of that, and went on. "I'm already on every capital list they've got. So're the Knights. Think, Sartora. How can you keep them from torching another city?"

"I don't know," she whispered, and there were fresh tears.

"By being fast." Rel leaned toward her, his smile grim. "If they stop to hit one town, you free four more. Very fast." His smile widened to show even white teeth. "I may not know magic or mysterious mind-matters, but I can move very, very fast."

Chapter Thirty-Two

When Dtheldevor woke up, at Senrid's urging the three decided to sneak back to Roth Drael to have a listen.

The rain hadn't ceased. It was heavier than before, which was an aid for spies.

Leander took the lead.

His woodcraft, with the help of prowling Fens, got them close. Limited visibility aided by Leander and Dtheldevor's knowledge of now-routine sentry patterns got them through what Senrid observed to be a nonexistent outer perimeter.

"Most of 'em are gone," he breathed, wiping wet hair out of his face and blinking away the rain.

"Huh?" Leander pointed to the Norsunder guards in the usual places.

For answer, Senrid indicated the diminished number of tents in the Norsunder camp.

One at a time they made their way up through the fallen, broken stones, then elbow-crawled over the roof to their spy spot.

For a long time nothing happened, if one discounted being pounded by driving rain. Inside, Siamis worked at the big table, reading reports. Beyond, the Warren twins sat glumly in a doorway staring out at the rain. Frederic and Deirdre weren't in view, but Senrid knew they were somewhere dully whiling away their hours, and his stomach clenched. So close, so very close he'd come to joining them.

The inner flash presaging powerful transfer magic caught his attention. "Not a sound," he whispered. Then he tapped his head: *mind-shields*.

At either side of him the other two frowned in concentration. Then they turned their attention to the new arrival.

Davernak transferred into the ancient Destinations square in that main room, shortly followed by another Norsundrian captain.

"Seen those two before," Dtheldevor breathed.

Leander recognized the captain, a huge man with gray-streaked hair. He wore a heavy sword and several knives.

Displaced air stirred the map on the table, but Siamis ignored it. "Well?" he asked, laying down his pen.

"Trade town called Loss Harthadaun is where she came out into the open. Broke the magic, right enough." Davernak's long face was tight with strain. "Town's smoking rubble."

He not only didn't get her, he didn't even see a body. Senrid winced against the man's thoughts, which were so loud it was like someone banging a pot right next to his ears. *He's terrified.*

"No one got by us," the gray-haired one said, his voice too loud for the small space. As if Siamis were hard of hearing—or had argued.

"You obviously neglected to capture her. Did you see her killed? Identify a body?" Siamis asked, still in his pleasant voice.

The gray-haired one said smugly, "No. Too chaotic. But no one got through. A few took to the river, but we caught a lot of 'em downstream, and they were all from the docks, not the Guildhall. We surrounded it first and made sure no one got out alive. I watched it burn to the ground myself."

Leander suffered an intense stab of anguish on behalf of the rulers he didn't know, who would someday wake up from their enchantment to this news of the slaughter of people they had done nothing to protect.

Dtheldevor quivered with fury. To her, the world ran right when battles were fair between more or less matched adversaries.

Senrid's anger stayed cold.

Davernak said, "During the day an unknown number of people, mostly children, did escape through some old tunnels. The river route was largely a decoy."

The gray-haired one glared. "You didn't tell us that."

"You should have secured it first, as ordered," Davernak retorted. He said to Siamis, "If she escaped, it was probably there. I searched the mid-town rubble myself, and of the twenty-six dead all were adults. The

Guildhall is still smoldering. I hadn't time to check that before you summoned us."

"She did not escape through your unguarded tunnels with the rest of the children," Siamis said, his gaze on the gray-haired one. "She was still in the Guildhall when you finally gave the signal. There was no need to wait for the eleventh hour."

Nothing but added scare-power, Senrid thought sarcastically. He squashed the urge to laugh, for he knew from Gray Hair and Davernak's scarcely concealed hostility that they'd been arguing over who got overall command. Probably also over whose followers had to be stuck on perimeter duty, and whose got to have the entertainment inside. Gray Hair and his gang wouldn't have given a snap of the fingers for Liere. Or for Siamis. All they'd be interested in was the chance to have some fun with live target practice after months of dull picket duty over the animated dolls Siamis had made out of the populace.

And *that* was why Siamis couldn't transfer down just for the attack. He couldn't risk being seen, or gossiped about where the survivors might overhear. He was supposed to be the big hero to the people. *The great peace-bringer can't be leading armies that slaughter civs.*

"You were told," Siamis said instructively, "to follow her into the town, and capture her."

"It took some time to shift down troops from other sites in order to surround and secure the town walls," Gray Hair protested.

Liar, Senrid thought. *And Siamis knows it, too. You probably had the town surrounded within two bells after Liere walked in through the gates, and you didn't even bother securing those escape routes. It was you against Davernak, squabbling for precedence. You're going to lose now . . .*

Siamis said gently, "You had time, and warriors, and only a single untrained adversary. I find your excuses . . . specious. At best."

Silence gripped the room, the tense silence of impending death.

Then Siamis spoke again, if anything more softly than before. "Your single order was to capture that girl. Or at least see to it that she died."

The other blustered, "She's got to be buried under a roof beam in that Guildhall. They're ash! You said yourself she was in there when we attacked, and no one broke the inner or the outer perimeter, no one!"

Siamis said, "Did any of your fools carry off prisoners or hostages?"

The Norsundrian bridled at his carefully picked bullies being called fools, but then he sidled looked at Davernak, who ignored him. "A few," he admitted, and it was clear that he would have lied if he thought he could get away with it. "Not many—"

"That's why I still hear her in the world," Siamis said, still gently.

She's alive, Senrid rejoiced. *I was right.*

"She probably took control of one of your fools. Like this." Siamis's voice hardened into that command voice, the one that sent white fire scorching down through the listeners' nerves and made their muscles twitch against their wills. "She walked right out . . . like . . . this."

The man jerked around and slammed face-first into the white stone wall. Then he staggered, turning around with a bloody nose.

Dtheldevor cursed, quietly and steadily. "A whole town. They really did it. A *town.*"

"Shut. Up." Senrid breathed the words directly into her ear. The rain was louder than their voices, but why take the risk?

She didn't even notice. She was far too angry. So angry, the only recourse was action.

Damn and blast those villains, there was one thing she *could* do.

"You failed a single order," Siamis said. "And now I must waste the time I needed elsewhere to recover your error, leaving no time for you. You may report your failure to Detlev, and see how much time he has to devote to your education in following orders."

Gray Hair's face blanched to the color of his hair. With a wave of his hand, Siamis forced him back onto the Destination square, and the man vanished.

Leander leaned close to Senrid. "At least we know Sartora got away. We better get moving—"

Senrid opened his hand in agreement. Then realized the cursing on his other side had stopped.

He turned his head. Dtheldevor was gone. Mentally he awarded her rank points for first-rate sneakery; on his other side, Leander muttered, "Oh, no."

Below, Peridot said dreamily, "Siamis, here comes Dtheldevor."

Dtheldevor sprang through the room from the door the Norsundrians used for egress, sword whirling. Davernak scrambled out of the way, pulling his blade.

Siamis leaned down, picked up the silver sword from where it lay on a side table, and easily parried Dtheldevor's strike.

Senrid whistled soundlessly. She was good, but she hadn't a hope against that guy. Senrid shut his eyes, and called out mentally for the Fens. Would it work?

In the room, Davernak attacked Dtheldevor from behind. Dtheldevor saw, or sensed, and shifted her step, though not quite fast enough to avoid the Norsundrian's point, which ripped into her shoulder.

Flash! She tossed her blade to her other hand and kicked the big table over, forcing Davernak to leap back. She whirled to face Siamis—who waited, smiling in appreciation.

But then he moved so quickly it was hard to follow. There was a blur of silver, and then he reached with his free hand. He took hold of her bad arm, and twisted.

Her sword arced away, spinning. Howling curses, she fell to the floor.

Senrid kept up his mental call for help.

Siamis said to Dtheldevor, "Now, where did you come from? Have we been introduced?"

Davernak stepped around the table, shortening his arm for a strike. "Shall I—"

A black flash in the door, and their lynx leaped in, all dark flowing muscle.

From another cracked wall came an explosion of crows, wings beating, harsh voices cawing. The off-world kids backed away, blinking, and Davernak flattened against a wall before taking a totally ineffective swing at the birds.

Two huge felines loped in, teeth bared, and the room turned into a maelstrom of fur and feathers.

In the center of the maelstrom Siamis sat down in the one standing chair, laughing. The animals leaped through various cracks and windows, the birds zipped up toward the sky and freedom, leaving the room a wreck. Dtheldevor—and her sword—were gone. Half a heartbeat later three Norsundrians appeared in the doorway, fanning out, heads jerking side to side as they tried to assess the confusion.

Leander pounded Senrid on the arm and whispered, "Dtheldevor dropped just beyond that hedgerow. They haven't spotted her yet. We gotta get moving!"

"Yes," Senrid said, and he looked down once more at that laughing profile. "Yes."

❧

An hour later, Dtheldevor woke up with a groan.

She cracked an eyelid. There was a pair of blue-gray eyes, framed by a wildly curling mop of sun-bleached hair. Senrid's smile was fierce.

"Uhn."

"Lie flat," Senrid said. "We got you patched up, but I don't know how long it'll hold."

She grunted, made an effort, and sat up.

"That was a spectacularly brave and even more spectacularly stupid stunt," Senrid continued.

Dtheldevor winced. "Looked t'me like only way we'll get a crack at him is t'take any chance we get. . ." That much talking winded her. "Ooogh."

Senrid said, "You want to know what happened? Save your breath, I'd ask the same. You made it just beyond the hedge to the old vegetable garden before you dropped. Leander and I hauled you the back way into the woods. The Fens obligingly kept the elevens busy."

Dtheldevor looked around. They were holed up in the lee of some mossy rocks. No fire, no food. But she did see Leander's knapsack.

Senrid said, "Soon's you're on your feet, we're heading north."

"Siamis—"

"I'm sure—almost sure—he knew we were there all along," Senrid said.

"That don't explain what he was waiting for here . . ."

"A power play between the surviving Norsundrians down south, maybe? See who comes out on top? I don't know. Whatever it was, we can just about guarantee it won't be good for us. I think we're outrun here."

Dtheldevor braced herself, and got to her feet. The world swam sickeningly, then slowly righted. "I can move." She sighed. "Let's."

"There goes the prescribed R&R," Senrid remarked.

"Where's Green-eyes?"

"He was talking to a Fen who was talking to a bird who . . . let me see if I got that right. Eh! He's doing some info gathering. That and netting us some travel grub," Senrid explained. "If those weird noises he makes that sound like gargled Sartoran is talking."

"The Language," Dtheldevor croaked.

"Don't feel you've explained too much," Senrid hinted.

Dtheldevor grinned. "More ye keep yer trap flapped . . . more ye learn. First rule . . . unh! . . . me dad drilled into me skull."

"My uncle beat the same idea into me. This probably explains why I talk as much as I can."

Dtheldevor snorted a laugh, then gripped her bound shoulder and winced. "Yer uncle a snot-brained butt-sniffer?"

Senrid snickered. "Worse. In thought, if not in deed."

"See?" She nodded with the air of one who has solved a conundrum. "Me dad weren't. All the difference."

Leander reappeared, laden with food.

"Let's put in as much distance as we can today," Leander said. "Davernak is mounting a search. Under his direct command. I don't think he's as simpleminded as those guards, and I'd rather not prove I'm right."

Chapter Thirty-Three

A heroic journey seldom celebrated by humans—because most are unaware—was that of a small black cat who traveled from the southern hemisphere all the way to the northernmost reached of the world.

Rina knew that taking many days and nights would worsen the danger, so she contacted other animals who could hear her. The result was two methods of travel that she did not like at all, but they were fast.

The first was a fierce eagle who came to her on one of the rocky peaks north of Wnelder Vee. His mind was full of rage against the evil humans: Rina received a stream of contact, showing the capture and magic-enchantment of once free-flying eagles. Now this eagle's brethren were forced to the wills of humans, flying controlled while spying, a horror that caused too many to pluck out their own feathers until they bled to death.

Rina let him know that the paper she bore would be a weapon in the fight. The eagle crouched down, spreading his mighty wings, and commanded her to climb upon his back.

Rina did, making herself as small as possible. Her hackles rose; she was miserable.

Do not claw me, the eagle cried.

I merely hold on, she yowled.

I will fly easy. You will not fall.

He dropped away from the stone, great wings spread wide, spiraling until he caught an updraft. Wind whipped through her fur, and hurt her eyes, but she did not fall.

The eagle made the journey as gently as he could, flying high over the Fereledria, where Geres magic sped him on, and drifting on currents when he found them. Rina fought the instinct to drive her claws deep into the bird's bony back. She crouched as low as she could, loathing the soughing wind over her fur.

He flew down slowly to one of the human ports where ships lay waiting, and landed on a dock.

Rina had learned about ships when she left Geranda. She must find a big one, with the towers of square sails that meant deep water sailing, and not the little ones with tall triangular sails, that stayed on coasts or traveled up rivers.

She sent her mind to local cats aboard the big ships, and found whose mental images depicted the far northlands.

She located the ship, and trotted on board, minding human feet as barrels were rolled aboard.

The ship's cats were wild, and smug, and loved the movement. Rina withdrew to the hold, enduring the journey.

After many days and nights, each colder, and then warmer, she understood that the ship had docked.

She traveled again on foot.

All the animals in Helandrias were interested in the alliance, and the mental image of Sartora, who was the human weapon against the ones bringing evil magic.

There have been magic battles between humans here, she was told.

There have been greater ones south, all the way south, she answered. *But the evil magic is coming back here again.*

The animals of Helandrias showed her the way to the human city Bereth Ferian.

At last she saw the blooming birches before the great marble palace the humans had made, and she found her way in, searching from room to room until she located Evend, the ancient human.

He took her letter, looked at it, and then his trembling old hands lifted Rina to his lap and he petted her with long, gentle strokes.

Chapter Thirty-Four

R el was as good as his word.

At first Norsunder sent every warrior they had in Everon, Imar, and Wnelder Vee to search for Liere. She knew within half a day that she never would have made it on her own. In fact, all her travels so far now seemed easy, compared to this terrible cross-country hunt.

That first day they must have had to hide twenty times, and more the next.

She never again spoke of going alone.

On the third day, the Knights met them at a designated place, with two bound and blindfolded prisoners who turned out to be the king and queen of Everon.

Commander Dei had convinced Mistress Hollem to leave with Loss Harthadaun's children through the tunnels, he guarding their flank. They were the last to make it to safety before the Norsundrians discovered this escape route.

His first action when they reached safety had been a command to the Knights hiding in Ferdrian, the capital. During the two days that Rel guided Liere and Devon south, the Knights smuggled the enchanted king and queen to this meeting place deep in dawnsinger forestland.

Reverent fingers removed the blindfolds.

Liere silently pulled out the dyr and held it before the ensorcelled eyes of the King and Queen. She watched the tall bearded man in whose blank face lines of pain had been grooved, and the short, plain, dark-eyed woman, as they gazed uncomprehending at the dyr. Liere said the spell, and watched their faces change. Question, puzzlement, desperation made them into people again as the Knights swiftly cut their arms free of the soft cloth bindings.

Then the air was filled with adults' voices—questions, answers.

Liere was afraid that the royal people would soon look for her, just as had the Guild Magister in Loss Harthadaun, to fuss over, and celebrate. And then . . . *and then.* The thought made her feel sick with anxiety. She looked around for Devon and Rel.

"Let's go," she said quickly. "Please."

Rel nodded. "I've arranged for some food, and horses. Now that all of Everon is free, Norsunder won't be able to track us until we get to Imar, and by then Mistress Hollem has promised that she will have unraveled the Norsundrian wards over Imar like so much rotten cloth."

Liere sighed. "Good."

When they reached their first town in Imar, while Liere did her spell, Rel arranged for food and horses. They ate on the road.

Then on to the next destination.

And the next, as spring ripened to summer. Liere liked moving fast. There was no time for people to force her into the center of celebrations, no chance for a vengeance-seeking Siamis to send an army to burn the city around her ears. As soon as she saw sanity in the eyes of those she disenchanted—question, puzzlement, curiosity, joy, anger, human emotions of any kind—she slipped away, Devon a quiet shadow at her side.

They did not go to South End. Liere had felt, and despised herself for, a wish to see her parents' faces when they realized who she was and what she'd done.

Instead she made sure that someone would go there, for she became adept at finding strong minds who could spread the word—and in spreading it, reverse the enchantment, a mirror of how it had propagated to begin with.

Rel never asked needless questions. He never seemed to tire, though once she sensed that he needed rest. She saw in his mind that he had gone out to make a food run that had taken all night, while she and Devon slept.

"You *are* tired," she said. "I see it. I can go on—" She remembered Everon, and shut her mouth.

His dark, deep-set eyes narrowed, his face blank, not the eerie emptiness of enchantment, but the blank of someone who didn't want to show what they were really thinking, as his irritation hammered her, with betrayal underneath.

He said, after a time, "Will you teach me that mental shield thing you mentioned once?"

It was another sickening new insight, that to trespass was inappropriate, even for others' supposed good. That the social lie was sometimes necessary for personal boundaries. She demanded her privacy, therefore she must permit others theirs.

Liere turned to Devon, sitting quietly by her side, and the insight hurt even more. She hadn't noticed how Devon had given up expressing her own feelings, or even talking about things that interested her. Why talk when Liere was always going to read her mind?

Liere stared down at her hands, which were grimy. Again. Her armpits prickled with embarrassment. She wondered what Senrid would say if he were here now, and was glad he wasn't.

"I'm sorry. Here's how you make a mind-shield," she said, and told Rel.

She did not check to see if he mastered it.

❧

Before they reached the great harbor at Jaro, Rel brought a wheelbarrow, and said, "Climb in."

Devon and Liere got in and crouched down. The wheelbarrow smelled dusty and salty, like moldy hemp rope and old wood. Rel wedged their knapsacks around them, and fitted over them a barrel sawed in half. It was horribly uncomfortable, but at least it kept out the thin, cold rain.

They tipped back as Rel picked up the handles. The wheels rumbled over the stones of the street leading down into the port, jolting the girls.

Liere was about to check on Devon, and stopped herself. "Are you okay?" she asked.

Devon's voice sounded surprised. "Sure!" Then came her higher, anxious voice, "Is there something wrong that I don't know?"

"Quiet in there." Rel's voice reverberated through the wood.

Unsettled, Liere tried a joke like the kind Senrid had made. She whispered, "Not unless Rel is secretly an eleven."

"Oh, *never*," Devon whispered passionately. "You don't *trust* him? I *told* you, I met him in Mearsies Heili. He travels with Puddlenose sometimes, and—"

"I know. I'm sorry, Devon. I was making a joke."

Rel's voice was quite close, as if he was bent over the barrel-cover. "Someone is going to notice if my load of luggage talks."

The girls fell silent. Now it was hot and stuffy. The jolting rumble seemed to go on forever, then it changed: they were rolling along wooden docks.

After a thousand years, Rel exclaimed, "I don't believe it!"

Liere's body flashed with alarm. She struggled against the impulse to invade his mind. How horrible, not to know.

Devon's breath tickled Liere's ear as she breathed, "I think he found something."

The rolling increased, jouncing the girls so their heads thumped the barrel. Then they were thrown forward, their faces pressing into the wood as the wheelbarrow went up and up, leveled off, then they were thrown back as they rolled down another ramp.

And came to a halt. Or so it seemed. The wheels no longer rolled and bumped, but the wheelbarrow itself swayed and jerked gently.

"We're on a ship," Devon whispered.

The barrel lifted away, and cold, sweet air rushed in to cool the girls' flushed faces as Rel and a tall, weather-beaten man in a green coat smiled down at them.

As the girls climbed out, Rel said, "I didn't even hope I'd find you here, Captain Heraford."

Captain Heraford said, "We may sit here longer. I can tell you the truth: I deeply regret setting young Senrid ashore a little farther north as soon as I caught word of him being hunted by Norsunder. I've been cruising this coast ever since, in hopes he'd make his way to where I dropped him, or to this harbor."

"He's safe," Liere said. "But he's very far north."

The captain's brows lifted, and Rel murmured, "She hears thoughts minds."

The captain's face tightened into revulsion, then smoothed, but Liere saw it, and her entire body flamed with embarrassment and regret. "I won't read yours," she said quickly. Then added, not quite in Rel's direction, "Not *anybody's*."

"Well, then," the captain said, his voice jovial, not quite hiding a tremor of laughter. He held out his hands, and dropped them. "Then tell me where you want to go."

"We'll talk about that," Rel said. "First, let's get the girls settled. It's been a rough few days."

The captain took in his scrawny, filthy passengers, in both of whose faces tension gave their eyes a haunted look, and his expression altered to sympathy. "Yes, I see that. Welcome, girls. As my guests, I invite you to sign the ship's log."

Liere concentrated on making her letters, but her scrawl looked like hen scratches underneath Senrid's neat printing above. She surreptitiously brushed her fingers over his name, glad that he was alive, then handed the pen to Devon.

Soon after that they were clean, and dry, and fed. Even their clothes were clean, for Captain Heraford had a cleaning frame on board his ship. They were given a snug cabin with two bunks, above which had been fitted little shelves with fine-carved wood rails. Books packed these shelves.

Liere pulled one down, thinking: *Soon—if I live—I will read, and read, and read. I will never again be ignorant. Knowledge must teach control, because I can't seem to learn it on my own.*

Devon knelt to look out the porthole at the gray-green sea. "I feel safe," she said finally, grinning at Liere over her shoulder.

Liere sighed with relief. Devon's volunteering that was the first time in a very long while that she'd spontaneously spoken of her feelings.

"So do I," Liere said, wondering if she ought to apologize. Except wouldn't that be a further trespass, to air the words just to assuage her own guilt?

Devon flopped back on her bunk. "Safe!" she repeated. "Clean, dry, safe, and lots of food, all at once. I hope I never forget just how wonderful those are."

Liere said, "Devon . . ."

The girl sat up, her face tightening into sharp worry again, so she almost looked like an old woman. Liere suspected she looked the same.

Liere shook her head. "Never mind. None of my business."

Devon's brow furrowed in puzzlement. "I thought you heard everything. *Knew* everything!"

"I'm trying not to. Hear, I mean. I don't know everything. Wish I did! Then I'd know when not to be nosy."

Devon giggled softly. "Well, what did you want to ask?"

Liere studied the younger girl. Devon seemed . . . yes, she was pleased at the prospect of knowing something that Liere might not know. She'd been denied that for so long.

"I've been hard to travel with. And you're friends with our rulers back in Imar, and they're no longer enchanted . . ."

"But not *safe*," Devon said, her mouth down-turned. "Not 'till Siamis is gone. And I don't want to go back yet."

Devon's gaze turned inward. Liere fought the impulse to send a tendril in the mental realm.

Devon was not going to admit to anyone how hurt she'd been after the Imaran prince and princess were unenchanted. Liere had left, but Devon had lingered, hoping for . . . she didn't even know what. But Karia hadn't even looked at her. She'd run shrieking to her noble friends, and oh, how much that hurt! Russy as well, but Devon didn't care as much about him.

"I want to go explore the ship," she said. "While it's still light out."

Liere started up, then realized she did not have to go. They were safe, and she did not need to guard or guide Devon.

"I'm going to stay right here," she said.

"Okay." Devon jumped up and scampered out.

Liere turned to the book she'd taken off the shelf. She puzzled over the words, sounding her way laboriously through a page or two, until her eyes burned. And then—with no pressing need preventing her, no threat, no responsibility—she stretched out and slept.

Rel watched from a distance as the days of the voyage passed into weeks, and a month. His two charges slowly altered from thin, frightened little wraiths to normal kids. At least young Devon did, sounding more like the child he'd met in Mearsies Heili not long ago. The older one, Sartora, *looked* more like a normal kid, but her manner, her expression, her interests, all belied her age. She carried a burden, one that never left her.

The only way to help that Rel could think of was to take her to Mearsies Heili. He knew she was anxious to reach land again, so she could continue her self-appointed job of freeing the world of enchantment. She might as well begin there—after meeting the Mearsian girls. Maybe they'd know what to do with a girl their age, who was in every other respect, unlike anybody else of any age.

Chapter Thirty-Five

Dtheldevor enjoyed the way Leander and Senrid talked through day-long marches and evening campfires; when she got bored with the endless talk of history and magic, she took off to explore on her own.

Only once did they touch on matters closer to home. Leader knew that his small kingdom wouldn't be of much use to Norsunder, but that wasn't true of Marloven Hess, and he could see Senrid's worry.

He said, "I think it would take a new and much more complicated type of spell to make the Marlovens useful to Norsunder. If they had such a thing, they would have used it long ago."

Senrid's mouth tightened. "Either my uncle had them enchanted, or he's holding executions to keep control."

That ended the subject.

Once Dtheldevor brought back horses with her. "Dawnsinger gifties," she said.

Leander suspected that Dtheldevor's sidekick Sarmonwilda had probably given her whatever kinds of secret signs and accesses that dawnsingers used to communicate with one another, but he knew better than to ask.

It was enough that the three got a couple of good rides through the hills southeast of the bend of the Silver Lake, and occasional gifts of food.

The weather steadily worsened. Leander and Dtheldevor were entertained by the spectacle, each time they came to a sizable pool or a river, of Senrid throwing himself in and splashing about in the cold water until he felt clean. Leander and Dtheldevor had both spent much of their young years under conditions of deprivation, and had thus learned to live with one set of clothing and long stretches between baths. They found Senrid's fastidiousness hilarious.

The three had reached a great river draining from the eastern mountains down into Silver Lake, a gleaming line along the western horizon, when Dtheldevor vanished again.

Leander sat on a fallen log, chewing wen-stalks, and watched Senrid splash with determination into a stream that had to be cold. "Looks like rain soon. Why don't you wait on that?"

"Because the dirt turns to mud," Senrid called, then splashed back into the water.

When he came up again, whooping from the cold, Leander said, "We'll get muddy anyway. So it makes sense to take a bath?"

"At least I'll only have one layer of dirt," Senrid retorted, climbing out and shaking himself all over. "Blast! Give me your knife, will you?" He slung his hair back out of his eyes.

Leander pulled out his knife and tossed it to land hilt-up near Senrid's foot.

Senrid gave him a sardonic look. "Why not between my toes?"

"Cause my aim isn't that good," Leander said equably. "Don't issue a dare like that to Dtheldevor," he added.

"Is her aim that good?" Senrid asked. He picked up the knife, grabbed handfuls of hair and sawed it off.

"I dunno, but a dare is a sure way to get her to try."

"I'll remember that." Senrid tossed the knife back. It split a knot near Leander's hand, which made Leander laugh silently.

Senrid didn't notice. He was busy burying his cut hair under a flat rock. "Why does the sun have to disappear now? Couldn't that cloud wait?" he complained, sitting back on his heels. His hair stuck up in curls all over his head, reminding Leander of ducks' down.

"Couldn't you wait?" Leander asked, sheathing his knife. "What were we talking about before you decided you had to become an icicle? Oh yes, Tdanerend and his—"

"Hey." Senrid stilled, head cocked.

Dtheldevor rode at a canter straight at them. She was astride one white horse and led two more.

"C'mon, you barrel-heads! Siamis sicced his blood-blisters on us!"

Leander snagged his knapsack and hoisted himself onto a mount.

Cursing furiously, Senrid thrashed into soggy socks, jammed his wet feet into his boots, took a few quick steps and vaulted onto the back of the third mount.

They splashed their way across the river, thoroughly soaking Leander and Dtheldevor as well as the already wet Senrid.

"What gives?" Leander called when the roaring of the river had diminished behind them.

"Dunno," Dtheldevor yelled over her shoulder. "Morvende said birds spotted 'em."

"If this river is the one I think it is," Senrid shouted, "we're in Lascandiar. Bet we've enchanted people ahead, and more elevens."

"Won't take that bet," Leander said. "Let's hope these horses can find us some areas that are human-free."

No one spoke as the horses raced away from the rolling hills into forestland. They kept up a steady pace, scarcely pausing until darkness had fallen.

By then they had reached the rocky foothills along the eastern edge of mountains covered with tall pine. The horses slowed, switching back and forth up a narrow trail. The kids' breath began to show, their noses tickled by the clean, astringent scent of resin.

The horses stopped before a treacherous precipice, and the kids slid down. Dtheldevor spotted the opening to the cave, low in a rocky gully that was partially obscured by young firs.

"I think . . ." Senrid said, trying to decide if the flickering images in his head were his own wishes or a kind of contact from one of the horses. "I think they're going to lead our pursuit away."

"Good," Leander said, looking at the fresh hoof prints in the dirt leading back down the trail. "Think it really is Siamis behind the pursuit, or someone else? I mean, there's been no pursuit before."

"That we know of." Senrid shrugged. "Can we risk a fire, do you think? I'm freezing."

"Let's see how deep this thing is," Dtheldevor called over her shoulder.

She was farthest down the rock-strewn cliff side. There was no path. They had to pick their way down, slipping and sliding.

But the cave turned out to be worth the effort. It was narrow—barely wide enough for one to sit with his or her legs stretched out—but deep.

Dtheldevor yelled, "Look what I found at the very back!"

The others crowded up. There was a neat stack of logs waiting, and a pile of flat, fire-blackened stones that had obviously seen much use.

"Outlaws," Dtheldevor proclaimed with satisfaction. "Bet anything. This-yere's a blast-gut fine hidey-hole."

"All we need is some kindling," Leander said, and as Senrid opened his mouth, he grinned and added quickly, "I'll get it."

Senrid snorted. "Well, how was I supposed to know that about green wood?"

Leander shook his head and vanished.

Dtheldevor busied herself with laying the stones in a ring, and then setting up the fire in the way she'd seen Leander do it so many times.

Leander returned, his arms laden, just ahead of another band of rain. He swiftly redid the fire, banking it so that it would burn steadily and long. Senrid watched this operation with interest, shivering the while, for he still had only his ragged shirt and trousers, one leg sporting a sizable hole. Both were still damp from his morning bathe.

Leander dug in his pack. "Here. Take my extra tunic." He pitched a dark green garment at Senrid. "I'm afraid it's, um, grubby."

"I'll live," Senrid said, his voice muffled. Then his head popped out, and he looked down at himself. "Is this a tunic or a gown?"

"On you, a gown," Dtheldevor chortled.

Leander said, "Anyone hungry? I found some scallops and mushrooms that I can add to these spuds, and I think I have a handful of olives left—"

"Cook!" Dtheldevor commanded. "Don't talk! Can't ye hear me gut growlin' from there?"

"Thought that was thunder," Senrid said. He'd crouched down as near to the fire as he could get, head on his knees, his feet bare again. He laid out his socks on the stones and watched them steam.

"You shut up, short boy," Dtheldevor said genially, "or I'll sit on ye."

Senrid made a face of fear, then Dtheldevor's slanted eyes narrowed. "Oh! Near forgot. Morvende says we ought to go t'the lake."

"The lake! The elevens won't patrol that, oh, no," Senrid retorted sarcastically.

Dtheldevor shrugged. "So we dodge 'em."

Leander said, "If we go to the lake, we'll probably get a transfer, which will save us time."

"Not necessarily," Senrid said. "The lake beings' transfers seem to be limited by the physical extent of their waters. True, we'd be able to skip dodging our way up the land route through . . ." He shut his eyes, then said, "I can't remember the names now, but there are three or four kingdoms around the lake, all north of Lascandiar, which extends on both sides of these mountains." He pointed with his chin east, and nodded backward west. "Problem is, there's a good chance they might put us in the mountains north of the lake. That isn't like the Fereledria, where the Geres seem to waft you along if they like you. We'll be floundering around in a huge range, probably under heavy snow, judging by the weather here. Now, if we cut east along the Lascandiar Pass—"

"Which will be stinking with Norsundrians," Leander said. "Especially if Siamis really does want us. Which we still don't know."

"Of course he does," Senrid said. His wide, derisive smile, his mocking gaze recalled the unpleasant, seemingly heartless Marloven boy king of the bad old days. "Because I know what he's doing next. And he knows I know. What bothers me is why he took this long to sic his hounds on us." His gaze went distant.

Dtheldevor said, "Back to the route. The sea along here, I know right good. Hier Alverian is north o' Lascandiar. We landed there a few times. Got less o' them blood-blast mountains to climb if we go the east way?"

"Yes, though it's a longer route," Senrid said, his voice absent. "At least, on the maps." He blinked, and faced the other two, palms out. "This is all new to me, too. Drawing it is very different from riding—or walking —it. But on the map, there are fewer mountains to the east of us."

"We might be walking it," Leander said. "I doubt we're going to find much help up here. And we have to dodge regular folk as well as the elevens." He stopped, watching Senrid, who was now staring at the fire, absently tossing a small stone from hand to hand. "Senrid?"

Senrid looked up, his round face blank in the ruddy firelight.

"Something wrong?" Leander asked.

"No."

Senrid was not going to admit worrying about Liere. "Just wondering if the dyr is doing its job. You haven't heard anything wherever you've been going, have you?" He addressed Dtheldevor, who shrugged.

"How long would it take to go over the entire world?" Leander asked. "Supposing, of course, that Siamis hasn't nabbed Sartora by now?"

Senrid's stone smacked against his palms with more force. "We're going to have to assume that either she's been caught, or she's gone to ground again of necessity. So it's up to us." The stone flew harder, slapping against his palms. "So . . . let's say Siamis went down to Everon right after the slaughter, to try to flush Liere. Either he pinpointed her by following her trail of disenchanted towns, or else someone had the wit to get her to the capital, where if I understand it right, if you free the monarchs, all loyal subjects would be freed. Not a problem finding loyal subjects in Everon," he added dryly.

Not a problem finding someone with wit, either, Leander thought, but he kept it to himself. He knew by now that Senrid thought most adults were either idiots or villains, and judging from his past, who could blame him?

"So she's either untraceable, or else she's been nabbed. If he oversees the search, there won't be squabbling minor bullyboys vying to make the grab and getting in each other's way, like that botched job at Loss Harthadaun."

Dtheldevor cursed under her breath, and Leander winced, saying, "It seems to me what we heard was bad enough."

Smack went the stone against Senrid's palm. "Of course it was! But remember the original orders that you overheard, Dtheldevor. If Siamis had gone himself, you can bet Liere would have been nailed, though his rep as the peace-bringing hero would have taken a direct hit."

"He'd enchant 'em again," Dtheldevor said.

"Of course. But he knows that individuals escape the enchantment, and they blab. Anyway, back to the botched job at Loss Harthadaun. From what we overheard, it sounds like most of the kids escaped, and probably a lot more of the adults than the Norsundrians were willing to report. I bet most of what they got were the drunks who didn't listen, because from the sound of it, everybody else had an entire day to evacuate before the attack. He's not going to make that mistake again."

Leander said, "All right, so we put Siamis next in the north. But all this is assuming that Siamis told you the truth about going to Bereth Ferian and making the rift up there. You yourself have said that telling the truth is way down on a Norsundrian's list of ethics."

"No," Senrid said. Then he frowned. Slap, slap, the stone smacked from palm to palm. "Well, I did. Aside from that, Siamis does seem to tell the truth. It's part of his superiority game. But he does it in such a way that he misleads."

"Howzzat?" Dtheldevor asked.

"He'll tell you three of five true things, but the two he left out change the meaning." Senrid flung the stone into the middle of the fire and scrambled to his feet.

He paced back and forth along the narrow length of the cave, stepping over Dtheldevor's outstretched legs and rounding Leander's knapsack. Leander doubted he even saw them. "I *wish* I knew why he let us go . . ."

"You're still sure he knew we were there all the time," Leander commented as he chopped the last mushroom, then turned to the scallops. "I know I was very careful to keep my mind shielded. The trick becomes a habit, doesn't it?" He turned his head, and Dtheldevor nodded.

"Didn't he say to Davernak something about how he thought you were rescued by magic transfer?"

"That could have been the mislead. Not quite a lie," Senrid said. "Just one interpretation of his words. 'Our shadows.' That could mean Lilith the Guardian's mage allies, or it could be the forest animals spying on him . . . or it could even have referred to you two."

Dtheldevor cursed again, and Leander shook his head, sighing. They'd been over this ground before. But he had to admit that Senrid thought faster than he did, and saw farther. "Then why didn't he grab us?"

Senrid said, "Why did he tell me the plan? And why . . ."

"It makes sense to tell you the plan if he was about to enchant you," Leander said.

"Yep," Dtheldevor said, adding in a meaningful voice, "You want some help choppin'?"

Leander realized he was waving the knife in the air, and laughed. Returning to his dicing, he said, "Stones aren't warm enough for the pan."

"Quiet, guts," Dtheldevor exclaimed, smiting her middle. "So the old pinch-soul changes his plans."

"He can't," Senrid said over his shoulder.

"Why not?" Dtheldevor and Leander said together.

Step, step, shuffle, turn, step, step, step, turn.

"Because—let's say Liere is free, and he's abandoned the search for her, which leaves her to unravel his enchantment. He's going to have to move really fast now. He can't delay the second phase of his plan."

"Second phase?" Leander repeated, then stabbed the knife into the air. "Oh. Rift."

"Chop, blast ye," Dtheldevor commanded, "or I'll dice ye myself and cook up the remains."

"Eat one of those cakes," Senrid said impatiently.

She shook her head. "We save those, if we got a long trip ahead. What's this second phase? I thought the blast-damn rift was already up there?"

"The permanent rift ready to move over armies."

"How many armies they got?" Dtheldevor demanded.

"Who knows?" Senrid said. "That place is timeless. One army I suspect is ready and raring to ride is the First Lancers of my many-greats grandfather, known to be unbeatable."

Leander grimaced. King Ivandred Montredaun-An had been so terrible that even Marlovens were afraid of his memory, and did not name their children after him. The image of him riding out of the maw of Norsunder made his stomach hurt.

Senrid waved a hand. "These dolts we all see running around at Siamis's command are only the recent recruits, who feel the pull of time just as we do. Norsunder needs that big rift."

"They did have one," Dtheldevor said. "Few years back, over on Goerael. Clair mentioned it once."

Senrid shrugged one shoulder. "Gone almost as soon as it was instituted. I heard that much. Did she also talk about how it was closed?"

Leander and Dtheldevor both shook their heads.

Senrid's lip curled. "Didn't think so. Back to Siamis, who has to establish the rift himself, because if he asks one of the other head snakes, he divides his power base."

Leander nodded, checking his pan for warmth. Norsunder commanders did not work for one another, they worked at best in conjunction with one another. Promotion meant taking another's position by force. Sometimes—as in Sartor a few years before—it was one of the few advantages beleaguered lighters had.

Senrid snapped his fingers. "In fact, what you want to bet Detlev isn't busy plotting behind Siamis's back right now? Remember, they just took a heavy fall down south, if we read the clues right."

Leander and Dtheldevor both said obediently, "No bet!"

Leander then said, "I still don't see why Siamis would bother with *us*. It's not like we could possibly be a danger, and he's got all those spells to renew, if Sartora is ruining them, and if that Detlev is trying to take over his plans. He's got to be insanely busy."

Senrid said, "That's what *I* thought."

"And now you don't?" Leander tipped his chopped food into the pan, which sizzled nicely, wafting the aroma of frying scallops into the cold, damp air.

Senrid whirled around. "It's too easy."

Leander was thinking that they had wildly differing definitions of easy, but he kept that to himself.

Dtheldevor shrugged. "So what's the plan?"

"We need to find a powerful mage. Someone like Evend, who could probably hold the magic while doing a dark-magic spell even if he wasn't trained to perform it. And we need a light magic object of power, something strong enough to hold all the binding spells without losing its own integrity. Liere has the hatpin now, but Bereth Ferian's gotta have a heap of 'em squirreled away over the centuries."

"All right, so we're right back to going north," Dtheldevor said, sighing. "Which way, is the question?"

"East," Leander said, stirring the food with his knife. "We'll be faster if there aren't many elevens." He cut a glance at Senrid, who hadn't answered.

Senrid had stopped pacing, and stood at the cave entrance, looking out at the gray veil of rain. "It all comes back to Siamis. He knew we were there. He knew you, Dtheldevor. There wasn't any surprise despite what he said."

Dtheldevor scowled. "Now I think on it, yer right."

"Yet he did nothing. Just played around with the sword—"

"That warn't no playing," Dtheldevor said, massaging the back of her head.

"It was playing," Senrid stated. "I only know the rudiments myself, but I've watched training all my life, and I know what's for fun and what isn't. He was having fun with you. Then he then stood by and let those animals attack, when he could have blasted them with fire-magic, or his mind. *Why?*"

Dtheldevor groaned. "I dismasted me own ship with that stunt." She rubbed her shoulder.

Senrid said, "I'm more and more convinced he knew we were there all along."

Leander stirred the sizzling food.

Senrid whirled around and resumed his pacing. "He has to go north. And he can take ages to make that rift on his own, or he can shorten it drastically by having a—"

He looked down, and absently rolled the cuffs of Leander's tunic back to his still-healing wrists. "'Family gift.' He knows all about me," he whispered.

Leander looked at the tunic, which sagged down past Senrid's knees. Though there was maybe half a year's different in their ages, Senrid barely came up to his shoulder. Short he definitely was, but there was nothing small about his brains. "Have a what?" Leander prompted.

Senrid turned around, his face grim. Just for a second, he looked disconcertingly old. "Look. It all follows. The off-worlders he can hold for just in case. They could probably do the magic to make small rift accesses, at the price of their lives, but they couldn't manage the big one. A big new one, away from all the others, that no one knows about, maybe not even Detlev or the other Norsundrians. So he will control it completely. To force it open he needs the life of someone who knows dark magic, can hold it. Someone—" Senrid grinned nastily. "—like me."

Leander's neck crawled.

"Why do you think we call it dark magic?" Senrid said with a strange smile. "The absence of light is—"

"Dark."

"The absence of life is death." Senrid whirled around again. "He *wanted* me to escape, because Detlev supposedly had me on some list or other. Maybe they had a cooperation deal with prisoners, but Siamis decided he had a better plan. If I ran, then no one in Norsunder would know what he was up to."

"Which is?" Dtheldevor prompted, frowning.

"If that's true, then everything he said is suspect. I think he wants me to run north, straight up the little rift accesses to Hier Alverian, and right into his trap. He's probably up there now, and the elevens behind us have orders to chivvy us north without ever quite catching us, because then we'd have to be handed off to Detlev."

Dtheldevor began cursing.

Senrid ignored her. " So we'll run straight into his arms, thinking we're ahead of them, bringing our news to Evend. He grabs me. And then I do his work for him, ending a short and unlamented life. But I have to arrive at the last moment, so he won't have to risk Detlev coming along to take me away if he holds me too long. That's why he didn't keep me that day, he wasn't ready!"

Dtheldevor leaned back, blowing a lock of hair that had come loose from her braid. She turned her head, narrowed eyes aslant. "So, what, ye gotta go back home, I take it?"

Senrid snorted. "I'm going north."

Leander said, "If he knows you're coming, what good does it do to go anyway?"

Senrid shrugged a shoulder. "Because . . ." He flashed the old toothy grin. "I know what to do to get around him."

Leander sighed. "I guess it's the mountains, then."

Senrid's eyes were wide, and steady, and filled with reflected light. "The danger is only to me. I can go alone."

Leander shook his head. "Nope. As a new lighter-ally you're going to have to get used to sentimentality like loyalty and mutual aid. May's well get the unpleasantness over with now."

"Besides," Dtheldevor added, snickering. "You're too short to make it up them mountains without us to boot you along."

Chapter Thirty-Six

"The queen here is not much older than you," Rel said to Liere.

"I told her, I told her!" Devon exclaimed, jumping up and down in her desire to get going, to show Liere off to the people she liked best in the entire world. And to show them off to Liere.

They stood on the white-sand beach, looking out at the *Tzasilia* moving slowly away, its sails belling in the southeast wind.

"Rose," Liere said, marveling as she stared at the waves. "It's the weirdest thing."

Liere leaned over the rail, gazing down at crimson, rose, peach, flame-colored sea plants fingering up toward the surface.

"The red stuff below is coral," Rel said. "That's what changes the color of the water."

"Coral," Liere breathed.

"Come on, let's go find the girls!"

Ever since she discovered their destination, Devon had filled the days with details about the Mearsiean girls, and no matter what subject was under discussion, she always had an anecdote be beginning with *Clair said...* and *CJ once said....*

Both Liere and Rel had been glad to see Devon so happy, and if it meant a lot of stories about kids who sounded like paragons, and whose names all sounded the same in the slurry Mearsiean accent that Devon faithfully reproduced—Cherenne, Irenne, Falinneh, sounding like *Shrenna, Renna, Flinna,* and Dha-na and *Dyah*-na nearly interchangeable to Liere's ear—it was a lot better than the worn, fearful girl they'd worried over at the beginning of the voyage.

Besides, Rel had some private misgivings about CJ—Princess Cherenne Jennet—who was trenchantly loyal to her friends, but he'd never met anyone so passionate about holding a grudge against someone she'd once thought an enemy. "I don't know what we're going to find here, so it's a good idea to start out carefully."

For glorious weeks they hadn't had to think about the enchantment. This reminder sobered Devon. She stopped chattering, and watched the road.

They walked westward into meadowland filled with dying grasses. A dark line of mountains jutted on the northern horizon. Occasional big raindrops spattered their faces from the iron-gray sky.

Seabirds cawed, circling overhead. Liere looked up just in time to see some of them flying rapidly inland. She watched in dismay, angry with herself that she could so swiftly forget to check. She closed her eyes, listened, and sighed with relief. Allies.

Slowly the clouds gathered, thickened, and rain began in earnest.

"She's here!"

CJ almost tripped over red-haired Falinneh, who was sitting smack in the doorway of Murial's little kitchen. "Falinneh, do you *have* to be *right there?*" She groaned, looking past Falinneh to Ben as he blurred into human form. "Who's here, Ben?"

"She—Sartora!" Ben exclaimed. His snub-nosed face was all grin from excitement.

"Here?" Sherry asked from her spot beside Falinneh, her big blue eyes wide.

"In the house?" Falinneh squawked.

"In Mearsies Heili?" Sherry put in, looking puzzled. Among the many faces crowded into Murial's cabin, there were no new ones.

"Yes!"

"And why shouldn't she come here?" CJ put her hands on her hips.

Irenne appeared behind CJ, and leaned on a chair, her long ponytail swinging forward. "Because she probably should go to all those big countries first. Or so all the big countries would think."

"Maybe she has," Sherry said reasonably.

Clair, sitting at a makeshift desk on the other side of the room, looked up at her aunt, who shook her head.

Gwen, the third member of the card game-inventing trio on the floor, asked, "What're we waitin' for?"

Ben turned to Clair. "Should I take 'em to the Junkyard?"

"Them?"

"She's with two others, one of 'em Rel."

"Rel!" CJ exclaimed, rolling her eyes.

"So that's why she's on her way," Sherry said. "Of course Rel would bring her to us."

"By all means," Clair said briskly, before CJ could unlimber some choice insults. "We'd better get bucketing, gang. If she's a kid, she'll want a kid welcome."

"Well, *we* would," Dhana muttered, her changeable face registering obvious doubt. "A great magician, even a kid, might want other great magicians."

"There aren't any here," Clair said, smiling up at her aunt, who nodded. Murial might be counted by some a great magician, but she did not care for the company of humans, especially strangers. "So she's going to have to settle for us."

"Then let's get our carcassi mov—*ow!* Falinneh!" CJ backed up, again nearly tripping over Falinneh.

Murial's cabin was small, and there was little space, so Falinneh and her group had perforce set up their game between the outer room and the kitchen, where CJ had been watching Seshemerria make a chocolate pie, as if watching it would speed it along.

Falinneh, Sherry, and Gwen scrambled up, Gwen snapping their cards together and plopping them onto a shelf. Clair had asked the Mearsiean girls to be neat, a rare enough request that all had been scrupulous to observe.

Kyale, the silver-haired princess from Vasande Leror, had carried on as she felt a princess ought. The others had quietly picked up behind her, some not without resentment, until, early in spring, one of Clair's friends had taken pity on the group and lured Kyale to the Tornacio Islands for a visit.

CJ dashed for her cloak, feeling an intense sense of relief that now—at last—something was happening. A whole year stuck in Aunt Murial's, with only quick sneak trips to check on the rest of the country, or to hide out in the Junky for brief times, had been confining to the spirit. They couldn't actually *do* anything, even after the elevens had seemed to be gone south. The people were still enchanted, and still compelled to report "strangers." Strangers, they'd discovered the winter before, had included Clair, the girls, and the regional governors.

They still could not use magic, save the smallest and most inconsequential spells. That meant a long walk north through the forest, in the rain, which pleased only Dhana and Seshemerria.

Devon had gone quiet. Liere walked with care, extending her awareness. So far, no Norsundrians.

They had walked for a while through meadows of rough grasses when a bolt of lightning shot out of the sky, slanting down in a sudden, shocking strike. It blurred when it hit the ground, and with a flash of silver-white light turned into a white horse.

"Ah," said Rel. "I was hoping Hreealdar would come."

Liere stared at the horse, who looked like the dream version of the white horses she'd met in the north.

"This is Hreealdar," Rel said, smiling. "It is from these beings, native to another of Erhal's worlds, I'm told, that our own white horses are descended. Climb up. He's safe." He smiled slightly. "'He' being a term of convenience."

Hreealdar turned his head toward Liere before deliberately lowering it. She hesitated, then gripped the silky mane and scrambled up onto his back. The horse *felt* like a horse—muscled, strong—but the hair was softer, and the smell was not horsy. If the creature had he or she parts, they weren't visible.

Devon climbed up behind, and grabbed Liere around the waist.

"He'll bring you to the forest hideout," Rel said. "Where I strongly suspect we'll find Clair and the others."

Liere, nodded, but she knew what must come first.

She tentatively contacted Hreealdar. The horse's mind was unlike any she'd yet found, but he understood her request: *Take me to the city*.

Liere stiffened, and felt only wind and light. There was no jolt, no burn. Suddenly Hreealdar pranced forward on a cobbled street lined with pretty, brightly painted shops.

Liere and Devon slid off, and made their way to the nearest house, where Liere took out the dyr and disenchanted the people. She asked them for the local leader, walked there, and disenchanted that person.

They could track the breaking of the enchantment by the noise of people talking, laughing, exclaiming questions.

And so it went, back to the familiar pattern, only easier, because of Hreealdar, and because there were no Norsundrians.

Mearsies Heili is a small country. It did not take long to free the kingdom province by province. Hreealdar's last stop was atop a mountain. The little city was dominated by a palace with spires. She sent a tendril in, and found only a few enchanted servants.

So she turned away, sweeping her eyes over the more ordinary houses and streets. Only this view, too, was disconcerting because the city seemed to extend beyond the mountain top into cloud, for wisps of vapor rose at the ends of the straight streets, and beyond those she saw only the distant sparkles of the Pink Sea way, way below in the east. A city in the sky?

The great moonstone palace reminded Liere of Roth Drael, only this one was beautifully complete, that series of towers, or spires, reaching upward in a style at once complex and austere.

She sent her mind within, and discovered that it was empty. So she walked into the town, marveling at the solid ground, and cheered by the houses with their brightly painted shutters and doors.

She disenchanted the first people she came to, moving away quickly down the street before anyone could talk to her. As always, they turned to one another and started talking, laughing, exchanging breathless comments, leaning out of windows over flower boxes, or running along pretty pathways to greet one another.

By now she was able to assess the speed of the breaking enchantment propagating outward like rings widen after one drops a rock in a pool.

When the magic 'ring' had passed her, she thought a summons to Hreealdar, and clambered upon his back.

The lightning flash brought them to a grassy sward near a sheer cliff. A waterfall splashed down into a wide pool from which iridescent bubbles and vapor rose. Liere stared, thinking that—like the Pink Sea—she should be repulsed, but the sight was as beautiful as it was strange.

She listened on the mental plane, and discovered that there were beings in the water. Echoing like faint singing was yet another kind of life, something very alien indeed, hidden deep within the mountain. She discovered by mental images that Hreealdar lived there, and that this was a place of very old power.

She tried thinking a question at the beings in the water. No words came back—they were too different from humans for that—but compelling images came that made her head feel like the natural boundary of her skull had dissolved.

She blinked, swayed, then sat down hard. The contact was gone.

"You got drunk without even falling in," Devon exclaimed.

"Drunk?"

Devon pointed at the water. "That's what CJ and the girls call it. You get kind of dizzy and dreamy if you swim in that water. Dhana comes from those people. I mean, before she decided to be a human."

They don't know how powerful these beings are, Liere thought.

"I think I know the way to the Junky. It's that way." Devon pointed west.

Liere had closed her eyes. Still sensitive from the strange contact, she said, "I sense other minds. They are coming."

"Oh, you're going to love the gang. I can hardly wait!" Devon plopped down on the grass. Overhead, rain began to rustle through the brilliantly colored late-summer leaves. The two girls waited in silence, Liere absently fingering the dyr, until they heard the sound of laughter.

"Where?" Clair asked.

"Hreealdar just brought her back to the Magic Lake," Ben said, still breathless.

"She must be finished breaking the enchantment, then," Clair said, smiling. She'd make her rounds to check, but first she must express her thanks to Sartora. She turned to the girls. "Well? Want to go with me?"

CJ groaned. "I *just* got on a dry dress, in time to get soggy again. I hate not being able to use magic transfer!"

"Just like every other person in the world," Irenne said, waving her hands airily.

"Except magicians," Diana said, looking up, her dark eyes amused.

CJ shrugged. "Everyday people aren't as dedicated to laziness as I am!"

"She's saving the whole world," Sherry said, her light blue eyes rounder than ever. "And she came *here*. To *us*."

"That was because of rock-faced Baglioni," CJ muttered.

A couple of the girls looked around guiltily, in case Rel might possibly overhear, but he was down in the room the boys usually used, changing into dry clothes. CJ didn't care. She never said anything about Rel, whom she considered entirely too perfect for his own good, that she wouldn't be quite willing to say—in detail—to his face.

"She didn't have to come here," Seshemerria said, ever the peacemaker.

CJ said impatiently, "I know what we owe her, and I'm proud she's here! I guess I want her to be proud to *be* here."

The news that Devon was traveling with Liere had reminded CJ of that snobby princess from Imar. Karia very definitely had looked down on little, rural Mearsies Heili, with its girl queen who had no sense of fashion, and its total lack of an aristocratic court. Sartora was from this very same country.

"Rain's slackened," Dhana said, her head cocked.

No one else knew how she could tell from underground, but they were used to Dhana's ultra sensitivity to weather, especially water.

"Well, let's fazoom," CJ said, hands on hips. "Get it over with."

Once she got outside her restless mood eased. There was a change in the atmosphere. Something . . .

She turned to Clair, whose grayish green eyes wore an expression that had not been there for a year. There was indeed a change, and CJ wasn't the only one to feel it.

CJ skipped, threw back her head, and stared up through the canopy of amber, gold, scarlet, flame-orange autumn leaves. She sucked in a lungful of the pure, rain-washed forest air, her heart expanding with joy.

She began to sing.

The walk to the Magic Lake took long enough for the girls to join her in all seventeen verses of one of CJ's songs. It had begun as a vivid imaginary account of a meeting between a silly kid villain, a goat, and a moth-eaten wig, but Siamis's name had been hastily substituted, as had other enemies' names in times gone by.

CJ was busy concocting an eighteenth verse, one suitably loaded with insults specific to Siamis, when they started down the gentle rise leading to the Magic Lake. " . . .' brainless grinch-faced sneeb'—What rhymes with sneeb?" CJ asked.

"There's the Lake!" Gwen called. "And I see Devon!"

"Greeb," Falinneh said, chortling.

Falinneh's happy laughter echoing brightly through the trees, and CJ's light voice that reminded her of bird-song was the first sound of the girls that Liere ever heard.

"What a great word! Fleeb, greeb, splareeb . . ."

"And verily and merrily they carried on . . ."

"Hey, Devon! Over here!" Irenne called.

Devon danced forward, her little face lifted upward, her mouth and eyes transformed with happiness.

Liere was startled to see long, curling morvende-white hair framing a square, calm face in the central girl. But she was no morvende, for she had ordinary fingernails, and her skin was light brown instead of fish pale. Meeting those light green eyes gave her another small shock: here again was someone close to making her unity, though as yet she did not know it.

CJ greeted Devon, then looked curiously at the mighty world-saver. She liked what she saw, which was unprepossessing enough: a thin, plain girl with raggedly cut hair in boy-style, wearing scruffy boy clothes. Her nose and ears were red from the cold. Liere's eyes were as large and round as Sherry's, only colored a light brown, like honey. When that gaze met CJ's, CJ felt as if her ears rang, but the reaction was so brief she thought she imagined it.

More disconcerting was the utter lack of humor in Sartora's face.

"Welcome to Mearsies Heili," Clair said. "I think you've already lifted the enchantment?"

"Yes. Are you Clair?" Liere addressed the white-haired girl.

"I am." Clair sighed softly and happily. "Thank you for lifting the enchantment. I must go check on things. People will have questions. Girls, why don't you take Sartora and Devon back to the Junky?"

Clair made a sign. A flash of light and there was Hreealdar, dancing forward, mane spilling silkily. Clair jumped on his back. Flash! They vanished.

"Sneeb," a girl with bristling, bright-red braids declared to Liere, her eyes crescents of mirth. She was dressed in green and orange striped pantaloons, and a bright purple shirt. "Do you know a good rhyme, better than greeb? It's for a song about Siamis. Plenty of insults," she added.

"Falinneh, I'll bet insults songs are too babyish," the girl with the vivid blue eyes said, and Liere sensed that she was being tested. Her expectations reeled.

"I don't know any rhymes," Liere said. "And I'm a terrible singer."

The blue eyes were a lot more friendly as their owner said, "I'm CJ." She introduced the others.

Liere knew their names already, from Devon's many stories: here was dark-skinned, dark-haired, dark-eyed Diana in her ratty old clothes, moving so quietly she scarcely disturbed a leaf. Devon had explained (several times) that Diana had been the first one Dhana met when she'd emerged from the Lake waters, and so the girls didn't know if 'Dhana' was the name of her people, an attempt to repeat 'Diana,' or her name, but the name stuck.

And here was tall, blond-haired Seshe, the oldest, the one who saw ghosts; there was Irenne who loved fancy clothes and dress-up and plays, and there was short, droopy-eyed Gwen who was good at mimicking voices, and curly-haired, blue-eyed Sherry, Clair's oldest living friend.

Except for Diana, whose beauty reminded Liere of a deer, they seemed like ordinary girls, and not the astonishingly witty, clever, gorgeous paragons she'd been hearing about for weeks, in such a voice of longing that Liere did not hold any of Devon's somewhat tedious brag against them.

They began the walk back through the forest, some still trying to find rhymes for various insults, others listening and laughing, she matched names to faces and personalities.

"You two hungry?" CJ asked presently.

"Sure," Devon said. "For your kinda food—always!"

"A wise philosophy," Falinneh put in, waving a finger instructively. "*Always ready for tacos* is at least as important as having several good insults ready for when you unexpectedly meet a villain."

"Important for what?" Devon asked with an expectant grin.

"Important for the life of the adventurer," Falinneh responded, as if it weren't immediately obvious.

Never had Liere heard kids talk like this. Silliness at South End had almost always been related to play-copies of adult life, or else teasing.

"Sing the song," Gwen said to CJ. "And when we're done snarkling at our own wit—"

"Snarkling means kind of laughing and snickering," Devon whispered to Liere, with a self-important earnestness that made Liere smile inside. This word, too, had been defined several times on board the ship.

"—then maybe they can help us finish the new verse," Gwen finished.

"Okay."

CJ's voice rose, echoing sweetly through the trees. Liere scarcely heard the words. What thrilled through her nerves was the glorious sound of a lovely singing voice, every bit as pure as the dawnsingers'.

CJ was a princess who didn't act like a princess was supposed to. She didn't dress like one, either. Her plain black wool vest, white shirt, and green skirt, her bare feet, didn't indicate any pride in mere self or status. So, too, her utter unconsciousness of the pleasing quality of her voice.

Then there was the fact that the Mearsiean girls had not treated Liere like a hero. In fact, at least a couple of them appeared to have expected her to act like one, a prospect that had made them wary, if not antagonistic.

Liere sensed the song drawing near its end, punctuated with the girls' laughter. When CJ finished, the others all chimed in with suggestions, some trying to outshout one other. Devon looked from face to face, grinning happily—looking, for the first time in so long, like a person her age.

Dhana ran off, moving with such grace that Liere turned around to watch in amazement as Dhana turned a handspring over a log, caught a tree branch and swung out over a mossy boulder, landing as lightly as a gull skimming water, and then, with a flick of light brown hair, she vanished into a running stream. Not splashed, but actually disappeared.

No one else paid the slightest attention.

Dhana rejoined them a short while later, her clothes and hair wet as she smiled skyward.

The group rounded a grass-covered rocky outcropping and ducked past a tree with low-hanging branches and droopy foliage. The girls scarcely disturbed the leaves with the unconsciousness of long habit, leading the way into a cave, which turned out to have a tunnel winding downward.

Liere followed, looking about in awe. It smelled of loam, wood, baking bread, and a faint trace of summer herbs. They emerged into a round room that was as snug and homey as a cottage, with brightly braided rugs on the hard dirt floor, a bookcase, and various types of artwork—obviously made by the girls—affixed to the walls. Chalks and paints were scattered around at one end. Roots and hard-packed soil formed the ceiling; magic protected the place. Fresh air ruffled slowly down from a hollow tree.

"Welcome to the Junky," CJ said, hands on her hips.

Liere turned to find all the Mearsiean girls watching her in expectation. This was their home, a home they had made themselves.

"This place is wonderful," she breathed, not hiding the harrow of envy in her bones. She had never imagined that such a place could exist, but seeing it made her think that she'd wished for something just like it, her entire life. The place, the people—above all, that sense of belonging.

The girls grinned in pride.

"C'mon, Sherry," Seshemerria said. "Let's fix something good."

"I'll help you clean up," Devon said. "I remember where everything goes."

"No, no, don't touch the paints," Falinneh cried. "Me and Gwen are right in the middle of an important masterpiece!"

"Okay," Devon said, snatching her fingers back.

Falinneh grinned at her. "Help me give Sartora a proper tour."

"A p-p-p-r-r-ropah too-ah," Irenne drawled, nose in the air.

"A Prrrrr—" Falinneh buzzed the 'R' sound like a bumblebee. "rrrropah! Tooo-ah! Now, here is the famed mural, depicting the usurper Queen Glotulae. We call her Fobo—and her snail of a son, PJ. She named him Jonnicake. Can you imagine? You don't have to look at it while you're eating . . ."

Gwen took over. "Now, up that way is Clair's room. That's the only high room—she likes to hear the rain on the ceiling. Mostly she stays up on the cloud top. On account of duty. Now, down this way are our rooms . . ."

Liere loved them all. Each room expressed the personality of its occupant, a contrast to the utterly plain one she and Marga had shared, with its bare walls and two battered pieces of furniture. Their father had forbidden his children any personal clutter—deeming anything but necessary clothing to be clutter, especially for girls.

CJ's room, with its forest-green rug and bedspread, the pictures on the walls, and the bookcase full of colorfully bound papers once evoked a sense of longing in Liere that she struggled to squash down.

"Food's on!" Sherry's voice echoed down the tunnels from above.

"I'll help set it out," Devon called. "I know where the dishes are."

The girls stampeded up the tunnel. Liere followed more slowly, her envy turning to regret when she noticed the Mearsiean girls dodge, hop, or side-step around Devon, who kept trying to do things for them, or who told them their routine in a busy voice, as if giving them direction.

Devon said, "I can take that around for you!" as she grabbed a bowl of grated cheese away from Sherry, and whirled away in triumph, nearly colliding with CJ.

CJ stepped aside, and sat as Devon set down the bowl, then rearranged the food into a circle, smiling contentedly as she fussed.

Liere's heart hurt. Devon had no idea that she was in the way.

Everyone sat cross-legged on the rug, wherever they wanted—again, so different from Liere's home, where each had had a chair and no one sat or was served until their father had filled his plate, and if there was not enough of a good thing by the time the dish reached Liere and Marga, too bad. They could make it up with vegetables.

"There's plenty," Seshemerria said. "Eat up!"

The girls grabbed and passed in a happy jumble. No one had precedence, not even CJ. Clair came in with Rel halfway during the meal, and everyone wiggled aside to make room. Rel sat in their midst, towering over them but looking perfectly at home—even when CJ teased him with insults, which she did half a dozen times. Rel just sat there stolid as a rock.

"Hey, Sartora," Diana said, her dark eyes friendly but curious. "Tell us about your adventures. Where did you go? What did you see?"

"I saw the Great North Forest, and Roth Drael," Liere said. "And some of Everon, and Wnelder Vee—" She had a sudden vision of Loss Harthadaun, and cut herself short.

They all saw the pain in her face.

"You don't have to tell the bad stuff," Sherry said quickly, her merry face sober for once. "Only the good things. Did you meet any interesting people?"

"Well, there was Senrid—"

"Eeeuw!"

"Ugh!"

"Yeccch!"

"NOT Boneribs Montredaun-An," CJ said grimly. "If so, how did you manage to get rid of him before he got rid of you?"

Liere shook her head. "He got caught by Siamis's people. Trying to decoy them from me."

"Huh?"

"What?"

"This is *Senrid*," CJ said, her eyes narrowed, her tone sardonic—much like Senrid's, in fact. "Montredaun-An. From that supreme grundge-pile, Marloven Hess. There *can't* be two of 'em. Kitty and Leander said he got slammed as a prisoner by the elevens."

"He escaped," Liere said.

Devon added, "He really helped us."

CJ scowled and Clair said, "I'm glad to hear that."

CJ said, "Glad a stinker escaped who tried to have Falinneh shot just because she helped someone escape that Land of the Stenches?"

"But he didn't want to kill me," Falinneh said. "You *know* that, CJ. His uncle made him do it, but he said he liked my jokes too much!"

"UGH!"

"He's insane!"

"*Anyway*," CJ cut in loudly, and when the others quieted, she continued, "I just like my villains to stay villainous. Then you know you're right when you get in a good hate." She sent a glare Rel's way.

"Yes," Irenne said airily, waving her hands in emphasis. "When they've done something rotten, then go oops, maybe that wasn't such a good idea, are you supposed to forget their rottenness and make them your best friend?"

"Puddlenose and Christoph like Senrid," Clair put in. "He didn't do anything awful to them when they traveled together that time."

"And we were pretty mean to Senrid when we all got stuck on that crazy water world," Falinneh said. "I say, fair's square. Unless he does anything rotten again."

"Meet anyone else?" Gwen asked. "Famous people? Siamis doesn't count. He's a famous poople."

Most of the girls laughed. CJ held her nose, and Falinneh began offering rhymes for *poople*, but shut up when Liere said, "Not famous people, but we did stay, many times, with morvende. And dawnsingers."

"Oh . . ." Seshemerria let out a sigh of pure pleasure. "What was it like?"

Liere hesitated, grateful when Devon began to describe them, using more detail than Liere would have. The most powerful impressions—the harmonies that dena Yeresbeth gave her access to—were impossible to put into words.

After the meal was over, the girls dispersed to various pursuits. They had not been in their home for a year, and each wanted to do little things to resettle, as Devon ran hither and yon offering to dust, to carry, and reminding people where things had been when she was here last, in case they wanted everything back as it was.

Liere's feelings veered between longing and envy and fascination, until she realized she was giving in to the weakness of emotion again, and so she sat down, shut her eyes, and began to meditate on all her mistakes.

Chapter Thirty-Seven

"**W**inn. That snappish monster of yours is harassing the mares again."

And that sums up life in Bereth Ferian, Meral Winzhec thought, turning his attention from the glowering young stable hand to Faris Apajhe's stricken expression: *continual wind-change from the tragic to the absurd.*

To the stable hand he said, "Those mares were flirting. Soot's too old to be a rake."

The stable hand sighed rather loudly, and, on finding that he was totally ignored, retreated to grumble at his subordinates, who had to listen.

Faris surreptitiously wiped her eyes, and Winn shifted his stance to shield her from the rest of the camp. Not that many glanced their way. All were too busy cleaning out the old hideout they'd all thought would be forever abandoned, except in the stories with which they'd thought to bore their children during the peaceful years to come.

"Problems?" she asked, straightening up.

"Naw. Just old Soot socializing."

Faris gave a wan smile. "Well, we could use more colts from old Soot, especially if things continue to get worse."

Winn sighed. "Come into my tent. We just got it set up. Tell me what happened."

Faris looked around at the steel-gray sky, already bright though it was not yet four in the morning. "If Norsunder had to come back in force, at least it wasn't in the middle of winter."

"Of course." Winn laughed. "They may be evil, but they're not stupid."

He meant it as a joke, but Faris's round face lost its humor as quick as a slap. She turned her somber gaze his way. Guilt goaded him. Time to shift perspective again. His own view of himself and his life so far required a large dose of humor, but he knew that others misconstrued, and thought he wasn't serious about what mattered.

The season was very early spring, the time dawn, but here in the northern reaches of human civilization what the denizens considered balmy weather was a wintry farther south: footsteps crackled on the frost and breath misted, falling before it vanished.

Winn looked around at the pearly light on tree buds, the pale green of new grasses poking through the mud, and smiled inwardly before he ducked through the heavy flap of his tent. So maybe Bereth Ferian as a polity was outdated and indefensible. This was still his favorite place in the world.

Faris plopped down on one of the pillows and wiped her eyes again.

"Shall I get something hot to drink from the cook tent?" Winn offered.

Faris shook her head. "Had some hot cider on the ride down from the city."

"Bad news, I take it?" Winn dropped on the pillow opposite. From outside came the hoof beats and yells of arrivals, probably a patrol.

"Yes. No. Oh, I don't think I can make sense," Faris said fingering the end of her long honey-colored braid. Her high forehead puckered, making her look like the small child Winn had first met back in the bad old days.

"Try." He smiled.

Faris looked at that smile, and her emotions veered. Winn was a familiar sight, someone she'd known since she was little, coming in and out (usually at night) with her brothers, during the nasty days when the Norsundrian Dzydes held Bereth Ferian. Of late her view of Winn had changed, for she didn't just see the smiling, reassuring fellow who had made her friends and family feel safe, she saw a handsome young man. Very handsome—long curling dark hair, dashing smile, the easy grace of one who is spectacularly good at riding, shooting, and sword work.

Oh, she knew what her changed view meant. She just didn't know how to express it. Or even if her admiration would be welcome. He was exactly as kind to her as he'd been since she was four years old.

She made a mental effort. "Evend is going to die," she said, roughly, to get the words past her lips. "You can see it in his eyes. Hear it in his voice. Oalthoreh knows it. All the mages know it. And there is nothing whatsoever that we can do."

Winn sat back. "Of course there's something we can do. There's plenty to be done!"

Faris shook her head slowly. "I don't mean fighting back when we find their scouting parties, or the mages warding against the little rifts the Norsundrians are trying to make. We'll continue to do those things. Must do them."

"But?"

"I don't understand it, really," Faris said, raising unhappy eyes. "But Evend feels that his world, everything he worked for, is past. And there has to be something to what he says, because Oalthoreh agrees. She says all the right encouraging things to him, but she's got that same look of defeat, of grief, in her face."

Winn thought of the tough gray-haired mage, and tried to envision her expressing grief. He couldn't do it. He suspected she felt it, but her usual expression was stone blankness. The fact that Faris had seen it made him uneasy.

"It seems to come back to the fact that there truly are Old Sartorans alive today, but they are Norsundrians."

"How about Lilith the Guardian?"

"She is so seldom on this world. That's what Evend says. And she's the only one we've ever seen on our side. How many more like Siamis are hiding in Norsunder, beyond time?"

"Ah." Winn waited patiently.

"And then there's the apparent fact that the only person who seems to be capable of fighting this terrible enchantment we've been hearing about is a child. With these same abilities that the Old Sartorans really seem to have had."

"I thought those so-called abilities were just the hyperbole of history," Winn said. "Well, that's what my pa taught me, and he knew if anyone did."

Faris spared a thought for Winn's father, dead before she was aware of him as anything but a tall, gray-haired memory. But the respect with which the mages talked about him made her nod soberly.

"Evend says that we might have been reading the old taerans wrong. We have so little left from those days, and so much of it was symbolic! He says that maybe they didn't talk about all those things because everyone was used to it, just as we don't write now about each breath we draw."

"Unless we came close to drowning."

"Oh, don't joke," Faris whispered.

"Your pardon." Winn made a gesture of peace. "It's not so much a joke as an observation. Clumsy! Go on."

Faris made a face. "Well, here's what's so, well, upsetting. Evend says that maybe these old abilities are coming back. Remember the white-haired girl who helped free us?"

"Oh yes. Clair of Mearsies Heili." Winn smiled when he remembered Puddlenose, the white-haired girl's cousin. Puddlenose was very much like Winn, and they'd become instant friends.

"Evend thinks maybe she has those abilities, too. So you know what it all really means?"

"No. What?"

"It means that Evend and his generation are not just seeing their world end, it's us, too. We're young, and yet we seem to be just a bit too old to have these mysterious abilities, or to be able to fight against Old Sartorans on their own ground."

Winn snorted a laugh. "Oh, is that all? Listen, Faris. Evend is still grieving over Dzydes having defeated him by magic."

"Yes, so says Oalthoreh."

"Bereth Ferian had been safe and peaceful for generations. So of course he's going to take the blame, even though the blame wasn't his."

Faris nodded unhappily.

"We all know that Bereth Ferian isn't a kingdom any more. It never really was. Just a federation for one purpose: guarding against the Venn, who've been quiet for centuries. So our peaceful existence was to blame, not an individual. You're good at guarding only if you have something to constantly guard against."

"But that fight was magical first," Faris said. "Then military. And we still lost."

"No, we defeated the enemy."

"An outsider did," Faris said.

Winn shrugged, conceding the point. "But it had to do with magic, and Dyzdes' arrogance, right? My point is, however it was done, he was defeated. He's gone."

"But it still weighs on Evend. Here's another thing. As you point out, we're no longer any kind of kingdom. We're a center for learning," Faris said, leaning forward.

"Right. And that's a problem?"

"It is if our knowledge has suddenly become outdated, especially now that the Sartoran Mage School is back in the world."

Winn waved a hand. "Weren't they gone for a hundred years? So they have to be outdated if anyone is."

"But that doesn't change the fact that the northern school is outdated, if Old Sartorans are coming back, loosing ancient powers."

He waved a hand as if shooing gnats. "These Old Sartorans, they still have to eat, and breathe, right? Still put on their riding trousers one leg at a time, just like us. Human beings, no matter how old. There's plenty we can do to fight against ordinary human beings."

Faris looked a little more hopeful. "True."

Winn laughed. "So we go on fighting against the making of those rift things, as hard as we can, with everything we can. And if the little one with the mysterious abilities does turn up, well, we'll put her to work, too. See if we don't smash Siamis when he least expects it."

Faris clasped her hands together. "I hope you're right."

Winn looked down at her fondly, wishing he could kiss away the lingering grief in her sweet face. But this was not an appropriate time to be flirting with his oldest friends' inexperienced young sister, so he gave her a friendly smack on the shoulder. "Then let's get busy rousting out the old maps and getting the old patrols back into the routine, eh?"

After a rough trip through the inexorable onslaught of a northern winter Dtheldevor, Leander, and Senrid reached the shoreline of the Silver Lake. This last leg of the journey had been made less miserable by the appearance of white horses to carry them—shortly after which they rode straight into the Norsundrians.

Both those patrols had been silently paced by phalanxes of watchers, four-footed and winged.

The alarm went up, winding horns that echoed cold and weird against the snow-covered hills behind them. The chase began, but those from Norsunder found themselves sorely beleaguered, and in ways they could not easily fight. Flocks of birds, a swarm of skunks, snakes hissing from tree branches to spook horses—against these swords and knives were all but useless.

The three rode directly to the Lake, pursued to the edge of the ice-cold water. The Norsundrians drove them into the water.

As soon as they ducked under the icy waters (to dodge flying arrows) they felt a ripple of vertigo, and popped up in an underground cave, climbing out to eerie greenish-silver lighting that seemed to come directly from the stone walls of the immense cavern.

The white horses were gone.

Gone, too, was not only the cold but the wetness of clothes and hair.

Dtheldevor was the first to break the silence, cursing as usual, and then interrupting herself to observe, "First time in days I ain't seein' me own breath!"

Leander looked back at the black underground pool, and shuddered.

Senrid rubbed his head, feeling . . . not dizzy, but almost. Something had happened, all right. Something more than a mere transfer from one location to another.

He lifted his head and scanned the cave, which was full of complicated paintings. He moved to the nearest.

Dtheldevor had pulled her sword and dried the blade out by performing warm-ups. Leander belatedly tended to his own, but his attention wavered between that and the walls, where Senrid paced, staring upward.

"Wow," Leander breathed.

The wall-paintings were enormous, unimaginably ancient, in a stylized form that he'd never seen anywhere before, either in person or in records.

He walked up to one wall, gazing at the letterings below a row of winged beings. Some of the letters were obscured by petrified mosses, but enough remained for him to determine that he had never before seen this alphabet.

"C'mon," Dtheldevor said, thwacking the flat of her blade onto his shoulder. "We gotta find out where they sent us. And git movin'."

Leander bit down against an angry retort. She was right. But how could she not be struck by the same intense sense of wonder?

In the faint greenish glow Senrid stood in a passageway, the rock smoothed by either time or ancient hands.

"Who—?" Leander asked, waving vaguely at the caves. "You recognize either the alphabet or the style?"

Senrid shook his head. "I think the real question is 'when?' Huh! I'll bet this was here before Detlev was an evil gleam in his parents' eyes."

"No parents," Dtheldevor pronounced from behind. "Hatched."

"Spores," Leander corrected.

"Fungus," Senrid stated. "Uh oh. No light up the tunnel there. I guess it's time for the blind line."

They took hands, Senrid going first, and fumbled their way upward.

After a time Leander imagined he saw vague lights, but nothing made sense. Sometimes sudden air currents, cold and wet and smelling of mossy stone, bathed his face. Once they heard—but did not see—a vast, thundering fall. At this point their path was a narrow ledge. With the falls thundering close by, they were forced to shuffle sideways, their backs to damp stone, the air cool and moist. The hissing roar of the water vibrated up through the stone into Leander's teeth.

For Senrid, the journey was nightmarish and challenging. He hated going first, but he knew he would like being the blind follower less. Besides, he was the main target so it made sense for him to risk falling into an unseen abyss, though he did take the precaution of taking off his boots and socks so he could feel his way with his toes first.

As he worked his way upward, he began to reach outward with more than his useless sight. When they came at last to a fork, he did not ask the others for opinions on which way to go. He followed instinct.

"Light," Dtheldevor exclaimed after an eternity. "Naw, I ain't drunk. Or crazy. I see it!"

Senrid discovered his eyes had been shut. There was faint bluish light just where he'd expected, up and to the right.

They emerged into a cloudy morning in deep cove-forest not unlike that along the western border of Everon and Wnelder Vee. Water ran everywhere: streams, drips from needles and leaves, trickles down tree trunks, while the drops scarcely reached the three travelers because of the thick canopy overhead, formed by ancient firs. But the air was filled with moisture.

Wisps of vapor drifted among the trees. The air was cool, not cold, and the trees burgeoned with springy life.

"We're way, way north," Leander guessed, looking around. "But . . . where's the winter?"

Dtheldevor shrugged. "Maybe it ain't here yet."

Leander snorted. "Impossible. The sun up here at this time of year goes south, to where we live. That's what winter *means*. Unless the Silver Lake pulled a nasty one on us, we've come even farther north, which by rights would mean it would be almost dark even in the day, and far, far colder than what we just left behind."

Senrid stood where he was, breathing slowly, his eyes half shut.

Dtheldevor shrugged again. "Well, I ain't seeing me no snow, and that there is light. If it was home, I'd say spring light, and that breeze ain't so cold, neither. A good topsail breeze, if ye get me drift."

"It's not winter," Senrid murmured.

"That's what I just said." Dtheldevor laughed.

"You aren't getting it," Senrid said slowly, as impressions added up, and formulated into words. "We were shifted through time as well as space. Winter is over."

"What?" Dtheldevor squawked. Then she grinned. "Now, how could I learn that trick?"

Leander shook his head slowly, and let out a long whistle. "I wonder if we somehow jumped to the time we would have got here if we'd toiled through those mountains?"

Dtheldevor shook her head. "We never woulda survived it, not in deep winter, not like we are now."

"Come on," Senrid said, running down the narrow trail marking the contour of the rocky hillside.

Within twenty steps the opening was already obscured, not that any of them noticed. They were too busy looking around in wonder, and breathing air so pure it made their heads feel light.

"Time," Senrid whispered. "How is it possible?"

"Never mind. It's done." Dtheldevor waved a hand. "Let's get a-movin'. Before someone finds *us*."

They began tramping along an animal trail. Here and there piles of blue-white snow lay in dark, greenish coves, but it was obviously old, and melting. Everywhere around them was the new growth of spring, even on the ancient firs—tiny sprouts of light green tipping old blue-green branches.

"Is there a ratio between distance and time when you travel that way, an immutable rule?" Senrid muttered.

"Who cares!" Dtheldevor answered. "What I'm interested in is eats!"

Senrid didn't even hear her. "Who made the decision to shift us here, and at this time?"

Leander's insides tightened. It wasn't just the magnitude of the power, but the fact that someone—some unknown someone—would act and not tell them.

Senrid turned, his brows drawing together. "Who is that powerful? And if they can do this much, why not smite the Norsundrians with that same power?"

Dtheldevor waved a hand. "Aw, Sharly and Sarmonwilda both say the old folks—you know, the ones ain't human—don't smite."

"But are we really being watched? By whom, at what cost?"

Leander and Dtheldevor exchanged laughing glances, both saying at the same time—just ahead of Senrid—"I need to know what's happening!"

Senrid clawed his hand through his wild hair, then sighed. "Am I really that much of a bore?"

Leander chuckled. "Never that. But you do say it a lot. All of us think it, Senrid." *You're the only one who seems capable of figuring out what to do about it.* But he didn't want Dtheldevor taking that as a challenge.

Senrid sighed, short and sharp. "All right. But if I become a bore, tell me to shut up, okay?"

"You're both bores, 'bout history and the like," Dtheldevor said cheerfully. "'s all right. I already knowed I'm a bore about m' ship. Who cares?"

"I wonder if we might be in Helandrias," Leander observed, frowning around at the gnarled old trees. "Fits the description in—"

"You would be right," said a scratchy voice.

They whirled. Blocking the trail was a deer with eight points. "Humans are not welcome here."

"We know that," Leander said. "But we were put here by the beings in Silver Lake."

"Why?" This new growling voice was from a huge timber wolf who emerged from the shrubbery, and stopped directly in the path ahead of them.

As more animals emerged from the shadowy forest Senrid closed his eyes. He tried to *listen* to the animals, and a kaleidoscope of sights and smells impacted his mind, making him dizzy. He shut his thoughts behind a mental wall, where he sorted through the images. These creatures were a kind of vanguard. He listened again, to find a dramatic change in atmosphere.

" . . . with Sartora?" That was the deer.

"Yes," Leander said, his fear easing into a wondering sort of relief.

The timber wolf growled. "We know of Sartora's mission, through one of our own kind."

Leander looked at muzzled faces whose expressions he could not read. "We are trying to get to Bereth Ferian as quickly as possible."

The deer turned, and with a flick of the tail and a dramatic, soaring leap, vanished.

"There will be help," the wolf snarled. "Use this path for now." And she vanished, a gray streak running northwards.

"On we go," Dtheldevor said cheerily. "Glad that worked. Weird, though."

"Oh, it's going to get weirder," Senrid muttered.

He was right.

❧

The word sped ahead of them, swift and sure as beak and wing could carry it.

Three days later, while low thunderheads rumbled away to the southeast, Oalthoreh, soon to be head of Bereth Ferian's mage guild, urged her tired pony up the last ridge toward the distant clump of cedar over which the gray hawk circled and circled.

Inwardly she braced herself for a task that she so disliked she could not permit herself to send anyone else. She clucked to the pony, urging it below the edge of the ridge so that she would not create a silhouette.

Her trail meandered as cold wind worried at her aging bones. Fifty years since she'd reached master-mage status, the same year she first saw the barefoot, nameless wanderer who had come seeking magic. How many years since Winn's beloved father had walked into the Ghost Lakes, never to return?

Among the sweet-smelling cedar, a shadowy figure motionless, watching northwards. His head turned, and there was the young version of that wanderer's face. How it hurt!

Oalthoreh tightened her grip on the reins.

Winn hid the urge to grimace. There was sour old Oalthoreh.

"Norsundrians down there. Doing magic," he said, motioning to the waiting mount.

Oalthoreh forced her stiff legs to work her up onto the animal's back.

As they eased through the cedar branches, Oalthoreh sniffed, then pulled her jacket tighter. Like his mother, before a Norsundrian blade killed her in the fight to defend Bereth Ferian, Meral Winzhec didn't seem to notice cold. That reminder struck Oalthoreh another inward blow.

Winn picked out a laborious trail that kept them out of the Norsunder perimeter's line-of-sight. Not that the Norsundrian scouts were very assiduous. They looked bored and cold.

They stopped above a little waterfall. Gazing through the crevasse into the little valley running along a river, they spied the Norsundrian mage. She was just finishing a long spell. The greenish shimmer in the air was visible even to Winn, but more palpable, as grit in the teeth, and an ugly hum in the bones.

The Norsundrian mage faced a new direction and raised her hands.

Oalthoreh put her fists together, thumbs up. Her eyes nearly closed, she began whispering, and drawing her thumbs toward her. Winn smelled a change in the air, a cooling, a ruffling of vapor from the stream running beyond the horses' feet. The vapor rose lazily, like smoke, twinned in greater volume down along the river, and there in the hazy distance again, beyond the Norsundrian.

The thumbs stopped, Oalthoreh intoned a long phrase, and Winn blinked, his vision hazing. Fog rose from the ground, white and thick and cold, all along the river.

The mage below broke off her spell, and raised a horn to her lips. The faint sound carried, like the caw of a rook.

"She suspects," Winn said. "The sentries will be searching now."

"Of course she suspects," Oalthoreh replied impatiently.

During this brief exchange, the fog thickened until they lost sight of the mage. Winn sat back to enjoy. The Norsundrians would search, but in terrain they didn't know they'd lose their sense of direction. That mage might even change her spells, but her magic would feed the fog.

Oalthoreh drew in a deep breath, and began her own spells. They were long, and complicated, that much Winn knew from having witnessed several of these minor rift-breakings.

"We can go," she said finally.

Winn led the way back. Any of the more experienced mages could have warded that beginning rift. The fact that she'd come, and alone, meant she had something to discuss. Probably something unpleasant. She would have sent a messenger for good news. She avoided Winn otherwise.

So they rode in silence until the fog thinned into distant fingers of smoke. Winn kept his attention divided between the trail before them and Soot's ears. The old trail horse would warn him long before his human senses were there danger.

"I have received a message," Oalthoreh said at last, when they were well beyond the area of danger. "From Helandrias. Comes a child who is being pursued by Siamis and the Norsundrians."

Winn slewed around in his saddle. "You mean that, um, whats-her-name? Sartora?"

"No."

The flat voice was a warning.

"The boy she was apparently traveling with. Good authority names him the heir to the Marloven empire."

"Marl—it's not an empire," Winn said, trying not to laugh. "Hasn't been for generations."

Oalthoreh made an abrupt, dismissive gesture. "You deny they use dark magic there?"

"No."

"Nor that they would be empire-building if they could?"

"That's probably true as well," Winn said, thinking of his single visit there—and his hasty retreat. He did a fast mental count of years, then grunted. "I guess the baby they all talked about would be about the age now to want his throne. Hmm. And you say he was *with* Sartora? And chased by Siamis? Not the other way around?"

"The messengers were very clear." Oalthoreh frowned. "So, too, the message from the morvende is to give our hand in aid of his plans."

"Huh."

"Apparently this boy has extensive magical knowledge," she said. "The word came to Evend by other sources."

"And?"

"And Evend wishes, most straitly, for Irtur and this boy to meet," Oalthoreh said. Reluctantly.

"Irtur?" Winn repeated the boy's given name, because the earnest older generation refused to use the nickname that the boy preferred: Arthur. "I thought he was to be kept hidden again."

"Irtur has . . . continued to exhibit signs of independence," Oalthoreh said, even more reluctantly.

As well he might, Winn thought. Sequestered by the mages so that he would not be tainted with military tastes, kidnapped by Norsunder, forced onto his own resources, thrown into world politics. Of course Arthur would question the old constraints.

Winn was interested in Evend's decree about the Marloven boy, who would be exactly the sort of person the mages would guard Arthur from meeting.

The Marloven regent certainly had been a raving bully, the kingdom seething with discontent, duels, corruption, and war-fever the time Winn passed through in search of better training. The Marlovan cavalry academy might have been great years ago, and was certainly world-famed, but all he'd seen there were bullies learning martial skills.

"Evend does not want us interacting with this boy at all," Oalthoreh said, in a tone of finality. "Or interfering with his plans."

"So does that mean Arth—Irtur is to come to our camp, then? You know we'll put him to work."

"That's apparently what Evend wants," Oalthoreh said. "For him to be kept busy. No patrols. He is not prepared for that. But he can help in the camp, and he can run messages to us, so that we may continue his studies."

"All right, tell Evend to hear is to obey. And we'll find something for the Marloven to do as well, once we figure out why he's here."

Oalthoreh rode off without another word.

Chapter Thirty-Eight

The Hervithe left Senrid, Dtheldevor, and Leander at the foot of the hills that formed a natural border between Helandrias and Bereth Ferian.

They were met by a handsome, dashing young man with long dark hair who rode a handsome, dashing stallion.

Senrid looked sardonic, and Dtheldevor squinty-eyed. When they neared Leander saw the expression of humor in the fellow's eyes, and said, in Sartoran, "We're apple-pickers. Is it harvest time?"

The fellow laughed. "Come! I'll show you some fine pluckings!" He spoke Sartoran with a lilting accent.

From the great ferns and broad oaks behind him several fierce-looking young men and women rode, leading three riderless mounts.

"Mount up," the young man said, his horse tossing his head and sidling. "We want to get back to camp before the next rain, and we have much to talk about. Ah, I'm Meral Winzhec. Everyone calls me Winn." The young man bowed over his horse's withers.

Leander and Dtheldevor liked his manner. Senrid reserved approval until he saw some action.

The three mounted up, and there followed a wild gallop through the hills. Leander was not used to rough riding, and so he did not even attempt to guide his mount. The smooth gait of the white horses on their occasional rides down in North Forest had been too easy; now it took all his concentration just keep his seat. From the looks of her profile (and the occasional curse) Dtheldevor was having the same problem.

Not Senrid. Riding was one of the few exercises his uncle had not denied him. It was too much a part of Marloven culture. He matched Winn pace for pace, leap for leap.

Leander kept the pace—barely—and was relieved to observe in Winn and Senrid as they rode into a camp surrounded by gentle hills grown over with towering aspen and young oak and maple, that whatever unspoken contest had taken place had been resolved to mutual satisfaction.

"This way," Winn said, leading them down to a tent village.

Senrid noted the camp with approval, as he had the perimeter.

Inside a tent, they dropped onto low cushions around a folding table.

"We have to get to Evend," Senrid said. "Norsunder is building a rift here."

"We know about the rift. We know all about the weakness between worlds here. Norsunder has been trying off and on, in various ways, to reestablish their access as long as history has been written." Winn shrugged. "What can you tell us that's new?"

Senrid gave him a concise report on what he'd understood of Siamis's plans, and then what he'd surmised.

Winn said, "Oalthoreh and the other mages have been finding and extinguishing these rift-points for months. But I've heard nothing about Siamis being here." Winn turned back to Senrid. "However, we've had a sudden increase in the number of Norsundrians riding about. So what's needed?"

"Three things." Senrid leaned forward.

Leander eased his aching legs and sighed in relief. Maybe convincing them wouldn't be so hard after all.

"First is magic harassment. And I know spells that are effective. Second, hit-and-run attacks to keep his bully-boys busy. Third, a wider plan of harassment in the other countries, to keep Siamis busy. All people have to do what they can, or the elevens will regroup and start in with kill-and-burn tactics to buy themselves time until the rift is ready. We have to keep 'em busy before they keep *us* busy—keep 'em separate and on the run. This is your territory, an advantage only if we use it. Siamis doesn't have a big force, not in world terms. He's spread thin. And if he has to run all over, then he doesn't have time to use his . . . considerable force to make the kind of rift he really wants."

"Yes," Winn said, wondering what Senrid had almost said, but hadn't.

Then he mentally shrugged off the matter. Even if the boy told them, it was probably magic-related. Winn knew nothing about magic.

So he'd talk about what he did know. "If the dyr-wielder can free the Gerandans and Toarans he's using down south for strong-arm purposes . . ." He snapped his fingers, then opened his hand. "Even more trouble for Norsunder."

"I like that!" Dtheldevor cackled.

"So let's talk specifics. I've got armies of birds waiting to disperse all over, and others who will spread the news farther, but we'll need to do a couple of things with our messages, if we expect to get the entire world to listen."

"Spell out the tactics for the civs to follow," Senrid said.

"You're ahead of me, young Marloven," Winn countered, and at the wary expression on Senrid's face, he laughed. "Of course I know who you are. And I've been to your cavalry academy, oh, 'bout ten years ago. Was not impressed, I might add."

"No," Senrid said, and grinned his toothy grin. "But try again in five years."

Winn smiled. "We shall see! For now you must remember, as the countries are freed, so the rulers will be busy at home. Magic I don't know, but politics I do. We need something stronger than home-instinct to turn their attention outward. A symbol, a leader. A way to bind them together."

Senrid's lip curled, then his expression smoothed as he reminded himself that though lighters needed symbols, he'd seen the effect.

More important, he had seriously underestimated the leaders of Bereth Ferian. Most of his time had been put to figuring out ways to get them to listen, to get them to think universally, without acknowledging the fact that Bereth Ferian was a world center of learning.

Senrid looked up to discover Winn studying him in a calculating way. "Whatever you pick for a symbol, it sure isn't going to be a short kid who wasn't even permitted to attend the corrupt academy of Marloven Hess. And Liere still seems to be hiding."

Leander saw where this conversation was going, and galloped his fingers across the table. "I think I know what you want. Winn's Charge."

Winn pressed his fingertips on his chest. "Not I!" He gasped in a parody of humility.

"You did well enough for us when we fought against Dzydes," the young woman spoke for the first time.

Winn groped in the air. "Help me think of a suitably modest denial."

Leander laughed, Senrid grinned, and Dtheldevor slapped her knee. "What's the use o' a hero unless he's out there doin' heroics?"

Chapter Thirty-Nine

Messengers winged across the world, sped by those who were capable of effecting transfers. Anyone near the Selenseh Redian caves was considerably startled by sudden flights of birds emerging, then spreading out in all directions to spread the word.

In Mearsies Heili, so near one of the caves, it was only half a day before a sparrow came to Murial. She promptly dispatched a summons to Clair, who transferred down to the Junkyard with the message.

"I want to go!"

"Me! Me! Me! Me!"

"Wahoo, an adventure!"

"Snorble grunch!" That was Falinneh, of course.

Since everybody wanted to go to Murial's, too, Clair gave everyone transfer tokens. As soon as they recovered, Murial pressed her hands together in the old-fashioned peace mode. "I am honored to meet you, Sartora."

Clair was dismayed at the way Liere hunched her shoulders, her mouth turning down at the corners.

"Thank you," Liere said in a flat, remote voice. "But anyone could have done what I've done. Probably better."

Clair wondered what to say to make things right, but her aunt forestalled her. "I don't know much about people." Murial made an apologetic gesture. "My study has been magic, my friends animals. And it's the animals who have befriended your cause."

"Oh," Liere said, slightly mollified. "They have saved us many times."

Murial smiled. "There is news from the north. It will affect you, if you are ready to go forth to unenchant the world."

"I think I'd better." Liere looked down at her hands. "I probably should have left the day I came." She turned Clair's way, her expression wistful. "It was so nice here." Her expression closed. "But I've been weak."

"You've been recovering," Clair said.

Liere knew it was untrue. She'd recovered during the long, peaceful sea journey. She'd stayed with these girls—a made family, rejected girls, runaway girls, lonely girls--because it was fun, because it was so easy to put off going back into danger just one more day, especially as the weather worsened.

And while she waited for the invitation that never came.

She looked up. "Clair, may I ask Hreealdar for help?"

"He already wishes to carry you," Clair said, wishing she knew Liere well enough to say *You haven't been weak, you've been normal.* But even after several days, she couldn't understand Liere, who sometimes acted like the rest of the girls, then she'd act like someone older than the oldest person in Mearsiean Heili. And then she'd hunch up wooden-faced. Like now.

"Thanks." Liere's relief showed in her pink cheeks, and her skinny chest heaved. "But what else, then? With Hreealdar taking me, I will be almost as fast as magic would be."

"You can carry a message," Rel said, speaking for the first time. "It's not enough to free people. We have to stay free. If your kings or councilors or dukes or guild leaders ask what's to be done, there's a plan. Straight from Bereth Ferian, arrived just today. Even if they don't ask, you must tell them, or it's not going to work. Everyone must rise at once, and attack the Norsundrians in concert. Or as close as we can get."

Liere chewed her lip, feeling her own inadequacy, her own arrogance. How could she think she was really fighting alone? "Tell me what to say," she asked. "And I'll say it. But I have to understand."

Rel explained Winn's Charge in simple terms. "Kings and queens and other leaders used to warfare will probably know immediately what to do," he finished. "Enough to let them know there's a general strategy, and a target date. Others will probably ask for the details, and sometimes the justification, for they're going to want to confine their attentions to recovery at home."

Liere thought, *My safe life is over.*

She did not dare to think about the future. It just brought all those horrible emotions that clouded clear thinking. "I'll leave today," she said.

Rel smiled. "The magic side is now your end, but this one is mine. I think I'll go out and see what I can stir up locally."

Clair said quickly, "Thanks, Rel."

He flipped up a hand in casual farewell and walked out of Murial's cabin into the night, his pack slung over his back, and *Daelender* at his side.

Liere said, bewildered, "What? He's gone? Like that?"

"He hates being thanked, or being made much of," Clair said, as CJ rolled her eyes, but stayed silent. "He told me once that it is usually followed promptly by requests for favors."

Liere sighed. "The magic side. What does that mean? I don't know any magic, save my spell with the dyr."

"That's all you need to be concerned with," Murial said as she sat in her window seat. "And that's plenty. The rest will concern others. It has to do with the ongoing trouble with rifts, now that Siamis has reappeared again, in the north. Apparently he vanished instead of helping in the south, and as you know, Norsunder was unable to establish their rift."

"I hope it means trouble between the elevens," Clair said. "That can only help us."

CJ rubbed her hands. "If the elevener stinkbombs squabble and fight among themselves, they do our work for us."

Murial said smoothly, "Conversely, if they get us fighting among ourselves, we help their cause. We seem to be very good at that. It takes so little effort on their part."

CJ flushed, arms crossed.

Liere felt accused, too, as if the world's problems were somehow her responsibility. "That is why you live alone?" she asked, then blushed for her daring.

Murial laughed. "It is. But I'm not the matter before us. Clair, this is where you are concerned. Keeping Norsunder busy is not just a military matter. We need mages making nuisances of themselves up in the north."

Clair drew a breath. "I could do that."

Murial turned her way. "You and CJ could both go north to Bereth Ferian. Mearsieanne and I can break the remainder of Norsunder's wards here, and watch the country. But there is a reason to send you—a young person—north."

The floorboards creaked as Mearsieanne entered the room from the little study.

Mearsieanne said to Clair, "I would like to stay here to help. I do not plan to usurp your throne. This is not my time, it's yours. But I need a cause."

Clair had been trying not to think about what it meant to have two queens. She understood Aunt Murial's *I am not the matter before us.* Clair had had nightmares about enemies stealing her kingdom from a girl whose land had no army, but she'd never thought to lose her throne to her own family.

"I'm ready," CJ stated, arms still crossed. "Just tell me where to go, and I'll pack some nasty pies, and my spell book."

Liere had been studying the ground. She said, "I'm confused. I learned . . . by accident . . . that the only way to end a large rift was if someone put magic on themselves and then sacrificed their life. So Norsunder couldn't get them and reverse the spell. They are afraid about a mage called Evend. Isn't there another way?"

Murial sighed. "It's been the most permanent way. It is a reversal of the way they are set up, but for light magic it only works on those who have extended their lives by magic. The magic falls apart if someone is forced, or whose natural span is not over."

Liere shook her head. "It doesn't make it right."

"No," Clair and Murial said together.

Mearsieanne stayed silent.

Liere wiped her clammy palms on her trousers. "I sent Evend a message. Telling him to wait. See, Senrid *told* me there's another way, that you can use a magical object. It gets destroyed. Maybe the same way as the life. I don't know how it works. As soon as I'm done with Siamis's enchantment, I thought I'd go to Bereth Ferian and find Senrid."

"He is there," Murial said.

"He is?" Liere's face lifted, and the others saw her rare genuine smile instead of her polite one.

Clair said, "Now that we've got a plan, let's go back to the Junky and get a good night's sleep. I've got to figure out a way to get us up north that won't take months."

"The Selenseh Redian," Mearsieanne said. "The messenger birds came via those caves. It seems that magic transfer is possible between caves. But you can only transfer to other caves. As soon as you leave them, Norsunder's wards detect you, as always."

"That's good enough," Clair said, thinking of that vast long distance northwards. "I know there is one up near Bereth Ferian. That's why the city was built there in the first place."

Mearsieanne said, "That's what I read as well. That all the Old

Sartoran cities were built near those caves." She turned to Murial. "Except, what about ours? There weren't any Old Sartoran cities here. Not in any records I've seen!"

Murial lifted her hands. "The ancient past in this area is lost. But have you ever considered who might have built our palace on the mountain? Though it is familiar to us as we all were born in it, I'm told there is nothing like it in all the world."

Clair snorted a laugh, glancing at the card game going busily at the other end of the room. "The girls are going to hate using the cave."

Liere looked at her in surprise. The Mearsieans really didn't know that what they called the Selenseh Redian 'cave' was home to another kind of sentience.

Chapter Forty

Back at the Junky, Clair outlined the plan. The girls cheered at the prospect of adventure (in spite of the weird caves), and Devon said with a little bustle of self-importance, "I can help you pack. I know where everything is."

The Mearsiean girls didn't see to hear her, or see her little hand-wringings as she looked about for where to begin first. CJ grinned fiercely. "They need *us* to decoy the slubbard elevens. No grownup magicians will be able to think of the *good* stuff. Why, they'll spend days poring over musty books in order to find a spell to stop the boulder-brains when a good, quick food spell and a rain of pea soup will do it much faster."

"Fire ants in the boots!"

"Itch-weeds in the clothes!"

"Prune-peach-pumpkin pies in the phizz!"

"Oh, this plan is going to be *fun*." CJ cocked her head. "Except I really think we ought to test those pies ahead of time, to make sure that we get ones that the villains can't possibly like!"

"Of course," Falinneh exclaimed. "Detlev couldn't possibly like a good chocolate pie, or he wouldn't be a villain."

"Right," Sherry agreed earnestly. "Now, when he thinks of tasty pie, what you want to bet his first choice is a rotten-banana-cabbage-cherry disgustimento?"

"No!" Gwen hooted. "A yam-spam-cram deluxe!"

"No, a mud-onion-spoiled-spud wazoo!" Falinneh declared, hopping from one foot to the other.

Voices rose, all the girls offering disgusting combinations, until CJ yelled, "Enough talk! Time for action!"

The Mearsieans dispersed in all directions. Devon turned one way, then back, and followed Sherry to the kitchen, where Liere could hear her piping voice. "Oh, I hoped we would get to do this. I wanted Liere to see one!"

Liere listened, uneasy but not certain why. Everything seemed friendly, but why did Devon's voice stand out so?

Clair waved Liere over to the side table. "We still can't use our magic for wards or outside purposes because of those Norsunder wards, but one kind of magic will get around that, illusory. Nobody wards illusions!"

Liere turned out her hands, not knowing what to answer.

Then Sherry reappeared, carrying a big tray of pies. Devon trailed her, hopping up and down.

Liere looked at the pies, which oozed a slime of jellies, buttered goods, and sauces that smelled awful in conjunction with one another. These were illusion?

Sherry yelled, "Testing!"

A stampede of bare feet brought the girls back up the tunnels.

"Okay." CJ whirled around. "Who's going to be Siamis?" And when no one spoke, "You get first pick of the weapons."

"I will," dark-haired, dark-skinned Diana said promptly. She reached down and reverently lifted a pie with a glutinous filling of boiled cherries, topped with mashed green peas and old banana. It looked revolting.

"Oh, Siamis," CJ warbled. "You are *so* evil and nasty. I am so afraid. I guess I'll have to give you the thousand year old crown of the Mearsian Empire—"

She picked up a pie that seemed to comprise orange filling mixed with prune-jelly, and threw it right at Diana, who ducked.

The orange pie landed on Falinneh's knee, making a squelching noise. Falinneh copied the noise with her lips, then convulsed.

Diana faked a throw, CJ ducked, and with practiced expertise Diana whirled her cherry-pea pastry-bomb underhand, right into CJ's face, where it connected with a satisfying *splorp*.

"Throw one at me! Throw one at me," Devon yelled shrilly. "It's fun, Liere, it's *fun!*"

It didn't look fun. Disgusting pastry fillings flew through the air, ensliming every surface. The Junky smelled of a horrible combination of over-cooked, over-ripe fruits, boiled vegetables, and strange spices.

The girls wheezed with hilarity as Devon tugged at Liere. "See? See?"

At first no one threw any at either of them. Liere understood those quick glances her way. None of the girls wanted to be the first to attack the Great Sartora. She suspected they didn't like her the better for the perceived distinction.

Now she understood what had begun to bother her, what seemed out of place. *It's not Siamis, or the situation in the world. It's us. Devon and me.* The Mearsiean girls were friendly, but they were a closed group. It wasn't even intentional. It just *was.*

The truth? Liere didn't belong here anymore than Devon did.

It was such a chilling, *sickening* thought. Most people in the world didn't know or care about you, but what if you met people you wanted to belong to, you should belong to . . . and they didn't want you?

It was like betrayal, and yet it wasn't. There was no rule that said people had to make you one of them.

Could she change that? She bent down and picked up a chunk of an avocado-pineapple nightmare that had landed near her foot. She flung it back at the nearest girl, and then wiped her slimy fingers off on Dhana's back. How angry her father would have been at such useless, messy waste!

"Whoo?" Dhana yelped, whirling around, and slamming something glutinous right onto Liere's head.

Liere gasped. Cloyingly sweet-smelling stuff glopped down her face, falling on her shoulders with soft splats. Then she rocked as another pastry hit the side of her head. It didn't hurt. This one seemed to be made of strawberry custard.

She scraped off the worst of it, and flung the mess. Falinneh crowed, "Got me!"

Liere was now a target. She picked up pieces and flung them indiscriminately. Though she didn't like the nasty feeling of gluey pies, the splatter, the sounds the girls made, caused a butterfly wing flutter behind her ribs, and when Sherry popped up, huge blue eyes gleaming out of a mask of drippy peace soup, and whapped a mashed potato pie in Liere's stomach, laughter exploded out of her like the birth of stars.

She grabbed pies, and pieces of pies, and then handfuls of goop, throwing it just to be throwing, whether it hit anyone or not. She laughed until she hiccoughed, and finally she fell flat in the mess, arms and legs out, breathing hard, a stream of giggles fizzing as girls slipped, splatted in the mess, tried to get up, and flopped down again.

Then Falinneh and Gwen ran and slid in the appalling mess on the floor, fetching up against the stone wall in an oozing tide of multi-colored goo.

That ended when the mess began to lessen in volume: illusory magic, just like they used in theaters. Somewhere was a pile of fine sand, or something like it, that the illusion changed for a brief time. Liere sat up to watch as the tide of slop diminished and then disintegrated back into its components, leaving only the rumpled rugs, and a scattering of paints and chalks, which Devon swooped on and tidied with quick fingers.

Liere thought wistfully, *They can do that anytime they want to.*

Next morning, she and Devon woke up to the smells of breakfast. There was an air of expectation. Departure was imminent. The girls were not thinking about Liere's quest, but about their impending journey.

"Can I see that dyr thingio?" Gwen asked.

"Yes." Liere took it out of its bag.

Gwen extended a small hand, then snatched it back. "It isn't going to turn me into a purple mushroom if I think the wrong thing, or something, is it?" Her forehead puckered above her sleepy eyes.

Liere shook her head. "No. It doesn't seem to do anything. I don't know why I have to use it, except as an object to catch the attention of the people I have to disenchant."

"It is kinda weird looking," CJ said, taking it and holding it up to the light of a glowglobe. "Looks like the one Wende had. Remember? Like silver mixed with white stone. Like our palace walls, a little, but more silvery."

"Huh," Irenne said, taking it. "It looks to me like it's melted moonlight."

Seshe took it, then passed it quickly. "It makes my head feel odd."

"Me, too," Clair said.

The girls passed it from hand to hand, giving it back when Falinneh bellowed, "Breakfast!"

They sat in a circle to share their last meal.

Liere's ribs ached. This emotion was different from the laughter during the pie fight. This ache hurt. *I will miss this place, the people—no, it's the way they bind together. I will miss that the moment I leave.*

"I'm going to fix you a nice fat food-pack," Seshemerria said to Liere. "Devon said she'd help me."

Devon smiled, reminding Liere of a bird about to chirp.

"You'll be in good shape for some days, and we'll also send along some coins for just in case."

Conversation was sporadic. Falinneh made jokes and laughed at her own wit. She also laughed when the others roundly insulted her, Irenne with dramatic emphasis.

Dhana punctured Irenne's persiflage with teases when she got too attention-demanding. Seshe ate quickly, then sped into the little kitchen, Sherry and Devon with her.

Clair sat next to CJ, who was delighted at the prospect of action after a long, horrible year of helplessness.

Clair's gaze kept coming back to Liere, so skinny and tense, carrying such a terrible burden. Liere had been places, seen things, talked to beings that Clair only knew from maps and books. Was her tension masking boredom? No, that wasn't right. She wouldn't be watching the girls so closely if she were bored. And she was watching, very closely. So much so she kept pausing, forgetting to eat.

"Done!" Irenne declared, jumping up.

That functioned as a general signal.

They helped clean and restack the dishes. Then they ran to get cloaks, or knives, or whatever they wanted to take north. Devon appeared from the kitchen to say good-bye to each girl. They each spoke quite kindly to her, friendly words, jokes, but then they turned away, their minds clearly ahead on their next adventure. It never occurred to any of them that Devon longed to be with them—and when they left, Devon flitted back down the tunnel like a little ghost, saying over her shoulder, "I'll pack my things."

Liere was alone with Clair. She looked at that calm face and asked quickly, "Is there really a spell against growing up?"

"Well, it's against the change that makes you an adult," said Clair. "Your body stays a child. Some of us want that." Her voice flattened.

Liere's nerves tingled. There was pain in Clair's soft voice. Betrayal.

Liere sighed. "That's what I want. I think. I—" She thought of her aunt saying on her ninth birthday, *She's plain as mud now, but you wait. She'll one day be a beauty, and you'll make a fine marriage for her.*

Liere had known for some time that she did not want a life like her mother's life. Now she understood that this, here, was the kind of life she wanted. Even if she couldn't share it with the Mearsiean girls.

"You can change it back," Clair said slowly, "if you want. Nothing is forever in light magic unless you want it to be. But you have to make the original spell before the change of puberty, or it's too late."

"Thanks," Liere said, waiting, wishing Clair would say, *And after Siamis is gone, come and live with us.*

But she didn't. They were a family, and didn't even know it, or think about it. It just *was*.

⚜

Lina Mellay walked slowly back across the tile floor, thinking over the messages from Clair that had just appeared on the slate in the workroom.

Hmmm, Lina thought, looking out one of the zillion arched windows at where her old friend Gutli, her new friend Kyale Marlonen, and some locals were playing in one of the gardens surrounding the rambling old building. It was good to see the kids playing, after a year of walking around like zombies.

Clair has her own reasons for doing things, Lina thought.

She was still thinking it over when the kids ran in, whooping in protest of a sudden frigid wind sweeping directly in off the sea. Lina glanced out the window at the tossing trees and the early spatters of sleety rain. That would probably keep people inside, which was just as well, until Lina could figure out what to say to Kyale about being left behind when Clair and the girls had gone north.

Clair hated gossip, especially negative gossip, and double that about girls their age. Well, Lina confessed (to herself) she thoroughly enjoyed hearing gossip, though she seldom told anyone besides Gutli, who was silent as a fence. Sometimes, in fact, Clair was so very reserved that she didn't always make her true feelings clear on what was to be done about a troublesome girl.

Like now.

Lina loved being the symbolic regional governor of the Tornacio Islands. It was an easy job, for there were only a few small villages comprised of fisher-folk or other sea-related professions. It was fun, because lots of youths on the Wander had been attracted to the Tornacios over the years, which was why Clair wanted a young regional governor. The islands had become a haven for runaways from some of the lands up north—like Ralanor Veleth—where, if you were poor and clanless, the military made you into a soldier or a servant. Lina's main job was overseeing the hostels where Wanderers lived and worked before they moved on.

Let them come, let them be wild for a time, Clair had said. *It's better if they do it with rough games here than they think the only choice is to go join up with Norsunder.* Many settled down to island life, or joined the crews on the ships coming and going.

Lina turned her attention to Gutli, her best friend for a very long time. They sure were pretty to look at, Lina thought: Gutli with her golden coloring and Kyale all silvery.

Lina grinned. She quite liked being scrawny and freckled and unpretty.

"It's great to have the enchantment gone!" Gutli proclaimed, running up to Lina. "Everyone's awake again!"

Kyale looked up, her silvery eyes round. "You said there was a message from Clair. Are we going to have a celebration now that we don't have to hide anymore? What does Clair say?"

Lina winced, wishing she'd known to keep her lips buttoned.

Oh well, she has to find out sooner or later, she thought.

"When they get back," she said out loud.

"Get back?" Kyale repeated blankly.

"C'mon, let's get some hot chocolate," Gutli suggested, after a quick look in Lina's direction. "My fingers and toes are still numb."

"Wait. Where'd they go, Lina? Let's go in and ask Clair on the slate."

"They're already gone. Magic workers are needed to fight Siamis," Lina said, hoping that that would end it.

Kyale was rather like a terrier with a rag. "Clair and CJ, sure, but did the others go?"

"They always go as a group," Lina said, shrugging. "We've got to stay here and make sure things stay safe."

Kyale's eyes narrowed and her lips thinned.

Lina and Gutli had brought Kyale to the Tornacio Islands ostensibly to help see that the kids and animals were all right, a job that had stretched out for spring, summer, and autumn. Kyale had been content to stay, knowing that news of her brother would have been conveyed instantly, as the magic slate was something so old it bypassed the Norsundrian wards. She had also enjoyed the advantages of the housekeeping spells that Clair had put over the rambling palace left over from centuries before. She wasn't expected to do unprincessy chores, like at Murial's, and she had her own room, something impossible in that tiny cottage. She and Lina and Gutli had played day-long games of hide-and-seek and treasure hunt, and Kyale had lorded it over the local kids as the Visiting Princess.

Now Kyale stiffened all over her small body. "Didn't they think to remember that *my brother* has to be up there, chasing Siamis? Why didn't they bother to tell *me*?"

"Maybe they don't think Leander is there," Gutli said practically. "That news was months old. Or they might not be anywhere near him even if he is."

"Huh! I could at least find him," Kyale said, her voice shrill. "Why didn't anyone consider that? If Siamis is going north, Leander will, too! Just because *they* don't have any brothers . . ."

"Clair's gone off to fight villains, Kyale," Lina said. "How about let's just wish her well? We can find plenty to do here."

Kyale sniffed, whirled around so fast her skirts brushed Lina's knees, and marched out.

She didn't appear at dinner, which was a relief—though no one said so.

At night, one of the local fishermen came to see Lina. "The little girl with the silver hair," he said. "I saw her walk right out into the sea and vanish." He looked worried. "Ought we to search?"

"Nope," Lina said, rolling her eyes at Gutli. "She's got some kind of magic armband she got on another world, that lets her breathe underwater. My guess is, the next place she'll be found is Bereth Ferian, or whatever shoreline is nearest."

When the man was gone, Lina shook her head. "We did our best," she said. "But she's gone. I couldn't think of a way to stop her."

Gutli said, "Maybe it'll turn out okay."

"Hope so. Fonei's fleas! Let's get bucketing on *our* chores!"

Chapter Forty-One

Five days' ride west of Bereth Ferian, Winn watched Arthur stick his head outside the tent flap, then pop back in hastily, rain dripping off his yellow hair. "It's rolling away south, just like usual," he declared, wiping the rain off his face with his sleeve.

"Good. Then we can ride t'night," Dtheldevor declared as she reached for the second roll on Arthur's plate. "Roust us some pinch-souls."

"Hai! Get your own." Arthur snapped out his fork and stabbed the roll back.

"I don't want to get into any fights with elevens," Leander said. "I have enough trouble staying on my horse."

Winn noticed Senrid Montredaun-An sending a fast look his way, but then he let his gaze go diffuse and kept stropping his knife on the whetstone, as if he hadn't a care in the world. Or a thought.

Leander glanced at the cheese-stuffed roll his hand, stretched out his legs, and winced. "Speaking of which I need a break from horse-riding." He did not add that he was tired of the eternal rye. That seemed to be what grew up here, and it was in nearly everything. Senrid wouldn't notice, because in Marloven Hess the good oats were given to the horses, and people ate wheat, barley, and rye.

"Aw, yer butt'll toughen up." Dtheldevor stuck her fingers in the apple tort and scooped up a portion. "Ridin's the right idee. Then maybe me'n you'll be almost good enough t'not fall off."

She obviously thought it a very good joke, the falls that the two had taken on some spectacularly rough rides. She crammed the pastry in her mouth, then licked her fingers.

Arthur sat quietly, head bent so all Winn saw was his damp blond head.

Winn remained quiet, trusting that his presence had become background noise again. He liked it that way. Made for better observations.

Evend would not like the next report, he was afraid. Winn had always thought it a mistake to keep Arthur mired up in the palace, studying day and night, instead of learning how to handle himself, but the mages had insisted. The Prince in Bereth Ferian was to be a Scholar King when he took his place as symbolic leader of the federation of northern kingdoms. It made sense if you considered that his so-called kingship had no political power whatsoever. Knowledge, mage-guild alliance, communication between nations whose rulers either practiced or had access to magic: those were to be his concerns.

But Norsunder could still march in, Winn had pointed out, or Arthur could be kidnapped—again.

He studied the kids. Leander and Dtheldevor talked. Arthur, the one forbidden to go on scouting runs, stared at his hands as if he could read something there, and he didn't like what he read.

The others never teased him, never referred to it, but Winn could see that Evend's single constraint was as effective a prison for Arthur as keeping him in the castle.

It was worse since Senrid came. Not that there was any trouble between the boys. The problem could be seen at a glance: two blond boys sitting side by side, Senrid eating with quick, neat motions, always checking the entrances, as if he would be required to leave at any moment. He casual familiarity with weapons. Arthur's careful manners, his attention to others' words. Senrid had been cheerfully blunt about his lack of military training, yet he went on every expedition he could. His lack of training was relative, everyone agreed when Senrid wasn't around to hear it. He might not be able to swing a sword, but he rode like the wind, he shot better than anyone, and he was a hard scrapper.

Arthur had no vestige of training, and had to stay behind.

The tent flap opened, and Faris slid in, shaking drops from her face. "My, it's brisk out," she said. "Venn weather!"

"That's what ya always say when those storms go down there." Dtheldevor pointed a broad finger southward.

"Well, the weather is much worse down there," Faris said, helping herself to the cider warming on the hearthstones. "The Venn haven't done anything terrible for ages, but their names still show up in all kinds of curses and nasty comparisons."

"We even have 'em in our own languages, down south," Leander offered. "Though most have long since lost the real meaning."

"Like?" Arthur asked, looking interested.

Leander grinned. "The word for a stubborn fool in Marloven, when literally translated, is 'westdoor', something so old they slur it and you can't pick out the words. Ask anyone what it means, and they look at you blankly. It took me a whole year to track it down, but what it means is 'builds his door on the west.'"

Dtheldevor rolled her eyes. "And *that* makes sense?"

She was just ahead of laughter from the locals. "It would if you knew anything about the Land of the Venn," Winn said. "There *are* no doors on the west sides of buildings in the Land, nor windows. All their storms come from the west, unless it's from the northwest. It has to do with currents."

"Killer storms," Faris said earnestly. "Dangerous and terrifying. Though Venn lies south of us, we're protected by a kindly current on the east coast, and most storms start on their coast in the west."

Dtheldevor slapped her knee, and dust rose. "Huh! That's new one on me! But I dunno know much about them people. I remember hearin' 'bout 'em, when I first took sail. Me dad was alive then." Dtheldevor flung her braids back. "Never did get over to that side o' the continent. Just as well, eh?"

"They are treaty-bound against empire hunting any more, but they are still formidable," Faris said, wrapping her hands around the ceramic mug.

Leander stretched again. "What I can't figure is why didn't Siamis use the Venn the way he did the Gerandans? You know, enchant them and put them out as guards and spies?"

"Too tough a rep," Senrid said, looking up from his laced hands. "And his spell's too flimsy."

Everyone glanced his way.

"But the Gerandans—"

"Gerandans are Venn descendants, though they don't have the rep the Venn have. Put the Venn out in key spots, lift the enchantment, and they're right where they need to be to take down the local leaders—and who says they'd obey him? Siamis has to have seen that one from the start."

"So that's why the rift up here, then? Send a big army to be sitting near the border to the Land of the Venn when the enchantment's lifted?" Arthur asked.

Senrid opened his hands. "Bet you anything they attack Veen first, after the magic lifts."

Leander winced. Arthur glanced away, his fine, fair hair falling forward on either side of his temples, hiding his puckered forehead. Winn chuckled to himself. *No military training? Maybe, but that is military thinking.*

Faris said, "Horses are ready whenever you are."

That started another conversation, as they waited for the last of the rain to patter on the tent and wind its way south. Senrid's abstraction vanished for a time as he and Faris talked about the horses. Horse training was important in Marloven Hess, that Winn had seen on his brief visit. They talked training until Dtheldevor made a bored comment, then Senrid fell silent again, and the conversation shifted to the night's plan.

Winn let them talk that out, too, and when Faris sent him an exasperated look and said, "I think we might as well go if we're going to," he followed along.

"I'll see you off," Arthur said, smiling.

"Me, too," Winn put in.

"What," Faris said to Winn as soon as the four kids were far enough ahead, "are you doing?"

"Two things." He grinned.

She saw that grin in the streaming torchlight, and gave his a skeptical glower.

"One, I just love watching that Montredaun-An boy in action."

"But you have to stay here with Arthur. It's time for the mage run."

"I mean planning. Assessing. You should watch him. There's a lot more going on in his head than he lets out, but he seems to anticipate every order, or conclusion, that makes sense. And I think he's nearly memorized my maps."

"Um." Faris lifted a shoulder in a shrug. "But?"

Winn's humor faded. "Something's wrong. I think it has to do with magic."

"Oh, it does," she said. "When you're not around, he keeps trying to get us to fall in with this plan of his."

"Why don't you listen to him?"

"Because Evend has given us orders. Also, because he doesn't want the risk of dark magic enchantments here, even if aimed at Norsunder. Too much possibility of being used by the enemy. Senrid has an amazing knowledge of magic, from what I can tell, but not as deep as he thinks."

"Interesting. He's certainly not guilty of over-assessing his other abilities."

Faris waved a hand dismissing the military abilities. "I have my orders. You have yours."

Winn sighed. "Tying Arthur down is not doing him the least good. He just has more time to brood, and he can't ask Evend or Oalthoreh questions."

Faris nodded soberly. "I'll tell them. You know they care deeply about him."

Winn forced a smile. *I know, or I would have cut him free a long time ago.*

He and Arthur watched Faris and the three visitors join with the rest of the patrol and ride out. They started back, the mud sucking at their feet at every step. As Arthur debated insisting on being permitted to go, and Winn wondered what to say if he did, they heard the *kek-kek-kek* of a stooping raptor, which was followed by a long cry: someone sighted by the perimeter watch.

Word ran ahead: *friends.* What was better, *aid!*

Then Winn was completely surprised when Arthur gave a whoop and exclaimed, "It's the Mearsieans!" as the scout on the northern ride led in a swarm of girls.

Winn's first reaction was dismay, for they so badly needed reinforcement, and who was going to watch over these ankle-biters? But then he saw the white head among them, and it was his turn to exclaim in amazement. "Clair of Mearsies Heili?"

She didn't seem to have her big cousin along, which was a shame, but the mages would be glad of Clair's help, wouldn't they? The girl who'd helped free Bereth Ferian?

"It's Arthur!"

"Ar-thur!" a girl with freckles and bristly red hair yelled, racing up. "Learned any new pocalubes? I need lots more insults, cuz Siamis is gonna have a whole chapter to'mself!"

Arthur said happily to Winn, "Falinneh is going to write a book about how to properly treat villains."

The freckle-face beamed at Winn. "Yep! Soon's I learn me a bit more about readin' and writin'!"

High, excited kid voices piped through the usually quiet camp, as people moved purposefully and torches wavered and streamed in the clean spring wind. Winn was amazed at the change that had come over Arthur.

" . . . so here's the current situation," Arthur was saying to Clair and a short girl with long black hair. "We don't have nearly enough people for patrol duty. Our plan is to find the elevens and see what they're doing, which so far is trying to lay rifts here and there. We have a tough time communicating, since the patrols go out for five day rides."

Winn watched, still amazed. It was the first time he'd seen Arthur take the initiative, and his sum-up was masterly.

Clair nodded. "I see. So there could be ten days lost in getting word out between groups, is that it?"

"Yes. Now, we do have the help of birds and in the north, at least, the animals, but the elevens have taken to shooting at them for sport, and we don't know how long they'll stay with us. Some think the animals will go right back into hiding from human concerns."

The black-haired one said, arms crossed, "And I wouldn't blame them. What about magic?"

"Norsunder can intercept messages. It's happened twice—that we know of. And we daren't use transfer."

"They need our slates, is what they need," the black-haired one said to Clair.

"Yes."

It was just a comment, but Winn saw Clair frown, and then her brow clear, and both she and Arthur turned his way, as if they'd had some kind of mental exchange. He knew they hadn't. The unknown, mysterious Sartora was the only one who could (supposedly) hear thoughts. But it was interesting how well they understood one another.

"Do you really need them?" Clair asked.

Winn gestured a little helplessly. "I—I don't really have much to do with the magic end of things. Oalthoreh commands, and Evend—"

"Yes," Arthur said. "We do."

Clair gave a firm nod. "Then we'll be back. Girls?"

The swarm of girls formed a quiet circle around Clair.

"CJ and I have to go back home to get our slates. They need people here for patrols. Arthur?"

And Arthur said, without hesitation, "The toughest area for ordinary humans is the Ghost Lakes. Dhana, you probably would do fine there. And Seshe."

Clair said, "Seshe? Dhana?"

Both girls nodded.

"I'll stay with 'em," spoke the beautiful one with dark hair and eyes. "I don't mind weirdies."

"You stay with them, then, Diana. The rest of us will get our slates. How's that?"

Arthur said, "We'll get you mounts."

As he sent them off, Winn mentally amended his report, thinking: *Oalthoreh, you're not going to like this sudden independence.* But he hoped Evend would, when he saw how happy Arthur was.

When the patrol rode south, Senrid peeled off. He didn't tell anyone he was going to scout his way to the city to talk to Evend.

It took him three days of hard riding. He shut out everything but the goal ahead, stopping for minimal rest, food, and water; the animals cooperated, so he always had mounts. He was too used to their appearance to be disturbed any more. But he wondered when the silent cooperation would end.

When he reached Bereth Ferian, he eyed the marble palace, feeling as if he was entering the camp of the enemy. He sensed powerful lighter wards in place, which explained why Siamis hadn't just blasted in and trashed Evend, since—to all appearances—the ancient mage was just sitting in his stronghold doing nothing.

Few people were about. Senrid practiced his inner listening, and located Evend in another wing. As he trod the quiet halls, glancing at old tapestries depicting historical occasions about which he knew nothing, and paintings of people whose identities he was ignorant of, he wondered why no one had stopped him. Did Evend really think that Siamis would only come in force?

And where *was* Siamis?

Senrid shook his head. Time for that later.

He found the room, and opened the door without knocking.

"I could have been Siamis," he said.

The old man was sitting in a wingchair, a great book on his lap. He turned his head. His long white beard drifted down onto his hands, and over the pages of the book.

"No," Evend said, his raspy voice calm. "He will not come until he is ready."

"And you're going to sit here and wait for him?"

Evend said nothing.

Senrid hissed a sigh out through his teeth. "Look. This method using your own life—it's very heroic, but unnecessary. I know another way. I'm warded against doing the magic, but I can tell someone how. I'm sure you can give up one of your light magic objects. Like that hatpin that Liere carries. Or you must have something or other lying around that has all kinds of heavy spells on it. Use *that* to bind your enchantment. It's just a reversal spell, right?"

Evend said, "I know enough dark magic to remove that mirror ward on you. It's a fairly simple spell, though lethal if done wrong."

"That characterizes most dark magic," Senrid stated with cheery irony. "Go ahead! Though I won't use my magic. I imagine Siamis has tracers against me, and you probably don't know how to break those."

"No," Evend agreed. But he performed the magic.

That done, Senrid said, "I take it you're not going to use my suggestion."

"I'm not stopping you from attempting it," Evend said. "There would be no proof like success, would there?"

Senrid gritted his teeth. Was the old mage humoring him? Senrid loathed being treated as if he were just an ignorant boy.

He liked Arthur, though. He'd only known Evend's heir a few days, but he had instantly comprehended that Arthur was unswervingly devoted to the old man. "Success as proof. Well, then, I'll be back with my proof, fair enough?"

Evend smiled, a sad smile. A disbelieving smile. "Fair enough."

Senrid walked out.

He cursed all the way to the edge of the city, and then grimly faced the long journey southward again in order to catch up with his patrol.

He needed a suitable magic object. When Liere returned, as everyone expected, he could borrow the hatpin or the dyr. She wouldn't need them anymore, right?

Chapter Forty-Two

For nearly a month, Liere and Devon lightning-flashed through the settled areas of the world. The Norsundrians were never able to predict where she would be next. By the time they discovered yet another population waking up and restless, she was long gone.

The girls whirled north and south over the world, never sleeping on the same continent, and seldom eating two consecutive meals in the same kingdom. Liere refused to talk to any adults, just did her job and vanished as quickly as she could.

When at last their food ran out, Devon made it her business to ask the adults for food and shelter when she thought it was time, because Liere wouldn't even ask for that. And she kept forgetting to eat or rest unless Devon suggested it.

It was good to do this work, but after a time the faces of the disenchanted blurred in their tired minds. They felt lonely and isolated, Liere driven by the terrifying memory of Loss Harthadaun, and her own guilt at having given in and permitted people to make a fuss over her. She lived in a fever of hurry, not wanting even to know the names of the people she faced: as soon as she saw awareness shape blank faces into persons, she ran for Hreealdar, tugging Devon after her.

As the month wore on, Devon longed for a quiet place to live, with friends and a cozy fire. She wanted to eat cookies again, and sleep in the same bed every night.

Liere longed for the last stop, because then she could go to Bereth Ferian, where she knew friends were. And conversation. And—
    She couldn't define the third 'and'. She just wanted to be there.

Chapter Forty-Three

After a month of patrols and rain and more patrols and more rain, Senrid and Leander rode in together to Winn's latest camp, tired after a week of hide-and-seek with the Norsundrians.

Leander had two thoughts: food and his bedroll. He watched Senrid assessing the camp—who was there, who not—and wondered what was going on in his head. Senrid had been sour for a couple of weeks after returning from a scouting foray about which he said only "Useless," but gradually his mood had shifted back to his usual restless cheer.

The left their mounts with the day's horse picket hands, then walked to Winn's tent.

"What news?" Senrid asked as they entered. "Where's Liere now?"

"Um," Faris said, glancing down at Winn's camp table. "Tivaree, Ormondeh, Shezla, and Barhoth have been freed from the enchantment. So far, in today's communications."

Leander said politely, "Thanks, Faris."

Senrid's eyes were half shut. He snapped his fingers. "North of Sartor. Mardgar River. She's fast!"

Faris shrugged, flicking her long honey-colored braid behind her. "The birds still insist she's riding a bolt of lightning."

"Whether she is or not, it's got to be confounding Siamis's people." Senrid clawed his wild curls back and peered down at the list. "Yesterday she was west of the Halian-Toaran land bridge. She can't be doing those kinds of hops without some kind of magic."

Faris pointed to Senrid's bandaged hand. Though she was a young woman, the boys found her a comfortable person because she didn't act like an Adult, appointing herself their authority because she was older. They'd learned that she was a magic student, but skilled with a bow, and a good rider. She and her two brothers—patrol leaders both—were old friends of Winn. And everybody liked Winn, partly (Leander had decided) because it was so clear that Winn liked everybody.

"Wound?" Faris asked.

Senrid shrugged.

Leander said, "The morvende we were with accidentally met up with some elevens who were nosing around looking for their geliath. We had a little sword-work and then led 'em a fine chase."

"And in the sword-work I was rotten, as usual," Senrid said grimly.

Faris and Leander exchanged looks.

"Any more news?" Senrid asked.

"Yes." Faris smiled. "The magic end I can give you more details on. We got a very, ah, colorful report from that black-haired girl, um, CJ. You'll find her and some of the other Mearsieans somewhere around."

"So the Mearsieans are back?" Senrid asked, crossing his arms. So far he and the Mearsieans had missed one another, each one's patrol returning just after the other rode out. Fine by him.

"Let's go ask for a report in person," Leander suggested. "Come on. You'll like Clair."

Senrid just smiled. His last encounter with Mearsieans had been memorable for numerous reasons, none of them being friendship. Of course he'd been doing a reluctant job of trying to kill two of them.

They crossed the camp, Senrid taking two strides to Leander's one. People were already busy breaking camp. Returning Norsunder harassers would be informed of the new location by birds, or a couple of Fen wolves who were running with the wilder groups—like the one that Dtheldevor had joined. This until every group could get one of Clair's slates.

Winn waved from the other side of the camp, then returned to his conversation with a pair of patrol leaders.

Arthur was in his tent, surrounded by half a dozen adults in mage robes, with CJ and Clair standing by, unnoticed. Leander and Senrid exchanged looks; something had happened. The mages usually stayed in their own secret camp.

Arthur gave a nod as the boys looked in. "So each of our people should have one of Clair's slates by the end of the week?"

The adults muttered assent, and Oalthoreh said to her companions, "I suggest we eat something and then depart. We all need to return to our own posts."

The adults walked out of the tent, deep in talk about mirror spells and enchantment key searches.

Arthur said wryly to Clair, "I think they still believe your slates were an accident."

Clair shrugged. "I don't really care what they think, as long as they use them."

"They're using 'em," CJ said gloatingly. "And they didn't invent them. One for us."

"Well, it did take me a long time to understand how they work," Clair admitted. "And it *was* happenstance to find out that we could transfer back to get them through the caves."

Senrid crossed his arms. "They don't know what to do about kids with good ideas. Or kid leaders."

Everyone looked up. CJ's made a comical face. "Hey! Is that you, Boneribs?"

Senrid said, "I have a twin somewhere in the world?"

CJ grinned. "Dunno—though maybe your spoon-faced gaboon of an uncle would know. And I wouldn't put it past that floob-nosed gnackle, either."

Senrid laughed.

Leander said, "Clair, this is Senrid."

Senrid met her calm, intelligent gaze, framed by odd blue-white hair. It was impossible to know what Clair was thinking, but she didn't look the least bit disapproving, scornful, or wary.

CJ's thoughts were, as usual, plain on her face. She grinned a challenge. "Last I saw, you were skinnier'n two twigs, and pasty-faced and boggle-eyed from five minutes of sleep a night. Now you look normal. Well, almost. You're still skinny."

"And you're not?" Senrid shot back.

CJ simpered, "Mine is but a delicate build . . ."

HAH!s from most of the others made CJ snicker. Leander breathed a silent sigh of relief.

Senrid was relieved as well, though he would never have admitted it to anyone.

Clair gazed at Senrid in interest. Why had he been wary? Well, he'd gotten over it fast enough. Maybe she'd even misinterpreted.

Arthur, a born peacemaker, was glad to see everyone getting along. But his worries about Evend would not be spoken, not unless a miracle happened and his mother returned from the mage battle in the south, now that she was no longer a prisoner. "I wish we could find out where Siamis is," he said to Clair as the others exchanged jokes and fake insults.

"Speaking as a former acquaintance," Clair said, putting fingers to nose, "I am just as happy we can't. At least I feel like we can do better against underlings."

Arthur rubbed his chin. "Right."

He left CJ and Clair planning magic tricks for their next foray, and dashed away to find Winn. Almost all the magicians had slates now, which meant immediate knowledge of their movements, but it was taking a lot longer to get the last slates to Winn's Chargers, who were spread out from east to west, wherever there were Norsundrians.

The plans seemed to be working, spirits were high, and the hit-and-run tactics had, so far, produced very few casualties.

But Siamis had yet to be heard from. And he still had the off-worlders.

And Evend stayed in Bereth Ferian, with his magic books, and gave his mages separate orders.

Arthur could not shake the feeling that there was another level to events that he was not seeing—that Evend did not yet want him to see.

And he could not get rid of his sense of disaster looming.

Frederic yawned as he watched Peridot jabbing stubbornly at a tree. *Emeth* flashed silver-blue in the spring sunlight; in this part of the world the light was gaining.

Frederic had little else to do but watch the light change. Life was so very boring. Siamis almost never had time for them anymore. After he'd gotten back from Everon he disappeared entirely, and Frederic overheard one of the Norsundrians saying that Detlev had ordered him to return to the Norsunder base to help in the fight to make the rift, but someone else said he went to Norsunder-Beyond. That meant he could be back in five minutes or five hundred years.

It was dreary when he was gone, but at least the Norsundrians didn't pick on the kids any more, not after Gloriel had repeated everything they said, and then rolled up her sleeve and showed Siamis the bruises. Since then the guards left the kids strictly alone, but the girls had nothing to say, not even Deirdre. Didn't Deirdre always used to be the leader, and think about things? She sat and stared at the horizon, unless someone talked right to her.

Frederic watched the light change. Sometimes, when they didn't notice him, he listened to the Norsundrians talk.

The Norsundrians didn't seem to know any of the kids' names, but Frederic had learned theirs. Long-faced Davernak seemed to be in charge again, after a time stuck with the worst duties. But he still didn't talk much, especially about whatever had happened to him before Frederic and the girls came along. How did they get here, anyway? Frederic couldn't remember.

So he turned back to the Norsundrians. That one with the light hair and the sharp chin, that was Effrath. He bragged a lot about Toar, and how tough they were there. The old one with the eagle-beak nose, his nickname was Nolv. He had a long name, impossible to pronounce. He only talked about killing. Parand was as tall as the men. She talked about weapons. And there was Laengal, the youngest. He said he'd joined up when he was ten. He was the meanest, even though he smiled a lot. But it was the sort of smile that made you back up a step.

Frederic stayed away from Laengal. The rest all acted a lot like the girls acted—just sort of sat around, only talking or doing something if someone talked right to them.

Laengal and his friends looked down on them, too, calling them recruits. Recruits and joiners. Laengal and his friends were joiners. There was obviously a difference, but Frederic couldn't figure it out.

He'd ask Siamis when he—

Oh. Siamis was back at last.

Things were going to be better. At least he'd stopped to talk to them and let them have *Emeth* to swing around in practice.

He was inside the house. The Norsundrians had taken over a house. Siamis left the kids outside for some practice. They each had taken turns with *Emeth*, squaring off with the one practice blade the Norsundrians let them have, until they got tired of it. Only Peridot persisted. To Frederic she looked like a robot—a robot?—as she switched from hand to hand, blocking, parrying, cut, lunge.

Frederic watched the light on the blade. Oh yeah. Siamis was back, wasn't he? Why did he sometimes have to remember something several times?

Frederic wandered inside the house, glancing with disinterest at a jumble of children's toys shoved into a corner. He hadn't seen what had happened to the cottagers who'd lived here. The Norsundrians took care of all that first, unless the people had vanished before their arrival.

Frederic drifted down a short hallway.

" . . . and in Colend as well," someone was saying. "Everon is hottest, next to Colend. All shouting 'Winn's Charge,' whatever that means."

"And Toar," said another. "And, same thing, Winn's Charge."

"That's six separate fronts," said Siamis. "Obviously coordinated through someone. Where did it break out first?"

"Middle of Toar is where we picked it up first. But within half a day it was everywhere."

"The Gerandans?"

"Broke the binding a week back. They're beyond our control. Those in coastal cities are strong-arming trade ships for home."

Siamis said, "You might go ahead and flush that despicable old man out of Chwahirsland and coopt some of his warm bodies. Their training is abysmal, but they can keep Colend busy—"

A sudden silence made Frederic peek in.

He felt the brief stir of air that meant magic transfer, and three new Norsundrians appeared, one by one, the last one causing that hot metal-stench that meant the air was burning, and magic transfer was unstable.

Frederic recognized the leader: Detlev.

Frederic didn't like Detlev. Wasn't there something in the past? Frederic only remembered having seen Detlev in Roth Drael one day, right after Siamis brought them there. From the back he looked like anyone else, a man with brown hair. He had gray eyes with green in them. You remembered that not because the color was anything special, but because when he met your gaze it made your head ache. You remembered those eyes like you remembered the shape and color of a scarred-over cut.

He always was the center of attention, even though he never seemed to wear any weapons.

"You seem," he said to Siamis, "to have misjudged the passage of time while you were sporting in the Garden."

The Garden, Frederic thought. That's the Garden of the Twelve, what the Norsundrians called the place in Norsunder where the real leaders hung out. The only thing he knew for sure about it was that nobody liked going there. Even Laengal looked grim the one time Siamis mentioned it.

"Is that an observation," Siamis asked, "or a warning?"

"Observation only." Detlev flicked three fingers up in a brief gesture.

The other Norsundrians were watching avidly. One of the newcomers, a very tall man wearing at least four visible weapons, snorted a laugh. This newcomer said, "His warnings are usually unequivocal."

Neither Detlev nor Siamis made any sign that they had heard.

Detlev looked down at a map that one of the Norsundrians had spread on a battered old table, and said, "Winzhec's camp is approximately here. They move it about daily, but so far have stayed in this area. Oalthoreh and the mages are still invisible to us. You will need to address that first."

Siamis said, "I take it you've not interfered."

Detlev lifted his hand, and turned the palm up. "This is your diversion. Not mine."

And then he made a sign, said something blurry, and vanished. It felt different than the other magic transfers.

The tall, heavily armed red-haired one said on the verge of laughter, "Do you want me to continue playing fire-and-drakes with Lilith?"

"Yes." Siamis's voice sounded like he wanted to sigh.

The red-haired man, and the one who had never spoken, walked out the door, and away. Frederic knew they would go a distance before using their transfer tokens, because the air still smelled like hot metal.

Davernak said, "We didn't know Detlev was in the area."

Siamis walked to the window. "You must always assume he is watching. Always. Especially now."

"What did he mean about a diversion?" Davernak asked.

"He's aware of the real reason I made my retreat to the Garden. They won't order him to release the Base to my control, even though he lost his rift. But they won't give him control over my rift here in the north. He knows it."

The Norsundrians looked angry. Two looked worried. Frederic just listened, wondering what it all meant.

"A diversion," Siamis repeated.

Frederic could only see Siamis's profile. He looked annoyed. Frederic felt annoyed.

The others began to speak, each trying to be heard. Their voices got louder. Frederic backed away a step.

He was glad when Siamis finally turned from the window. The others shut up, like a TV turned off. A TV? Frederic thought. What's that?

" . . . what is clear is that we need to move swiftly," Siamis said. His voice sharpened, and Frederic frowned. He wanted Siamis to be happy. Then Frederic and the girls would be happy. "I would have liked to accomplish our goals with as little interruption as possible. The lighters really do seem to prefer bloodshed. So be it. We will finish forming the rift here, and then we'll give them bloodshed."

Laengal laughed. Frederic backed away three steps.

"Now. Our focus is going to stay local for the immediate future. Laengal, you and the other three are going to keep Oalthoreh and her minions busy here. Davernak, be patient. Once we have my arrogant young Marloven friend with us, you may do what you like with your four dead-weights, but until then, we do need them as backup."

"How are we going to lure him?"

"No need." Siamis smiled. "Senrid will find us. So. We first . . ."

Marloven? Frederic thought. Senrid? Why did he know those words?

Well, he'd forgotten them now. Frederic sighed, and wandered out. Orders were always boring.

He saw a carved rocking horse, and stood there kicking at it with his toe, and watching it creak back and forth, back and forth.

Chapter Forty-Four

Senrid drifted around the new camp, listening. The military side of Winn's Charge was a stopgap. So far it had been successful, according to the reports the mages were receiving. Siamis's forces were divided, distracted, spread too thin. But that would end the moment Siamis brought in a considerable force.

Senrid was convinced that the magical side of their efforts was the most important.

The adult mages ignored Senrid, and a few made it clear that they distrusted him. Not overtly. But somehow he never could find them whenever they held conferences. And though they now came often to the camp, and interacted with Faris and the mage-apprentices, Senrid was increasingly convinced that they spied more than they actually helped. They were obviously busy with their own plans.

So he shrugged them off. It gave him freedom of action.

At least Arthur and Winn understood that time was limited.

Siamis has to be feeling the pressure, Senrid thought. His obedient population base was vanishing every day, which had to mean he was gambling all his resources on effecting his big rift and then cutting Norsunder loose for total warfare.

What pressures might he be getting from Norsunder? "Gotta use 'em for us," he muttered, rounding behind a tent.

He nearly tripped over someone.

"Hey!" CJ sat with her back to a tree, her legs out, and a plate in her lap. She gave him a sour glare. "Watch where yer going!"

"What? All alone?" Senrid countered, quite ready for battle if she offered it.

She grimaced. "Clair asked me to skip the meeting. I can't stand the way Oalthoreh keeps looking down on the odd little white-haired kiddie." CJ grinned. "So I made a comment or two, only to be helpful, but apparently the ol' bat didn't like 'em. Clair will tell me whatever they decide, but she says we don't have time to be squabbling with those grownup mages."

"She's right," Senrid said. "Though they don't even let me have the chance to squabble. I didn't know about this meeting."

CJ shrugged. "Probably the only reason Clair did is because she was here before, and happened to accidentally break that big spell. Or maybe because she's got white hair. Who knows? They don't talk to me, either, just to her."

Senrid snorted.

"So anyhoo, what's the hurry?" CJ said. "Can't we just keep on doing what we're doing until either you or the grownups find a way? Find some other way," she corrected herself," to make sure Siamis doesn't get a big rift made?"

"Other way?" Senrid asked.

CJ made a nasty face. "There's a way. It mirrors your g-r-r-eat old dark magic, but it costs a life—"

Senrid let out his breath. "So you do know about that."

"Everyone knows about that." CJ's expression changed again. "Well, maybe not everyone. The mages do, and Clair heard." Her fine black brows drew into a line. "Clair also overheard some people worrying that Evend might be planning something nasty like that."

"He is," Senrid said. "I thought you all knew it and didn't care. Thought it a noble sacrifice, and all that."

"Wrong," CJ said. "Haven't you talked to Arthur at all?"

"Oh, I know he doesn't want it to happen, but I thought he was the only one. Seems to regard that old man as a kind of father."

CJ squinted up at Senrid, her blue gaze wide and speculative. "You think we're stupid."

Senrid shook his head. "I've learned plenty about the 'ignorance of the lighters' but there are some things you seem to regard as noble and necessary and I think of as . . . unnecessary." When her lips parted, he added, "If you're about to shove my past in my teeth, I'm gone."

CJ snorted, obviously unimpressed. "It's just that you looked so surprised. And I remember all that gas you blathered about idiot lighters, last year."

"Then forget it," he said. "Here's what I see shaping up. All of us under the age of sixteen, say, are hearing the same sort of stuff about how things are changing but we kids don't know what we're talking about, listen to those with experience, talk, talk, talk. It's not a coincidence that there are a lot of us—"

"Sartora said the same thing. To Clair. I'm the first to squawk if some grownup treats me like a stupid little kiddie," CJ said, "but we don't *know* all the stuff they know."

"Maybe alone," Senrid said, urgency making him restless. This always happened when his mind followed two paths of thought, or rather, when one seemed clear but the important one was hidden, revealing itself in shadows and subtle signs.

He began to pace back and forth, from the tree to the tent. "Maybe when we're alone. But when we work together, kids can out-think adults. That's what I've learned. *I* can out-think an adult. I did. I out-thought my uncle all the time, but until the end I never had the power to act on anything. You saw what my life was like."

"It stank." CJ held her nose.

Senrid grinned."I know I will out-think him again when I go home and boot him out."

"And you'll change some of his wonderful rules?"

"No," Senrid drawled. "I'll spend *all* my time killing lighters."

CJ grinned unrepentantly.

"Enough of that." Senrid snapped his fingers. "We have to out-think Siamis. And we can. He's arrogant, so arrogant he let Liere thrash through half his enchanted kingdoms before he even took her seriously. Arrogance doesn't change overnight. And I think he's also pressed for time. By us, and by his allies."

"Hah!" CJ snorted. "So what's he doing, then?"

"I think this is what's going on. He's sent flunkies out to make as many rift accesses as they can, to keep us busy putting them out. Like setting little fires."

CJ said, "Will you sit down? You're making me dizzy. So what is it we need to figure out?"

Senrid dropped to his knees, smoothed the dirt with a couple quick swipes, and began drawing a map with his finger. "Where the real accesses are, as opposed to the fake ones he's making to keep us busy. We have to figure out where he plans to make the big rift, and that will tell us where he's got the off-worlders stashed."

"Oh. That's soooo easy."

Senrid didn't mind her sarcasm any more than she minded his. She set aside her empty plate and crouched opposite, her chin on her knees, her bare toes just touching the northern edge of his dusty sketch of Helandrias.

"You know how rifts work."

"Yes. No. I know that at eleven their magic is strongest, so the Norsunder gabboons can bring their snilches over."

"One or two at a time, through the rift accesses, which are kind of like doors. It takes a tremendous amount of transfer magic to move people anywhere. As you know. It's apparently worse from Norsunder, and considerably worse if they try to do it repeatedly, due to the drag of time."

"I don't get why," CJ said.

"Think of it a little as jumping back and forth from a moving ship to another ship, both of which might move at different speeds."

CJ closed her eyes. "Okay. And the big rift is real long, like a tear in the world, Clair said. See, she was there a while back, when they closed one by the city of Bereth Ferian."

"You can't make a big one without having at least two small ones to join. And a really big one will join a line of them, close together as they can get 'em, kind of like stringing beads. That's why in the past, when there were big rifts, they could move numbers back and forth just like marching from here to that hill over yonder."

"So where do the off-worlders come in?" CJ asked.

"You know that lighters can destroy a huge spell by ending their own lives, but it only works for those who have already extended their lives by magic, and are truly ready to let that go. And of course they are dead, and so beyond the reach of Norsunder, so the rift ward holds forever."

"Got that."

"Rifts made by dark magic can be bound to a person who can hold the magic long enough to be murdered. They get stashed in Norsunder, and if the lighters can't get to them, then they can't break the magic. Mirror image."

CJ looked sick. "Siamis wants to do that to the off-worlders?"

Senrid nodded. "The drawback is that if they aren't strong enough to hold the magic, they die anyway, and end up in Norsunder as soul-bound, where they'll never regain their identities. And Siamis goes looking for more victims."

"Ohhhh," CJ said, her eyes distant. "Now I see it. Groanboils! That really stinks!"

Senrid smiled sourly. "Right. Normally death takes you beyond the temporal realm. In Norsunder-Beyond, you're stuck there. whether you want to be or not. And it can get worse, if the soul-eater turns up."

CJ shuddered.

"That's why they don't often do that kind of magic, using a life. The really strong victims tend to come back and make trouble."

CJ narrowed her eyes. "So why hasn't he used the off-worlders, if he's going to?"

"Because of the drawbacks, is my guess," Senrid said. "The rift probably isn't going to be big enough for an army to cross, even using all four of them. They don't know any magic, and they're enchanted so their wills are half in a dream world. They won't be able to hold the amount of power he needs. Now, if he had someone who knows dark magic, who can control a lot of power, but who is under his control . . ."

CJ's gaze was now uncomfortably direct. "Someone like you."

"If he can catch me." Senrid curled his lip. "Anyway, the question we have to answer is, where is the real rift going to be? Here's the coast, along which we've got Hier Alverian, and so on, down to Chor, and the big bay. West of this land, down toward the Venn, was a huge rift, millennia ago. Mages are all busy there, trying to negate attempts to reopen that old rift."

CJ shrugged. "That's not news."

"I haven't finished. I don't think he's going there. Too many mages expect it. I think he's making a new one, but where? He's not going to make a rift that will put his emerging troops in front of a huge body of water and no way to cross it quickly. Or in front of a big mountain range, or anything else that'll slow 'em up right at the start. That's where those mages are starting out wrong. They know nothing about military thinking, and they won't listen to Winn, who does."

"And Clair doesn't know anything about war junk," CJ said, "so she won't be able to tell them."

"That's my part," Senrid said, with his old grin that showed too many teeth. "We all have our own special knowledge. Clair did her part with the slates. This way we keep track of everyone."

CJ nodded.

Senrid looked down, his gaze distant. "Has to be this coast, here, in the north. He won't make it too far south, because then he'd have the Venn to face before long. If Liere's made it over to the Venn side of this region, they're going to be worse than an angry wasp nest, and even Norsunder respects the Venn in the field."

"Even the Marlovens respect the Venn?" CJ asked, digging a little.

He looked up fast—and saw the tease in her face.

"Even the Marlovens respect the Venn," he said. "We tangled with 'em all up and down the coast of both continents, back in the bad old empire days. Where d'you think we come from? Marlo-ven, Marolo-Venn, Outcasts of the Venn, though we once blurred it by calling ourselves Mar-lo-vahn. Not that anyone was fooled."

CJ snorted.

"Anyhow. Gotta be this coast. . . . no big river, but a good port for putting in warships. Big enough . . . Hier Alverian has plenty of good spots. But which?"

"Don't ask me," CJ said. "My way of catching elevens is to sniff the air and see which way the stench comes. That is, if I'd ever want to catch any, which I haven't. So far my preference has been to run soon's I smell 'em!"

"I need a good map." Senrid straightened up. "Back to harassing Winn for his."

"I'll go with you. I hate sitting around waiting for a giant boot to squash us." CJ snagged her plate, to be dumped in the barrel outside the cook tent. "I want to be doing something."

The afternoon shadows were at their longest slant. Soon they'd blur together into the long northern twilight. Another day gone, Senrid thought.

CJ said, "What I want to know is, why do you want to get the off-worlders back? Besides foiling his plan, and rescuing them, I mean."

"Because they could also break a rift. I'm pretty sure."

"Ugh!"

"Oh, not that way. See, they weren't born here, so they exist outside of magics that ward natives. So they could do the spells and bind a powerful white object, which would get destroyed in destroying the dark magic rift. But isn't that a good cause?"

"Sure," CJ said. "And if it doesn't work, no one gets hurt, right?"

"Except," Senrid said, "then we're still stuck with a functioning rift. And he might be making it *right now*."

CJ sighed.

In the west, the sun rimmed the distant mountains.

Chapter Forty-Five

"I like this country," Devon said, looking around the capital city of Silver Wood, as she and Liere walked away from the city center. "I sure like it better than that huge, scary place this morning!"

"Land of the Venn," Liere said.

This city was full of flowers, in gardens, along the streets, in window boxes, even visible along balconies and roof terraces. Devon sniffed the balmy air. "Roses!" She loved the glowglobes set on metal poles with brass leaves twining all round them. In their light, though, Liere looked tired.

"It was kind of strange, wasn't it?" Liere said. "Strange, but not at all ugly. Who would have thought the Venn would have a city above the ground and another underground, like morvende? I wonder if 'Venn' and 'morvende' are related, the common thing being those underground cities."

Devon ignored Liere's speculation with the ease of long habit. "I thought they were scary."

"Scary? Their city is very old. I want to learn about their history."

Ugh, Devon thought. But she didn't say it. Her knees ached and her neck felt as if someone had put an invisible iron band round it, and when she looked up at the glowglobes, they had rings around them.

The streets were full of people laughing, talking, some angry, busy with one another. The girls had left so quickly that no one knew who they were. Liere had gotten very good at that.

Devon sighed as she tried to see past all those adults. "Where's Hreealdar? I'm so, so, tired."

Liere took Devon's hand. "I'm sorry, Devon. But we're done now. This is the end, for we dare not go to the east coast. Siamis and his elevens are there."

Devon didn't ask how she knew. It was enough that she did, that the job was finished.

Liere knew better than to tell Devon that she felt Siamis's presence in her dreams, as if he *wanted* her to know where he was.

Each day of the past couple of weeks seemed to have gotten longer, and all the places they had visited blurred together in her memory. Where was it the people all had rainbow coloring? What was that place where the queen had fixed them a meal with her own hands, in the hollowed-out goldenwood tree she said reached a thousand years of age before it died in a lightning blast? Devon couldn't remember any more.

They reached a bridge. Liere leaned against the rail and looked back at the people in the square, their faces reflected in the light of glowglobes, and of windows in cozy-looking houses with arched, diamond-paned windows.

Liere made the sign, which was followed by the familiar flash.

Devon forced her tired body up onto Hreealdar.

"Last time," Liere breathed.

And they transferred to Bereth Ferian.

The minds around her were bright, clear, a jewel box of emotion-colors, instead of the muted-gray sameness of those under the enchantment.

They slid off Hreealdar. Liere leaned against the horse that wasn't a horse. She closed her eyes. *Thank you,* she thought. *Thank you.*

And from Hreealdar came an outflowing of benediction.

Then the creature vanished.

The girls looked up at the night-lit palace, the windows like golden lacework through the leafing birches. From somewhere came the bracing scents of an herb garden.

They walked inside. A woman in blue and white met them.

"Is Evend here?" Liere asked. Her voice was going hoarse.

"She is Sartora," Devon added, and Liere hid the sharp jab of irritation at the pride in her voice.

The woman gave them a slight smile. Devon thought of her mother, though this lady looked only a little like her mother: gray eyes and thin. But this lady's smile was a real smile, not painted, and she looked right at you, and not at your clothes and then away to find her own reflection. "You are most welcome," the lady said, and the memory disappeared. "Come."

The girls followed her swaying robes down a long hall to a room with windows on all sides, and double door. They were open.

"Here he is," she said, and she walked away.

Devon watched her go. That slim back, the gold-glinting hair, again reminded her of her mother, one of the times her hair had been that color.

Does she miss me at all?

Probably not. Do I miss her? I don't know. I hope she's nicer to my baby brother. But even as she thought it Devon knew that her mother's interest would last exactly as long as she had an interest in the baby's father. Then she'd ignore him just as she had her, while she looked for a new husband, always richer than the one before.

Liere had gone inside. Devon followed down a hall lit by tiny glowglobes to a room with lamplight spilling out. A tall, stooped old man sat in a carved chair, reading

"Welcome, children," he said. "I am Evend."

"Isn't it dangerous for you to be here?" Devon burst out.

"I await Siamis." Evend spoke the words with calm conviction.

Devon hunched up, shoulders to her ears, as if Siamis lurked in the corner, waiting for mention of his name.

Liere said, "There has to be another way. Can't you use this thing? I'm done now, or nearly." She pulled the dyr bag from her tunic. "It's a dyr."

"I know what a dyr is. At least, I know as much as anyone knows these days. It was I who trained Erai-Yanya in its protection."

"Take it, then. Use it, please. I'm done." Liere held it out.

He shook his head. "It is not going to help. Its purpose seems to be restricted to distorting, or augmenting, or manipulating interactions between people, as far as we can discover. It's useless for anything else."

"How about the Guardian's hatpin?" Liere unpinned it from the hem of the dyr bag.

"That is even more useless, I'm afraid."

Liere's insides tightened. She'd been so certain that she had the solution. She remembered, with almost overwhelming shame, sending a little cat on a long perilous journey. How many beings, human, animal, and non-human, waited confidently for Sartora to rescue them yet again? Yet here she stood, ignorant about magic—ignorant about everything, even where she'd been. She was done breaking the enchantment, but there was no feeling of triumph, or even the power she'd feared. How very arrogant that seemed now! She had never felt more stupid in her life.

"Is Rina all right?" she managed, fighting the sting of tears.

Evend smiled. "Rina is fine. She stayed a long time with her cousins in Helandrias, and the Lake beings sent her home to Geranda."

Liere's eyes burned as she struggled against the stupid, *useless* feelings. Weakness! How could one kill them forever, and be free to exist in a mental realm of calm rationality?

Think!

She lifted her hand. "Senrid Montredaun-An was sure there was another way."

Evend said, "He knows little about our forms of magic. In the meantime, there is danger. You cannot remain here."

Liere stared back at him, blinking hard. All this time, all this way, and nothing had happened the way she'd planned. Evend was kind, and good, but he wouldn't listen to her. She was just an ignorant little girl in his eyes, and the adults would go right on doing what they wanted.

"You must leave," Evend said again.

"Where would I go?" Liere asked, whispering.

Evend leaned forward, compassion and regret clear in his old face. "Surely you, of all people, would find a welcome anywhere you chose."

Liere drew in a shuddering breath. "No. Sartora would. Not me. Nobody wants stupid Liere Fer Eider." *Not even my family*. She didn't say it; she knew it wasn't true, or at least not completely. The truth was she no longer wanted them, or rather, she no longer could bear being shoved into the back of a shop to count yarns, and beat dust out of rugs, and sweep floors after her brothers ran in and out on deliveries; she could no longer bear her father scorning her for inappropriate curiosity about the world outside South End, could no longer bear her mother's hurt silences when Father's temper smashed the family harmony she longed for, could no longer bear Marga's unquestioning happiness—or Brother Elesier's silent unhappiness at being kept away from the kitchens.

Was there no one, besides little Devon here, who wanted the company of Liere Fer Eider?

Senrid. She could see his face, so vividly. His near sacrifice.

She looked up. "Is Senrid is *here*?"

"Near enough." Evend said kindly, "He's with my heir, helping with the efforts to deflect the Norsundrians. My allies will transport you in a wagon. It will take all night." His old eyes took in Devon's drooping form. "You can rest during the journey."

Devon's pleading gaze decided Liere. "Thank you," she said.

And very soon they lay on quilts under more quilts, with empty baskets piled on top to hide them.

Devon dropped promptly into slumber.

Liere lay awake, her body exhausted, her mind reeling. Someday she would be able to remember the places she'd been, the people she'd encountered so briefly. But what to do about Evend? *Don't think about the rift . . . don't feel. There has to be a solution.*

She'd find Senrid, and ask him.

Senrid.

Liere thought of Kerendal, Prince of the Venn, a boy not much older than she. He'd had Senrid's coloring, only more intense: golden hair instead of blond, and eyes so dark a blue they seemed violet. But there the resemblance ended, for Kerendal, though young, was already tall, and strong from whatever training had fashioned Rel to move the way he did. The physical resemblance ended there, but not the intensity of personality.

Show me on the map where you've been, Kerendal had asked, there in the awe-inspiring halls of his ancestors, gazing at her with the kind of hungry focus Liere knew from her own days of mental starvation. And when she had to confess she could not name the kingdoms she'd been in and out of so swiftly, he'd nodded, in sympathy, not scorn, and said, *Show me the magic object? We are forbidden magic here, because my forefathers always used it to make war.*

Amid images of the wind-battered ancient city of Twelve Towers, she slid into sleep.

❧

That same morning, not far distant, a figure emerged from the ocean onto a beach, having spotted kids her own age.

The four kids she'd seen from the water stared in somewhat muddled bemusement to see a girl more or less their own age swim to the shore and step up carefully, as if she found walking difficult, her dress soggy with brine. Nobody had seen her go into the water.

One of the four disappeared up the beach; by the time the girl had paused to wring out her hair and skirts as best she could, the kid was back, leading a man.

Kyale Marlonen was relieved that the grownup didn't look like any eleven or Marloven or other such creep.

The man walked down the shore to join her. "Had a long swim?" he asked.

He seemed friendly enough. In the background, the kids all smiled.

Kyale said, "I have. A month! At least. Maybe longer! It's hard to count days when you're in the ocean bottom. The sea folk don't really talk, except if you go up for air."

"Why would so young a girl undertake so long a journey?"

"I'm a princess," Kyale replied, chin elevated. "It's my duty to see to the safety of my brother. Who's a king! No one else will. Not that they even know what a princess is down there, but they did know where Bereth Ferian is, and pointed me in the right direction, and the last time, said this beach was the best place for me to come up to land."

"I see." He smiled. "Well done, your highness."

She grinned, pleased *at last* to be properly addressed by someone with a notion of proper protocol!

"So when I was swimming in, I saw those kids over there. I figure, I'm safe where there are kids. And all the rest of the coastline is all rocky and full of weeds and things."

"It is," the man agreed. "That's why we're here."

"As for which princess I am," she went on importantly, though the man had not asked, "I am Her Royal Highness Princess Kyale Marlonen of Vasande Leror, and I'm looking for my brother, His Majesty King Leander Tlennen-Hess of Vasande Leror."

"I regret to inform you he's not here, your royal highness," the man said.

Kyale loved it when people were impressed—if they really were impressed. Was he laughing at her? He was definitely smiling, and so were all those kids.

She wondered if she might have sounded maybe a little pompous. She had an uneasy feeling that the Mearsiean girls would have thought so, and she admired them. But a person had a *right* to be proud of her birth! Even if her mother had turned out to be a rotter.

"Well," she said, "you can call me Princess Kitty if you don't like long titles, and some of my royal friends don't. Anyway, can you direct me to where Evend and all the others are? I've got to keep an eye on my brother to make sure he doesn't get cabbaged by that picayune pickle-face Siamis and his nasty bunch of bunions."

"I can tell you where Evend is," the man said. "I believe he sits in Bereth Ferian, protected by formidable magic."

"Yes, magicians are like that," Kyale said airily. "But I don't really care about him so much as I do about finding my brother. He needs looking after. Especially if that disgusting Senrid is anywhere around."

"I think . . . I really believe I met your brother briefly," the man said, looking up at a line of high-flying gulls. "But that was some time ago. Do you think if you find Senrid—or he finds you—your brother might not be far behind?"

He fell in step beside Kyale, who walked up the shore to where the row of kids stood.

"Oh, he probably would," she said briskly. "Just to keep Senrid from causing too much trouble, you know."

"Indeed! Now, tell me more about your brother and Senrid," the man said invitingly, and nothing could have pleased Kyale more.

She described in detail how he was prone to forget things like food and sleep when he was busy with his stupid magic books, and he also was much too absent-minded to remember his position in life around people of lesser status. And kind hearted! He was nice to every fathead who walked in and asked a favor. If she weren't on hand to remind him, he probably would have become best friends with that horrible, evil, disgusting, nasty, ravening beast of a Senrid Montredaun-An . . .

The man's eyes were friendly and interested, and his voice was nice to listen to, but more important, he seemed to find *her* interesting. Nobody did, she found herself complaining as they joined the four silent kids. *Everyone* seemed to do everything better than she did, and it wasn't *fair*.

He agreed with all her statements, until she found herself agreeing with him.

And by the time Kyale remembered to ask the man's name, and found out that he was Siamis, she'd forgotten exactly why he was to be feared. All she could think was that he was kind, with a nice, smiling voice, and he was much, much, preferable to that horrible Tdanerend Montredaun-An, who was the biggest villain in the universe—except maybe for Detlev.

And stupid Senrid was third on the list.

Chapter Forty-Six

Dawn brought a summer shower. New Year's Week was nigh.

Arthur woke up and looked out of his tent, his heart expanding with the sense of rightness that came with the clean, cool scent of gentle rain in lush greenery, while one was cozy and warm.

But then the old worries gripped his skull like invisible steel fingers. He sighed, folded up his bedding, and walked out into the misting rain.

"Arthur!" Sherry waved from across the camp. "Sartora's here!" She vanished in the direction of the horse pickets.

Arthur ran, enjoying the squish of mud in his toes.

He arrived at the same time as a crowd of other people. A wagon had just pulled up, driven by old Hagan from the Bereth Ferian palace stables. The man spotted Arthur at the same time, and called a greeting.

"Safe journey?" Arthur asked.

The wrinkle-framed eyes squinted down at him. "Safe enough, safe enough, your highness."

Arthur winced internally. He still was not accustomed to the stupidity of titles, which Evend claimed were as much a part of social habit as any other manners. Arthur had spent his early childhood running barefoot among the ruins of Roth Drael with animals and morvende (who paid no attention whatever to political boundaries and terms), with a mother who changed her gown maybe once a year (a step through the cleaning frame when she woke and before she went to sleep being the extent of her interest in appearance) and kicked off her shoes the first day of spring.

"Let me see to the horses," Hagan said.

"Did you see Evend?" Arthur asked in a low voice. "How is he?"

Wiry old Hagan was already busy at the traces. "Saw him indeed. Bade me say that you are doing very well, your hi—"

"Thanks, Hagan," Arthur said hastily.

He turned around, to find the rest of the wagon blocked entirely by a huge crowd. Half the camp seemed to have arrived in the brief time he'd spoken with Hagan. The mist was now steady rain, but they all ignored it.

Arthur ducked elbows and squeezed between damp raiders and mage-apprentices—most of whom gave way when they saw him—until he spotted two skinny girls. Or was one a boy?

From every side came eager questions. The taller kid said, "My name is really Liere. I'm sorry. I don't remember," to someone.

Arthur recognized acute embarrassment when he heard it.

He thought, *Why doesn't his highness use his 'highness' and issue a few orders?*

"Here," he said, raising his voice. "Haven't we all things to do? Let's give Sartora a chance to get out of the wagon, at least, and then maybe a bite of breakfast?"

Miraculously they listened, wandering off in clumps, with backward glances and whispers.

Sartora's downcast eyes and her flat voice probably helped send them along, Arthur thought with an inner laugh. It would be hard to find a more unlikely-looking or sounding hero than this skinny, scruffy girl. Especially for those used to Winn's dashing grace.

"This way," Arthur said, pointing to the cook tent. "Um, which is which?"

The boyish one looked up. Meeting those eyes, Arthur felt that same painless flash-through-the-head he'd felt when he went swimming in one of the Ghost Lakes once.

Her lips parted. "Another one," she said. Then she flushed, her thin, flat cheeks mottling with red. "I'm Liere. This is Devon."

"Liere Sartora?" Arthur asked, confused. "And, uh, another what?"

The blush reached her ears. "Sartora's something our allies thought up. I agreed, hoping to sidetrack Siamis. It's meant as an honor—"

"But honorifics are like wearing somebody else's clothes," Arthur finished, understanding thoroughly.

Liere's brow cleared. "Oh, yes. Someone's *fancy* clothes, and I feel like a, a, thief!"

"Like a fake," Arthur said. "But—if I can ask—I'm another what? Not something disgusting, I hope."

"Another ready to make his unity," came a wry voice from behind.

Liere looked up quickly, then she gave a happy laugh. "Senrid!"

"How's the world saver?" Senrid asked. He was also grinning. Arthur stared in amazement. He'd never seen that kind of expression on Senrid's face before. "Eh, Devon?" Senrid asked.

From him, apparently, the imputation of heroism wasn't embarrassing, because it was a shared joke.

"Tired," Devon said, rolling her eyes. "But we are *done*—" She uttered a shriek. "The Mearsieans are here!"

"Where's Siamis?" Liere asked quickly, as rain began to tap the ground. "Exactly, I mean. I know he's . . . that way." She pointed vaguely east.

"That's what we've been trying to figure out." Senrid looked around, his eyes narrowed. "You say that Siamis is to the east. Along the coast?"

"I think so."

Senrid's expression hardened. He looked old for a startling and unsettling moment. "Arthur."

"Yes?"

"That's what he's been waiting for. *We're all here.*" He pointed to Liere, Arthur, and himself.

Liere held up her hands. "You mean, by my coming, I did something wrong?"

Senrid shook his head. "Never mind that. It's better, or will be, if we act fast. Arthur, let's plan. Now. Just us, no adults. Let's pool what we know—right now—without any adult on hand to interrupt and tell us we're wrong, or inexperienced, or just children, or of a questionable background, and hand out orders right and left. But we'll just call it a breakfast, not a conference. So they won't feel the need to nose, or to break it up for our own good."

"I'll go get Clair and CJ." Sherry had been standing behind Arthur.

"I'll come with you!" Devon said.

Liere looked after, wondering if she was wrong to feel relief as Devon ran off with someone else.

Arthur blinked at the coolness trickling on his scalp. He shook his head and fingered his hair back. As they walked toward the cook tent to get their food, they were in time to see Dtheldevor come from the other direction. She stomped in the mud, shaking herself like a dog, then turned her face up into the steadily increasing rain.

CJ appeared, and shouted, "Get your food and come to our tent!"

They began crowding in, with plates and gently steaming mugs. They sat in a circle, their camp plates on their knees.

"Grownup cooks," CJ was heard muttering. "All they make is tea or coffee. Sickness stuff! Horse-wash! No chocolate within three kingdoms. Ugh!"

"Speak for yourself," Senrid said. "I like coffee. Hot chocolate tastes like sugared mud."

"That's because you haven't had ours," Sherry said earnestly.

"Something he can try," Arthur said, "if we defeat Siamis."

"'Nother words," Dtheldevor cut in, "shut yer flaps!"

Arthur looked around the expectant faces, then he waved a hand at Senrid. "Okay. All yours."

Senrid leaned forward, his quick gaze assessing every face. "I think we have to act fast. The adults all seem to think they have lots of time. They think that if they keep finding and negating the little rift accesses the Norsundrians put up, we'll eventually wear them out and they'll go home. I gather that's what happened in the south." He turned to Clair. "You've been the only kid besides Arthur included in their sessions. Am I right?"

Clair said slowly, "I haven't been to all their planning sessions, but so far, I think you're right. But sometimes I get the sense that there's something they don't discuss, except maybe with each other. Out of our hearing."

Arthur's insides squeezed with the familiar gnaw of worry. "And I get the same sense."

"Because we're kids." Senrid's lips curled. "We're just too young to understand their great and powerful thinking."

Arthur grimaced at his toes; he hated the sarcasm Senrid used about people he'd known and respected all his life . . . but at the same time, Senrid was right. And the way CJ snorted, Arthur knew he wasn't the only one who thought so.

Senrid went on. "I think Siamis is keeping the mages busy with some of his underlings, making rift accesses over the old rift site, just as he's keeping Winn and the rest busy chasing small ridings all over the hills. He gets two things out of it: he keeps the mages out of the way, and he's got to have an idea where our camp lies."

Arthur leaned forward, elbows on his knees, his food forgotten. "I heard Winn tell Faris that, a few days ago. He ordered their group to make shadow camps."

Senrid flashed a grin. "Okay, here's my next guess. I think Siamis himself is making the rifts he's going to use. And we have to find him, and act before he can finish. Because now he has everyone he could possibly need, all neatly gathered for him. We have to act before he can send his force to round us up."

Silence, as the kids looked at one another.

"Where?" Leander asked. "I mean, where is the rift?"

Senrid pulled a folded paper from his shirt pocket. "I made a copy of Winn's map last night."

He spread the paper out in the middle of the circle where all could see it. Some scooted closer to stare down at it. Others glanced down at the painstakingly neat writing, then returned to their breakfasts.

"It has to be here. Along this coast. If you agree with my guess, then the next step is, we need a plan," Senrid said.

"Always," Sherry put in. "A good plan to ignore will always footle up the villains."

"Sherry," CJ said sharply. "That's *us*. I bet those Marlovens make a plan and stick to it." She dusted her hands on the last three words.

"Then they don't win," Sherry responded with calm certainty.

Leander smothered a laugh, and Dtheldevor snickered. The Mearsieans promptly launched into descriptions of past plans that had flubbed on them, and Dtheldevor, Leander, Arthur, and Liere listened with interest.

Senrid fought impatience. This was what it was going to be like, dealing with people who had little or no regard for chain of command or discipline. But he enjoyed the freedom of his interactions with the lighters. Trade-off. So he found patience—and his sense of humor.

"Sherry, you're free to footle the villains any way that works. For the rest, here's what I think. If someone has a better idea, that's why we're here. But I think we have to act now. *Today*." He glanced at Liere, whose thin face paled to the color of oatmeal. "Arthur?"

"Yesterday," Arthur said, in a low, fervent voice. "Before they close in on us. I think Senrid is right, that has to be their next move. And I think if Winn were here, he'd agree."

"That settles it. I'm in." Dtheldevor smacked Arthur heartily on the shoulder, and Arthur clutched at his plate to keep it from flying out the tent flap. "Well? Spit out yer idee! Want me 'n Leander t' try to assassinate the old soulstealer agin?"

"No. I want you searching. I'm going to be the only decoy—roam around to flush out his searchers. What you've got to do is find and spring the off-worlders while Siamis is busy chasing me. Liere can unenchant them, then we can get them to do *our* spells. I'll write them out. We'll use Cassandra's hatpin, or the dyr, or whatever works, to close the rift."

"But Evend said the dyr isn't useful for that," Liere said, wringing her hands together. "Or the hatpin."

Senrid said, "Lighter magic can't. But dark magic is all about force. I know how to do it." Senrid drummed his fingers on his map. "So we find the rift. Find the off-worlders and spring 'em. They can break the rift. I think they'd go for this plan if they had their wits."

"Thass right," Dtheldevor exclaimed. "Gloriel and Peridot, I know 'em. They'll be fair gutwrenched t' find out they been livin' next'r nigh that stenchifyin' Siamis, and not even holdin' their noses."

"I can vouch for Deirdre and Frederic," Arthur said. "When I was kidnapped and taken off-world, they saved my life before they even knew me."

Senrid said, "So that's my plan."

Clair said, "If you write out the spells for me, too, I could help. In case I get to them first, and they need coaching."

Liere said, "I can, too, if you tell me, Senrid. I can remember it, even if I don't know what any of it means."

CJ looked squinty-eyed. "Any reason why you have to be the noble martyr—" Her tone made that no compliment. "—who has to decoy Siamis-the-Stench?"

"The way I see it," Senrid said, "is I have the easy job. See, he wants me alive. He likes my background. Thinks he's going to use me as a shortcut for his big rift, which is why he went out of his way to mention this rift, and then didn't really chase us northward, not like they could have. The elevens have no orders to spare your lives, so you're going to be in the most danger. That means you have to be fast. If he does catch up with me, all I have to do is concentrate on his middle shirt button and try to keep him from enchanting my brains out until the rest of you get the off-worlders out, and they do the spells."

CJ chewed her lip, then glanced up, her blue eyes suspicious.

Senrid waited, holding his breath. He worked hard to hide how much he wanted everyone to fall in with his plans.

Liere said in his head: *You figured CJ out.*

She wasn't praising him.

Senrid thought back: *Everyone to the job best fitted, and reasons they'll understand, even if they aren't my reasons.*

Liere's awareness vanished from his, like a candle being snuffed.

"Anyone have a better idea?" Senrid asked, looking around.

CJ whispered to Irenne, "I thought he looked Siamised, there, for a sec. Yeccch!"

"Where do we begin the search?" Leander asked, studying the map.

Senrid was still listening in the mental realm. Leander had doubts, but he was not going to voice them. His nature was to be cautious.

" . . . said something about needing access to a good natural harbor as well." Leander was still speaking.

Senrid shut his eyes against the dizziness caused by that inner listening shifting abruptly to outer listening. He shook his head impatiently, and knelt in front of the map. Putting his finger on the representation of Hier Alverian's coast, he said, "Here. And maybe here."

"Then we better get moving," Dtheldevor said. "But where do we find ye?"

"I have the last two slates in my tent," Arthur said. "They were meant for the raiders who rode down the coast to Chor. They might not be back for a week."

"We'll take 'em." Senrid folded his map and pocketed it. "And divide into two groups. Get your gear and let's move."

He dashed out, followed by everyone save the Mearsiean girls.

As soon as they were alone, CJ turned to Clair. "What do you think? You didn't say much."

"I think it's too easy," Clair said.

"What?" Irenne flung her arms out dramatically. "Decoying elevens? Trying to keep our minds out of Siamis's mucky spell?"

"The plan." Clair shook her head. "Everything in steps, like the elevens will go right along. Our plans never worked because we always ended up being surprised by something we didn't know about the enemy. Senrid seems to think they are all alike, all stupid—except for Siamis. That is, now he thinks Siamis is stupid, and he'll just stand there villainizing at Senrid over *there*, while those kids do that spell over *here*."

"Well, aren't they stupid?" Irenne demanded.

"Of course. Or they wouldn't be elevens," CJ chimed in.

Clair sighed. How to articulate what she meant? She'd had so little experience with Norsundrians—a good thing. But during her year of trying to protect her country, she'd watched from a distance, and listened carefully to what Ben had reported hearing.

Norsundrians weren't all alike. Some were smart, and some acted almost like the enchanted people did, like they were caught in a dream. In a nightmare, maybe, except they weren't scared. They weren't *anything*. Some were old, some young. Some were even funny, Ben had told her in private. They were mean, but funny. Others were just bullies who'd gone to the Norsunder Base in order to get away from rules about being nice and helping your fellow human. Some wanted to live forever and get more and more power, at any price.

She was sure that some of the ones Siamis had working for him now would figure out the kids' plans as fast as the kids figured out theirs, and who had the weapons and the strength? Not kids.

"I'm afraid Siamis might guess our plan," Clair said.

CJ grimaced ferociously. "But Boneribs *sounds* convincing. He certainly knows plenty more about war junk than we do."

"That wouldn't be hard," Diana put in, grinning.

"I don't want to know any," Sherry said, her face earnest. "I just want to throw yukky pies at 'em, or give them itchweed sandwiches, and annoy them so much they'll go away and leave us alone."

"But they don't go away," Irenne countered. "This whole year cooped up at Aunt Murial's showed us that."

"We'll never be good at sword-fighting a bunch of grown-ups—" Sherry said, then she looked puzzled. "Why are most of them men?"

"Remember Dejain?" CJ countered.

"She was one woman. And she didn't like fighting."

"She liked power," Clair said. "Fighting's the easiest way to power, if you're born big and strong. She's smart, so she's doing it through magic, and it doesn't matter what size you are to be a magician."

"I think kids—girls—are too smart to become elevens," Irenne said loftily.

Clair said, "Our ancestors' wars were mostly men. They are better at it." She mimed hacking and stomping. "But women got power other ways, and not all those were good. I'm sure there are plenty of female Norsundrians, but I hope I never meet them. What worries me right now is Siamis."

"But we've got Boneribs to spot the war-signs, and Sartora to do her mind junk," CJ pointed out. "If we all do our jobs, we should be able to splorch one villain. When *we* got splorched, we've always been alone."

"That's *right*," Irenne declared, as if anyone had been arguing.

Clair looked from one to another. She didn't see disagreement in any of the girls. "Well, how's this. I wish you girls wouldn't do anything—or go anywhere—alone. Go in pairs, or threes. If one person runs into trouble, the other can go for help. Okay?"

Little gestures, words, and nods of agreement reassured Clair. They separated to grab up some camping things, and then ran out to find the others gathered at Arthur's tent.

"One more thing," Arthur said as soon as the Mearsiean girls joined the group. "Sartora will teach everyone a mind-shield. Practice it as we travel." He turned to Liere. "Go ahead."

CJ watched Sartora take a deep breath. She looked stiff and angular in her grubby boy's clothes and worn out shoes, her fingers trembling. *Poor thing*, CJ thought with a pang of sympathy. *She looks as worried as Clair was.*

"Here's one way to do it . . ." Liere began.

Faris and Winn stood in the opening of the empty command tent, watching.

They'd each seen the kids slink off to their private conference. They'd said nothing to anyone else, just finished their separate tasks, and then found one another.

Finally Faris said, "You know they're going to make a run on their own. And Arthur's probably going to go with them."

"Let him go," Winn said.

The wind drummed gently over the tent top, bringing the soft, high murmur of children's voices. Winn resisted the impulse to go closer to listen. What would be the point?

"How strange it is," he said finally, smiling at Faris's questioning expression. "We're both under thirty, though I think I have half a year left, if I remember right. But that's not old. Yet all of a sudden we are too old. As outmoded in all our training, our outlook, our abilities, as Evend and Oalthoreh."

Faris fingered the end of her braid. "I realized that the day I saw Arthur with those Mearsiean girls. It was like someone else had taken over his body. Someone happy."

Winn was seized by a fierce impulse to press her close, and kiss her. How long had he been fighting that instinct? *Wherever you are, my love, there is home.*

"What do we do?" she asked.

"We'll do our best to lead our people against whatever forces Siamis is sending. He has to have been waiting for that girl to show up. Let's rouse the camp and start causing some trouble for the elevens as backup, as soon as those kids leave on whatever mission they've set for themselves."

She turned to face him, and smiled.

The trust in her steady gaze, the warm hint of a smile on her lips, slipped past his guard at last, and his arm drifted round her sturdy shoulders. She did not bolt, or stiffen, or move away.

One breath, two, and then she leaned close, and he breathed in the dusty scent of her hair. Bent and kissed the top of her head.

She reached up and with one strong, capable hand pulled his face to hers.

They kissed. And kissed again, more fiercely, until breathlessness forced them apart, and they remembered they were standing in the opening to the command tent, nor were they unnoticed: a couple smiles turned their way, and one of Faris's friends, next to the cook tent, raised her fist in triumph, laughing out loud.

Winn flashed his grin, then took Faris's arm and they walked a little ways away. His face sobered. "The children are going to force an ending, one way or another, and Siamis is waiting. And if a miracle occurs and we are left alive, let us marry, and do what we can with what abilities we have. And maybe our children will join these children, and carry on the quest for peace."

Faris slid her arm around his waist.

Chapter Forty-Seven

"I think someone's been doing magic down that way." Leander pointed through the wind-twisted pines.

"That's by the water," CJ said. She'd glimpsed blue between the trees, and the piny breezes carried the scent of brine. "How can you tell? You said you don't dare do magic."

"They'll land on us if we try," Leander said. "Arthur said the whole region is laced with tracers. Everywhere outside of Bereth Ferian itself—"

"—which they can't touch. Yet."

"Anyway, it's a sense. Like you know where the sun will come up, even if you've gotten all turned around in the night."

"I can't do that, either," CJ said. "Not up here, anyway, when those pretty hissing lights are going all over the sky. When it's not raining."

Leander grinned. "I like those, too. But you're right, if they cover the stars, they're confusing."

CJ nodded. "Never mind. If you think we should check, we'll check. 'Sides, Sartora and the girls said they were going to look *that* way. And Sartora said when we woke up that she smells Siamis somewhere around, so maybe you're right."

"She said that?" Leander asked. "Smells?" His green eyes quirked with enjoyment.

CJ grinned. "Well, no, not exactly. You know how she talks. Means the same. I figure, Norsundrians gotta have a mental stench, same's the villain-stench."

"Which is also mental," Leander said.

CJ just laughed as they picked their way downhill, CJ hopping to keep up because she would have turned herself into a mushroom rather than admit a boy moved faster in the woods than she did—even one who was a foot taller, and who had lived most of his life in such surroundings.

"Tell you what surprised me," CJ said, once they reached the shelter of a clump of willow trees. "Other night, before we all split up. Her and ol' Boneribs and Arthur yakkin' half the night. Arthur, it makes sense. He's a little like her, in some ways. But Senrid? You'd think you couldn't find two people more different." She shrugged.

Leander thought over that last evening, when the group had camped after the long walk east from Winn's camp. He hadn't seen much of Sartora yet, but so far, she seemed painfully reserved and self-effacing—until someone made a comment about dena Yeresbeth or Old Sartorans. Then she talked with passion, and everyone listened respectfully. Even Dtheldevor, who tried heroically to smother her yawns.

All listened respectfully, that is, except Senrid, who argued, questioned, or even teased. From what Leander saw, Sartora didn't seem to resent it at all. Not the way she resented the careful treatment she'd gotten from the adults just before they left the big camp.

"There's a cliff," CJ said, pointing downhill. "Shall we go down there and eyeball around first? I don't want to have to squelpsh all the way down this snorfling mountain just to have to slog our way back up again."

"I don't know," Leander said, scanning in a slow circle, as his insides quaked silently. *Squelpsh.* The rocky hillside behind them was silent, the rolling hills they glimpsed to the south seemed peaceful, and what they could see of the rough palisades leading down toward the shoreline seemed empty. But. "I don't think we should break cover."

"We can stay in the bushes and wiggle out," CJ offered. "We're already muddy, and at least the air is warm. Ho! I do wish we were at home, snug in the Junky, getting ready for New Year's Week. I miss the snow, and hot chocolate, and going out to play without worrying about the stenchiferous flap-brained elevens snilching up the landscape."

"I miss my desk," Leander said. "I had at least three interesting projects going. And two of them would have helped us, I think, if I could have just learned the magic. And I miss a morning ride, no worries that I can't solve, and First Snow."

"I miss chocolate pie." CJ groaned with artistic fervor. "You'd think someone could figure out how to fix it for camp!" She paused, looking southward. On the distant hills, she made out a flock of sheep moving, cloudlike, through the tall green grasses. She turned away. "You checked the slate?" she asked.

"While ago. Nothing."

CJ wasn't sure which she dreaded most, Senrid's group finding Siamis first, or her own. The thought of happening on him was nasty, and so was the notion of deliberately going to face him and his creeps. But that had been the agreement: whichever group saw him first would apprise the other, and wait, so all could act together.

And she would show no more fear than any stupid boy would.

CJ slapped the rough bark of a young pine tree. "At least you don't worry about elevens. Or do you?" she muttered, studying the tree.

No answer from the tree.

Leander made the sign for silence, and they picked their way down a steep, rocky incline, staying within the close-growing greenery.

Below was the cliff CJ had pointed out.

Leander dropped down into the long grass and snaked forward, the sharp astringent scent of broken grass tickling his nose. CJ followed, her black head rising cautiously as she tried to peer downward.

From far above and to the north, they heard the harsh "Kek! Kek! Kek!" of a hawk. Farther away, the cries of seabirds answered.

Leander stilled.

"What is it? What is it?" CJ whispered, peering upward frantically.

"The hawk. A warning. They *are* here."

They elbowed forward, then peeked downward, taking care not to disturb the line of growth along the cliff edge; Leander silently demonstrated how making that rustle and wiggle would be visible from below.

CJ ducked her head in agreement. She peered cautiously, trying to see with one eye between the gently nodding ferny leaves of a plant, and a tuft of sharp-smelling grasses. At first all she could perceive was a weird sheen to the air all along the coast.

Leander drew in a long, audible breath.

CJ inched a bit closer to the edge. Several human figures milled around on the sandy shore. She counted the Norsundrians—three—and the rest were kids. Three . . . four . . . five. Two kids busy with swords, two not. And . . . one of them twirled lazily, her embroidered and lace-trimmed lavender and gold gown belling in the breeze.

I know that dress. CJ was astonished. *And that silvery-blond hair.*

"Kitty." Leander sighed, and rubbed his hands over his face. "What have I done?"

"Nothing. She was perfectly safe with Lina, like we told you. C'mon, we gotta find the others." CJ poked Leander. His profile made his feelings clear: he blamed himself for whatever had landed Kyale in Siamis's clutches.

I left her too long, he was thinking. And he knew why. It had been so much fun, so free, not to have to act as her guardian.

The result of his selfishness? Kyale was Siamis's prisoner.

CJ writhed with impatience. She knew that Siamis had not gone all the way back to Mearsies Heili just to pinch this girl who was sometimes a little tiresome, though she certainly felt the right way about villains. That only left one possibility. Kyale had managed to pick a quarrel with easygoing Lina, and had dusted off, straight into Siamis's arms.

Didn't that sound just like her!

"Slate," CJ said, when Leander still hadn't moved. "We gotta find Sartora."

He jerked, as though woken from sleep, then began wriggling backward. CJ followed, and when they had reached the shrubs, they got up, turned—and stiffened in shock.

Two Norsundrians stood there, the light-haired one a little older than Leander. Both smirked

"Siamis wants to have a word with you," the big dark-haired one gloated.

"A word," CJ snarled. "I'll give HIM a word—" She sucked in her breath and shrieked, "AAARGGGH!"

❧

A scream echoed in broken shards of sound off the rocky cliffs above the narrow forest path where Sherry, Irenne, and Liere were walking.

"Uh oh," Sherry exclaimed.

Irenne raised a finger. "That," she pronounced, "is CJ."

Terror made Liere's heart thump. "They found *Siamis* instead of the kids. Has to be."

Irenne laughed, her ponytail swinging as she whirled around. "Let us seek the sound of pocalubes! Cause I think old snore-face Siamis found *her.*"

"Pocalubes?" Liere repeated, following Irenne's quick steps.

Irenne stopped short, hand raised. "Didn't we explain?" she asked with dramatic surprise.

"It's a very exact insult form," Sherry said earnestly. "You have to have at least seven describing words before you get to your insult. We got really, really good at pocalubing the Chwahir villains."

"You did. And Devon also told me about those."

Sherry nodded quickly, her expression odd—half-frightened, half-laughing. To Liere she was clear and uncomplicated as spring water. Irenne was more like lace work, all knots and complexities.

She sounded heartless, but Liere had already figured out that Irenne—most of whose days involved playacting of various forms—really wouldn't believe CJ was in actual danger until she saw it. Everything in life seemed to be a play to Irenne, and she was always in the center of the stage.

Liere had to introduce reality right away. "Let's run."

The two Mearsieans looked startled, but complied.

Liere pressed the slate against her chest so it and the dyr wouldn't thump She had better write to Senrid as soon as they had a location on the Norsundrians.

Already, it seemed, his plan had gone awry.

❧

No animals came to rescue Leader and CJ.

In fact, it seemed to Leander, who looked about covertly, that there were no animals about at all. Even the seabirds who'd been circling lazily overhead had vanished. Maybe it was because of the oppressive sheen of dark magic shimmering subtly all about them, either that or those had been spy birds.

His steps lagged as he tried to scan the sky, but a sudden, vicious thump between the shoulder blades made his head rock back and he staggered forward.

" . . .knock-kneed bile-faced pilch-brained . . ." CJ's mutter increased in volume.

"Shut up," came the inevitable command.

"YOU shut up," she snarled right back.

The urge to snicker—mixed with fear —made Leander's insides shivery. The Norsundrians had searched them and took everything, both their knives and Senrid's carefully written spells. Leander had practiced the spells, but he was not so sure he could risk coaching the off-world kids in dark magic without a prompt. Where was Senrid?

"—STUPID gnackle-nosed grouse-mouth—"

Smack. CJ fell down. She scrambled up, holding her cheek. Leander winced and looked away as the Norsunder shoved CJ ahead down the path. Leander's mind veered like a wingshot bird between CJ's running insults (now just mutters) and a jumble of observations: that sheen in the air; the fact that he and CJ were still alive; Kyale's astonishing presence; the quiet little bay.

Senrid was right, Leander thought. Or, almost right. He was right about where, and even when, because the sheen had to be a rift access. But he hadn't been right about the kids managing to stay unseen.

Sick at heart, Leander wondered if Siamis was killing time until eleven o'clock, when their magic would be strongest, to make that sheen into a rift. And he was waiting for someone whose death would force the magical transformation.

Senrid was right about that, too. About everything—everything except us being able to thrash Siamis's plans.

Shut up. Shut up.

There had to be something to try. *Think.*

The opportunity to escape narrowed with every step that brought them close, then face to face, with the tall blond man with light-colored eyes who waited, smiling gently.

"You both are very far away from home," Siamis observed, as the Norsunder handed over Senrid's neatly-written spells.

Siamis knew who they were.

As CJ's high, clear voice started in with insult-laden bravado, Leander sidled a glance sideways to locate the others. All five were in sight, Kyale and a boy holding swords—doing a slow kind of playacting fight—and the others watching. So no one had been forced into any kind of killer spell. Yet.

Yeah, Siamis was waiting for someone.

" . . . and if it weren't for you, I'd be home right now, enjoying a piece of chocolate pie, and making up a new song about how gum-brained you Norsunder pustules are!" CJ finished, whooping in a shaky breath.

Leander looked down at his shaky palms. You had to admire CJ's thorough-going pigheadedness!

"You're welcome to do both with us." Siamis smiled broadly as he scanned Senrid's papers. "While we wait for the rest of your friends to come along."

CJ fumed. Siamis's lack of anger—and obvious amusement—seemed to be the most effective way of routing her.

The two kids with the swords turned around. Sunlight gleamed down the silver blade in Kyale's hands as she dragged it in the sand, making wavy patterns. That was Siamis's own rapier from Old Sartor.

Kyale's blank eyes met Leander's gaze. "Hi, Leander." Her indifference chilled him to the heart.

CJ crossed her arms. "Kyale. I can see off-worlders getting snaked by this splat-banana, but *you*?"

CJ said it mostly to be goading. Ever since a harrowing misadventure, she had a horror of even remotely seeming to compromise with villains. Scared, angry, determined, she would mouth off until something happened, either to the situation—or to her.

Siamis didn't seem to care, but Kyale frowned. "Who do you think you are to judge *me*? I'm Princess Kyale Marlonen, and I can take care of myself. And Vasande Leror," she added, nose in the air.

CJ's thoughts dashed about like singed butterflies. This wasn't the real Kyale, it was a caricature of Kyale.

"What happened to your brains?" she asked. "Can't you *see* those elevens uglying up the landscape?" She jabbed a finger toward the armed men ringing the group.

A thought not her own darted into her brain: *Keep them talking!*

Sartora!

CJ crossed her arms more firmly, straightened her spine, and dug her toes into the sand. "So what do you think these fatheads are good for?" she asked Kyale in her most sarcastic, snide voice. "Holding petunia pots?"

"Better that than following that stupid girl around who likes to get cities burned just so she can be famous," Kyale fired back, her eyes wide.

"That's it," Siamis said encouragingly. "Let's get to specifics."

From behind, one of the Norsundrians guffawed.

CJ gulped in air. *They're just hanging around. Waiting for . . . what?*

No time to consider. She settled in for the performance of her life. "Kitty," she said, "it looks to me like you left your mind back home. Or maybe Siamis leaked it out while looking for a replacement for his flat tire of a brain, but before we get to the 'I am not' and 'You are too'—and I can do it longer and louder than ANYONE ALIVE—let me just tell you a few truths about Norsunder. And believe me, I know plenty about just how stupid, cowardly, mud-brained, not to mention slug-nosed they are . . ."

Senrid stared in blank horror from his slate to the evil sheen over the distant Klenal Bay. Then back to the slate.

Irenne's slanted letters still glowed there.

SARTORA SAYS—SIAMIS IS AT THE BAY, AND HE'S GOT CJ.

The rift accesses were exactly where he'd thought. Maybe so were the off-worlders. Who Siamis had used as bait.

What now, o brilliant one?

He cursed.

Dtheldevor snickered.

Arthur said, "We're going to have to go back."

"We can't make it in time," Senrid said furiously. "It's happening *now*."

Arthur looked around carefully. Nothing was in sight except breeze-tossed cedars, and an old, overgrown orchard whose blossoms carried fragrantly on the wind. In the distance, cotton trees stippled the contours of the hills in neat rows. All peaceful, oblivious to the human dramas.

Arthur swallowed in a dry throat. "Someone is pacing us," he said finally—reluctantly. As if speaking the words would make it real. "All day. I haven't seen anyone, but I've felt it."

Senrid's eyes had gone narrow as he scrawled on the slate *We're coming*. He said, "I think we're going to have to risk a transfer."

"Is there an answer?" Liere asked. "Did Senrid say anything?"

Irenne stared fixedly at the slate. "Just 'We're coming'."

Liere gulped. Her throat hurt. "Not how long it will take?"

"But they're a day's hike away!" Irenne wailed.

The three girls crouched on the edge of the high palisade and peered down at the tiny but recognizable figures in the bay.

"He might not know that," Liere whispered. "He doesn't know this land any more than we do."

"What do we *do*?" Irenne whispered, her hands held out wide.

Liere turned her gaze to the dyr. Her hands trembled, so she stiffened her fingers as she tucked the dyr into its bag. "I know what I have to do," she said. "But you two better run for help. Go!" She pointed northward, and they fled.

Liere got up and shoved aside the ferns. She hesitated on the edge of the steep cliff, her heart thumping, then she put her bottom on the ground and began slipping and sliding down the tree-dotted escarpment toward the bay.

Leander stared in bewilderment.

Siamis seemed to find rare amusement from CJ's unstintingly sarcastic, pungent, and detailed opinions of himself, Detlev, and a number of prominent leaders among the Chwahir. She did not stop with their looks, manners, and brains, but went on to expatiate on their motivations and goals, never once betraying even a vestige of approval. Or repeating herself.

Leander did not know what to do. Action as well as inaction seemed equally dangerous.

Kyale argued just to be arguing, interpolating insults of her own, but it was CJ who definitely carried the conversation, without pause or repeat.

It was a wonderful show. Leander, snickering in dizzy helplessness, wondered—if a miracle happened and they escaped this impossible situation with lives and brains intact—whether CJ might let him read her records of these past encounters that she described so vividly.

Mostly, though, he was acutely aware of the exquisite cruelty of the wait. Once Siamis met his eyes, and though Leander hastily looked down, his laughter dying, the after-image of that awareness, the superior smile, were burned against the insides of his eyelids like the sun at midday. Siamis could—and would—end this little scene whenever he felt like it, and they both knew what would happen next.

Keep yourself blocked, Liere thought as she ran hard, pressing her hand against her side to minimize the stitch. *Don't try contact. Just stay hidden.*

She stumbled through the sparse trees, her mind homing on the awarenesses gathered . . .

There.

She reached the lowest palisade, directly uphill from Siamis and the others. She paused at the edge of a tumbling stream that emptied down into the bay. She tried to catch her breath as she peered between trees down the little gully. No Norsunder guards in sight, except for those ringing the kids. She checked twice. No humans, but lots of hidden wildlife. Including some very big creatures.

Think. I have no weapons, and I am alone. A diversion . . .

She moved forward, shaping images in her mind.

Arthur said, "There are wards against the light-magic transfer."

Senrid checked, and checked again. There were no wards for the dark-magic transfer.

It was an open invitation.

He stared eastward, struggling with the realization that he had guided his friends right into Siamis's trap. He hadn't been a step ahead, but behind.

"I'll do the magic," he said, and did.

Leander felt the moment that the Norsundrians shifted from entertainment to boredom. The two girls had gone from history to the personal. Everyone wants to hear about himself, but no one cares what a couple of brats think about each other.

Scarcely a heartbeat later the underbrush rattled along the base of the palisade, and a golden, leonine head poked out, yellow eyes staring at Kyale.

That beast looked a little like her tame lion from home.

Leander turned to Kyale. She'd seen as well. She stopped talking, blinked, and her vision focused beyond the lion to a glint in the bushes. And then she said in a small voice, "Conrad?"

CJ whirled around as gray shapes streaked out of the shrubs.

The Norsundrians were flanked by big gray timber-wolves who waited with unnerving quiet. Not a few. Fifty—or more.

A small, crimson-faced figure thrashed her way through the shrubbery.

"Sartora!" Leander yelled. "The hatpin!"

Now was the time to act. There was no chance of reaching those off-worlders. What would happen if *he* tried Senrid's spells? Disintegration in dark magic fire would be better than whatever Siamis had planned.

Liere ran forward, then stumbled to a halt as a hand clamped with bruising force on Leander's shoulder and a knife pricked his neck. CJ let out a yell of fright and rage, abruptly cut off as she was held in a similar grip.

Liere gasped, her eyes wild, but her gaze was not on Leander, or CJ, or even Siamis.

Leander felt a cold, weird breeze through his bones: dark magic transfer!

Senrid and the others appeared.

"Ah, at last." Siamis smiled in welcome. "You know what comes next," he said to Senrid, gesturing toward Leander and CJ, who writhed in a guard's tight grip, her face purple. "The same thing, incidentally, your uncle did to your father with you. Their lives, and if they don't work, hers." He indicated Liere. "Your life, just like your father's, is the price. Make your choice."

Leander watched Senrid's face blanch. "Liar." His voice cracked.

"Try me." Siamis laughed.

Senrid's skinny chest heaved, and then he took a step forward, another. And another.

They all saw it. He was going to give in—trade his life for everyone else's. Senrid's mouth trembled, his gaze bitter, but he stepped forward deliberately.

Leander wanted to shout *Don't do it!* but when he sucked in a breath, the knife pressed harder into his neck. In impotent horror, Leander was forced to stand and watch.

Senrid was almost within Siamis's reach when Leander became aware of another voice, a husky, old voice, accompanied by the coruscant wind of building power.

Siamis's chin lifted.

From the shelter of a tall pine stepped a white-haired old man.

"You will not set foot in Bereth Ferian," Evend said. "And you will make no bridge to damnation here. I only needed the site. Here it is." He raised his hands, and intoned swift words.

Leander shivered, his skin prickling at the tremendous surge of magic coalescing. This old man's voice was the voice he'd heard—

"As you will," Siamis said, and he lifted a hand in a casual sign.

Davernak whipped a hand to his belt, pulled a knife and threw it, all in a swift motion, sending it speeding across the trampled sand to bury hilt deep in the old man's chest.

But not before Evend made another sign.

He staggered, swayed—and vanished.

So did the green glow arcing over the sky.

Liere held out the dyr on her hands. Her fingers trembled, her nose ran, her face was slick with sweat, but she locked eyes with Siamis for a long, agonizing moment—and then, quite suddenly, he was gone, he and his Norsundrians.

Gone.

Reaction hammered the kids, some falling to the sand, others frozen as the animals vanished, and the endless waves crashed and hissed on the beach.

Liere gave a sob, and a hiccough. When everyone turned her way, she said numbly, "Evend took their entire rift with him."

"He did it," Arthur whispered. "After everything I said. He did it anyway."

Liere went on, "Norsunder wouldn't back Siamis. Not against that kind of spell. I—I heard him. Heard them. For just a moment." She sucked in a shuddering breath. "The Guardian, and the Geres . . . and . . "Her voice wavered, and she stiffened. "And all the powers here were willing to back us."

Arthur walked over to Kyale, who stood blinking, still holding the silver sword *Emeth.*

Arthur took it, and crossed to Liere, passing the place where drops of Evend's blood still marked the sand, and he handed her the sword.

Her wrist promptly bent, and the point buried in the sand.

"You won it," he said. "Fair and square."

Senrid dropped onto a tree stump and put his head in his hands.

Chapter Forty-Eight

"**I**s it the city? Or me? What is it you object to?" Arthur asked a day later.

Liere stared at him. Grief still ringed his eyes and pulled his mouth awry even when he seemed to be smiling. She knew very little about Arthur, but she did understand that old Evend had been a better parent to him than her own angry father had even been to her.

He'd been enough of a parent to keep his plans from Arthur, including ordering his guild of mages busy running around looking like fools to deflect the Norsundrians in a way that camouflaged his great weaving, from old rift to new, covering each and every access. And he'd been enough of a parent to shadow Arthur and Senrid, suspecting Siamis's plans to entrap them, while he readied his spells.

And that had meant that Evend could choose the right moment and end it all at once.

All the northern rift accesses were gone now, and with them Norsunder's wards and preliminary spells. There was no trace of them in the entire region.

Liere sat down on one of the fine carved chairs in the little room. "There's nothing wrong with you, or your city," she said to Arthur. "I feel like I'm pretending to be something I'm not. And if I ever stop feeling like that, I'll hate myself."

"How do you think I feel?" he countered, hands wide. "'Prince' in Bereth Ferian. It's a stupid title. It means nothing. Evend as king was all right because I was used to it. Every mage in the world was used to it. But the titles don't mean anything anymore, because not only do I not have any kind of power, I don't even mean anything, symbol-wise, the way he did. Not with all things changing. The mages all want you to be Queen in Bereth Ferian because everyone in the world knows your name—"

"But they don't know my name. I'm not Sartora."

"That's a *symbolic* name. Same as the title."

"I know. But can't it be someone else?"

"It's just a title," Arthur pleaded.

A new voice spoke at the door. "Cowardice, Liere?"

They turned.

Senrid sauntered in, his face at its most sardonic, framed by the wild curls he'd sawed at with a knife.

"You know how I feel," she said.

Senrid dropped down into the window seat, overlooking the garden. "You won't have any real power. All you have to do is put on the old crown from the anti-Venn Empire days, gas on a little about a new era of peace and magic learning, and then start working on reading lessons."

Arthur flushed at Senrid's tone, but he didn't speak.

Liere clutched at the bag round her neck as she cut a glance Arthur's way. "Can I give this dyr thing back to your mother?"

"Soon's the southern mages finish in Sartor. Oalthoreh says it'll require a day at most. Then she'll come here and take it off your hands."

Senrid said, "What else would you do?"

Liere turned to him.

"What else?" he repeated. "You said you can't go back to South End."

Liere looked down at her brother's ruined shoes, with her toes almost broken out the front, and then back at Arthur. "Do you really think it will help?"

Arthur said firmly, "All the adults think so. They even got a message from Tsauderei, way down in Sarendan. And the Queen of Sartor. Who is our age."

Liere closed her eyes. All right, she couldn't go home, but it wasn't as if no one wanted her. They did want her, right here, even if it wasn't Liere Fer Eider they invited.

But couldn't they get to know Liere Fer Eider? She wondered if her objections were a form of fakery. "All right," she said. "But I won't promise to do this queen stuff forever."

Arthur sighed in relief. "I'll go tell the others." His smile was sad. It made her heart hurt. "The parties will be fun!" He ducked out the door.

"Thanks," Liere said to Senrid, who shrugged, then looked out into the garden.

"The least you can do is listen to me," he drawled, "since I nearly managed to get us all killed."

Liere sighed. "You don't know that."

He turned to face her, but for once, did not get up and prowl around. Yet she could feel how tense he was. "I was outmaneuvered by both of 'em, Evend and Siamis. Anything else is fart-noise."

Liere sighed again, longer and louder. His rudeness was a measure of not just tension, but how upset he was, though he now blocked off his emotions much better than she did. "It was the only way," she said. "The only way to keep Siamis from sniffing out their plans was to keep his attention on you, and me, and the other kids."

"Oh, I know I was a big help. All I had to do was lead everyone to Siamis's trap so Evend could pull off his magic." He sounded sardonic again, instead of savage. "I hate how I underestimated everyone." Senrid got up and began pacing the length of the small room.

"Except us." Liere tried to smile. "You overestimated us."

"Since mine were the worst mistakes, I'm not pointing any fingers. The Mearsieans tried to tell me what they can do—" He stopped, shook his head, resumed pacing. "You have a lot to learn. I have a lot to learn. But I have to go home first and throw my uncle out of my land, and if I live through that, I can get busy at my end."

"You won't stay? For the, the—" She could not bring herself to say *coronation*. It was embarrassingly silly, the mere idea. "Celebration?" she finished, knowing it was just as silly.

Senrid shook his head. "Lighter speeches about the Blessed Twelve and New Eras and Great Magic and all that, I think I can miss. They won't want to see me snoring in the background. Wouldn't look good in the forty-eight verse ballads I'm sure the local poets are busy scribbling up for the morale-lifting of the world."

Liere's emotions veered between dismay and laughter, and laughter won. "It's so stupid! Me. Here."

"No stupider than anyone else." Senrid backed toward the door.

"Wait. Will you visit? When you're done?"

He smiled, a real smile. "Sure. If. A big if. If the if comes true, I'll visit, and we can argue over whatever they tell you about history. And you'll have to come south for a personal tour of the Evil Marloven Hess."

There it was, a true invitation. Not for Sartora. For herself.

"I will come," Liere said. "Soon's you get all your own things done. Happy New Year, and fare well."

He left.

჻

A month later, Liere sat in her reception room with her friends, as outside, lightning flared and thunder rumbled.

She wasn't watching the ridiculous word-game that Falinneh and Sherry had invented. She was assessing her life.

She still felt like she was playacting, only not in front of Town Hall in South End, but in a real palace. She had several rooms to herself, and if she wanted could have more. She shared the palace, and the "royalty," with a boy she'd only met four weeks before, but they got along well.

The very first thing Arthur had shown her was the library. She smiled, thinking back to that day. They were hungry, and tired, and dirty, and he'd been crying so much his nose ran, but he just had to show her the library first.

And he'd been right. Somehow the idea of living in a palace had been a lot less awful once she'd realized how close she'd be to all those books of knowledge, wisdom, wonder—answers to all her questions, at long last. And all right there for her whenever she wanted. Nobody would chase her out to go fold dried sheets, or to sweep the shop, do proper girl chores as defined by her father.

She had a real royal anteroom, with a carved and gilt ceiling, and fine furnishings in the old carved-and-curved Sartoran style, and its own fireplace. The warm air smelled of the fresh berry buns they'd all just been served.

Arthur was perched on a hassock, listening to the game. One of his ever-present books lay near his hand.

He studied constantly. Despite what he'd said about meaning, he really believed that Bereth Ferian was a center of magic and learning, even with Sartor and its ancient mage guild back in the world. Evend and his two predecessors had been collecting histories, and magic books, for many years. Arthur seemed determined to master every single one. And he knew his map at least as well as Senrid.

Senrid. How was he doing? Liere had heard nothing.

The days had been filled with studies, and reports of recovery from all over the world—these latter at first sporadic, then frequent, now rare again. It seemed that, just as Winn had once said, as life returned to normal people focused on concerns close to home.

Liere smiled, thinking of Winn and Faris now off adventuring somewhere to the south, their marriage-trip being a quest for causes that required their skills.

But where was Siamis?

Liere thought of the silver sword lying in the old treasure room at the other end of the palace.

When she remembered the great alliance, she could believe that Norsunder was truly defeated, and that the great New Era was nigh. Except that no more animals came around with messages, or anything else.

Quiet, definitely. Peace? She hoped so.

"No! Gnackles are *not* the same as grackles," Irenne cut in.

Kyale Marlonen put her hands on her hips. "I can call a villain a grackle if I want to. They are stupid-looking birds."

Falinneh nodded. "Kitty gets her point."

Diana snorted. "Then I can use bear, or cat—"

"But those aren't funny," Deirdre Weiss said reasonably.

Deirdre was happy after Oalthoreh had accepted her as a magic student. *I'll never get bespelled again,* Deirdre had said, after Liere disenchanted her. Then she burst into tears, and no one knew what to say, or to do. Liere sensed how the adult mages all knew how they would feel, to discover that they'd been bespelled to follow a Norsundrian around for months, and nobody had said anything mean to any of the four off-worlders.

Deirdre hugged her knees against her chest. "Grackle is funny!"

"You keep changing the rules." Irenne sighed loud enough to flutter the curtains.

"Of course," Falinneh agreed, looking surprised. "It's more fun that way."

The girls—except for Dhana—went on arguing happily. They were waiting out the thunderstorm so they could continue an outside game that had been running for days. Dhana was out dancing through the rain, and reveling in it.

Liere felt cozy and wistful. She knew she'd miss them all, Kyale included. Kyale was a lot of fun when she forgot to be Princess Kyale.

Liere had asked the Mearsieans to stay with her and Arthur, to help her adjust to a new life. Aunt Murial had insisted that Mearsies Heili was quiet, and that Clair might learn some magic if she stayed up there.

Leander had gone home to clear away Norsundrian spells and make some wards. Faced with the prospect of him being busy day and night, Kyale had gladly volunteered to stay and take her part in the continuous games.

Liere had given up hoping that Clair would suddenly invite her to come to Mearsies Heili and be one of the girls. Could she ever *be* one of the girls? Even when she ran and laughed and threw pies, the shadow of Sartora was stuck to her. She saw herself trying to act like the others, just as she'd copied Marga's friends during her horrible life in South End.

She had also seen the way Devon had tried constantly to insert herself into their lives. Kyale and Devon had taken an immediate dislike to one another, Devon wanting to organize everything, even when people didn't want to be organized, and Kyale resenting what she saw as attempts to be the center of attention.

Gloriel and Peridot had vanished right away with Dtheldevor, more than ready to scoop up Joey and Ellen from Roth Drael and settle in at Dthel Rendm, this time for ever.

But Deirdre and Frederic had needed time to recover from the nasty shock of the enchantment. Not that they talked about it much, except to each other. Deirdre would soon move over to the mages' wing, and Frederic had asked Winn if he could join the Chargers.

The one who seemed happiest was Devon. Good food, no worries, no arduous traveling, and the company of the Mearsiean girls balanced out Kyale's jealous dislike, before she received a message from Princess Karia inviting her back to Imar, which she'd showed everyone, as if she had to prove that she was needed.

Liere suspected that Princess Karia was interested in Devon now that her name was in all those ballads Senrid had made fun of, but she kept that to herself. Maybe things would work out.

The important thing was, in Devon's view, the bad days were over, and peace was here to stay. They had worked hard for their happy ending.

I hope we get one, Liere thought, looking out the window at the slanting rain.

The door opened, and Leander Tlennen-Hess walked in.

Kyale jumped up. "Leander!" She looked apprehensive. "Is everything all right down home?"

"Yup." He rubbed his eyes, woozy after the long transfer.

"Kits all right?"

The 'kits,' Liere had learned, were six feline friends of Kyale, Conrad being the one for whom she'd mistaken Evend's Helandrias ally the day of

Siamis' defeat; her looking for Conrad had distracted her attention to Liere and the dyr, breaking the enchantment. Kyale didn't seem to remember being enchanted, which made Liere privately grateful.

Leander said, "Everyone's all right, and everything's as safe as I can get it. Want to go home?"

Kyale looked around, obviously not wanting to miss anything. "Do we have to go *now*?"

"Not this moment," Leander laughed. "I's rather not do two long transfers right in a row."

"Then siddown and play," Falinneh offered.

"Or give us news?" Liere asked.

Leander threaded his way through the kids on the floor and sat down cross-legged next to Liere's chair. "What news do you want? You have to hear more than I do."

"About general things, I might. Kings and mages and such. But not about other kids. How is Senrid, do you know?"

"Yep. He's been borrowing my magic books. He asked Hibern, a mage friend, to tutor him. And we get together and compare notes when we can. But he's busy. Up to his neck in cleanup as well as magic studies."

"Cleanup? You mean he did have to have a war?"

"Oh, no. When Norsunder pulled their people out, Tdanerend had to go, too. He picked his allies, and now he gets to pay. Lilith the Guardian cleared out the wards. Like brooming old spider webs, she said. The Guardian I guess wanted Senrid's country waiting for him when he got back."

A gift, Liere was sure—the only gift Senrid would want.

"So . . . what's the cleanup?"

"Administrative stuff."

"Oh." Liere couldn't imagine what that even meant, much less where he'd start.

Leander looked at the kids sitting about on elegant, aged furniture. The Mearsieans and Kyale were busy with the game, watched by Arthur, Deirdre, and Frederic.

"Everyone's settling down, then," Leander said, smiling.

Liere shook her head.

"No," she said, drawing in a deep, slow breath. "Everyone's just beginning."

About Book View Café

Book View Café Publishing Cooperative (BVC) is an author-owned cooperative of over fifty professional writers, publishing in a variety of genres such as fantasy, romance, mystery, and science fiction.

Since its debut in 2008, BVC has gained a reputation for producing high-quality ebooks, and is now bringing that same quality to its print editions.

BVC authors include *New York Times* and *USA Today* bestsellers. Our authors have also won the following awards: Agatha, Campbell, Hugo, Lambda Literary, Locus, Nebula, PEN/Malamud Award, Philip K. Dick, RITA, World Fantasy, Writers of the Future, the Academy Nicholl Fellowship, and have been nominated and represented in even more.

www.bookviewcafe.com